THE Dori O. PARANORMAL Mystery SERIES

# LOST
# IN
# THE
# LIGHT

## BOOK ONE

# MARY
# CASTILLO

REINA BOOKS

Lost in the Light. Copyright 2012 by Mary Castillo. All rights reserved. No part of this book may be used or reproduced in any manner whatsoever without written permission except in the case of brief quotations embodied in critical articles or reviews. For information address Reina Books, 1048 Irvine Avenue, PMB477, Newport Beach, CA 92660.

ISBN-13: 978-1479255917
ISBN-10: 1479255912

Print Edition published October 1, 2012

Cover photos: iStockPhoto.com
Cover design: Mary Castillo, Reina Books

# DEDICATION

For every reader who reached out via email, Twitter and Facebook. You'll never know how your messages of encouragement shone the light when it seemed there was no hope of finishing another story.

For Aunt Irma, your spirit carries on through Grammy Cena.

This book is my gift to you.

# PRAISE FOR *LOST IN THE LIGHT*

"Dori Orihuela is a detective with a gunshot wound, a ghost, and a Grammy who needs her own book. *Lost in the Light* is the entertaining answer to the question, 'What would happen if Kinsey Milhone met "The Ghost and Mrs. Muir"?'" – **Deanna Raybourn, author of *Silent in the Grave* and *A Curious Beginning***

"This book captivated me. The ending might have been my favorite. One of my favorite mystery reads of the year, and one to get your to-read list!" – **Samantha March, author of *The Green Ticket***

"*Lost in the Light* is an enchanting story that takes the reader from present to the past. Full of mystery, emotion, and a plot that keeps the readers on their toes, I couldn't peel my eyes away. Ms. Castillo, you've got a new fan. I can't wait for more!" - **Storm Goddess Book Reviews**

"The story is a page turner with old flames, sexy ghosts, family obligations that we all contend with, humor, and bonds with new female friends." - **Sandra Ramos O'Briant, author of *The Sandoval Sisters' Secret of Old Blood***

"Castillo created an interesting, and expertly woven tale that is fraught with romance and mystery. Dori's guardedness, Vicente's rough edges and Grammy's spunkiness all made for very real characters and good story telling. Castillo knows how to dish up a story with some spice, and I'll be looking forward to more adventures from Castillo in the future." - **Cellar Door Lit Rants & Reviews**

"Mary Castillo has written such a rich and compelling novel... I was pretty much glued to this book. To say I was behind Dori the whole way is an understatement. I love her!" - **Whoopeeyoo! Reviews**

# CHAPTER ONE

No one visits the dead in the rain. Parking would be easy to find at La Vista Memorial Park.

Dori turned up the steep hill and the wipers scraped against the windshield. Shafts of pearlescent light punched through the clouds. Grammy Cena was right. They just might get a break from the rain.

"Now don't get out until I come around with the umbrella," Dori said while Grammy checked her lipstick in the visor mirror.

"Who are you to tell me what to do?"

"It's still drizzling outside."

"So? I ain't no wicked witch. I ain't gonna melt."

Pulling into a parking spot, Dori repressed a sigh so not to start an argument. As she pushed open the door and twisted around to step out, white hot pain exploded at her left side. While Grammy primped and fussed in the mirror, Dori held her breath. She slowly stood up. By the time she reached Grammy's side of the car, sweat rolled down her back.

Shielding them from the light mist with the umbrella, Dori offered Grammy her arm.

"Wait, this is your bad side," Grammy said.

"It's okay."

"Give me your other arm."

"Just take my arm."

"I will when you turn your ass around."

This time Dori didn't hold back an exasperated sigh. She switched the umbrella to her left hand and did what she was told.

Grammy took her arm and eased out of the car. "You okay with this?"

"Yeah. I owe Grampy a thank you."

Dori steered Grammy over the uneven pavement towards the mausoleum. Her eyes squinted against the sun reflecting off the puddles. Cars whooshed up and down the 805 freeway and the scent of the eucalyptus trees sharpened the cold wind. La Vista Memorial Park stood at the top of a hill. On clear days, far beyond Sweetwater Road and the wetlands, she could've seen a ribbon of ocean.

"Don't let the flowers get wet," Grammy said, leaning on Dori as they took the steps down.

"I won't."

"Hold the umbrella straight. I got my hair done."

Dori cracked a grin, welcoming Grammy's bossiness as a distraction from her stiff side. "Sorry."

She glanced at Grammy's freshly colored and coiffed up-do. Rhinestone earrings glittered at her ears, ropes of pearls hung over her reinforced bosom and her mango-colored pant suit could've beaconed ships safely into harbor. Grammy had gone all out for her weekly visit with Grampy.

The clouds swallowed up the sun again by the time they arrived at Grampy's crypt. Stopping in front of him, Grammy let out a long sigh. Her hand reached out, shivering in the cold. She hesitated just before she caressed his name, Joaquin Gregorio Orihuela, 1929-1985.

"After visiting you on a day like this, you better be waiting for me when I die, mi amor," Grammy said.

Dori put her hand next to Grammy's, her fingers bumping over the letters of his name. "Hi Grampy," she said. "Thanks for watching my back."

She'd had more years without her grampy than with him. But right now, when she was supposed to be a strong, capable woman, all Dori wanted was to press her cheek against his chest and hear him tell her everything would be okay. Dori's throat tightened and she pulled her hand away, stuffing it in her pocket.

Grammy shifted her weight off Dori's arm, taking away her warmth. "Mija, get some water for the flowers. I want some alone time with your Grampy."

"You want the umbrella?"

"I don't need it."

Dori checked the sky for rain before she left them together. She carried the metal vase to the sink located right outside the cemetery's office. Miniature American flags flapped against the white marble.

Ever since Dori had been put on leave pending an investigation, this was her fourth time out of Grammy's house. She'd met with her therapist twice, taken Grammy to the grocery store and now they were here. She felt rickety on her own two feet but tonight she was determined to sleep in her own house and get on with her life. She tried not to think about what she'd do when Grammy would be laid to rest beside Grampy. The vase clanged against the sink and her bones nearly jumped through her skin.

Time lurked just around the corner and then Dori would really have no one and her dependency scared her. Mom was caught up in her new boyfriend. Sela was now living in New York but kept in touch through phone calls and texts. Their brother, Robbie, sent two emails and flowers but he wasn't interested in rejoining the family after his disastrous wedding. Dad was somewhere in Mexico with his new wife who, according to Aunt Delia, was five years younger than Dori but looked twice as old.

Grammy and her sergeant were the ones who had been sitting by her hospital bed when Dori emerged from the drugs and trauma of having been shot. After her supervisor left, Grammy had held her as Dori cried after telling her about the woman she'd shot and killed in front of her two kids.

Something caught in her throat and Dori choked. She braced her hands on the edge of the cold sink, trying to catch her breath. She'd been doing this a lot lately. She held on to the sink as if it would keep her from exploding into a million, irreplaceable pieces.

She stared down at her boots and wondered how she, Dori Orihuela could've ended up a mess like this. The department might clear her of any legal wrongdoing in taking the life of Kaylee Matthews, but she wasn't so sure about God. Dori tried to remind herself that she didn't believe in God anymore, but that didn't make her feel any better.

Her hands eased their grip on the sink and Dori breathed in slow and deep. She focused on rinsing the vase and then refilling it with clean water. She walked back to Grammy and Grampy and the sun returned, spotlighting the old section of the cemetery. Massive granite gravestones rose crookedly out of the grass. The Victorian wrought iron fences that sequestered the city's founding fathers were crumbling with rust.

"There you are," Grammy said. "Grampy and I were getting worried."

Dori stretched her lips into a grin and unclenched her fist. It was a front but she hated the worry in Grammy's eyes. "I had to give it an extra rinse," she said, sliding the vase into the holder.

"It's crooked," Grammy said. "The flowers will fall out."

Dori made an adjustment.

"It's still crooked."

Dori nudged it just so.

"Psh! Let me do it."

Grammy shouldered her aside and jimmied the vase. "I was telling him about that house you just bought," she said. "He thinks you should stay with me for another week."

"I'll be fine."

"It's too drafty."

"I've got all those blankets you gave me."

"But it don't got no heat. That little thing you bought might burn the place down."

"If that happens, I'll move back in with you."

Grammy turned to Grampy. "Will you talk some sense into this child?"

"Fixing it up will be good for me," Dori said even though she wondered if closing escrow on a 120-year-old eight-bedroom mansion had come at

3

the worst possible time in her life.

Her throat closed up as she stared at Grampy's name. This is why I need you again, she thought as if she could will him back to life and help straighten her out.

"You see what I gotta deal with?" Grammy said to Grampy, holding out her hand towards Dori. "You were the only one she ever listened to."

Dori opened her mouth to argue that the last time she'd listened to Grammy, she'd tussled with a guy in the kitchen at the Hotel Del. But Grampy probably knew all that and she could see him shake his head and tell her in his deep whispery voice, "You know your Grammy."

His name plate blurred. Dori made a choking sound and clamped her hand over her mouth.

"There, there, mija," Grammy said, sliding her arm around Dori's waist. "See you gotta let it out. Stop holding it in."

They stood there quietly as the wind shoved against their backs. Grammy's tender encouragements only worsened the pain. Dori clenched her jaw tight, forcing the sobs back to that dark place where they'd come from.

"I'm ready to go," Dori said, pulling away to stand on her own.

Grammy sighed. She kissed her fingertips and then pressed them to his name plate. "See you soon, amor." She then closed her eyes and bowed her head.

"Bye Grampy. I still keep my back to the wall like you told me to."

They got to the car when Grammy asked, "You'll call me when you get home."

"Yes."

"Keep your cell with you at all times."

"Okay."

"I don't like you being there all alone. One of your cousins should stay with you."

When Dori didn't say anything, Grammy added, "You said it's a big house."

"Not that big."

"Will you just cry or beat someone up or drink? You gotta stop bottling it in or it's gonna eat you alive."

Dori held the door open. "I don't need to advertise my suffering. It's time for me to move on and that's what I'm doing."

When she was firmly ensconced on the passenger seat, Grammy muttered, "Then at least get laid, mija."

After making sure Grammy was safely in her house, Dori checked the time and figured her prescription was ready. Her palms began sweating as she turned into the shopping mall off Sweetwater Road, remembering the Old

West theme it sported back when she rocked leg warmers and three-inch high bangs. She bought her Go-Go's albums at the old record store and her Grammy's romance novels from the Book Nook.

As she walked through the automatic doors of CVS, Dori replayed the conversation she'd had with her therapist the other day. The Lexapro didn't mean she was defective. It was a tool to help her get her footing. Dori hadn't filled the prescription until today and she wouldn't change her mind or chicken out this time. If she wanted her job back then this was part of the process. It didn't matter that-

"Well lookey whoo just walked in! Dora Orihuela!"

Dori stopped so suddenly she nearly fell forward. Cleve, her mother's boyfriend smiled and waved from the other side of the pharmacy counter. She very nearly ran for it, but then she'd just visited Grampy, and he wouldn't like her turning tail.

She sucked in some air and rolled her shoulders back. "Hey, Cleve. How's it going?"

"Not bad. They cut my hours so it's a little tight. What can I do you for?"

She'd been trained to shoot to kill. She'd wrestled drunks in the gutter and had been called names that would shrivel a lesser man's balls, but Dori couldn't summon up one teensy lie to get herself out of this situation.

"I'm here to pick up a prescription," she managed.

"Here lemme look you up," he said. She watched him flip through the plastic bags hanging along the back wall.

"Or-hee-well-ah," he said, mangling her last name on the ticket. "I just called you Dora, didn't I? Sorry 'bout that." He tore open the bag to scan the paperwork and then paused to wink at her. "My mind ain't what it used to be. A few more years and you'll know what I-"

When Cleve read the prescription, his grin flattened. Dori felt the ping in her gut. He looked her in the eye, all humor gone. "It's not my place, but is everything all right?"

He knew she'd been shot. He'd brought her hysterical mother to the hospital. How the hell could everything be all right? Dori slapped her credit card on the counter. "How much do I owe?"

"Oh, right I-" The bottle fell out of the bag and rolled off the counter. Cleve dived down to get it.

"You need help, Cleve?" one of the pharmacists asked.

Dori wanted to pull her head into her coat and never come out again as the older blonde snapping gum walked over. Her badge said, Berta.

"No thanks, I got it," Cleve said, slipping it back into the bag. It took him four agonizing tries before the scanner read the bar code.

It was bad enough that her therapist had put her on anti-depressants. But within the hour, he'd tell her mother who then would call up her aunts and then they'd tell all of her cousins. They'd crow that Miss High and Mighty couldn't handle her problems.

Not that Dori planned to take the pills. They were like insurance in case yoga, exercise and the guided meditation she downloaded onto her phone didn't work. Still, she should've done what she used to do in high school when she'd fill her birth control pills at the pharmacy on Coronado Island where none of her family or their friends would find out. But she'd forgotten Cleve worked here. She needed to think more clearly from here on out.

He mumbled the total and then asked if Dori had a CVS card. Dori slid it across the counter that suddenly turned blurry.

"Here you go," he said. The bag appeared in her line of sight. Her hand shot out for the grab but he kept his hold on it.

"Wait, I have to ask you to hang on for a consultation," he said. "This is a, a you know — one of those things and-"

Shame or no shame, Dori leveled that cold Orihuela stare that everyone said she'd inherited from Grampy. "I'm fine."

He flinched but held her gaze. "I can't let you go without a consultation first."

She could make a scene and then he'd really think she needed drugs. She pulled her hand away and stuffed it in her pocket. "Okay. Fine. Thanks."

He nodded as if he appreciated what she was going through. She didn't want his damn pity. She just wanted her bag so she could get the hell out of there.

"If you need anything, you know you can-"

"Sure thanks." Dori moved out of the way for the next person in line behind her.

Dori slowed to a stop at East 24th Street and she tried to shake off the guilt that she'd blown Cleve off. At the hospital, when he'd walked her crying mother out into the hallway, she had heard him asking her mom to calm down, to be strong for her daughter. Then again, like Grampy used to say, sometimes you had to front so no one would mess with you. Maybe, just maybe, Cleve would keep the prescription to himself.

From her experience, Dori doubted it. She knew she couldn't trust anyone, not even herself.

With the rain pattering on the roof of her car, she pulled up the semi-circular drive of the house the county of San Diego declared was legally and financially hers. Her Rav-4 looked ridiculous in front of the three-story, 19th-century mansion that stood tall and proud even though one earthquake could send it into a smoking ruin.

The police tape Dori had draped across the sagging front porch fluttered in the wind. But she would fix it. Together, piece by piece, both she and the house would be put to rights. Staring at it through her fogged up window, she remembered the very first moment she saw this house and thought, this will be mine.

The memory was so clear that for a moment she was nine years old again, sitting in the backseat of her dad's Scout, imagining what went on through the murky, mysterious windows. There were three other 19th Century mansions in this neighborhood that had been beautifully restored. But this one was special. She'd came back to it through the years, even when she visited from Denver. Now it was hers.

Sighing, Dori reached across the seat for her CVS bag. Goosebumps sprang up her arms. She tensed; the back of her neck tingling with the awareness that she was being watched. Locked inside her car, she scanned the back seat and the yard.

No one lurked behind the dead boxwoods. The grass had dried up, and not even one weed sprung up out of the dry earth. The plastic bag crinkled as she closed her fist around it. The house wasn't in the best of neighborhoods but she refused to think about Grammy's worrying.

The weeks she'd first lived in the house, before the shooting, Dori never felt weird or scared. But it was good to be aware, she told herself as she pushed the door open and paused, sniffing chimney smoke from the neighbor's house. It was quiet up here, the traffic on Sweetwater a soft hush that rode on the winds sweeping clouds across the sky. She shut the door and the alarm beeped. The bay windows in the front parlor reflected Dori as she walked up to the house.

Idly wondering what to pick from the meals Grammy had prepared for her, Dori plugged her key into the lock. Her heart gave a painful jolt when she looked up into the face of a man. He stared at her from the other side of the wavy glass window of the Dutch door.

His dark eyes narrowed. In one motion, Dori dropped her bag, stepped back and reached for her weapon. But she only felt the bandage under her shirt where her Smith and Wesson should've been. She swayed in momentary confusion and then remembered she'd locked it away. When she looked back up into the window, he was gone.

Dori stood there with her pulse kicking against her neck. He couldn't duck faster than the blink of an eye, nor was the window shade moving in the wake of a sudden movement. It hadn't been that long since she'd been with a man that she'd start making one up as Grammy had repeatedly warned. Warning pricked at her nerves. She pulled up alongside the edge of the door and peeked into her dark kitchen. She strained her ears, listening for movement in the house. Against her better judgment, she reached over and turned the key.

She pushed the door open and the smell of cologne stopped her short of walking inside. Dori instinctively rocked her weight onto the balls of her feet, her muscles tensing for a fight. Night crept across the yard behind her.

As a cop, she'd been in much scarier situations than this. But back then, Dori had a gun at her hip and a radio for back-up. Unlike real bad guys, figments of her imagination couldn't send her to the hospital. Dori told herself to go out to her car and call the cavalry.

Instead, Dori propped the door open with an old brick. This was her house damn it and it might feel good to kick some ass.

Dori made her way through the gloomy kitchen and flipped on the light switch. The fluorescents flickered to life and their hum filled the silence. She crossed the kitchen and then poked her head through the door leading into the butler's pantry. The air held still as if the house held its breath.

She crept across the floor, scanned the dining room and then reached in to turn on the dining room chandelier, which thankfully had survived the architectural rape and pillage of the 1970s. His shadow moved across the wall in the hallway. Fear shot up her spine.

"I'm armed," she called out, backing into the kitchen for a knife. Her Mossberg was upstairs in the safe. Then she remembered the knives were still packed in a box. She had a spork from her and Grammy's KFC lunch earlier today.

"Walk out the front door and you won't get hurt," she ordered, clutching the spork in her hand as she tiptoed back to the dining room. Her voice echoed.

She pressed the light button and the hall lights switched on. "Go out the front door."

The hall was clear. With her back pressed to the wall, Dori held her breath as she waited for an answer or a creak of a floorboard that would give away his position. She should go for the Mossberg. But she peeked into the front parlor, the room that had suffered the most damage in the house. Something slammed against the front door and the lights snapped off.

# CHAPTER TWO

The spork dropped to the floor and Dori's fingers buzzed from the jolt of adrenaline. She couldn't move as the blood pounding past her ears.

She was out in the open, vulnerable to whoever was in her house, watching from the shadows.

The door thudded again. One moment Dori was frozen; the next she fumbled with the locks and dead bolts. The door swung at her. She leaped out of the way, her lips pulled tight, baring her teeth at whoever waited on the other side.

The porch was empty and so was the yard. The trees hissed and swayed from the wind. Fingers traced down the back of her neck and Dori bolted outside, the porch floor bowing under her weight. She ripped through the crime scene tape and then stumbling, turned back to see if he was coming after her.

She blinked but no one appeared in the hallway or the gaping door way. Her hair blew in her eyes and she pushed it out of her face. Thank God none of her neighbors were looking out their windows, shaking their heads at the crazy neighbor who just flew out of her house like a bat out of hell.

Rain dotted the top of her head, tapping impatiently on the ground. He could be anywhere in the house. Dori reached for her cell phone but it was in her purse by the kitchen door.

She jogged over and then sidled up to her purse and her CVS bag, keeping clear of the open doorway. When she was back in the safety of her car, she dialed National City PD.

An hour later the cruiser pulled into the driveway, the rain now coming down at an angle in the headlights. The officer pulled behind her car where Dori had told the dispatch she'd be waiting. Now she was beginning to second guess her decision.

"Thanks for coming out in the rain," Dori said, rolling down her window as the officer approached.

Holding a black slicker over her head, the officer didn't look happy. "You have an intruder?"

Dori nodded, hoping the man left some trace of breaking and entry so she hadn't come out for nothing. Then again, on nights like this, what else would the officer do except work traffic calls? "I'll come in with you."

"Did you see him leave?"

"I didn't."

The officer looked at the dark brooding house and then Dori. "Stay here. I'll clear the house."

Dori watched as the officer's flashlight beam moved through the house. She went from the front parlor to the living room and then a few moments later, the bedroom next to Dori's. The lights came on, room by room. After what felt like forever, the officer stepped onto the porch, her arms shooting out to catch her balance as the floor boards threatened to give under her. Dori got out of the car and ran across the drive.

Officer Cruz had her jacket and slicker pulled open over her duty weapon. "No sign anyone came through the windows or the back door. Did you see him leave?"

"He disappeared when I unlocked the door." Dori gave a quick explanation of how she'd seen him through the kitchen window and then followed him down the hallway. She left out the spork and her panic at the lights turning off.

"Well, I checked all the rooms upstairs and downstairs. No one is here."

"I know I saw him," Dori said, her voice shaking. She cleared her throat. "I smelled his cologne when I opened the kitchen door. I followed him into that room."

She pointed to the front parlor.

"Come in out of the cold." Dori knew from having been in Officer Cruz's shoes what was going on in her head. "Do you live here alone?"

"I do."

"You see this guy before? Is he an old boyfriend or something?"

"No. Nothing like that."

Officer Cruz took her time before asking the next question, her eyes scrutinizing Dori's face and wet clothes. "This happen before?"

Dori glanced over and saw the spork lying on the floor where she'd dropped it. She held her breath as she thought of all the ramifications that could come from just one stupid phone call. Officer Cruz would write a report, which would find its way back to her sergeant and the homicide supervisor who was investigating the shooting. Dori would have to explain herself.

"Detective Orihuela, are you all right?"

She opened her mouth to answer but her throat went stiff. Her fingers were so cold they hurt. Dori forced herself to focus on the officer's face, not quite meeting her dark eyes. "No, I- Nothing like this has happened before."

An 11-83 call for accident no details on the Sweetwater Road off-ramp came over the radio. Officer Cruz never took her eyes off Dori. "I'll go with you to lock up the doors. If you see anything, you can call us again."

"Thanks. I appreciate your time."

When Dori didn't move, Officer Cruz pointed to the front door. "You want to start with that one?"

They asked Dori to dress as close to what she'd been wearing on the day she shot and killed Kaylee Matthews. The doctors had cut away her blouse and pants. Her jacket had been trashed by blood. Only her boots had survived and she wished they'd been tossed out as she pulled the zippers up her legs.

She had been calm and focused during the walk-through of the scene with Lt. Llevanos of Homicide and her sergeant, Dean Carr. Dori had already given her statement in the hospital. She had no flashbacks walking through the front door in the apartment. Just nerves boiling in her stomach. The place had been cleaned and shut up for weeks. Sweat bloomed over her skin when she breathed in the smell of the chemicals that the clean-up service had used.

Dori pointed where everyone stood as if she were staging a play. The little boy had been curled up on the couch against the window, wrapped in a dirty beach towel. The daughter sat on the floor in front of the TV, twisted around to look over her shoulder at Dori, her partner Elliot and the social worker.

Kaylee stood by the television, no expression on her face as Dori explained their business.

The walk-through had taken only an hour. Dori shook their hands as they prepared to leave the place for the last time. When she reached the threshold, she hesitated.

"Everything all right?" Lt. Llevanos asked.

"Yeah, I-" She patted her pockets as if she'd left something behind. Dori walked out onto the balcony overlooking the cracked and stained driveway. As he locked the door, she wondered what the next tenant would think if they learned what had happened here.

"You saved those two kids' lives," he said when they reached the sidewalk. "She was probably one of those who would've killed them and then herself before letting them go."

Sergeant Carr placed his hand on her shoulder. "You did a good thing."

Dori nodded and then said good-bye before she crossed the street to her car. She'd planned to tell them about last night's encounter with National City PD. But they'd been more concerned about her state of mind leading up to the shooting.

Their blue, unmarked sedans headed west towards downtown and she wasn't sure where to go or what to do with herself but return home. She just started driving, thinking of the how Officer Cruz talked to her last night. Her cheeks flushed and there was this strange shakiness starting in the center of her chest. For weeks, she'd been in a state of total numbness and just as Grammy had predicted, the dam was now leaking. Dori pressed her hands against her chest until it hurt. But the shaking increased and the muscles around her mouth quivered and jumped.

She slammed her palm against the steering wheel. She shouldn't be driving with tears in her eyes.

Dori pulled into her driveway. She realized she had no memory of driving home from East San Diego. She had no control over the keening sounds that broke through her clenched teeth. Ever since her second day in preschool, when Angel Lopez ran over her hand with his tricycle, Dori controlled her emotions. The humiliation of showing weakness had been ingrained in her by Grampy, who after she'd come to him crying over what Angel had done, leaned down and looked her fiercely in the eye. "Don't ever come crying to me again. You cry like some baby and you're meat for the coyotes."

He'd shoved her away from him and refused to speak to her until she stopped sniveling.

Dori had promised. She wasn't one of those women went crying to their girlfriends with her broken heart. She sure as hell wasn't one of those cops who lost it on the job or even in the ladies room. She was the tough Orihuela her grampy had molded her to be; that her fellow officers respected and admired for keeping a cool head, returning fire and allowing two kids, her partner and a social worker to walk out of that apartment unscathed.

She grasped at the broken pieces of who she had been. But they slipped through her fingers. She wasn't supposed to be this sniveling, crying, weak woman. She'd done her duty.

But she'd taken a life. Good or bad, it didn't matter right now. She had a mother's blood on her hands and it was unraveling who she had been to the point where she now saw "make-believe" men running through her house.

Wrapping her arms around herself, Dori rested her head on the steering wheel until the burning in her chest slowly died out.

It had rained. Dori smelled it in the air. Moisture seeped into her shoes as she walked across the grass. Spent clouds crowded against the mountains and faint wisps of steam drifted up from trees under the morning sun. She stopped at a circle of rose bushes bursting with blooms so vivid that they might drip their colors on the grass. A stone bird bath stood in the center, reflecting the house in the still water.

Startled, she looked up. The house – her house - glowed with a coat of fresh white paint. The windows reflected the trees as if they'd just been washed with vinegar and newspaper. Fresh gravel had been laid on the semi-circular drive and smoke drifted out of the chimneys.

A crow cawed and swooped overheard, the wind rustling its wings. She watched it land in the middle of the road where a man in a gray suit stared up at the house.

He straightened the sleeve of his jacket over a glittering watch. He looked like he'd taken a tumble through the dirt with a ripped-out knee. He wasn't much taller than her but he had thick shoulders and powerful arms. The sun glimmered off his polished shoes and as he passed her by, she recognized him as the man she'd seen in her kitchen door window.

Without moving, Dori stood beside him at the front door. His hair was brushed back off his forehead; his profile proud and sharp against the white house. She smelled stale smoke and cologne.

The door swung open and an unsmiling short guy scowled. "Your kind usually tries to run," he said.

"Only after our enemies are dead," the gray-suited man replied, his deep voice hushed and accented like her Grampy's.

Dread uncoiled in the pit of her stomach. Dori was pulled into the house behind the gray-suited man, and the hall went dark as the door slammed shut. She shivered even though a fire crackled in the marble fireplace. Cold seeped out of her bones as she stood there alone with the gray-suited man. He stood in front of the mirror over the fireplace as if memorizing what he looked like.

Her heart jumped when the double doors slid open behind them. A large man with curly black hair stepped out of the front parlor.

"Let's go, Vince," he said, his eyes so piercing and blue that Dori thought he could see her. He watched Vince back away from his reflection in the mirror and walk down the hall.

"Before you go in, I need to tell you that-" He paused and laid a meaty paw on Vince's shoulder, squeezing as if they were father and son. He wore a blue sapphire on his ring finger. "I didn't want this. When you come out, I'll have a place for you. I promise."

Vince stood absolutely still. He started for the parlor and the large man moved his hand as if to stop him.

Dori reached out to grab Vince and pull him back. But her arms wouldn't move. She opened her mouth to shout, but nothing came out. She struggled to pry her voice loose, but she could only stand there as the doors slid shut. Voices rose in anger, and then something slammed against the doors, nearly rattling them off of their tracks.

The doors pulled her closer until they melted away. Dori wasn't prepared for what lay on the floor.

Two red-faced men stood over Vince, laughing as he fought for breath. His jacket was half ripped off, dirtied with boot prints. A pool of blood oozed off the rug and onto the wood floor. His fingers were so broken and mangled; they were more pulp than skin and bone.

"No one's gonna miss one more grease bag Mexican." The two men laughed. Dori saw the deputy stars on their leather belts. One had a bloody chain wrapped around his fist.

They giggled and wiped sweat from their brows. Another man with a mustache watched from his leather wingback chair by the marble fireplace.

Dori choked on the horror of their amusement.

"My God, what did you do?" The blue-eyed man now stood in the doorway. "You were supposed to arrest him. Not- Not this! You'll frame me for murder."

"It'll keep you locked up good and tight. You got your deal, Jimmy," the mustached man said.

Dori felt something wet land on her foot. Vince groaned as he pushed with one leg to crawl out of the room.

"Look at him," one of the deputies said. "Let's just shoot him like a dog."

"I would if he were dog," the mustached man joked, and the others, except Dori and Jimmy laughed.

Vince lifted his face from the rug. Dori never would've recognized him if it wasn't for the suit. His mouth gaped open, with bits of teeth floating in the blood and broken flesh.

Through the swollen folds of skin, she made out his eyes, staring straight into hers. "Do you see me?" he wheezed. His cold, bloodied hand squeezed her foot.

# CHAPTER THREE

A hand smacked the window. Dori jolted awake. The seat belt still strapped her against the seat. Her neck felt like a wilted stem.

"If you don't open this door right now, I'm throwing a rock through the God damned window!"

Heart pumping, she turned to see Grammy frowning at her. Confusion as to how and why she was in her car came and went as Dori realized she had been dreaming.

"That's it, I'm gonna find me a rock," Grammy muttered.

"Wait!" Dori struggled to get free. Her hands shivered.

"What the hell is going on here?" Grammy demanded when Dori managed to open the door. "You finally go out for a bender?"

"No." Panic burbled under the surface. The cool air felt good on her face that was sticky with dried-up tears. She scanned the yard for signs of Vince and the man named Jimmy. "What time is it?"

"I'm retired. I don't keep the time. Why are you sleeping in your car?"

The mental fog cleared and Dori took in deep breaths to calm the fear racing under her skin. But as she stepped out of the car, she winced from the stiffness of her side.

"Looks like you need a Tylenol and bourbon," Grammy assessed, coming over to help her straighten up.

"I didn't sleep last night. I must've just closed my eyes and-"

"Mija, you got to take better care of yourself with a gunshot wound!" Grammy shook her head and then grabbed Dori's arm. "Your grammy knows all about these things. You need to be lying down with a St. Jude candle burning."

Dori looked down at the Big Ben grocery bags next to Grammy's car.

"What's all that?"

"Your groceries," Grammy said. "I don't like you eating all that tofu garbage. You need meat to make your blood strong."

"You didn't have to do that," Dori said, pulling away to help carry the bags inside. She needed to do something normal. But Grammy sank her claws deeper in her arm. "Ow! That's not helping."

"Get inside. I got a little cart thingy I use."

Even if Grammy drew blood, Dori dug her heels in. "You're not carrying that in by yourself."

"You're thirty-six years old and I still have to remind you to say thank you?"

"Thank you. But you're still not carrying all of that in by yourself."

Grammy muttered something about letting people go ahead and kill themselves if that's what they wanted. But she let go and Dori went over and picked up three bags with her right hand. "How long was I asleep?"

"I got here maybe five minutes ago." Grammy pulled out a fold-out wheeled cart. Dori put the three bags in it before reaching for the last two. "I thought you'd wake up when I honked the horn, but then I got worried."

Shame curled her insides at the thought of scaring Grammy.

"I'll pull it," Dori said as Grammy reached for the cart.

"With your good side," Grammy said as they started towards the house. "By the way, you got twenty minutes to powder your nose."

"Why?"

Grammy waved her hand around her face. "You got the greasies, mija."

A greasy face was the least of her problems. She hadn't even taken her anti-depressants and she was already hallucinating. As they approached the house, her chest felt tight at what she'd witnessed in her dream.

"Wait." She stopped, remembering Vince staring at her through the Dutch door window yesterday.

"What?" They stood just two paces from the corner of the house. All her senses were on high alert. What if she saw him again, but Grammy didn't? In their family, fisticuffs at Easter, misdemeanors and certain felonies, extra-marital affairs and children born out of wedlock were par for the course. But Grammy didn't truck with mental illness. To her, craziness was weakness.

"Did you lock your car?" Dori asked.

"Why would I need to do that?"

"Just in case."

Grammy looked back at her car and Dori took the opportunity to hurry to the kitchen door. No one glared back at her through the window as she approached.

"I've called you paranoid before but baby, are you all right?" Grammy asked in that voice she used when one of the cousins had an unsuccessful court hearing.

Dori inserted her house key, but before she could give it a twist, the door swung open. Her heart paused for a second and then resumed at a

16

pounding gallop.

"I locked that before I-"

"Hoo! What have you been drinking?" Grammy waved her hand under her nose just as the alcohol smell flowed out and smacked Dori in the face. It was like someone had rearranged a liquor store with an Uzi.

"Did you bring your cell phone?" Dori ordered, reaching for her off-duty weapon.

"Damn girl, what you packing?"

Grammy pointed to the Smith and Wesson M&P9 in Dori's holster.

"You can't have it."

"That a .45?"

"9mm."

"9mm? Pshh! That's for pussies."

"Stay outside. I may need you to call 911."

When Grammy didn't answer, Dori turned to see her pulling a chrome-plated piece out of her purse. "Your grammy don't bring no damn cell phone to a fight."

She then marched into the kitchen before Dori had the presence of mind to say, "Put that away!"

Grammy's eyes glittered at the prospect of a rumble. In her youth, she'd carried a switchblade in her bra and a razor in her pompadour. "Mija, you let your grammy handle this!"

Dori stepped in, careful to keep out of her grandmother's range. "Seriously, put it down and- Wait, you smell it, too?"

"I'm not that old!" Grammy lowered her gun. "God damned safety! Can't trust these stupid things."

Even though everything was as she'd left it this morning, someone had been in this house. Dori knew it.

She bypassed Grammy fiddling with her gun, figuring two guns if she needed them were better than one. She walked into the mud room at the back of the house. The back door was locked. She crept up the servants' staircase and searched the rooms upstairs. She came back down the main staircase and then cleared the bottom floor.

Holstering her weapon, Dori went back into the kitchen. The smell had dissipated.

"Show me how to take off this safety thing," Grammy demanded.

Dori took the .45 out of Grammy's hand, admiring the inlaid pearl handle before removing the magazine. She pulled the slide open and emptied the round into her hand. She pocketed it and then lowered the hammer before handing the gun back to Grammy. "There you go."

"Give me back my bullets!"

"Is that registered?"

Grammy pursed her lips. "We shouldn't leave the groceries outside."

"Everything was locked when I left. Nothing's been moved and I know the windows were-"

"Honey, no one's been in this house. Not anyone who's alive."

"What?"

"You heard me." Grammy stuck her .45 back in her purse and then dusted off her hands. "How old is this place? Hundred years or so? Bound to be a ghost or two."

"But the smell. I don't get it. I don't have any alcohol in the house."

"Once we bring in the groceries, that won't be a problem no more."

"Aren't you afraid?"

"Are you?"

"No," Dori lied. Then again, a ghost was better than going crazy and calling the cops only to find out it was just her imagination. Even though she was still a little shaky and her eyes ached from crying, she felt safer now that her grammy was here.

"Come on now," Grammy said, making a shooing motion with her hands. "Go out there and bring those groceries inside. We got ice cream that needs to go in your freezer and I need a drink."

# CHAPTER FOUR

After they put the groceries away and Dori made them tea, they sat down on her IKEA couch in the living room.

"This is one helluva place," Grammy said after blowing the steam off her tea. "But it's haunted. I can feel it."

Dori shivered, even though the living room was stuffy. All the windows were stuck and she didn't feel comfortable about opening the French doors until she had a fence around the property. "You say that about everyone's house."

"We're Orihuelas and Mexicans. The spirits talk to us."

From a bottle, Dori thought to herself. "You won't tell anyone that I was sleeping in my car, will you?"

"Give me back your Grampy's billy club and my bullets, and you won't hear nothing out of me."

A shiver shot up her spine at the memory of those men beating Vince in the room across the hallway. "I told you that it's illegal to own a billy club."

"You better not have thrown it out or else I'm taking those groceries to your cousin Chuy's house and you know I don't like that woman he's with."

"I have it," Dori said. Tension bit into her neck. "But with my investigation, the billy club needs to stay where it is, okay?"

Grammy rolled her eyes. "Fine. Now, go clean up. I got a strawberry pie from George's."

Dori was instantly suspicious. "Why?"

"I thought it would help you feel better, and I found you a contractor!"

"What?"

"You said you wanted to fix this place up. Anyway, he's good with his hands and if you're smart, you'll let him use them on you, too!"

Grammy cackled at her own joke. Dori took in what was supposed to be a deep, calming breath. Judging by the dubious architectural state of

Grammy's house, the last thing she wanted was her contractor touching this house.

"I know what you're thinking-" Grammy held up her hands as if placating Dori. "But let me tell you that he's-"

A footstep sounded in the hallway. Springing to her feet, Dori hissed at her to be silent. The person stopped and then started towards the living room.

Dori tiptoed towards the doorway, every muscle ready for battle. "Who's there?" she called out, her hand yanking her jacket aside to reach for her holster.

"Put that thing away," Grammy hissed. "It's probably him!"

The man in the doorway was solid, breathing and looking just as surprised as she was to be standing nearly nose-to-nose. When she looked into his eyes, dark and slightly titled at the corners, she pulled her jacket closed.

"Hi Gavin," she said, her gaze dropping to the floor.

"Dori," he said.

He'd filled out since high school. His red shirt hugged a nice chest and was neatly tucked into dark blue jeans. The sole of his black motorcycle boot rubbed against the floor as he shifted his weight. Dori looked up and he caught her checking him out. A knowing grin formed on his lips.

Ex-boyfriend or not, he let himself into her house without knocking. If she wasn't under investigation for a shooting, she'd introduce him to her Smith and Wesson just to see that grin fall off his face.

"So you're the cop granddaughter," he said, holding up one hand and wiggling his fingers. "I'm the guy with the good hands."

"Mijo, you startled us!" Grammy pushed Dori out of her way to get at him.

"I knocked, but the kitchen door was open," he said, eyeing Dori over Grammy's shoulder. "Sorry if I startled you."

"Oh, now don't you worry about that. You're so dark, mijo," Grammy cooed, petting his muscular arm. "You should wear that sunscreen so you don't burn this nice skin."

Resisting the urge to bolt through the nearest window, Dori held her hand out. "How are you?"

He leaned forward to take her hand. His eyes were brown like brandy held up to candle light. "Good," he said simply and Dori felt the warmth of his hand all the way to down to her toes. "So where do you want me to start?"

"I'm sorry?"

"With your house. It needs some work."

"It's my gift for her fortieth birthday," Grammy said.

"I'm thirty six!"

"Forty'll be here before you know it, mija."

Gavin cleared his throat, toying with the pork pie hat he held in his hands. "Well, let me start with the big stuff. You got a lot of stuck doors and windows and that means the foundation needs work. See out here-"

He turned and walked down the hallway. Grammy trotted after him like he was the Mexican Marlon Brando. He turned and looked at Dori like he expected her to tag along and pretend everything was normal.

"Come, mija," Grammy ordered like Dori was four years old. "Gavin knows what he's talking about."

Dori followed because the sooner she got this over with, the sooner she could take her pain meds and eat the entire strawberry pie.

"See this?" He put his hat on the mantle of the marble fireplace that was sinking into the floor. "These old places shift with time and with the proper retrofitting, we can jack up this fireplace so it doesn't end up in your basement. Now, here's a really big problem."

He reached for a tiny flashlight riding in the back pocket of his jeans.

"Let me hold that, mijo," Grammy cooed, taking his hat off the mantle and caressing it. "Are you thirsty? Hungry?"

He smiled at Grammy but never once looked at Dori. Not that she blamed him. "No thank you, Señora Orihuela."

Gavin went back to business. He aimed the beam of light at the staircase. "See the third step there? And the fifth and that one and that one-"

Dori distinctly felt a hand between her shoulder blades. Grammy shoved her forward and she bumped into his solid shoulder.

Gavin recoiled as if he didn't want any contact with her. Even though it had been 20 years since they broke up, humiliation flashed hot then cold. He'd once stood before her with a bouquet of roses and hope in his eyes. Now she was the evil high school bitch who cheated on him.

Dori righted herself and folded her arms over her chest. "Sorry, you were saying?"

She deliberately stepped back, keeping a distance between them. "Hey, watch it! That's my foot!" Grammy exclaimed.

Dori glared at her over her shoulder. "Well, I'm just all sorts of clumsy today, aren't I?"

Gavin cleared his throat. "This staircase shouldn't be used anymore until it's been retrofitted. Also, you're missing some lalley columns in the basement and the foundation is literally crumbling to pieces."

"When did you see my basement?" Dori asked.

Instead of answering her, Gavin went back and crouched down in front of the marble fireplace. He poked his head under the flue and aimed his flashlight into the chimney.

Dori turned to Grammy who had risen up on the balls of her feet with the hope that his shirt would ride out of his jeans. She refused to be ignored. "I'll ask again when did you-"

"Sorry. While I waiting outside, I took a little trip into your basement," he said, his voice echoing in the fireplace. "You should have your basement door locked up."

Just as she was about to get pissed off, Dori realized that Gavin gave her the perfect explanation for the man she'd seen in the window. Maybe he'd gotten in through the basement. Maybe his face had gotten all mixed up in her head and her nightmare had been nothing more than some weird psychological thing.

As Gavin and Grammy talked about bricked-in chimneys, Dori broke away and walked to the basement door. Even though she hadn't seen the guy run off, nor had she heard his footsteps after he'd vanished from the window, it would make sense that an intruder could get in through the basement.

The doorknob was cold and when she twisted, it was locked. She pulled and tugged.

Her mind yanked at any logical explanation it could find: the man she'd seen had locked it on his way out. Or maybe the lock caught when he'd slammed it behind him.

Then she realized she had been left behind. Gavin and Grammy were talking on the front porch. Dori was about to hurry over before her grandmother sexually assaulted him, or fell through the rotting porch floorboards. As she walked by the front parlor, she couldn't help but slow her pace and look in that dark, cold room that she'd seen in her dream.

She was about to reach for the door knob when someone in the front parlor walked across the floor towards her. Awareness shot up her spine and when she turned, her whole body flashed hot then cold. No one was in the front parlor, except for spiders and their desiccated victims. She was alone.

Dori waited for the sound again. Then, the floorboards made a cracking sound right in front of her and she felt the distinct sensation of something cold and sticky pressing against her. Dori staggered back. She breathed in the smell of blood and nearly gagged on it. Her breath came in short. Her thoughts scattered in every direction as this horrible cold suffocated her.

She opened her mouth to scream for Grammy when two hands shoved her out of the room.

Just like that, the walls pushed back to their proper places and the cold swept back into the room. Whatever had been in her face had vanished and took with it the smell of blood.

Dori took one step back and then another, waiting for the sensation to come back. But nothing happened.

Drawing her shoulders back, Dori pressed her hand against her chest, feeling her heart hammering through skin and bone. Still shivering slightly, she was just a few paces short of the front door when Grammy's voice drifted out to her.

"You think you can handle working with my girl?" Grammy asked.

In spite of being wobbly on her feet, Dori leaned forward to listen for his response.

"I can tolerate anyone as long as they pay on time," Gavin finally said.

She swallowed the lingering nausea and forced herself to walk out the front door and down the steps.

"Hi," she said. They both whipped around in surprise.

Gavin turned away and ran his fingers along the peeling siding. Dori needed to gain control of this situation before he thought he could swagger around her house.

"We were wondering when you'd come out," Grammy said.

"I've got a lot to do today, so let's do this another time," Dori said.

"Mija, Gavin here builds big houses."

"You know I grew up down the street from here," he said and Grammy nodded. "I'd like to take a crack at this."

"Then it's done," Grammy said. "You're hired."

Dori's eyes burned from the brilliant sunlight and she swayed on her feet. Two panic attacks within a few hours of each other were taking their toll and her stomach gurgled in warning. But she stared at him with a confidence she didn't feel.

"The thing is you can't do this half-assed," Gavin said, looking at Grammy as if Dori didn't scare him. "You need to take in the whole picture and not just patch things up here and there."

"What if I just want to make it safe and livable?" Dori asked.

Gavin gave a short laugh. The kind of laugh that wasn't all out rude, but still patronizing. "What do you mean by that?"

She patiently explained. "I'd like to open my windows and not fall into the basement when I come downstairs one morning."

"Let's start with the lalley columns and pour you a new foundation," he said, not looking her in the eye. "Didn't you get a home inspection report?"

"Yes, and I read it, too."

He grinned at the acid in her voice, but he was toying with his hat. "I'd like to see it. Please," he said with exaggerated courtesy.

"I didn't say you were hired."

Grammy's spine stiffened and she did a slow turn at the tone in Dori's voice.

Dori counted off on her fingers. "I want a written bid for the roof, the staircase and the column things within three days. Do you think you can you do that?"

He finally looked at her fully. Contempt shot across the distance between them. "If you don't mind my asking, what are your plans?"

Dori straightened her spine. "Give me the bid and we'll go from there."

She could see exactly what he thought of her: ball-busting bitch who didn't know what she'd gotten herself into. "And next time we meet, I'd like for you to call and make an appointment so I know when to expect you," she added.

He shot a glance at Grammy as if hoping that she'd save him in case Dori took him down to the ground. "Sure thing."

Dori turned to Grammy. "I'm going to take a shower. Can you tolerate him?"

Grammy gave a slight shake of her head as if wondering how Dori could verbally bitch-slap a beautiful hunk of man like Gavin. But if Dori hadn't turned and walked inside, she would've seen admiration, too.

"Oh yes, mija," Grammy said, taking Gavin by the arm. "I can handle him just fine."

# CHAPTER FIVE

## The train, April 1932

Eighty-something years is a long time to go without a drink.

Vicente paused in raising the coffee cup. Where had that thought come from? He shook his head to clear it; not having slept last night because of the dream in the white house.

He concentrated on the coffee shivering with the swaying of the train. The silver spoon rattled on the table. He looked out the window, framed by green velvet curtains to see where they were between Los Angeles and San Diego. From the looks of the writing on the buildings, they were chugging through an Italian quarter. The sunlight peeking over the hill seared straight into his eyes.

"God damn," he said, slamming the coffee cup on the mahogany table.

"More coffee, Mr. Sorolla?"

Vicente looked over his shoulder at Andy Munemitsu, who like him, had been recruited from the orange groves to transport product from the midnight deliveries along the coast. Now, Vicente was James McClemmy's personal secretary and Andy served as the butler and gunman when needed. They and a few heavies Vicente had personally selected traveled in the private Pullman car.

The bright sun had blinded him. All he could make out were Andy's white coat and his silhouette against the open windows facing the hazy ocean. "Go to hell."

"Very good, sir," Andy replied. He almost kept a straight face but then snorted out a laugh.

Vicente fought to keep from smiling.

"Good thing he's not here to see this," Andy said, whipping out a towel and then mopping away the few drops of coffee.

Rubbing his aching forehead, Vicente asked, "When are you heading back?"

"Right after I make sure you're fed and diapered."

"Well, I won't spend all your money all in one place."

Andy didn't live up to the stereotype of his race. He couldn't play poker for shit.

"I'll get it back and some." Andy held up the cup. "You done messing up my private car?"

"Not by half."

Andy muttered something in his father's tongue as he walked away. Vicente had long given up demanding the translation years ago.

With all these wild colors swirling and fading and reappearing before his eyes and the swaying of the train, his stomach felt as if it were crawling up his throat. He was almost home. His shoulders and neck tightened like screws. Six years of having vanished like a ghost, he was on the train from Los Angeles.

The train slowed and the brakes screamed against the wheels.

Ever since Mr. McClemmy had given him this assignment, Vicente hadn't slept. Would he face his grandmother and sister again, having left them all those years ago? And then there was Anna. They were three women he'd loved and hated; the ones he'd promised to take care of, but abandoned. They probably wouldn't even recognize him.

Vicente pushed himself up to his feet and walked to the windows facing the ocean. No point in thinking of them right now. Repeal was coming. With Mr. McClemmy's appeal hanging in the balance, Vicente had been sent to consolidate their territory and make sure they had import agreements in place. Once he accomplished his mission, he'd worry about the women.

"The conductor just informed me that we arrive in fifteen minutes," Andy said, shouting from the kitchenette. They never would've been this informal if the boss had been on board. But with the trial underway, Mr. McClemmy couldn't leave the county.

Vicente stared across the new airport tarmac at the San Diego Bay. It was a hazy blur of blue. He could almost smell the brine and feel the give of the sand under his shoes. If he closed his eyes, he might feel the wind and see her-

He staggered when the train pulled to a stop.

"Here," Andy said, holding the camel hair coat open for Vicente to slide his arms into the sleeves.

"Give it over."

"Let me do my job while I still have it."

Vicente gave him a dirty look and then yanked his coat free. He nearly caught his watch on the satin lining. Andy sighed. "At least let me open the door."

"See ya later," he said to Andy and then stepped out, letting the sun slide over his head before he put his hat on.

He was the first off the train. The porter ran over, holding his hat to his head. Andy's whistle cut sharp through the grumbling of the engine. He shouted at them to collect the trunks. Vicente walked across the tracks eager to stretch his legs and get to work.

He pushed through the crowd into the Santa Fe Depot. He paused under the giant bronze chandeliers. It was so small and quiet in comparison to the cavernous station in Los Angeles. To think he'd once thought this place glamorous when he'd admire the glossy Pullmans as he came to and from his job cleaning street cars. He shook his head and found the car waiting for him. He nodded to the driver as he stepped into the back. The walk to the US Grant Hotel was an easy one, but he wasn't a kid hustling papers anymore.

The doormen called out good morning as Vicente walked up the carpet and through the main entrance. He didn't recognize them from his days selling the afternoon paper. His shoulders tensed, expecting someone to quietly ask him to leave as if he were a mongrel who wandered in off the street.

But with a slight bow, the desk manager said good morning and they'd looked forward to his arrival. He then presented Vicente with the ledger and a silver pen. "If you'd sign here, please."

Vicente signed his Americanized name, Vincent Sorrelle.

"Welcome to San Diego, Vincent."

He glanced over his shoulder. Two feds stood behind him. The desk manager cleared his throat and kept his gaze on the ledger.

"Agents." Vicente handed the pen to the manager. "I'll be up in my suite later this afternoon."

The hotel manager kept his eyes averted. "Thank you, sir."

Vicente faced the agents, about to invite them to coffee as his boss had done when the U.S. Treasury goons had searched his wife's modest bungalow. Always be a gentleman to the men who were about to arrest you, was Mr. McClemmy's rule. It pissed them off.

But his smile froze on his face when he recognized the blue-eyed, curly haired agent. The older guy looked like a boxer who gave it up for a more lucrative line of work. "You come with us," he said loud enough to startle the guests in the lobby.

Ignoring his command, Vicente turned to the younger officer. "Good to see you again."

Agent Rick Campbell held out his hand. "I thought you looked familiar.

Come back home?"

"On business."

"This is Agent Hollner," Campbell said. "Agent Hollner this is-"

"I know who this spic is."

Vicente nodded a greeting to Agent Hollner, whose face turned the same color as the red carpets he had just trod upon.

"We know exactly what kind of business you're in," Hollner said.

"Yes, the dairy business," Vicente said, glad that Andy had stayed on the train. He would never have kept a straight face.

"Right," Agent Campbell said. "Minding the farm for the boss."

Vicente liked Campbell. He always thought of him with gratitude after he'd arrested him with decency.

"Your boss needs all the help he can get," Hollner cut in. "At least he's an honest crook, spilling his guts to his arresting officer."

"How can I help you?" Vicente said, almost offended that Hollner thought he could be baited that easily.

"Go back to the Mexicans," Hollner offered. "The sharks will move in and eat you alive when your boss goes to prison."

"Our dairy business is here in the U.S., not in Mexico. Far as I know, milk, eggs and butter aren't illegal," Vicente replied.

"San Diego's a small town, but we're not small time. After the Aqua Caliente killings, we've got a zero tolerance policy-"

"Your mayor and the coroner learned the hard way," Vicente said in a perfect imitation of his boss. He then strolled away from the desk and Hollner followed him like a dog in heat. "But my interests are of no concern to the law."

"We'll make sure of that."

"If you're not going to arrest me, I have to go to work."

Vicente held out his hand to Campbell in a friendly gesture as if Hollner weren't ready to boil over. "Glad to see you made something of yourself," Campbell said.

"The feeling's mutual."

As Campbell loosened his grip, Vicente bore down with all his strength and leaned in. "I'd like to contribute to the fallen officer's fund. My secretary will personally deliver the check."

He released Campbell and turned his back on them.

They let him walk out the main doors, but they'd stick a tail on him. Vicente made a bet with himself that it was the man in the blue suit sitting in a wingback chair by the door, reading the paper. The doors opened as he approached and he had two tens in his hand to tip the doormen.

Vicente froze in place. The doormen vanished. The sounds of the taxis honking and the gentle murmur of conversation abruptly switched off. The cool, damp morning was replaced by a stale mustiness. A moment ago, he'd headed out the door of the fanciest hotel in town. Now he stood on a scarred wood floor in a small room with sickly yellow walls. The fireplace was cracked and stained, its black mouth hanging open like some sleeping drunk.

He looked around, trying to remember how he'd gone from the lobby to here. His coat was missing and he now wore a pale gray suit streaked with soot and a ripped-out knee.

Voices sounded from the next room. He stepped forward. Then he stopped, not sure if he wanted them to know he was here. He had no idea what day it was, or why he was here.

But then it looked familiar as if he'd been here a long, long time ago. He was dreaming again. Was this the white house again, or had he passed out? He couldn't remember what he'd done between dismissing Agents Campbell and Hollner and walking out the door. Had they gotten him and dragged him here? Vicente felt the back of his head. He then brought his hand to look for blood. It was clean.

The voices started again. Two women and a man. He looked down at the floor as he heard them moving closer.

Vicente flexed his fingers and then curled them into fists as he looked around the room. No curtains hung in the windows and yet all he could see were blurry shapes through the glass. His gut tightened; he knew something terrible had happened here.

Then he was on the floor, his body on fire with pain. Two men leered down at him, their lips drawn tight over their teeth. He heard the clanking of the chain but he couldn't move his arms to shield his face as it came down at him.

He was then on his feet, the men gone but the agony remained. Someone approached the room. Before he could move, she stood in the doorway. She wore men's pants and strange, soft looking shoes. There was nothing delicate about her compact figure. She stood proud and defiant as she cautiously stepped towards the room.

Vicente felt his teeth swimming in blood. He shifted his weight and the floor creaked under his weight. She looked right at him. Their eyes met and fury erupted in his chest.

"Who are you?" he asked. He moved towards her, now standing right in front of her.

She jerked back. Her eyes flashed up and around as if she couldn't see him crowding near her. When he looked behind her and saw the wide hallway, Vicente knew this house. He'd been here before, but he couldn't-

This had to be a nightmare and if it was, it was a helluva realistic one. "What am I doing here? Talk damn it!"

Vicente reached for her. "Where am I?" he demanded. "Who brought me here?"

She acted as if she couldn't hear or see him, but she knew he was there.

He raised his mangled hands to wrap them around her neck, to somehow release the pain by squeezing the life out of her. But he wasn't that kind of man. He'd never hurt a woman, no matter how low she was. Instead, he planted his hands on her chest and shoved her away.

Her arms flailed out. When she caught her footing, she looked in his eyes, trying to catch her breath. Vicente dropped his hands, drowsy on his feet. As he came to his knees, he had this feeling that he knew why he was here and who those men were. But he was losing consciousness as it started to come back at him like water, slowly rising up his body and then over his head, from which there was no escape.

She backed up, fading into the light. He was about to call out for her to help him when everything around him blurred and all went quiet again.

# CHAPTER SIX

Dori's eyes snapped open. She grabbed her neck, the raw meat feel of his hands lingering on her skin.

"Holy-" She couldn't finish from the tightness in her chest. Her tank top was plastered to her skin. Even her hair was wet with it. For one horrifying second, she thought it was blood. She pressed her hand to her chest and then pulled it back, staring at it in the moonlight. Her hand was clean. Only sweat.

It was the same dream. Again. She'd followed Vince into the house and watched him die. Dori pulled air into her lungs, shivering so bad that she couldn't move to turn on the lamp by her bed.

Downstairs, the pocket doors slid open. Her fists curled as she listened to shuffling directly below her room. One of them made a sound that sounded like a curse as they bumped against the wall.

"Here," a man's voice said.

Dori held her breath to be as quiet as possible. She heard the men moving towards the back of the house. They were talking but she couldn't make out the words. The hairs on the back of her neck prickled as the back door opened and they moved out into the yard.

She then lunged for her cell phone. Her hand smacked the nightstand. Just then, she had a clear memory of setting it on the kitchen counter after she had walked Grammy to her car.

Using the moonlight that came in through the windows, Dori got down on the floor and reached under her bed for the lock box. Careful not to make a sound, she pulled it out. She stabbed in the code.

Finally, the weight of her off-duty weapon gave her some comfort. She grabbed the SureFire flashlight and then turned towards the blade of light at the bottom of the door. She'd left the hall light on before going to bed. She slowed her thoughts until her head went into that place where instinct took over. Standing with her back against the wall, she aimed at the floor, counting to three before reaching to open the door.

After waiting to hear if they'd come back into the house, Dori stepped out into the hallway. Her gun aimed forward as she scuttled alongside the wall.

Her bare feet whispered along the wood floors. She peered down the main staircase and then headed towards the servant's staircase that spiraled down into pitch black. No one moved; the house was silent. Dori switched on the flashlight as she descended the stairs.

She took a deep breath as she approached the mud room. Expecting to see the back-door open, she froze when she saw it was still shut. Scanning the floor, there were no recent markings or prints. She tried the knob. It was locked.

Her blood pounded past her ear drums. She then heard gurgling and desperate gasps for air. Her gun swung up as she moved towards the sound. The chill in the air swept over her before she turned the corner into the main hallway. The flashlight caught him in the beam. It was Vince. She shook her head. This was a dream. She wasn't fully awake. But the gun grip in her hand and the cold floor under her feet were real.

He lay sprawled face down, a blood trail evidence of his agonizing crawl from the front parlor. Dori recognized the high-pitched wheezing breath of a dying man.

"Wake up Dori," she said to herself. "Just wake up."

If this wasn't a dream, she had to help him. But the guys who did this could easily overtake her. He let out one last hissing breath and then went completely still. Screw it. She couldn't just stand here.

Ignoring years of training and experience, Dori ran over to him, completely exposed to whoever waited in the shadowed rooms. As she bent over him, she saw his gray suit, ripped and stained with blood. His black hair hung over his face.

A floorboard popped and Dori swung around, aiming her gun and flashlight into the darkness. No one stood there with evil intent. No one jumped her. She then looked down. The dying man and his blood were gone.

Her knees gave out and the gun clattered against the floor.

Dori began trembling, shaking her head in denial of what she'd just seen. She drew in her feet and wrapped her arms around her shins, horrified that she'd just emerged from an elaborate hallucination.

For the first time in her life, Dori prayed that she'd just seen a ghost.

The good thing about discovering a guy lying in a pool of blood in your hallway - only to realize that he wasn't real - was that it roused a girl into cleaning her house.

At four in the morning, Dori had enough of shivering on the floor. She refused to sit there another second and deny what she'd seen. So, she did what any self-respecting woman would do. She walked into the kitchen, drank straight from her bottle of Herradura Silver and tried to catch her breath from the might of 80 proof.

If this were a movie, she'd jump into her car and never come back. But it wasn't. Dori had invested a hefty down payment and she'd sent in her first mortgage payment last week. She paid her insurance and her property taxes. If she walked away, she couldn't afford rent until the house sold. Her only alternative was to live with Grammy.

The thought of going back to her grandmother's house had Dori reaching for the tequila again. When she came back up for air, her fingers and toes tingled and she had to blink a few times to see straight. The kitchen lights pushed back the darkness. Her heart jolted when she saw the wide-eyed, wild-haired woman staring back at her in the reflection of the window.

She twisted the cap back onto the tequila bottle before she became one of those cops who drank to get through the night. At least she hadn't started taking the Lexapro.

Dori had the bandage to prove that she'd survived worse than seeing a dead guy vanish from her floor. Then again, what had she expected when she bought a 120-year-old house? To be honest, she'd thought she'd get some disembodied voices, footsteps, a door or two opening and closing; maybe a nice old lady ghost who died peacefully in her sleep.

Laughter burbled out of her mouth. Tears of hysteria, in the privacy of her haunted house, were better than blubbering in her car so Dori went with it.

When she'd cried out the tequila and despair, she stared at the boxes piled in the butler's pantry. She washed her swollen eyes and dabbed her face dry with a paper towel. She might as well get some cleaning done. She yanked on some rubber gloves.

Unpacking, dusting, wiping and vacuuming unearthed more dust and dirt. But her unending, obsessive quest for cleanliness was the only way to break up the wad of hysteria that threatened to take her down to her knees. With each stroke of the vacuum, she convinced herself that what she'd experienced was a ripple effect of her own real-life trauma. With each parry and thrust of the duster, she told herself she'd do yoga or even meditation to straighten out the tangled wires of her mind.

By seven that morning, Dori had set up the bookcases in the living room. Her blend of antiques and Ikea stuff looked like doll furniture in the cavernous room with ceiling medallions and Tiffany glass windows.

By nine-thirty, she finished what would've normally been an easy workout before she'd been shot. She limped into the showers at the gym, her side aching but her mind calm. Looking forward to a hot shower in a place where no dead people would show up, she opened her locker. Just as she set her towel and shower bag on the bench, her cell phone rang.

Out of habit, Dori answered without looking at the display. "Detective-" She caught herself. "Dori Orihuela."

"Dori, this is your mother."

She nearly crushed the phone in her hand. "Oh, hi. Uh. How are you?"

"Cleve and I would like to meet you," Brenda said in a voice that dripped with judgment.

Her blood iced over as she thought about what Cleve might have told her mother.

"Dori?"

Sinking down to the bench, Dori realized she might as well face the inevitable. "So, when do you want to meet?"

# CHAPTER SEVEN

Even though she tried not to, Dori arrived early at Casa d'Oro. The restaurant was tucked into the far corner of the Sweetwater Mall. She watched the woman slapping masa between her hands and then tossing it onto the hot iron comal to blister and puff up with steam. Her face was blank with peace or most likely, boredom. Either way, Dori thought it must be nice to have a job where you weren't likely to get shot.

Her phone buzzed in her pocket. Hoping it was her mother calling to cancel their lunch plans, Dori glanced at the screen and then grinned. She opened Sela's text and read, "Why would you answer mom's call?"

Sela's face then flashed on the screen. Dori answered, "I know. Next time I'll let her go to voicemail."

"Dude, like when in doubt call me first," Sela said.

The tension in Dori's stomach loosened. The longer Sela lived in New York, the stronger her California parlance. "I will."

"It's not too late to flake out. You don't have to do lunch with mom."

"I'm already here."

"You're too principled for your own good," she said breathlessly. Dori could hear the sounds of the city and imagined her sister walking up from the subway to her Greenwich apartment.

"How's your gig?"

"Mariah Carey came in last night or this morning. Anyway, she didn't tip but I was doing my Alicia Keys cover and so…"

Dori relaxed against the wall, listening to her sister's excited chatter. For once, she appreciated Sela's self-absorption. It was a relief not to be asked how she was feeling if she was having nightmares or what she'd do if she wasn't reinstated.

"So enough about me," Sela said, slightly out of breath. "You'll call when Mom is finished with you?"

"Won't you be sleeping?"

"Yeah, but I'll make an exception."

"Turn off your phone. Get some rest."

"Okay," Sela said, yawning. "You'll be all right. I know you will. You always land on your feet."

Dori's eyes teared up. "Night night," she said, her voice husky from keeping her emotions in check.

"Later." Sela ended the call. Dori slipped her phone back into her pocket, her throat burning. She wasn't quite sure why her sister had set her off. Sela had meant it as a compliment. But Dori felt like her sister had been talking about a stranger; someone they once knew a long time ago. Her chest felt hollowed out as her thoughts touched on the possibility that this time she might not land on her feet; she might continue free falling.

Cold air swept in and curled around her legs. Dori turned. The moment she saw her mother's face set in tense lines, she knew she was done for. Cleve shook rain off the umbrella.

"There you are," Brenda said. A tight grin flashed across her face as she came at Dori with her arms held open.

When she released Dori from a minimal contact hug, she did a quick evaluation and pronounced, "You look terrible. Are you not sleeping?"

Dori adopted a relaxed smile in an effort to seem natural and unconcerned. "Hi, Mom. Cleve."

"Dori, good to see you," Cleve said, his eyes apologizing for what was about to happen.

"You, too," Dori said evenly.

Her mom sniffed and shuddered with revulsion. "This place always smells funny."

"Let's sit by the window," Dori suggested.

"There's nothing to see but a rainy parking lot," Brenda said wearily. "It's better than sitting next to the kitchen. Did you hear that your cousin Jenny was accepted into fashion school? I don't know what practical skill that girl will learn there."

They sat down while her mom gossiped and critiqued and aired her grievances, only stopping to breathe when the waitress came for their orders and returned with the food. Dori and Cleve politely avoided eye contact.

As Dori crumbled oregano into her posole, Brenda asked, "What about you? How is the house coming along?"

"It's still standing," she said, immediately seeing Vince in her hallway. She blinked and pushed him out of her mind.

"When can we see it?"

Dori reached for a lime wedge. "Anytime."

"I know you don't care for my opinion, but I don't think you should be living there in your condition."

The lime wedge dropped into Dori's posole, splashing her hand with scalding broth. Here it comes, she told herself. "What condition is that?"

"You're a single woman with a- Well, you know."

Sweat bloomed under her shirt. Dori lifted her gaze from her posole and aimed straight into her mother's eyes. "A what?"

Brenda leaned in close, even though the waitress had disappeared into the kitchen. "You got shot," she murmured as if it was as sinful as cooking meth in the basement.

"I don't see how that affects me living in my house," Dori replied, her calm tone rankling her mother.

"You're all alone."

"I've lived alone for fifteen years."

Brenda straightened in her seat. "What are you saying?"

"Nothing. Just that I've been on my own for a long time and I'm fine."

"You don't look fine."

"You already said that."

"Everything else is good?" Cleve cut in, reminding them he was at the table.

"Yeah. No problems."

He smiled weakly. "Good."

"So, does this mean you're finally giving up this police work?" Brenda asked.

"Excuse me?" Dori asked.

"Well, after what happened."

"I'm not giving up anything."

"Are you sure? It's not too late to do other things."

If Cleve hadn't looked so miserable, Dori would've let her mother have it. But he'd apparently said nothing about the Lexapro or else Brenda would've pounced on that the moment she came through the door.

Dori swallowed a caustic reply, and it shredded the back of her throat. She normally loved the plump corn tortillas. But she stuffed one in her mouth and tasted nothing but bitterness.

They ate in wounded silence. Dori and her mother had never been particularly close. Even when she was a kid, Dori always had this sense her mother was afraid of her. She'd heard stories of her frighteningly strong mind as a toddler. Grampy and Grammy celebrated it, while her mother felt victimized by it.

Still, now that they were adults, it would've been nice if they could at least be friends.

Without warning, the sun came out from behind the clouds, washing the parking lot and the trees with a brilliant light that streamed in through the windows. It bisected half of the table, warming the right side of Dori's face. The light bounced off of her knife and seared straight into her eye. She covered it with her hand and slid it into the shaded half of the table.

"If I were you, I'd rip the house down, subdivide it and then sell the lots," Brenda said. "You might as well make money while you can. Just in case."

The spoon stayed poised in Dori's left hand, her right fist balled in her lap. Betrayal lodged thick in her chest, sending out tentacles that choked off her breath. She carefully placed the spoon next to the bowl. She could no longer force herself to eat. No one spoke, nor ate their food.

The waitress returned, and Dori nearly threw her credit card at her so she could get away from them.

"You don't have to do that," Brenda said. "It's our treat."

Dori grinned and her cheeks hurt from the effort. "No, no. It's mine," she said thickly and then cleared her throat.

The waitress took her card, and Dori clenched her jaw to keep herself steady.

"Well, if you say so. Gosh Cleve, we should've ordered dessert."

Dori caught the apologetic look in his eye as he said, "We're still trying to lose weight."

Brenda turned to him. "What are you saying?"

While her mother bickered, Dori turned to look out the window, no longer caring to hold up her end of the conversation. Trees were whipped around by the wind. A white plastic bag tumbled and sailed across the blacktop.

She just wanted to go home as her mother filled up the silence with chatter. But then she remembered the dead guy roaming around the place.

The waitress returned with her credit card, and Dori scribbled her signature.

"When do you think Cleve and I might come by to tour your house?" Brenda asked as they stood up and put on their coats.

"I'll be busy for the next few days."

"Getting a manicure, I hope."

"Brenda," Cleve said, quietly. "That's enough."

Her mother sat there open-mouthed with shock. Dori took the opportunity to get up and grab her jacket. "See you guys later."

Cleve hurried around her mother and blocked Dori from leaving. He hesitantly held out his arms for a hug, and Dori did nothing to stop him. "You take care all right?" he whispered in her ear.

"I will. Thank you."

They made eye contact, and he nodded that he understood that she was thanking him for keeping her secret.

"Where's my hug?" Brenda demanded but Dori pretended not to hear and left a tip for the tortilla lady.

# CHAPTER EIGHT

Her dad used to joke that the only thing Dori had in common with her mother was that they didn't know how to have fun.

Dad would wake them up on Saturday mornings with the announcement they were spending the day exploring. Her mom would pout, determined to clean the house and then scream and cry at them for not helping. She'd say things like: "Let's just call our maid so the place won't be a sty when we get back," or "Laundry doesn't wash itself."

But back then, when Dad still played with them, he would wait out Mom's testiness. Eventually, under the influence of the open road and the car radio blasting out Hendrix, the lines in her mom's forehead would ease. Dori would look through the gap between the two front seats and see her parents holding hands.

Those were the good times. Christmas on the Prado at Balboa Park, riding the carousel at Seaport Village, exploring the tide pools at Cabrillo National Point and playing charades to the light of bonfires on Coronado were the backdrops when Dori had a family. Then Grampy died and left nothing to her parents, choosing to leave it all to Grammy. To be fair and with the perspective of an adult, Dori saw that Grammy had lorded over her parents; not bothering to keep her opinions about how they were raising their kids and managing their money to herself. Dad's cruelty broke through the soil of disappointment and from that point on, Mom wilted under the stormy clouds of his anger. Dori and Sela went wild just to be noticed, while Robbie worked hard at being the good son.

Home was a battleground on which Dori fought to be her own person. She and her sister became those wild Orihuela girls, the bane of every boy's mother especially their own. But it hadn't been fun. Not in the true, free sense of the word.

You're an embarrassment, Brenda would yell when she'd catch Dori sneaking in through the window at 2 a.m. Boys rape girls like you.

Then one night, her mother's words almost came true. After a house party, Dori got into a senior boy's car just for the thrill of seeing the other girls envy her. They took off, the car vibrating from the bass, and then he went crazy, pretending to crash into cars and veering into oncoming traffic. At first, Dori kept her cool, determined to impress him until he reached over and grabbed her breast, squeezing like he'd yank it off.

Her stomach still clenched at the memory of the nasty promises he'd made to her; the things he was gonna do when he pulled over where no one could see them. She was gonna like it, he'd said.

She froze with terror, convinced that she was being punished for all her misdeeds. Her mother had been right. Dori desperately grasped onto the unlikely hope that Wonder Woman would land from out of the night sky to rescue her and she would never ever do something this stupid again.

But a miracle of a different kind occurred. Light burst into the car, and cursing, he pulled over. While they waited for the officer to approach his window, he told her to keep her mouth shut if she wanted to go home without a black eye.

It wasn't Diana, Princess of the Amazons, who shined her flashlight into their faces. It was Officer Ellen Gutierrez who asked him to step out of the car. She'd arrested him for possession among other offenses and then sat with Dori at the station until Grammy came to pick her up.

"Is he your boyfriend?" Ellen had asked, pulling up a chair and sitting face-to-face with Dori.

Dori shook her head, still shivering from the violent images his promises branded in her head.

"Then why'd you get in the car with him?"

She had shrugged and nearly had a heart attack when Ellen barked, "That's not an answer!"

Dori hadn't trusted herself to speak. She dammed up her terror, determined to keep her cool façade intact.

But Ellen had waited her out. She appeared like she could do anything in her winter blues with the heavy belt at her waist and thick black boots.

Finally, Dori replied, "I thought he was cute."

To her surprise, Ellen had leaned back in her chair, a wistful grin on her face. "Honey, the worst ones usually are," she'd said, and that was when their friendship and Dori's career had begun. She left her party friends and her see-through lace tank tops behind and became an officer Ellen was proud of.

So why did anything that came out of her mother's mouth still hurt?

Dori blinked and came back to the present where she stood with her elbows resting on the metal railing of the pier. The bay rippled between her and Downtown San Diego. The ferry pulled away from the pier, carrying a few tourists and hardcore bicyclists away from Coronado. She breathed in the smell of fish and a pipe that one of the fishermen had clenched between his teeth.

She walked off with a whole afternoon stretching barren and pointless before her. She should be at the range or calling contractors for bids. She should've been more like Ellen, who was now retired but still barking at teenaged cadets.

"On your left!"

Dori scooted over as a bicyclist whizzed by her, waving a friendly thank you and then continued down the bike path that went around the island.

She stopped in her tracks. How long had it been since she'd done something as simple as ride a bike? Her mother would never do something like that.

Fifteen minutes later, on a pink beach cruiser with streamers on the handles, Dori pedaled down a street that looked as if it had been freeze-dried in the 1920s. The leafy trees let in spots of sunlight between the bungalows, stuccoed Spanish fantasies, Cape Cods and Tudors. She looked a little funny riding around with a flowered pink helmet on her head, but she was smiling with the simple pleasure of the wind against her face and the little basket that held her purse.

She burst out of the shade, the sun blinding since she'd forgotten her sunglasses in the car. A yellow Victorian stood on the corner, its nose turned up at the cars that raced towards the Coronado Bridge. Immediately, the image of her house from the dream popped in her mind: the scrubbed windows, the roses planted around the bird bath and of course, Vince.

When she got a break in the traffic, she hurried across the main thoroughfare and back into the quiet neighborhood. She drifted along, trying to outrun the memories of finding Vince lying in her hallway. Had it just been a dream or had she witnessed something that had happened in the past?

She shook her head no. But if-

No. Never. Impossible, her rational mind insisted, closing off further argument.

But her instincts hinted otherwise. It wasn't some random nightmare. The suffocating feeling she'd experienced in the front parlor wasn't her damaged psyche. Dori had seen a man's last moments and there was something in that room.

The weight of it, the impossibility of it in the light of day pressed down on her. She pumped her legs faster, the wind roaring in her ears, her eyes smarting and starting to tear. Dori needed to pull her head out of her ass and get back in the moment where she belonged. But her questions were like dust motes caught in a beam of light, lingering, floating, too many to count and pointless to wave away for they'd settle right back where they'd been.

Her heel slid off the pedal. The bike veered straight for a parked car but she yanked it back in time. The questions refused to leave her alone until Dori wound up on Orange Avenue, Coronado's main thoroughfare. She rode under swaying palm trees until she pulled up to Bay Books, which beckoned her inside with the promise of sanctuary.

Dori paused in the doorway to breathe in that soothing book smell. Her fingers tingled from the warmth of the store. She wished she'd brought a backpack to carry all the books on the tables that promised a romantic journey in which heroines prevailed and had great sex. She couldn't remember the last time she'd indulged in a good book. Maybe that's why she needed antidepressants.

Drawn deeper into the store, she picked out her old favorites: Nora Roberts, Victoria Holt, Isabel Allende and Anne Rice. As she touched their spines, memories of the stories and the characters contained within drifted into her mind.

She wandered to the very back of the store, reserved for children's books but then stopped when she came upon the local history section.

"May I offer you a cup of tea?" the bookseller asked, tugging her beaded cardigan closed.

About to politely decline, Dori decided not to be like her mother and nodded. "Thank you. Do you have any books on National City history?"

"Let me see." She pursued the shelf and then shook her head. "No, sorry. No one's written a history about National City yet."

"Oh, okay. Thanks."

"May I ask why you'd want a history about National City?"

Dori bristled with the implication of that question. Some people considered National City to be the drunken cousin among the cities in San Diego County. "I bought a house there," she replied coldly.

"Really?"

Just when Dori was about to turn on her heel and make for the door, the bookseller's face burst into a smile. "My sister's son just bought a beautiful Spanish house there that was built in the 30's. It needs so much work, but it's such a nice little street. Is your home historic?"

"It is."

"Really! Well, make sure you go to the Local History Room at the library. My nephew's wife has been doing research there and she found the original owner of their house. Do you have pictures?"

It was just a house, not a kid, Dori thought. "No, I don't."

"Well, if you're looking for inspiration, we have a great architecture section over here."

Even though she knew better, Dori followed her to a section of coffee-table books on design and gardens. Even after this morning, she still had boxes of books on Victorian architecture, design, and gardening as well as five years' worth of Victorian Homes back issues in storage. She could tell the difference between an Edwardian and Victorian and spot a Queen Anne or an Eastlake at first glance. But this time, she would control herself.

"With so many lovely homes on the island, we sell these titles like hot cakes," the bookseller said. "I bet we have something on- What style home did you buy?"

"A Carpenter Gothic built in 1888."

"Which one? Is it that neighborhood on the hill overlooking the golf course?"

"It is."

The woman's eyes gleamed behind her glasses. "How exciting."

Dori smiled, thinking of the dead guy who crawled out of the front parlor this morning.

"Take a look. We have a nice comfy seat there. I'll be right back with your tea."

Dori stopped herself reaching for a book on Downton Abbey style. Now, she had to wait for the lady to return with the tea. To walk out would be rude. Coming here was such a stupid idea. She should've been calling up her colleagues to meet for lunch to get a feel for how the investigation was going.

She wandered away from the décor section and found herself dangerously close to the self-help books. Dori sneered at Deepak Chopra and Pema Chödrön. What the hell did they know what it was like to get shot and bleed on a filthy floor?

The topper was the book cover, *Ghosts Among Us* by James Van Praagh. Sneering, she pulled it off the shelf and would like to have lobbed it across the store. Instead she read the first few pages.

"Have you ever attended one of his spirit circles," the bookseller asked, sneaking up on Dori. "I've always wanted to."

Dori accepted the paper cup of tea, smelling summer apricots and honey.

"No, I haven't," she said, sliding the book on the shelf.

"Do you have any 'friends' in your home?" she asked, not letting Dori off that easily.

"Nope, it's just me."

The bookseller stared at Dori too long to be polite. "Well, don't be surprised. A home that old can't help but have a few extra residents."

Under the sleeves of her jacket, chills raced up Dori's arms.

# CHAPTER NINE

The fog bank crept out of the ocean, chasing Dori inland. Her legs still felt rubbery from her bike ride across Coronado Island, and the apricot tea turned bitter on her tongue.

Her house came into view, daring her to come back. Dori sucked in her breath and held it. She waited at the stop sign. If she was a normal person, she would've checked into a hotel room.

But running away was not what she did, and so she parked in her driveway. Her heart hammered as she stepped out of the car, determined to see this through. Electricity hummed in her fingertips as she searched the windows for the guy named Vince.

Was it the light or did the house look as weary as she felt? The windows stared vacantly as if it no longer cared that its façade was pocked and scarred from neglect. Maybe like Dori, it wanted to collapse in on itself and forget about starting over again.

Dori walked up to the windows of the front parlor and laid her hand on the wood. She silently told the house that she'd try. In her dream, she'd seen what it had once been. She'd do whatever it took to bring her back to her younger days.

"I was just going to slip this under the door."

Dori jumped, snatching her hand back as if the house, not Gavin, had just spoken to her. "What are you doing here?"

He held up an envelope. "My bid that you asked for," he said, holding it out. "This is negotiable, just so you know."

Dori didn't take the envelope, swamped with embarrassment that he'd caught her in such a personal moment.

"I called your grandma since I didn't get your number," he said. "She told me it would be fine if I dropped it by."

Dori reached out and took it. "Thanks," she said, not in the mood for polite chit chat or talking about the night he found her making out with another guy. "I'll call you after I take a look at this."

She started for the kitchen door.

"Do you mind if I ask how much you paid for it?" Gavin asked.

"What?"

"Your house."

"I'll tell you if you take twenty-five percent off your bill."

Rocking back on his heels, Gavin grinned down at her. "But you haven't looked at it."

"I'll call you after I do."

Now that she was able to breathe again, she noticed he wasn't all squeaky clean like he'd been yesterday. His arms were covered in dust, and his baseball cap had been discolored with sweat. The fact that he wore shorts in spite of the chilly afternoon irritated her.

"I'm not trying to be nosey, I'm just curious because I made an offer and they turned it down," he said, in no hurry to leave.

She stared at him. "You tried to buy my house?"

"I'd just got back from surfing in Australia, but I was too late." He gestured to the giant mustard-colored mansion across the street. "I love this neighborhood. I used to climb up the canyon wall with my buddies just to walk by these places after school."

She remembered the night she made him drive by this house after they went to the movies. He'd told her that very same thing.

Dori nodded her head. "I remember you telling me that," she said.

His expression never changed from the polite mask. "Right."

The fog was getting closer.

Too tired to revisit her sordid past, Dori held up his bid and said for the last time, "Thanks for the bid. I'll call you."

She turned and kept walking. Either he was hard up for a job or he had some horrible plan to exact vengeance on her. As she walked by the chimney, she ran her fingers over the rough bricks thinking about that night they'd parked his car across the street from her house and walked past the old houses in the neighborhood. Maybe he still cared about these old places. He knew a lot about history and things that at the time, she'd thought were nerdy and boring.

But then Gavin had kissed her under one of the pepper trees across the street from her house. He wasn't so nerdy then. Her stomach tingled at the memory.

Maybe he would be the person for the job but how could they stand to be around each other? Would they have to talk about what she'd done? Remembering the look on his face when he caught her with that other guy, Dori shuddered. Strange that she couldn't even recall the other's name much less his face. The refrigerator gurgled and then switched on. Dori blinked and realized she'd gone on autopilot as she opened the door and walked into her kitchen.

She froze in her tracks, listening and waiting for a sign that a dead guy named Vince waited for her. She took a step forward. Nothing. She'd never been so afraid to make a noise and possibly awaken the dead. Finally, she took a deep breath and closed the door.

Just in case, she cleared her throat and squared her shoulders. Grammy always said that when dealing with ghosts, the living had to set the rules or else break out the holy water.

"Okay, whoever or whatever you are, do not scare me," she shouted into the empty house. She then remembered Gavin might still be lurking outside, looking for more things to fix. If he was and he'd heard her, good, maybe he'd think she was too crazy and count himself lucky that they'd broken up all those years ago.

When nothing happened - not so much as a disembodied footstep - Dori let go of the breath she was holding. She then ripped open Gavin's envelope. She rubbed her side, testing how tender it was. She'd need a pain pill in a couple of hours. Maybe if she didn't wake up tomorrow too sore, she might get a bike. Her pants were starting to feel just a tad bit tight and-

Taking in the blunt force of Gavin's estimate, Dori thought about having a slug of tequila. Then she remembered that she didn't want to become one of those lonely ladies who drank.

Instead, she pulled an Amy's Pizza out of the freezer. Now her decision was made for her in that she couldn't afford him. She twisted the dial to preheat the oven and it broke off. She tried to jam it back on, but then how would she know if she had the right temperature? Cussing out the stove, she felt the ripple pass through the room. The microwave display went blank and her answering machine beeped. The kitchen lights flared and then died.

Dori braced one hand on the stove. She could hear the blood rushing through her head. Maybe it was stupid, but she heard herself call out, "Look, just come out and show yourself. Don't play these little tricks."

The air went still. The most primitive part of her went on alert, muscles tightening in preparation to run. Something was coming. She swung her gaze around the shadowed kitchen - her table, the empty chairs, Gavin's bid and the open doorway to the kitchen - looking for some sign that what she was feeling wasn't make-believe.

Just when she was about to crush the oven dial in her hand, from somewhere in the shadowed butler's pantry, a voice said, "It's not like we've got nothing else to do."

Jumping back, Dori slammed her elbow into the refrigerator. Heart pounding, she realized it was on. She'd called him out for a spiritual mano a mano and now she got it.

The shadows in the butler's pantry shifted, gathering until they took

46

shape. Dori couldn't move, even though her brain screamed at her to turn and run.

Before her eyes, he stepped into the kitchen, the linoleum crackling under his footsteps as if he were real.

Dori began to shake. She had no Bible, no holy water, no nothing in case he went poltergeist on her. Maybe if she closed her eyes and said nothing, he'd go away.

He came to stand a few feet away from her and then shoved his hands in his pockets. He lifted his chin to arrogantly stare down his nose at her. "Does your elbow hurt?"

Dori looked down at her elbow. It occurred to her that yes, it did. "What do you want?"

He stood there studying her with his dark eyes.

She shivered from the cold that radiated from him. She tried to remember her prayers from Catechism. The only one she could remember was Hail Mary and she wasn't sure if that would work but it was better than nothing.

The floor creaked and her cop brain kicked in. His dark eyes were deep set under blunt, angry brows. The suit he wore was beautifully cut but ripped and stained in places. The bloodied, toothless face was gone, thank God. He was, or rather had been, a wickedly handsome man.

"Are you going to say something?" she asked.

His chin came up, and his eyes locked with hers. "You have to find her," he said, his hushed voice vibrating with intensity. "I don't know who the hell you are, but you're all I got."

She managed to ask, "Find who?"

"I left her and they-" His voice dropped out like a weak radio signal.

"Give me a name and I'll-"

His voice whipped out at her as if someone cranked up the volume. "You have to-" Suddenly he stood inches in front of her. She flinched, pressed up against the stove, high on the balls of her feet.

"You have to promise me," he growled in her ear. "I have to know I can trust you."

Dori couldn't punch, maim or shoot him. But she could stand her ground even if she was so terrified that she might throw up. "Back off!"

He flinched as if the force of her voice shoved him away.

"Here's the thing, Vince." It didn't occur to Dori, until an hour later, how foolish it was to yell at a man who could walk through walls and see her naked without her knowing. But she continued, "I own this house and I pay the bills. You don't get in my face."

He tilted his head as if puzzled by her. Keeping his eyes locked on hers, he deliberately stepped back. Dori cleared her throat, sliding down until her feet were flat on the floor again.

"Find her," he said.

"A full name would help. Let's start with yours."

"What year is it?" he suddenly asked.

Dori told him and then asked, "What year did you- I mean, how old were you when you, well uh-"

She stopped herself from asking what felt like a rude question.

"It was 1932," he said, humor softening the grim line of his mouth. "We were this close to going legit."

She wondered what he meant, and then the Kevin Costner movie, The Untouchables kicked in her memory. Prohibition had been repealed in the 1930s. She'd have to Google it.

"I'm Vicente Sorrolla," he said sticking out his hand. "And you?"

"Dori Orihuela," she answered, eyeing his hand. He raised his eyebrows, daring her to take it. She did and grasped frigid air that zapped her with a sharp, almost painful shock. She hissed and yanked her hand away, holding it against her chest. Vicente chuckled and then he was standing by the table, one of the chairs pulled out.

"At least I haven't lost my effect on the ladies," he said, hitching up his pants and then sitting with his legs sprawled out.

Dori shivered. "I'm dreaming," she said to herself. "Or I hit my head riding the bike." She expected to wake up in her car or something. But he laughed.

"Okay then, I'm awake." She pressed her hand against her chest. "Why are you here? Do you get off on scaring women?"

His eyes narrowed and Dori held her breath.

"The last time I was-" He paused. "The last time I was here, there was this other woman. I tried not to scare her or nothing, but there was something about her that woke me up, I guess."

He lifted the corner of his mouth, eyes traveling over her. "You're the same way," he said seductively.

"I need a drink."

He lifted a shoulder and then dropped it like he could care less.

When she didn't move, he said, "Well? Go get your drink. I won't bite."

"I can't move."

"Whatever you do, don't tell me to go away. Please."

"Why?"

"Look, lady, I don't want to be here anymore than you want me around. I'm not supposed to- It wasn't my-" He looked down at the floor as if he were trying to put his thoughts together.

"I understand."

"Like hell you do."

Dori grinned, moving her hand from her chest to her side. "Yeah, I do."

"Find Anna and maybe I'll-" He quirked his lips. "Who knows? Maybe

48

I'll be sent straight to hell where villains like me belong."

"Who's Anna?"

"Anna Vazquez." He lost his posturing and for a moment their gazes met before he stared down at the floor. But she caught the vulnerability in his eyes. A million questions crowded in her head. So, she started with the first. "Was she your wife?"

He shook his head.

"Then who was she?" Dori must've blinked because just like that, she was alone again.

She stared at the chair he'd just occupied. She thought about touching it to see if it was warm and then realized he was dead so it maybe it would be cold. Either way, she was too afraid to move.

"Hey, where did you go?" Her voice rang in the hollow room. "Is that it?"

As if it were a tangible thing, like an ocean wave, the cold air receded. The tiny hairs on her arms still stood at attention. Dori covered her mouth with both hands and squeezed her eyes tight.

Her heart pumped so hard that she swayed with each beat. Her knees folded, and she sat on the floor. He'd really been here. She'd really talked to him. He had been so human and yet, he literally stepped out of thin air. She reached across the room and placed her hand on the chair to check that her conversation with him wasn't a hallucination. Sure enough, it was cold, but what if that didn't mean anything?

Then it occurred to her that not only had he refused to answer her question, he hadn't the courtesy to turn the power back on.

"Do you mind?" she demanded.

As if he'd heard, the microwave beeped, the refrigerator hummed with life and the light blinked on the answering machine.

# CHAPTER TEN

After Vicente vanished and the lights came on, Dori switched off the oven that apparently didn't work and drove to Grammy's house.

Excitement rang through Dori, she felt as if it would burst out of her skin if she kept it all to herself. If there was anyone who could understand, it would be her grammy.

She barely remembered driving across town. When she stepped up to her grandmother's small porch, someone had dumped a box of pumpkins by the door.

"You're lucky I don't have my shotgun by the door," Grammy said, opening the front door. "What's going on? Who died?"

Dori held up her hand for Grammy to give her a moment. Through the white noise in her ears, she tried to think of where to start. What bugged Dori was not that she'd just spoken to a dead man; although in truth, yes that was weird. The thing that got her was that she wasn't afraid of seeing him again. He hadn't threatened her. He'd freaked her out, but he hadn't done her harm. Her gut told her she could trust him.

"Maybe you oughta come in and sit down," Grammy said. "It's cold out here."

Dori looked at her bare arms, prickled with goose bumps. The yard had grown dark as the sun sank behind the fog bank. A thin layer of mist hung in the air.

"Did you fight with your mother at lunch?" Grammy asked.

"What? No." Dori realized she was pacing again. The dogs watched from under the tree. "How did you know we-"

"Well then, what the hell is wrong with you? Did you get fired?"

Dori stopped pacing. She shook her head no.

"You can stand out here all night by yourself. Or, come inside. Joan Rivers is gonna be on QVC."

"I don't know," Dori said, her voice shaking from the adrenaline rush. She held up a fluttering hand and then shoved them both into her pockets. She needed to get warm and think this through.

"Well okay-" Grammy started to close the door but Dori stopped her, walking into the warm house that smelled like cinnamon from the candles glowing in the fireplace.

She flopped down in Grampy's lumpy and stained recliner.

"You got ten minutes till Joan starts selling her jewelry."

"Okay," Dori started, and then her mind veered off into ten different directions. She opened her mouth to say one thing and then shut it thinking maybe she ought to start with the first time she'd seen Vicente in the window.

"Mija, you're scaring me," Grammy said.

"I have a ghost in my house." There. She said it. Now she waited for Grammy's reaction.

"I knew that."

"No, I mean a ghost who just a few minutes ago walked into my kitchen."

One of Grammy's penciled eyebrows lifted. "Was he a good-looking man?"

"He was a Hispanic male. Between 25 and 30 years old, five nine and approximately 150 pounds."

"Ay yi yi, you sound like a cop."

"I am a cop."

Grammy shook her head as if she'd been reminded of something unpleasant. "So, we bring some candles, La Virgen, maybe some sage and you'll be fine."

Dori pulled her feet under her and wrapped herself up in the chenille blanket draped over the back of the chair. "I don't think that's gonna work."

"Well, I know someone who can help," Grammy said. "He's an ex-priest."

"Before you go any further, why is he an ex-priest?"

"I don't know. I didn't want to embarrass him with awkward questions," Grammy said, reaching for the remote and turning off the TV.

Dori shivered in her blanket cocoon. Grammy believed her. But just in case, she asked, "So you really believe me?"

"Of course, I believe you." Grammy thoughtfully tapped a black and orange fingernail to her chin. "Whatever you do, you can't just leave him there."

"I can't exactly pack him up in a box."

"He was a human being once, mija. Maybe he appeared to you for help."

"He asked me to find someone," Dori muttered.

Grammy tilted her head. "Hold on. Did you say he talked to you?"

She nodded and both of Grammy's eyebrows went up as high as they could go.

"You always say you see Tío Fermin."

"I only smell him. That's different."

Dori's heart started to shrink. Grammy thought she was crazy. But she wasn't. She really had talked to Vicente, just as she now spoke with Grammy.

A shudder rang through her as she thought about the symptoms for PTSD, which included hallucinations. What if it had all been in her head? She'd dealt with people who lived in fantasies complete with make-believe husbands or wives, friends and even enemies that were out to get them. Unlike her, they usually slept on the sidewalk and kept all their worldly goods in a shopping cart.

"So, what else did he say?" Grammy asked quietly.

Dori stared down at the ends of the blanket she'd twisted together. "Nothing. I mean, I thought I heard him say something, but it happened so fast you know."

"What happened so fast?"

"I came home and I saw him."

"And you talked to him?"

Dori cleared her throat and burrowed deeper into the recliner. "Like I said, I heard him."

"Mmm hmm."

Dori could tell from her tone that Grammy was looking for a way to chisel out more details. She tried to tamp down the doubt rooting deep inside her. She thought of the Lexapro waiting in her medicine cabinet. Maybe she could go a day or two longer and see if this whole Vicente thing was real or not.

"Okay well, let's get back to practical matters," Grammy said. "If Gavin starts working on that house of yours, el fantasmo might get cranky. So, let's get this taken care of before it gets out of hand."

"I can't do that."

"Do what?"

Dori stopped herself from telling Grammy that Vicente had asked her not to send him away. "I got Gavin's bid. I can't afford him."

"How much is he?"

"Eighty thousand."

"In my day, I could've gotten that in one weekend," Grammy said with a proud sniff. "Marijuana wasn't illegal then. Your Grampy and me were farmers. You might say we were organic before it became fashionable."

Unless Dori raided the drug closet at work or took up her grandparents' version of the American Gothic, she could never afford Gavin even if she wanted him.

"Let me call my sources. Don't you make that face at me! You want a ghost around your house or not? Cuz he'll be watching the likes of you in the shower."

"Why don't you think I'm crazy?"

"You want me to? I got lots of experience in dealing with your Tío Fermin's ghost, that little pervert. I know he was staying around to see me naked. Did I ever tell you he tried to seduce me back when your daddy was still a little boy?"

"Is that why he mysteriously drove off the road?"

"No! Your grampy fought man-to-man. If he was gonna mess you up, he did it with honor." She sighed like a dreamy teenager. "I felt sorry for Fermin being your Grampy's baby brother and all, so I didn't say nothing. Fermin was puny, you know, and he thought as an older woman I could make a man out of him."

Dori flattened out the twisted blanket ends, hoping she'd successfully diverted Grammy away from her encounter with Vicente. "If anyone could, it would've been you."

"Damn right. Maybe that's what you need!"

"Need what?"

"A young boy you can make a man out of."

"Been there, done that."

"With who?"

"All the guys I've dated. That's the problem with them these days. They're boys masquerading as men. They don't make them like Grampy anymore."

"Mmm, true," Grammy said sadly. "So, you staying the night?"

Dori thought about her dark, cold and now haunted house. "I'll stay and watch QVC with you."

"You hungry?"

She nodded. "But you stay put. I can help myself."

"So, let's think like your grampy. What are you going to do tomorrow?"

Dori counted on her fingers. "I'll get up, workout, go online to research my house to see who lived there and then find a contractor I can afford."

Sitting here with Grammy, she almost felt like she did on the bike; she could breathe. Her shoulders no longer felt shrink-wrapped under her skin. The edge wore off from her encounter with Vicente. She started a mental to-do list starting with verifying that someone by that name had died in her house. There were records and old news clippings that could be researched.

"Good girl." Grammy turned the TV back on and sat back. "Man, I wish I'd bet you a hundred bucks that you had a ghost. I woulda won."

"If you had, I never would've told you."

# CHAPTER ELEVEN

One moment Vicente was in the middle of talking to Dori. Then the next, he stood now at the window watching her talk to another man.

He tried to orient himself. The house's shadow lay across on the ground. If he remembered correctly, the house faced west so it was now morning. Had an entire night or a week passed since he talked to her in the kitchen?

Dori looked up at the house, but she didn't see him. He smiled, feeling himself take form. Even though his body was long dead and probably nothing more than dust, he sometimes felt the sensations of being inside it. He could see and hear. He could feel emotions, especially the ache of having been lost to those he had loved so many decades ago.

He used to wonder if they'd found his body somewhere and buried it proper. He doubted it but still, it would be nice if someone had placed flowers on his grave.

Dori's voice rose in anger. Vicente leaned closer to the window, sensing the exchange between Dori and this strange man intensify. She walked away, the man calling after her. She flung up her hand in dismissal and something clenched where Vicente's heart had once been. The gesture was so reminiscent of what he done to Anna.

The man stared after Dori, shook his head and then walked away, fading from Vicente's view.

Curious, Vicente turned from the window and then he was in the downstairs hallway. He stayed put, waiting for Dori to walk through the door. She was tough and he admired that. When he got in her face, she barked at him like a man. No crying and screaming and hand-wringing like most women.

But he needed to play this carefully. If he scared her off, who knew how much damn longer he'd be stuck in this bullshit purgatory.

He looked down the hallway, remembering what this house had looked like on that last morning of his life. The once pristine marble fireplace now

54

sagged into the floor of the dingy hallway. The mirror he looked into was long gone.

Then, as if it he went back to that morning, Vicente saw himself as he had once been: hair disheveled and face rough from having missed his barber's appointment. But his body still carried the languid heat from the night before. When he stood before the mirror that morning, he had been thinking of Anna and her ferocity when he pushed her out the back door.

He blinked and the memory vanished when Dori slammed the door. She stomped through the kitchen. "Doll? Who the hell does he think he is calling me doll?" she muttered to herself.

"I wouldn't and I'm already dead," Vicente said, appearing behind her.

Both her feet came off the ground. Dori turned to see him standing in the butler's pantry, arms crossed with his shoulder leaning on the door jamb.

"You handled him pretty good. You made him feel about this big." Vicente pinched his thumb and finger together to illustrate.

She looked him up and down. At least this time she wasn't climbing up the stove to get away from him. "Is that how I make you feel?" she asked.

Vicente laughed and shook his head. "Nope. And you can put down your dukes. It won't do you much good."

She looked down at her fists and then opened her hands. "Oh, right."

"What did he want?"

"Who?"

"The man you were talking to."

"You saw us?"

"I wouldn't ask otherwise."

They stood there a moment, not quite sure how to proceed. "I called him to come look at the house. He said I should level it and then work with him to subdivide it."

Vicente tensed. "And?"

"I told him no thanks."

"And he wouldn't give up."

Her eyes narrowed. "He told me I was making a stupid decision."

"See now, I know how to respect a strong woman." Vicente deliberately drifted his gaze down the length of her body and then back up, hiding the fear of what would happen if she'd leveled the house. Where would that leave him?

Dori crossed her arms as she lifted a skeptical eyebrow. "I've had bigger and better than you," she said.

"But nothing like me." He then crossed the room in the blink of an eye, standing close enough that he could make out the freckles sprinkled over her cheeks.

Dori flinched but she stood her ground, meeting the challenge in his eyes. She even lifted her chin.

"Man, you're tough," he said. "No wonder you're not-"

"Not what?" Dori asked.

"Afraid of me," he said easily.

She made a face as her shoulders slumped down. "I'm more afraid that I'm crazy and you're not really here and I'm actually talking to an empty kitchen."

"I'm here," he said suggestively, and she couldn't help but smile.

She walked around him, moving towards the dining room. "All right then, you need to answer some questions. You never gave me the day you died or the time or place you were born."

"I don't want you to find me. I want you to find Anna."

Dori paused in the doorway. She looked at him as if she wasn't quite sure if he was made up. He couldn't say he blamed her. After a moment, she nodded to herself as if she decided he was the real deal. She walked out of the kitchen and he quickly followed.

"Where are you going?" he asked, making himself appear to walk alongside her. It felt more normal that way.

Dori noticed. "Would it be easier for you to float or something?"

He glared at her, but she lifted her eyebrow as if she'd lost her fear of him. He wasn't sure how he felt about that. To be feared was a necessity in his line of work; it allowed him to easily control people. "I don't need a tour of the house."

"I know, but my notebook is in the living room." She hesitated before asking, "So where do you go when you're not here?"

He abruptly halted in the middle of the hallway, feeling the pull from the front parlor. "I don't answer stupid questions."

She turned and met his eyes. He held her gaze, familiar with this power play. Dori looked over his shoulder and just when he thought he'd won, she asked, "Is there someone else in that room?"

"What room?" he asked, knowing full well what she meant.

"The front parlor where you died."

"I don't know." He slipped his hands in his pockets as if he could hide the fear and rage reaching out for him. She wouldn't help him if she knew he'd been the one in there who'd wanted to kill her.

"If you think my questions are stupid than find someone else to hunt down your girlfriend."

He wasn't going to back down and neither was she. Truth was he didn't know where he went. He had no control when he woke up and fell asleep. All he knew was that he'd been consumed with pain and humiliation when he was in the front parlor and he sure as hell didn't want that again.

"Come on," she said with that superior grin women had. "Let's sit down."

Even though he didn't technically have one, he nodded his head. She led him to the room she'd made for herself. The sofa and the chairs appeared more comfortable than he remembered from his time. A flat box hung from the wall and he wondered if it was some kind of mirror. She'd stacked novels and magazines on a kidney-shaped table. He wanted to jumble them up just to see what she'd do. A rug lay underneath and brightly colored pillows rested on the sofa.

He made out the indent of her shape in the corner of the sofa next to a reading lamp. This was a comfortable and private space. As the tension eased, he thought about how he'd been rolling in dough and lived in some swell places. But he never had his own personal place like this.

She sat in her corner and dug a notebook out of a canvas bag that was a smaller version of what citrus pickers had used in the fields. His lips curled as a brief memory of that time in his life sparked to life. The only thing that had made the humiliation bearable was Andy's laugh. Even though it was against the rules, no one could shut that guy up.

Vicente lifted his trousers and sat on the chair next to the sofa. He missed Andy. He hoped he didn't end up like him.

"Okay, give me some facts I can use," Dori said, bringing him back to the present. "Tell me what you know of Anna: her date of birth, when you knew her, when you last saw her, where she lived-"

"I never knew her birthday. She was a year younger than me."

She brought up her chin. "How can you not know her birthday?"

"My memory doesn't work like that anymore."

Dori placed her pen in the fold of her notebook.

He didn't know where to begin. Her questions stirred up flashes of memory and feelings: an image of Anna's face, the smell of the eucalyptus trees in the barrio and the wet, salty breeze against his cheeks.

"The first time I saw Anna was the morning I woke up on a bench."

## National City, 1925

The roosters hadn't crowed yet and late-blooming stars still sparkled in the sky. His old grandmother slept sitting up, with Eugenia's head on her lap. Vicente's legs ached as he straightened them from the ball he'd curled into.

They had travelled two weeks from Douglas, Arizona to National City, crammed into the back of a truck and then on a bus with others like them who'd received letters from California promising work and a place to live. It happened so fast after the last time their father showed up drunk, demanding to see them. The old lady said it would be the last time. Vicente took his little sister, Eugenia to lay a clutch of flowers on their mother's grave. Without a word to their father, who was either down in the copper mine or spending his paycheck across the border, they left town to meet the old lady's nephew who worked for the railroad.

Up till then, they didn't know they had other relatives. Their mother died when Vicente was four and Eugenia almost two. Their grandmother had packed them up after the burial. They never lived with their father who visited on the rare occasions he was sober.

The sun beat down on them across the Arizona desert; dirt scratched their eyes and shriveled their throats. In Yuma, the old lady paid a man to write a letter to her nephew, even though Eugenia and Vicente could've done it for free. She didn't like them to know anything: her nephew's name, his address, or even the town they were going to.

When the bus had dropped them off here at the pool hall last night, her nephew wasn't waiting. The men, women and children with their rope-bound boxes and bulging suitcases had shuffled past them, absorbed into the dark barrio.

"Where are we going to sleep," Eugenia had said, her voice trembling with fear as she tried to pull down the sleeves of her dress to stay warm.

"We wait here," the old lady said. "He said he would come for us."

Vicente ground his teeth at the old lady's stupidity. "Did he know we were coming?"

She glared at him to shut up.

"I'm going in for a smoke," he said.

She'd hissed at him to come back, but Vicente ignored her. The man in the pool hall sold him a cigarette and offered him a shower with a clean towel and soap for twenty-five cents. Vicente handed over his last nickel that he'd made shining shoes in Yuma and then walked out onto the sidewalk to smoke. The pool hall closed up for the night, which was how they wound up asleep on the street.

Vicente winced as he stood on numb feet. He swayed as his nerves came back to life. The sun climbed up the backs of the mountains, outlining them in gold. The air was cold and wet, smelling of tar and damp earth.

He watched some of the windows of the tiny houses light up as women started the stove fires and prepared breakfast for their men who would go to work in the slaughterhouses, tanneries and the factories that made railroad ties. Beyond the barrio that mushroomed around the train tracks, the sleepy town spread out east. Unlike the converted rail cars and wood shacks where the workers lived, the east side was made up of a few two-story homes that rose over red-tile roofed bungalows. Paved streets were laid out in neat gridlines. It was the first time he'd ever seen palm trees.

Vicente limped alongside the pool hall to get the blood into his feet again. Unlike the other halls where he'd picked up laundry for his grandmother to wash, this one didn't stink of urine or beer. The shallow steps were swept clean and the windows shined to reflect the mountains.

He swallowed his fear of what would happen if his grandmother's nephew had done a runner on them. They had nothing but the old lady's irons, his mother's oval-shaped portrait and a few clothes. She'd refused to pack Eugenia's dolls and the only way he could stop his sister's tears was a promise he'd buy her a new one.

Vicente tucked his fists under his armpits, calculating how long it would take him to get a job as an errand or shoe-shine boy. He wasn't old enough to work for the rail road and at 15, he'd already finished school. The one thing he wouldn't do was work in a field. He wasn't above pulling a harmless grift for a few extra nickels, but he wasn't a dumb animal.

"You can't sleep here," a voice cried out behind him. "Go! Get!"

He spun around, and for a moment, he couldn't move as a strange woman wearing an outdated feathered hat swatted at his grandmother and sister with her leather purse. Her pale, fleshy face reminded him of bread dough.

"Mama, stop," a man said, appearing behind the crazy woman.

"They're on our property," she exclaimed in a high-pitched, panicked voice. "They're nothing but filthy hobos!"

Her husband caught up with her, breathing hard from the exertion. "Stop it now," he said, grabbing for her arm and nearly taking her elbow in the eye.

Vicente heard the woman's purse smack his grandmother across the cheek. She cried out and her hands shot up in defense. Holding both arms in front of her face, Eugenia cried out, "Vicente!"

"Leave them alone," Vicente ordered, stepping in front of his sister in case she went after her next.

The lady screamed. They stood eye to eye, even in her heeled shoes. He puffed out his chest and stepped towards her, forcing her to back down. "We arrived late last night, and we had nowhere to go."

"You're trespassing on our property," she insisted, her jowls quivering righteously. "We'll call the sheriff if you don't leave."

Vicente took a few steps closer and the old bitch stepped into a muddy puddle. Fear, humiliation and exhaustion boiled up from the pit of his stomach. He clenched his fist to keep it from smashing into her face. Eugenia scrambled off the bench, murmuring to their grandmother.

"My wife, forgive us," the man stammered, recognizing how close Vicente teetered on violence. He said something to his wife in a strange language. Whatever it was, he seemed to be ordering his wife to shut the hell up.

He then held his hands out in peace. "Tranquile, tranquile," he said, switching back to Spanish. "I'm so very sorry. This is your grandmother, you say?"

"And my sister."

"Come. I can provide you with coffee."

"Jakob!"

"We don't need your charity," Vicente said.

"They're filthy. They'll tell everyone we give everything away for free," the old bitch wailed.

"Enough," Jakob said and then gestured behind his wife. "Anna, come. Take your mother inside."

Out of the corner of his eye, Vicente saw the girl appear at her mother's side. His first impression was the graceful line of her jaw and lush pink lips that made him take a better look. Then his heart came to a sudden stop. All of the anger and the violence boiling inside him vanished.

Her face glowed like an angel's in the tender morning light. Her hair was pulled back and twisted low against her neck. He'd never seen anyone off a movie screen as elegant and regal as her. She took in his too-tight shoes and working her way up to his wrinkled and dusty jacket with sleeves that stopped inches short of his wrists.

Vicente stood frozen with shame at how he must appear to her. Then his stomach grumbled.

"Come, mama, let's go inside," Anna said in her deep, quiet voice.

"Jakob, you're too soft on these types of people," the old bitch said as she was led away. "They always take advantage of you."

Vicente wanted Anna to feel the same stunned recognition that clenched around his chest. But she lifted her chin and her blue eyes were almost ghostly in the dim light.

"Excuse us," she asked Vicente.

"She said get out of the way," her mother shouted. In his haste to move, he stepped on an untied shoe lace and staggered into the muddy street.

Anna noticed and rather than giggle, she merely walked by him as if he weren't worth her notice.

"Señora, please. Allow me," Jakob said to his grandmother.

She covered her eye with her hand where his crazy wife had struck her. Eugenia hovered over her. Vicente's throat clenched with frustration.

"You must please come in," Jakob said, blocking Vicente's view of his wife and daughter, who turned the corner. "Anna will take my wife into the back office. I will make you something warm to drink, yes?"

His grandmother said, "We'll be on our way."

Vicente couldn't speak. He watched his grandmother painfully rise to her full height. She looked like a witch in the pale light with her hooked, crooked nose and long, outdated black clothes. Ashamed that they'd been caught like beggars, that this illiterate, mean old woman had put him in this position, he dropped his gaze to the ground.

"I wish there is some way I could help with this," Jakob said.

They hadn't had a decent night's sleep in two weeks. Vicente still wore the same clothes since his last bath three days ago. His stomach cramped with hunger and desperation that such a beautiful girl had taken him for a bum.

"Do you know Salvador Cardenas?" the old lady asked.

Jakob frowned and then his face lit with recognition. "Yes, yes of course."

"He's my nephew. He told us to come out here for work."

"I see. But he has left."

"Left where?" Vicente demanded, his heart hammering with a fresh wave of anger.

Jakob flinched, startled by Vicente's sudden intrusion on the conversation. "Up north. A whole group of them left to pick the crops."

The old lady dropped her bag and then snapped at Eugenia not to just stand there and look at it.

"You must go here," Jakob said, taking out a notepad and pen out of his pocket. Vicente caught the flash of a silver watch pinned to a gray wool vest. "They will help you."

He ripped off the paper and handed it to Vicente.

"Give it to me," the old lady ordered even though she couldn't read or write.

Vicente could, and he knew she'd rather have them live in the street than take charity. He wasn't about to sleep another night on a bench or on a bus and snatched the note out of Jakob's hand.

"Thank you, sir," he said, stuffing the note in his pocket.

"Of course. But don't come here for a job, understand?"

Vicente stared at Jakob and knew the old man had seen the way he'd looked at his daughter.

"Please, there are many places to work. Just not here. We are only a small family business."

He jerked his head in a polite nod and then walked off as fast as he could.

Jakob sent them to St. Anthony's Church where they were fed pan dulce and coffee. The priest listened to the old lady's story about her nephew and then made it quite clear that after their meal, they were to get work and only return to receive penance and then mass.

By the time they left the priest's office with directions to the boarding house, the day had turned brilliant but with a chill that clung to the air. His grandmother limped slowly, leaning on Eugenia's arm. His sister nibbled on pan dulce the priest gave to her when their grandmother suddenly knocked it out of her hand.

"You're fat enough."

Eugenia stared at bread laying in the dirt. He could see the tears welling in her eyes.

"Move!" The old lady demanded.

Eugenia stumbled along. He swung around to deliver a verbal blow. But he saw his sister's face was gray with exhaustion. She was the buffer between them and bore the bruises and marks from the old woman.

"I'll go first," he said. "I'll get everything ready."

Eugenia looked up at him with fear that he'd leave them. The old lady scowled, preparing to call him back. But he already ran down the street, eager to get away. The air felt good and fresh over his dirty face. The cracked handles of their suitcases cut deep into his cold fingers, but with the beautiful swaying trees overhead and the snap in the air, the world had opened up and personally invited him to take what he wanted.

Knowing that Anna was just a few blocks away, Vicente imagined all he needed was a good job and a new suit. Perhaps her father would give him permission to visit her on account of the way his loca wife had beaten up his old grandmother. As he walked by the houses, he wondered which one was hers.

As they settled in the barrio, his grandmother resumed her laundry business and complained of her back, Vicente's laziness and Eugenia's stupidity. The old lady found him a job cleaning the trolley cars at dawn. As if she needed to make sure he knew the leash was fastened good and tight, she arranged with his boss to receive his earnings. Vicente found himself a job selling the evening editions of the newspaper to set some aside towards the new suit he needed to meet Anna again.

He kept his mouth shut around the other men at work, giving them the impression he was slightly dangerous if provoked. But with the women, he stoked their favor with smoldering looks and suggestive banter that made the starchiest giggle and preen. He kept a keen ear for their gossip. He knew better than to ask direct questions, for fear of being teased. He picked up bits and pieces, finally learned that Anna's last name was Vazquez. Her father was a German who came from somewhere near Mexicali. Her mother was slightly mad having lost of all of her children except for Anna during the epidemic. Each time theirs or Anna's name popped up, his heart clenched tight.

"Her owner came back yesterday," Louisa said to her friends. Her kiss curls flopped about her face as she polished the wood benches. "He walked in with flowers and presents."

"That'll end the second he marries her."

"He doesn't have to. What do you think he does when he takes her on drives? Her mama doesn't go with them."

"Yes, she does!"

"No, she don't."

A finger drove into the soft place between his shoulder and neck.

Vicente jerked up his shoulder and turned to see Fernando, the self-appointed boss of his crew.

"Hey, we got the next car to do," Fernando ordered and then turned away.

The ladies slowed their polishing to watch what Vicente would do next. He winked and they got all coy and giggly. But their talk sickened him. Who was this owner, this man who brought flowers and drove his own car?

As he walked home, Vicente didn't want to believe any of it because how could he compete? He had nothing and from what he heard, that man had everything. Vicente walked by Anna's house, a two story, white house with long windows at the crest of Billy Goat Hill across the street from St. Anthony's. His hands went sweaty as he slowed to a stop, directly across the road. He'd deliberately avoided it for the past month, hoping she'd forget he was the filthy bum who nearly cold cocked her crazy mother.

She and her parents were working at their pool hall. Lace curtains hung in the windows and their garden was filled with rose bushes instead of chickens and vegetables. There was no sign of this other man. He thought again of the morning when Jakob warned him off. The girls' gossip seethed in the pit of his stomach. He hated them for their glee.

Vicente couldn't stand to fight with the other newsboys over his corner, or go home to the old woman's bullying and Eugenia's tears. Even though his stomach ached with hunger, he skirted the edges of the barrio towards the tidelands. He followed the path that cut through the sage brush and the bush mallow that resisted the wind pushing them down against the spongy ground.

He followed the creek and then the short rise until the San Diego Bay lay flat and sparkling under the fall sun. He closed his eyes against the glare. The wind buffeted against him. When he opened his eyes, shading them with his hand, he saw her standing at the very edge of the water, a slender column of white.

Vicente headed straight for her. He didn't know what he'd say or do as shells crunched under his boots. He had nothing to offer her. What little he made scrubbing other people's dirt and trash was given to his grandmother. As he got closer, he curled his hands into fists so he wouldn't chicken out and run away.

The water lapped the tips of her bare toes. Her shiny black button boots lay on the sand a few steps behind her. Her dark hair was pulled up and twisted near the top of her head. A gold chain twinkled against her neck. Vicente stared hard at that place, tracing the path of her necklace where it slid down into the front of her dress.

"So, this is where the world ends," he said.

She jumped at the sound of his voice and turned. Her lips were red from the candy she'd been sucking on. Her eyes narrowed at him, and she pointed at him with the candy stick that he noticed was still wet from her mouth. "You're the one who nearly punched my mother."

# CHAPTER TWELVE

Vicente laughed softly to himself. Dori watched him fading as he sat in her chair.

"I said, 'I'm sorry but she was hitting my grandmother.' But inside I was thinking how I'd love to be that piece of candy."

Dori was hardly a blushing spinster, but the way he said it made her toes curl.

He looked up at Dori, not really seeing her or the room. "Anna had this way of smiling like she was wise to you. And then she says to me, 'I wished you had. Sometimes I'd like to punch her in the face, too.'

"She didn't seem to mind me there. She just turned back to stare at the water. She always smelled very sweet, like candy. Probably because if she didn't have a piece stuck in her mouth, she carried it in her pocket."

Dori could now see the chair through him. She didn't dare ask any of the factual questions in her head for fear she'd pop him like a bubble.

"We didn't say a word for a long time," Vicente said, his voice growing fainter. "I was shaking in my boots, so I didn't dare try to hold her hand or say anything. Finally, she finished her candy and then asked me, 'Do you ever wonder what it's like on the other end of the ocean?' I shrugged because people like us didn't even think about stuff like that. We were too busy trying to find work and survive."

Vicente's form flared just before dissolving. Dori released the breath she'd been holding and slunk against the back of the couch. She rubbed her arms, vigorously trying to get rid of the goose bumps on her skin and hoping wherever this Anna Vazquez was that she was worthy of such devotion.

There was no way she could just hang out alone after Vicente's story. A few minutes later, as her house receded in the rear-view mirror, Dori decided she had to find a concrete fact that would prove Vicente and Anna had been real.

Her usual channels of investigation were closed to her. She couldn't just type Vicente into the system to call up his arrest records – of which she had no doubt existed in some dusty archive – because the digital records only went back so many years. Dori tried to remember what year Social Security began. If he or Anna were in the system, she could locate their last known address.

Remembering the lady at Bay Books, Dori wound up at the new and improved National City Public Library. The automatic door swished open, and she immediately missed the shabby, cozy living-room feel of the original library set among pines and eucalyptus.

After she met Ellen and became a police cadet, every Thursday afternoon Dori would ride the city bus to the old library. She'd do her homework and then carry home an armload of novels and biographies. The old library had that soothing book smell and felt like more like home than her real home did. She remembered the catalog cards had felt soft, almost velvety under her fingertips. This new library smelled like new carpet and buzzed with computers and printers.

Dori knocked on the glass door of the local history room, feeling slightly ridiculous to be researching on behalf of a dead guy. In this 21st century building, with the sunlight streaming through the walls of glass and free WiFi whirling all around her, it was a little hard to believe she'd spoken to someone who faded into thin air.

Dori was about to turn back and check out the romance section when the door yanked open. A brunette stared at her with the outrage perfected by librarians through the ages.

"You don't have to knock," she said crisply. "Just come in."

Dori wondered how a British girl ended up working in the history room of the National City Public Library. Instead she walked inside. "Thanks."

"So, what can I do for you today?"

"I'm just researching family history."

"Really?" The librarian scanned Dori from head to toe and back as if she were highly doubtful. "How far does your family go back?"

"The 1930's or thereabouts."

"Who exactly are you looking for?"

Dori rolled her shoulders back, remembering she was a detective and she could lie to the best of them. "My great grandmother."

"And what was your great grandmother's name?"

Anna's name burned in Dori's throat. She cleared her throat and managed, "Anna Vazquez."

"Well, let's see." The librarian turned on her Victorian style heeled boot and then sat down behind a painfully tidy desk that was in stark contrast to the dreadlocked hair twisted at the nape of her neck. Clear plastic folders were labeled and laid in ruler-straight lines. Unlike Dori's desk at work, there were no coffee rings on the paperwork or sticky notes pasted along the edges of the monitor.

The librarian pushed her glasses up higher on her nose. As she typed, Dori noticed she wore a tiny tea pot ring on her left middle finger with a matching tea cup on her ring finger.

"She's not in our oral history list," the librarian said crisply. "Was that her married or maiden name?"

"Maiden name."

"Do you know her married name? Most women, unless they were widows, were listed under their husband's name in the city directory."

"Oh. I don't know."

The librarian lifted a skeptical eyebrow. "She's your great grandmother, you said?"

"Yeah." Dori shrank within herself. She had no idea where Anna lived, when she was born or even where she had been waiting for Vicente to return. Dori could tell the librarian what Anna had looked like, what people thought of her and that she smelled like candy. But she had nothing factual.

Then again, she was a detective being questioned by a librarian for God's sake. It wasn't like the woman was going to put her in library jail.

The librarian stood up and gestured at Dori to follow. She took her to a bookshelf crowded with hardbound books, all listed in chronological order from 1899 to 1984.

"Try the city directories. See what you find."

Dori wished Vicente had told her the year he'd come to National City. She randomly chose 1926 and then sat at one of the tables. The clacking of a keyboard filled the silent room, and the librarian stared intently at her monitor.

She opened the book at the letter V. Three entries down her finger stopped at *Vazquez, Jakob*. Dori held her breath at the cold jolt of recognition.

He and his wife, Emilia had lived at 1929 Harding Ave. His profession was listed as proprietor. Anna's name wasn't listed, but holy crap, there were names that matched Vicente's story. She looked up Sorrolla, but found no listing. He'd only referred to his grandmother as "the old lady."

She jotted down Jakob and Emilia's names and address in her notebook. Then for the hell of it, she looked up Orihuela. With a chill she spotted her real great grandmother listed under *Orihuela, Francisca (wid)*. Her profession was listed as laundress. Dori smiled to herself. If that woman did any laundering, it was money.

"Find what you're looking for?"

Dori looked up from the book. The librarian had snuck up on her, perching one hip on the edge of the table.

"Excuse me?"

"Oh." The librarian's hurt tone made Dori wish she'd been a little less defensive.

"Sorry," Dori said, softening her tone. "Yeah I did."

"Was there a death in your family? Because most people who come in here are researching family histories after someone has died." She paused, tilting her head thoughtfully. "I don't know why death always stimulates interest in the family history. It just does."

Dori took in the woman's dreads, the black dress with a fitted gray vest and the oddly tarnished silver jewelry. "I bought an old house," she said, closing the book. "I'm doing research on someone who might have lived there."

"Your great grandmother lived there?" the librarian asked.

"Not quite," Dori said, clearing her throat. "She might have known the person who owned it."

"Where is your home, if you don't mind my asking?"

Dori hesitated. As a cop, she never told anyone where she lived. "It's off 24th Street."

"No shite," Meg said.

Dori blinked. Were librarians allowed to say "shite" in the library?

"Meg Yardley." She stuck out her hand.

Dori took her hand, and Meg squeezed. "Dori Orihuela."

"We don't have much information on that particular house in the collection."

"Do you have any files on bootleggers?" Dori asked.

"In National City?" She brightened and held up a finger as if calling up a lecture in her head. "Well, there was a rather famous murder in 1929 but-" She waved her hand dismissively. "It was an armored car robbery. This town already had a prohibition in place that I believe started in…"

Meg turned and headed to the bookshelves.

"You don't have to look it up."

"1908," she called out. "Yes, that year the city passed an anti-alcohol law, which was typical of the period. Have you seen the Ken Burns' documentary?"

That was a good idea, Dori thought. She wished she'd thought of it before. "Thank you. You've given me a good start."

"You don't have to leave. Not that many people come up here anyway."

"Should I put this back?"

"Please no," Meg said. "I always reshelve materials. That way nothing slips into a backpack, if you know what I mean."

Dori left the book on the table, feeling as if she'd left a part of herself in it. "What information do you have on my house?"

"Oh, here's something." Meg hurried over and pulled out a thin pamphlet. "It was built for Wallace Boal by his father who lived in that yellow pile across the street."

Dori scanned the text under the photo taken in 1888. She hoped for a list of owners but it only detailed the architectural style and when the original owner moved back East.

"How can I look up the owner in the 1930's?"

"You could try the county records. Here's my card." Meg held it out and Dori toyed with the idea of handing over hers just to see how she'd react. "How long have you owned the house?"

"Maybe a month."

"What are your plans for restoration? If you don't mind my asking."

After her meeting, this morning with the contractor who told her to tear it down and subdivide, Dori didn't know how to answer that question. A week had passed since Gavin delivered his estimate. He'd never called or followed up and now, she wondered if he was her best bet.

"You know, people find all sorts of goodies when they tear out walls. You should start a blog."

"I'll think about it," Dori said, edging towards the door. "Thanks for your help."

"Would you care for a lunch?" Meg asked.

"Lunch?"

Meg sucked in her breath. "I brought enough to feed an army, but most people here think my cuisine is a touch on the exotic side. Then again, do you think it's my accent? I thought Americans would be much friendlier but all they really seem to want to do is work. And the second I open my mouth, they ask if I'm from England, which is fairly obvious and then they shut up as if I'm about to correct their grammar. I'm banging on about, aren't I?"

Dori thought about her lunch prospects of which there were none. She hardly knew this woman. What would they talk about and should she trust the food made by someone who wore a tiny tea set on her fingers?

"Well, I understand if you need to shove off," Meg said quietly, taking a step back as if to give Dori an escape.

To cover the awkwardness of the whole thing, Dori found herself asking: "What did you bring for lunch?"

"I'm sorry?" Just like that, Meg's face went from confusion to delight. "Oh! Stuffed red bell peppers. They're a specialty of mine."

"I'd like that. Thank you."

Meg popped up on the balls of her feet, as if Dori had produced a cake with candles. "Perfect! Let's hie to the lunch room."

Meg kept a friendly chatter as they left the history room and went down a short hallway to the lunch room. Dori tried not to think how uncharacteristic it was of her to have lunch with someone she barely knew. Most people she had lunch with were from work. Only a month ago, her days and weekends were filled with barbeques and get togethers. After the shooting Elliot and his wife visited. She got offers to go out and talk about what happened, but she turned them all down. Now her phone hardly rang and she got the occasional email.

Dori thought up conversation topics in case she ran out of things to talk about. She couldn't exactly lay down the last few weeks of her life to someone who worked in the safe, quiet world of a library.

"So how is Anna Vazquez connected to your home again?" Meg asked as they walked into the lunch room.

All of her hoarded conversation topics popped like bubbles. It took Dori a moment to come up with, "She might have had a relationship with someone who lived there."

"An illicit relationship, I hope?"

"I think so. May I help with anything?"

"Of course not," Meg said, opening the refrigerator. She bustled about, explaining how she made up her own recipes as she prepped and microwaved. Dori nodded and listened, thinking how similar this was to talking to Vicente. Except for the fading in and out parts and that she'd seen how he died, there wasn't much difference to interacting with people dead or alive. She almost reached out to touch Meg just in case.

Meg set a steaming plate in front of Dori. "It's ground turkey with wild rice and my homemade marinara sauce. What do you think?"

Dori politely dug out a piece on her fork, blew on it and then put it in her mouth.

"Oh wow," she said, surprised as it melted deliciously on her tongue. "It's good. Thank you."

Meg beamed as she sat down.

"How did you end up working here?" Dori asked.

"How much time do you have?"

"Plenty."

"I'm a graduate student and I'm interning here."

"You're from London?"

"Norwich."

"So why here when you live in a country with amazing history?"

Meg smiled mischievously. "My grandmother had much looser morals when she was a girl. My grandfather was an airman with the Liberators of 453rd Bomb Group and well..." She twirled her fork in the air. "He died during an attack on aircraft plants in Germany before he and my gram were properly married. My poor mum hates the story but ever since Gram told me, I've been fascinated with the whole idea."

"So how did that bring you to San Diego?"

"Well that part all began with a Naval officer I met in a Starbucks in Kuala Lumpur. Like my grandfather he was from San Diego and we had great plans until he decided not to divorce his wife."

Meg looked down at her vest, dabbing at a spot with her napkin.

"Do the lattes taste the same in Kuala Lumpur?"

"They do," she said. "I couldn't let a perfectly good green card go to waste and so here I am." She grinned but her eyes were sad. "What about your family?"

"We've been in National City since the dawn of time. I was in in Denver for five years up till two years ago."

"Doing what?"

"Law enforcement."

"A lady officer. I thought that was the case."

Dori grinned. "Did not."

"Okay, I didn't. But I had a feeling." Meg nodded to Dori's plate. "Would you like more?"

Drinking her iced green tea, Dori shook her head.

"I've been here in San Diego for almost a year," Meg continued. "I'll be honest that I have no family and many acquaintances but no close friends, which is why I dragged you here at the slightest sign of interest. You didn't think I was trying to hit on you, did you?"

"If you had I would've let you down gently."

Meg smiled and leaned back in her chair. "Well, that's good to know."

They lapsed into a comfortable quiet for a moment. Except with Sela, Dori had never been one for chatting over lunch, or having girl time. She'd always had more important things to do than shop or get manicures or gossip. The only other person she confided in was her eighty-something grandmother. Sitting her with Meg made Dori wonder if she'd been missing out on something all this time.

"Well, if you don't mind my forwardness, I'd love to meet for a coffee or a movie."

"I'd like that, too."

"It's done then. We're officially mates. My, you really did like my cooking, didn't you?" Meg asked as Dori collected their empty plates.

"I've been eating out of bags and boxes for weeks."

"Then we should do this again. I'd hate to lose a new friend to death by manufactured food products."

"Thank you."

"As for Anna Vazquez's illicit affair, I'll poke around some more. What else do you know about her?"

They were back on shifting ground. Dori wasn't like Sela, who pranced through life by sprinkling white lies in her path. "Not much," she said, trying to stick to as much of the truth as possible. "Her parents owned a pool hall and lived in a big house across from St. Anthony's Church."

"Check the county records of your home. Research, I find, leads you from one point to the other and then suddenly you land on one detail that pulls it all together." She smiled at Dori. "I suppose your line of work is the same."

Dori put her hand to her aching side and then eased it back, not wanting to call attention to it. She'd take a Tylenol when she got to the car.

She glanced at the clock and realized she'd spent two hours with Meg. She didn't know where she would go now that they had finished lunch. "So, have you found your grandfather's family here?"

# CHAPTER THIRTEEN

The rain started again that night. Dori looked up from her e-reader on which she'd been reading James Van Praagh's *Ghosts Among Us*. A tapping sound pulled her out of the narrative and she expected to see Vicente.

Instead, she saw water dripping from the corner of her ceiling. She threw the e-reader down and ran upstairs to the third floor. For a moment, she remembered she should be scared at being alone in a cold, freezing house with a ghost who could appear out of the walls. But then she looked up and saw hundreds of water drips coming through her roof and then knew true terror. Dori couldn't move as she realized she didn't own enough pots, pans and bowls to catch it all.

She shut the door and went back to her bedroom where she stuck the bathroom trash can under the leak. Dori picked up her phone, weighing it in her hand to the sound of drip, drip, drip. She called Gavin's number and got his voicemail.

Dori thought about sleeping downstairs but she felt safer up here. She cleared her throat before she called out to Vicente, "Are you here?"

Only the water tapped into the trash can.

When Gavin didn't call her back the next morning, Dori drove to his office, which was a 19th Century townhome on Brick Row. Ten individual row homes were linked by a white painted porch roof. Tall, skinny windows reflected the Jacaranda trees lining both sides of the street. The wind blew cold and sweet from the lavender colored flowers that fluttered down to the ground.

She walked up to his office, located at the front corner. His truck wasn't parked in front and a sign hung in the door with his cell phone number.

Before she could talk herself out of it, Dori pulled her phone out of her purse and called him again. Hoping to get his voicemail, she scrunched up her face when he answered, "I was just about to give up on you. Enjoy the rain last night?"

She almost choked on the flare of anger. "So when can you get started? Do I write you a check or something?"

"I collect at the end of the month."

"Good. I uh, now have an urgent project for you."

"Really?" He sounded like he was enjoying this.

"My roof leaks."

He left her dangling in silence. "So, when can you start?" Dori asked.

"Sorry but my guys are on a new job. They'll finish next Monday."

Dori wondered how much longer she could go before her ceilings and floors were irreparably damaged.

"But I'll have my roofer stop by tomorrow with some sheeting for the roof."

"Thank you," she said, relieved. "But here's the thing, I can't afford half the things on the bid."

"I figured that." He cleared his throat. "If you're going to start with anything, reinforce the foundation and save your roof."

She'd never heard anyone make the word roof sound quite like that.

"When I went into your basement," he continued, "I saw that the house is off what is left of the foundation, which is typical for a house that age. You've even got a few places where someone stuffed wood blocks to hold it up."

"Are you saying my house is about to fall into the earth?"

"Well, yeah. It's only a matter of time."

Dori felt slightly ill.

"Look, if you want the job done right-"

She took a deep breath. "Let's just get things started."

He cleared his throat. "I'll draw up our agreement and drop it off tomorrow. You need anything else?"

"No, we're good."

"You don't sound so sure about that."

"What do you mean?"

"I know the cost is a lot for a single woman like you. Maybe we can work something out."

Her mouth dropped open at his insinuation. Then again, not all of Grampy's teachings on negotiation had been lost on her. A deal was a deal.

"Like what?" Dori asked.

"You sound suspicious."

She could hear the gloating in his voice.

"Let me propose this. How about if you put in some sweat equity? Because I like your house, I'll eat some of the profit."

Her anger snuffed out, leaving her with guilt twisting her insides. She ran her fingers along the rough bricks. "Why would you do that, Gavin?"

"You have a house that's gonna fall to the ground if there's so much as a tremor in the earth," he replied as if they'd never held hands or kissed. "Where's that going to leave you?"

She didn't mean to but she sighed.

"I don't need to make money off you," he continued. "And it'd be a shame to see a house like that be torn down."

She almost asked, why would you help me after what happened all those years ago? But she was afraid of his answer. Dori swallowed but the lump in her throat wouldn't budge. "All right," she said, one hand cupped around her eyes so she could better see the polished wood floors and antique furniture in his office. "What do you want me to do?"

She could almost see his smile of victory.

If Dori had any dreams last night, she couldn't remember them. The moment her head hit the pillow, she fell into a black hole. Then suddenly it was morning again. She shut her eyes with the hope of a few more moments of sleep. But she was wide awake and sore.

After talking to Gavin, she'd made good on her promise to feed his crew in exchange for a discount. She'd nearly worn out the shocks on her Rav-4 from all the stuff she bought at Costco. It had taken an hour to haul it into the house, and her side burned as she now eased up to sit on the edge of the bed.

Showering and dressing for the appointment with her therapist, Dori congratulated herself for not taking the meds. Last night before bed, she'd Googled Jakob and Emilia Vazquez's address. The house was just as Vicente had described, except now old and run down. She almost cried at finding more evidence of his tales. Meg had given her a list of websites to help her locate their birth and death certificates. Hopefully she'd find Anna and, perhaps, Vicente.

A few moments later, she was downstairs, stretching the sleep out of her muscles on the porch outside the kitchen. Her breath made clouds in the early morning chill. The fog licked wet trails on the ground and left translucent beads on the windshield of her car. If she was – no – when she was fully cleared and back at work, Dori wondered if she'd miss Vicente.

She turned the corner and her stomach lurched when she saw him staring up at her house. She almost tiptoed back inside. But that would be cowardly and incredibly awkward if he caught her.

"Find what you're looking for?" she called out.

"Oh, hey." Gavin started at the sound of her voice and then snatched the ball cap off his head. "Any more problems with the roof?"

She grinned, pleased to have caught him off guard. "I dried everything as best I could."

"I thought I'd let you get a few winks in before we started demo today."

"You're starting today? I thought the roofer was coming with the sheeting."

He shifted his weight from one foot to the other. "Yeah, well, I thought you'd want to get it started sooner than later. We got our job up to speed, and I pulled a few guys to start in your basement."

"Oh. Thank you." Dori took a deep breath, guilty that she'd been so bitchy with him.

"I hope that's okay," Gavin said. "I meant to call you last night, but time got away from me and it was too late."

"It's fine. Thanks."

"Can I ask you a question?"

Dori now wished she'd tiptoed back into her house. "Uh sure."

"Is one of my guys already here?" he asked.

It took her a moment but then she finally said, "No, why?"

"I saw someone in that window."

Dori stared at him, not quite understanding. He stepped close enough that his arm brushed against her shoulder. He pointed up at her bedroom window. "That one. When I got out of my truck, I could've sworn I saw a guy standing right there watching me."

The curtains hung motionless. Dori could see the outline of her headboard. She pictured her bedroom as she'd left it this morning, the blankets and sheets left in the swirl of her departure; pajamas tucked under her pillow and the tea cup she'd forgotten to bring down to the kitchen sink. Then it hit her: Vicente.

"You okay?" Gavin asked.

"Yeah. I have to go back inside. I left my phone and-" She stepped back, not sure why she had to keep Vicente a secret. If Gavin saw him, then that was one more check in the box next to "Dori is not crazy."

Gavin cleared his throat, toying with his hat. "He was up there for a couple of seconds," he said after a brief moment. "We stared at each other and then you came around the corner."

"Huh, I don't know what to tell you," she said, looking him straight in the eye without blinking.

"For a second, I thought maybe he was your boyfriend or something."

"I don't have a boyfriend."

"Oh. Okay."

Dori crossed her arms over her chest. "What? You don't believe me?"

"I do." Gavin held up his hands in a conciliatory gesture. "I mean not like that."

Dori knew she was acting weird. Hell, she had a prescription for it. An apology for her prickliness clogged her throat. But then she'd have to explain everything and while she had proof that Vicente was more than a figment of her imagination, she didn't want to expose herself in that way with Gavin.

76

She glanced up at her bedroom window, expecting to see Vicente laughing down at her. But he'd apparently seen enough.

"There's food in the kitchen," she said. "I stocked up the downstairs bathroom, too."

"Thanks. I don't want to run you off, but it's gonna get real loud."

"I'll be fine."

"You might want to cover your furniture, too."

"Okay."

She frowned as a camouflaged school bus turned into her driveway.

"They're here," he said.

"What is that?"

"My foreman's bus. He carries everything in that thing."

The noise was deafening from both ends of the house. The floor rattled and dust exploded up in the cracks of the walls. As the roofers nailed in sheeting, it felt like she was inside a drum. Music screeched from a boom box and Dori escaped with her ears ringing. She went back to the library to kill time before her appointment, but it was closed. She drove up to South Park and settled into a window table with her laptop and a cup of Hibiscus Breeze at Halcyon Tea on Beech Street.

She was waiting for her laptop to fire up when her phone buzzed. Dori frowned at her mother's name on the text message. Against her better judgment she opened it and read: *I would appreciate a return phone call.*

Dori had been ignoring her mother's calls. She punched out a quick text that she was busy and she'd call later – which was a total lie - and then tucked her cell phone into her bag.

As steam curled up from her cup, she typed Jakob Vazquez's name into the International Genealogy Index. When she saw the immense list of possibilities that popped up, she narrowed it San Diego and reduced her list from 500 to 350. She sat back against the chair and breathed in deep. No stranger to investigation, Dori realized it was a lot easier when her persons of interest were alive.

She flipped open her book on Prohibition and checked the date of repeal. She then narrowed her time frame from 1924 to 1933 and the system spat out his death certificate.

"Holy shit," she said out loud.

Two women with their toddlers in strollers glared at Dori.

"Sorry," she said and typed in Emilia's information.

Emilia had died in May 1, 1927. Jakob followed soon after on October 14 of the same year. She made a note so she could look them up in the obituaries. She then found them in the 1900 census in Anthony, New Mexico. Jakob was listed as a business man and they had five children. Anna's name was not among them and if she was a year younger than

Vicente, her birth year had to be 1910. Dori searched for their marriage and birth certificates, but her search ended there. She could call the local cemeteries to find where they were buried. If Anna was dead, she might be buried with them or nearby.

For the hell of it, she typed in Anna Vazquez and the list was so extensive, she checked the time. "I know you exist," she muttered to herself, shutting down her laptop.

When Dori returned to her house, two dumpsters blocked her driveway. The camouflaged school bus was gone. An ancient red Ford Pinto was parked behind Gavin's truck.

Feeling like the rubble that had once been her basement, she considered pulling back onto the street and going to the movies.

Walking into the kitchen door, she reared back at the reek of incense. Her sensitive eyes burned while Gregorian monks chanted from the other room. Gavin lay under the sink.

"Is that your music?" she asked, setting her laptop bag on the table.

"She said they'd be done blessing the house by the time you'd get back," Gavin said, his voice muffled.

Dori didn't have to ask who "she" was. "You let her in?"

"You hired me to work on the house, not keep your family out."

"Why are you under my sink when I hired you to fix my foundation and the roof?"

He sighed and then scooted out from under the sink. "Your grandma asked me to fix it."

"What's wrong with it?"

"The hot water wasn't working."

Dori sighed long and hard, debating if she should turn around and leave, or put a stop to the pagan rites in the other room.

"The good news is that it wasn't your water heater," Gavin continued. "Although, don't be surprised if it dies in the near future."

"Of course," she muttered.

"You want me to have the guys install a new one? It'll save you on the water bill."

"Do I have to?"

"Do you like cold showers?"

She held her up hand. "Okay fine."

Leaving him under the sink, Dori followed the music that switched from Gregorian monks to Tibetan ones chanting to her living room. There she found Grammy wearing all black with a mantilla covering her from head to her black-and-white converse sneakers with sequined skulls. She was really laying it on thick, praying piously alongside a woman who was flicking water all over Dori's coffee table.

Dori rolled her eyes. She was about to go back to the kitchen when Vicente said, "When I was alive, I wasn't into all that church stuff. I sure as hell haven't changed now that I'm dead."

She flinched and turned to find him standing with his shoulder resting on the door jamb, one foot crossed over the other.

"Aren't you going to do something?" he demanded.

Dori gestured to Grammy and the Holy Water lady. "This wasn't my idea."

He opened his mouth to answer when the chanting switched off.

"What are you doing here? We almost had him going to the light," Grammy demanded.

Dori quickly stepped between them and Vicente, not sure if she was protecting them or him. "What's going on here?" she demanded, crossing her arms over her chest.

"La luz, mija," said the lady with the plastic water bottle. "The light. Where we are all destined to go when-"

"Who are you?" Dori interrupted, having questioned enough crack heads and drunks to know where this conversation was headed.

"This is Bernice," Grammy said. "She owes me a favor so, instead of using it for myself, I brought her here to help you out with el fantasmo."

"Azucena, is this the one who-?" Bernice hurried over to Dori, arms held out. The sleeves of her black sweater fluttered like wings. "Oh, my baby girl! What you've survived!"

Before Dori could get away, she was grabbed in a gut-squeezing hug. She glared at Grammy over Bernice's shoulder.

Bernice then yanked her away, holding her by the shoulders before reaching down to take Dori's hands in hers. "Tell me, did you see the light? I can tell by your aura that the angels have sent you back with so many gifts to share with us."

"What the hell is she flapping on about?" Vicente asked, now standing right beside Bernice.

Dori tensed, waiting for Grammy and Bernice's reaction. Apparently, they couldn't see nor hear him.

"Many of my clients have had near death experiences. Tell me everything. Did your Grampy send you back?"

Anger choked off her breath. How dare this woman try to manipulate her? Dori hardened her stare and leaned forward. "I blacked out, and then I woke up in the hospital."

"Oh." Bernice tried to pull her hands away, but Dori held on wanting to put some fear into her. She had half a mind to shove her into the front parlor and see what would happen.

"Why were you in the hospital?" Vicente asked, distracting her.

"I got shot," Dori answered without thinking.

"Oh, that's makes sense," he said knowingly.

"What does that mean?" Dori asked, releasing Bernice's hands.

He pointed at Bernice to remind Dori that they couldn't see or hear him.

"It makes sense that you didn't see the light," Bernice said, thinking Dori was talking to her. "You weren't meant to go. You have unfinished business on this plane."

"See, Bernice knows what she's talking about," Grammy chimed in. "And she saw him right away. Your ghost told her that he died right here."

Grammy pointed to the floor and Bernice nodded regally, as it were proof that her powers were undeniable.

"Really?" Dori asked, remembering the night she found Vicente sprawled on the hallway floor. "Right here in the living room, he told you?"

"I've been able to communicate with them since I was a tiny little girl. He's a sentient being. Very troubled. Much gray and black around him. He needs to cross over."

Dori slid a glance in his direction. He stared at Bernice, devoid of any expression. He reminded her of criminals and cops alike when they had their game face on.

"The way I understood things is that you have to ask the homeowner's permission for this to work," Dori said, with the authority of having read James Van Praagh's book.

"Azucena, the energy is no longer right for this work," Bernice said as if Dori hadn't spoken. "Perhaps another time."

"Thanks, but I don't think so," Dori said. Even if Bernice was a phony, she couldn't take the chance that she'd accidentally send Vicente into the light or whatever. She'd promised to find Anna, and she would do it.

"Mija, you don't know what you're dealing with," Bernice said with a sniff. "Unlike a residual haunting, a sentient being is stuck; trapped by strong emotions or violence."

Grammy's eyes grew wider as she edged closer to the psychic who was oblivious to Vicente mad dogging her.

"The longer you keep him here, the greater dangers you face," she said. Dori thought of that day when she smelled blood in the front parlor and the cold that seemed to suffocate her. "He may have appeared to you, but some spirits just want you to believe they won't hurt you so they catch you off-guard."

Even though she didn't like it, what Bernice said corroborated James Van Praagh's book. But that hadn't been Vicente in the front parlor. It seemed to fit the definition of a residual haunting.

"Who the hell is this broad?" Vicente demanded, now standing beside Dori. She tried not to flinch at the searing cold that radiated from him. He jerked a thumb in Bernice's direction. "She's a high-hat phony."

"I know she's a phony!"

Bernice gasped and held her hand to her chest in an exaggerated pose of offense. Dori realized she'd said that out loud. She might as well take it all the way. "Bernice, I didn't invite you into my house."

"But-" Grammy started.

"This is my house, and when I'm ready for you to send my ghost into the light, I'll let you know."

"You think I'm going to let some woman tell me when and where I can go?" Vicente demanded.

"Mija, you have no idea what you're dealing with," Bernice said darkly. Dori half expected her eyes to glow red. "But if you insist, I'll leave you here against my better judgment."

Grammy sighed and rolled her eyes, coming over to reassure her.

"Leave me the bill," Dori said. "I'll be in the kitchen."

She made it to the hallway when she realized Vicente hadn't moved. She cleared her throat.

"Do I look like a dog to you?" he sneered.

With Grammy and Bernice turned away from them, Dori flapped her hand at him. When he refused to budge, she shook her head and went to the kitchen to see if Gavin was finished.

"Fine, what do you want?" Vicente said, appearing right in front of her. She stopped just short of walking through him.

Just then a power drill started up and made an awful high-pitched whine that threatened to peel the enamel off her teeth. It shut off, and Gavin cursed.

Dori muttered to Vicente, "Follow me."

She led him into the butler's pantry and then shut the door. "I didn't ask her to come here."

He crossed his arms over his chest.

"Was that you who shoved me out of the front parlor?"

He didn't react.

"Was it?" she insisted.

"What are you saying? I've done a lot of things in my life-"

"I can just imagine."

"I bet you can." He lifted his chin, grinning like a predator thinking how good the prey tasted. "But I never hurt women. I mean, I used one or two and-"

"What's in that room? I felt like something was trying to strangle me."

He lifted a shoulder. "I don't know."

She waited a second longer and then backed off. "Sorry. I had to be sure."

"That's because you don't know me."

"I know your kind well enough."

"Really?"

She grinned back at him. "I've had the honor of putting them in jail."

He made a dismissive sound. "The cops only came close when I handed them their monthly cooperation compensation."

"Is that why they, uh-" She summoned her courage to say it. "Killed you in my house."

He took in her measure and then uncrossed his arms. "We were preparing for repeal and setting up legitimate operations, but the sheriff and his KKK friends wanted part of the action."

"The KKK lived in my house?"

"One of them."

"Is that what's in my front parlor?"

He lifted a shoulder as if he had no idea and could care less.

She'd later deal with the possibility that it was a Klansman ghost haunting her front parlor. "But why did they beat you like that? There are easier ways, I mean, moving a body isn't that-" She caught herself from saying something insensitive.

His jaw stiffened, and then he finally said, "What do I look like to you, Dori?" He advanced towards her, but she knew better than to cower. "I was nothing more than a greaser monkey in a suit to them, someone who made twenty times what they could in their whole damn career. The fact that they had to open the door to me was an insult to them."

"Sorry. You know, I'd rather find them-"

"I don't care about them. I need you to find Anna."

"I found her parents. They died in 1927."

"I know that. What about her?"

Dead or alive, people were impossible to please. "I'm working on it. It would help to have hard facts like dates and years and addresses."

He closed his eyes. Dori dared not blink in case he vanished on her again.

"I want to help you," she said. "I don't even know where you lived or when you were born or where you're buried."

His eyes snapped open, and he swelled with energy, making the pantry go cold.

"None of that matters," he said in a big hurry, as if he needed to get it all out before he disappeared. "Once they were done with me, they would've gone after Anna. She was vulnerable and like most women, wouldn't listen to a damn word I said."

# CHAPTER FOURTEEN

## National City, 1925

"Where have you been?" Anna demanded when he came up to her on the beach. She gestured for him to follow her into the brush. "Look. I found something."

He stood a bit taller at the knowledge she'd been waiting for him. The low-lying grass crunched under her boots as she crept towards a patch of black slimy water.

"We have to hurry before she comes back."

"Your mother?"

"No," she said as if he were slow. "Look there."

She pointed and he leaned forward, only seeing mud and a bush of spiny, pointed limbs.

"What am I looking at?"

Anna edged closer and her hair tickled his cheek. He stared down at her ear, tracing down to the edge of her dress that came up to her neck.

"See it?"

Vicente traced the length of her arm, itching to rub his hand down her smooth skin to the tip of her pointed finger. The breeze ruffled the feathers stuck into a nest of twigs and mud.

"I saw the mother. She has three eggs in it."

"You're not going to eat them, are you?"

She swung around, about to chastise him and then realized how close they stood. "Shut up!"

He held up both hands. "I was joking. It's very uh, natural. I've never seen a nest this close."

Anna looked at him like she knew he was humoring her. He didn't give a crap about birds' nests, but if she put a lot of store in them and stood close enough that her hair caressed him, then he would, too.

"Here," she said, reaching into her pocket and pulling out a candy stick. "Not that you deserve it."

She turned and marched with arms swinging towards the water. Vicente tore off the paper and stuck the candy in his mouth. He wondered how long she'd pout. He jogged ahead and caught up with her.

"Are you going to the wedding?" he asked.

"What wedding?"

He thought for a minute, trying to remember the names of the couple getting married. The women at work talked of nothing else. What caught his attention was that whether you knew the people or not, weddings, baptisms and wakes in the barrio were fair game.

"You don't know their names?" Anna asked, laughing as she sat down on the sand and unlaced her boots.

He joined her. "The food is free and so is the music."

"My parents just send a gift if they get invited." The wind blew the ends of her hair against his arm as they sat side-by-side facing the water. "I hate going to those things."

"Why?"

She shrugged and then stuck a piece of candy in her mouth.

"It's because you can't dance, huh?"

"No, it isn't!"

"Dance with me and prove it."

She straightened her spine. "At the wedding?"

"Where else?"

Even though he teased, his question hung between them. She was fourteen, too young to be out with young men. But he'd do things properly. He eased back onto his elbows, forcing himself into a relaxed pose. He was asking for more than a dance, and she knew it. His hands clenched tight when she didn't answer his question.

They'd met here for the past five Thursdays. Always by chance, or that's how he played it. Little by little, she stayed a bit longer and lost that quiet, blank look on her face. The last time when he showed up, she held out four sticks of candy. His heart doubled in size that she'd brought them for him. It was the best gift anyone had given him because it meant she thought about him when they weren't together.

He still had two hidden under the floor where he kept his stash of newspaper money.

She sighed and then finally said, "They won't let me go."

"But they let you come here."

She grinned as she drew circles in the sand. "It's nap time. Mother thinks I'm sleeping."

The thought of Anna sneaking out of her big white house just to see him made his heart stop and then resume beating at double time. "Then come to the wedding."

Her finger stopped. "People will tell."

"Then don't go home. We both won't go home."

She didn't look away. Before she could say no, he sat up. "We could move to Hollywood. You could sell candy and I'll be-" He looked off at the bay, squinting against the harsh sunlight. "I'll be in the movies."

She snorted and then pressed her hand to her mouth, covering up her laugh.

"It could work," he said, his pulse kicking against his throat.

"I think it's ridiculous."

"Not if we do it. We could-" He stopped himself. He said too much.

She shook her head. "When I turn fifteen next year, I'm getting married."

Even with the sun burning his face, Vicente went cold. She hadn't moved from her spot, but she was slipping away from him.

"Everything we have is because of him. Our house, father's business, the doctors for my brothers and-" She brushed her hands over her light blue skirt and then dropped her gaze to the sand between them.

"What's his name?" Vicente managed, even though it felt like he was being held by the throat.

"Albert. He was supposed to marry my sister but she died during the epidemic with our brothers and sisters, so my parents they-"

She clamped her lips into a tight line. He thought she was going to cry, but she went very still. "I sometimes dream that my sister is mad at me for taking him from her."

"How old was your sister when she died?"

"My age." Her eyes softened. "She was the one who took care of me and I had to sit with them when he came calling. He seemed old then, too."

"Do you want to marry him?"

"I have to."

"But-"

Anna rose up from the sand. The wind blew her dress against her legs. "I'll see you at the reception," she said. "I'll try but-"

She shook her head and then started off.

"You will?" he called.

"I will."

She'd left her boots behind. He picked them up and ran after her. He saw her flinch when she heard him coming up on her. She swung around with the look of uncertainty of what he'd do.

"You need these," he said, holding them out.

She looked from the boots to him. "Thank you."

When she reached for them, he held them over his head, laughing.

Anna didn't seem to know what to do, as if she'd forgotten how to play.

She planted her fists on her hips. "Give them!"

He danced back, clenching his candy stick between his teeth.

She stalked over. "Vicente!"

He almost handed them over. It was the first time she'd ever used his name. "Don't just stand there."

"Come on. I'll be late."

He wouldn't see her for three more days. He wanted to make this time last. She leapt up and he tensed to spring back at the last minute. Instead of snatching at her boots, she ripped the candy out of his mouth.

They stood there, both of their eyes wide with surprise. She covered her mouth, laughing.

"Give it back," he said.

She put his candy stick behind her back, lifting her chin. "Only if you say you're sorry."

He could've easily tackled her for it, but he liked seeing her eyes alive. "What if I don't?"

"Then I toss this in the water." She wiggled the candy stick.

"No, you won't."

Her grin burst into a full smile.

He launched at her. She sprung out of his way and then ran around him, racing for the water. He gave her enough time to think she might get away. The sunlight burned straight into his eyes, and for a moment, she disappeared into the light.

It was the happiest moment of his life.

Everyone brought chairs from home to sit and watch the dancing at the church hall. Mariachi Calderon, all the way from Guadalajara, performed at the front of the room, their faces shining with sweat. The tables held homemade tamales, rice, beans, tortillas, nopales, cakes and a bowl of punch. Men who wanted something more, went around the corner to Ulalio Riley's backyard for a glass of whiskey. It was brewed by his Irish grandpa, who would tell anyone how he came across the Atlantic Ocean for America's promise of fortune only to end up Mexico.

Vicente stood outside between the church and the hall, selling papers and tobacco to the boys. They clung together in a tight circle, the smoke rising from their eager pulls. His attention flicked about the churchyard in time to the thrumming of the guitarron. The husbands were already swaying under the influence of the Riley whiskey. Children yawned and slept in their mother's laps. The old ladies in their stiff, old-fashioned black dresses watched with disapproval and envy as the young girls danced with their suitors.

Alex ran up. "Look, look," he said and held out a dented flask. Vicente stepped forward to stop the infringement of his business, but Alex was giving it away for free.

Jorge was the first to grab it and drink. His eyes bulged out, and he spat the whiskey.

"Cabrón, that cost me five cents!" Alex flicked off beads of spit and whiskey from his white shirt.

"You paid five cents for horse piss," Jose said, shoving Alex so hard that he dropped the flask. Vicente jumped out of the way to keep his new suit clean.

The first fight of the evening began as the boys shoved each other, their oiled hair falling in their faces and lips pulled back, revealing teeth.

Vicente picked up the forgotten flask, sniffed the inside and then thought a sip might ease the tightness in his chest. It was like swallowing fire. Alex grabbed the front of Jose's shirt and with the sound of the fabric tearing, they fell to the ground.

The police would be prowling the party if these two didn't finish up soon. National City had gone dry before prohibition, and cops here loved nothing more than a Mexican with whiskey; especially when they'd been tilting back a bit of their own during patrol.

Vicente tossed the flask into the Father's roses. He edged away from the noise and clamor.

The collar of his new shirt stuck to the back of his neck, and he held his arms away from his sides so his armpits wouldn't soak the dark blue wool of his coat. His new pants hung the right length over proper dress shoes. His grandmother nearly brained him with her iron when he stepped out in his new suit this morning before the wedding.

"Where did you get the money? Why would you spend it on yourself when your sister needs a new dress?'

Vicente used his newspaper money. He had bought Eugenia a new doll, which she'd hidden from their grandmother. He bought the tobacco and papers to make back what he spent on the doll and the suit. When he tossed a few quarters on the table, the old lady shut up real quick like he knew she would.

Hands grabbed him by the coat. "You! Watch where you're going!"

Vicente was yanked up to the balls of his feet, staring into an angry face. The next moment he was tossed back, landing hard on his ass with a bounce. He snarled up at the broad-shouldered man who held Anna's fist against his chest.

"You almost stepped on Miss Vazquez," he said, as sweat trickled down his florid cheeks. "You should apologize."

Anna stared down at him, her hair hanging long and loose with two pink bows stuck behind her ears. Her dress was white with a panel of lace running down from the high-necked collar to a pink sash tied low at her hips. Long sleeves and thick stockings covered her arms and legs, and instead of heels, she wore flat pink slippers.

In this childish get up, she looked ridiculous.

"Do you know this boy?" the man ordered. Tiny rocks bit into the heels of Vicente's hands as he pushed himself up to standing.

Anna's chin stayed level, but her eyes dropped to the ground. She shook her head.

"What kind of answer is that, Anna?"

"I don't know him, Albert."

Albert stared at her, leveraging silence to pry open the truth. Vicente willed Anna to admit that she knew him, that she'd brought him candy and they'd chased each over the sand until they both had stitches in their sides and could hardly breathe from laughing.

Vicente stared at her, willing her to look at him and step away from Albert and stand beside him. I'll fight for you, he wanted to say. I'll take care of you.

"Beg your pardon," Vicente said, nearly choking on his apology. Tonight, he'd such hopes he and Anna would dance, that he'd finally get to touch and hold her. In his head, she would gaze up at him in such a way that he'd finally know she wanted him as badly as he wanted her.

She now refused to look at him, to give any indication that they knew each other.

"Come," Albert said, giving a sharp tug on Anna's arm. She didn't follow. "Anna, I said come."

Vicente watched Albert escort her past the boys who'd been pulled apart by their friends.

Standing there with dust on his ass, Vicente held his breath until his chest nearly exploded. He stalked across the yard and into the dance hall. He kept to the edges of the crowd, pain making his chest go cold.

Albert walked Anna around the edge of the dance floor, showing off his prize while nodding to the old ladies. She kept her gaze straight ahead, not bowing in shame even though hands shot up and covered whisperings in their wake. She stared unblinking as if she were sleepwalking.

When they finished the circuit, Albert reached into his white suit coat and held out cash, waving it to the band. The singer nodded in appreciation, and they began a waltz. Vicente watched as his whole body froze over. He should've felt some spark of anger or something. He felt nothing.

Albert danced her into the center of the dance floor, a smug grin pinned to his fat face. He had a square-shaped head that seemed to sit right between his shoulders. He couldn't dance worth shit and his chubby fingers clamped tight onto her back. The two of them in their pure white glowed in a sea of dingy gray, brown and black. He smiled down at her as if about to bite her. Every time Anna turned towards Vicente, she kept her gaze on Albert's shoulder as if to pretend he wasn't there.

He watched them dance four dances. Albert walked her to sit with two old ladies and then headed out the front door with a silver cigarette case in his hands. Vicente wheeled around into the darkness, not seeing Anna look up at the last moment to see if he was still there.

He let the moonless night swallow him up, not caring as he splashed through the reddish water collecting in the center of the road. The wind roared by his ears as he pumped his legs faster and faster away from the barrio, along the train tracks.

The train's light burned his eyes, but he kept running towards it. His heart was about to explode out of his chest. He couldn't get far enough away from her in that man's arms. The train's whistle screamed and he veered off to the right. Grass and dried shrubs scratched and tore at his new shoes and pants. As he came over the rise, his ankle collapsed. He hit the sand hard. The train rattled past, car after car and then it was only a red swinging light that disappeared into the night.

Vicente could hardly breathe through the agony in his chest. He felt a fool in his new suit; so, obvious in his attempt to rescue her.

"You gotta reason for being here?"

Something poked him in the arm. Vicente looked up at the shadow of a man holding a shotgun on him.

"I said-"

"Yeah," Vicente snapped, his stomach boiling for a fight. "I got every right to be here."

"Stand up."

Vicente refused to get up.

"You're at the wrong end of the barrel, kid."

Vicente surged to his feet. The man stepped back. "Hey, take it easy!"

"Don't stick a gun in my face unless you're going to use it."

"Hell, kid. I don't wanna shoot you."

The man backed off, and Vicente saw there were two more unloading barrels onto the beach. His mouth dropped open. He'd never seen real bootleggers. They weren't small time or grandpa with his still in the basement. These were the real deal.

Vicente held up his hands. "I don't want to get shot."

The man lowered the barrel. "If I were you, I'd head back where you came from."

Vicente counted six barrels on the sand, and one of the guys waded out to the boat for more. From his newspaper sales, Vicente read that the caves in La Jolla and along Point Loma were getting too hot. But on this silent stretch of beach, they had to roll those barrels up the rise and then across almost four miles of tidelands to the nearest road.

"I can get you guys closer to your truck," he said.

The shotgun came up, aiming at his chest. Vicente quickly explained there was a sandbar up north. He could fetch the truck, drive it up and meet them.

"Who the hell are you?" the gunman asked.

"Just a guy who wants to help."

The man turned and hissed over his shoulder. "Hey Mario, come here."

Vicente heard the crunching in the sand.

"What's the problem?" another voice asked in the dark.

"We gotta a kid here who knows where we can make the drop."

"We got half the load on the sand."

"From here, you have to walk up the rise and cross the tracks and then the swamp to get to the nearest road," Vicente explained. "I'll help you reload, show you the place. You can send your gun with me to make sure we're square."

"Hell, there's cops up there."

"There's a dance at the church," Vicente said. "They'll be there waiting to break it up."

The two men stayed silent. "Go with him."

"Are you sure?"

"Cops patrol about the main road because it heads straight to and from the border," Vicente said, making it up as he went along. This was better than running away to Hollywood. His chest ached at the memory of her but he lifted his chin. "They keep an eye on it all day and all night."

"You know what you're getting into, kid?"

"I'm no kid."

"You better be on the money," the gunman said. "Or it won't be pretty."

# CHAPTER FIFTEEN

Dori flinched when someone pounded on the door.

"Anyone home?" Gavin called.

She blinked, having been engrossed in Vicente's story. How long had she stood in the now dark and empty pantry? If she kept this up, she'd wind up like crazy Bernice.

Her cheeks puffed out as she released her breath.

She yanked the cord from the bare bulb in the ceiling. The light stung her eyes and she squeezed them shut and opened them wide so it wouldn't look to Gavin like she'd been standing in the dark for who knows how long.

Dori opened the door and was nose-to-nose with Gavin's solid chest. She breathed in and thought he still smelled the same.

"I heard you in there talking," Gavin said. "I didn't mean to scare you."

"You didn't. I was just-"

He glanced behind her. "Were you on the phone or something?"

"Yes," she said, seizing the perfect excuse.

"Oh. Well I finished up with the sink."

She shoved her hands in her pockets and then crossed her arms over her chest. "Great. Thanks."

"Your Grammy and her friend left."

"I figured that."

Gavin craned his neck to look behind her. "It's kinda dark in there."

"Yes, it is," she said. "Are you done for the day?"

"Yeah, but we'll be back bright and early tomorrow. I didn't want to leave your house unlocked."

"Okay. Thanks."

"In a week, you think you'll be ready to get to work?"

"Yes, but-"

"No buts. We made a deal."

Dori wished she had just a pinch of Sela's entitlement. But Gavin was right, and he had access to the vital organs of her house. With no work or other engagements, Dori could find Anna in a week. "Fair enough. What do you want me to do?"

"Strip."

Dori didn't blink.

"I mean the paint," he said, his face relaxing into a teasing grin. "In the hallway."

"After I strip it, who's repainting it?"

"You are."

"Wait a second-"

"Hold on." He held his hands out as if to ward off a blow. "Let me show you."

He turned and walked towards the hallway. Dori noted that he had learned his way around her house pretty quickly. He waited by the door and swept his arm to indicate she should go first.

She did, keeping an eye open for Vicente appearing out of thin air. Dori cleared her throat, hoping the ghost would get the hint: no pools of blood or walking through walls.

Gavin led her into the hall, held out his arms and said, "So where should I start?"

Dori realized that Gavin was right: the yellowish pink walls looked sick. Brown stains scarred the plaster ceiling and some sadist had flanked the mantle with cheap bookcases. Everything was scuffed and chipped and down at heel. She felt Gavin watching for her reaction.

"I see what you mean," she said, keeping a stoic face.

"If this were my place-" He stopped when she turned to him. "Never mind. I'll bring paint samples tomorrow. But don't touch this wood. Only the plaster walls."

"I won't."

"I know a guy who specializes in this stuff. It's redwood that was shipped down the Columbia River."

"How do you know that?"

"Or, it came from Northern California. The guy I was telling you about, his grandfather built the flumes that they used to transport the trees from the mountains to the river." There was an awkward pause before he asked, "You want to see what we did today?"

"Sure."

"Unfortunately, we found some more problems," he said, opening the basement door and reaching into the pitch black. "I managed to get your sink working for now, but I'll bring in my plumber tomorrow."

Dori sucked in a sigh. He found the light switch and she went down the steps. She came to a slow halt, astonished by what she saw before her.

Lights hung from the ceiling by hooks. What had once resembled a hell mouth had been stripped down and swept clean. Tools were neatly piled under the coal shoot against the wall.

"It's so clean," she blurted out.

"A clean site is a working site," he said. "And a safe one."

He cleared his throat. "I wanted to show this to you. See that bottle?"

She bent down to peer at an old wine bottle shoved between the river rock foundation and the floor. "Yeah."

"Someone thought that could help hold up your house." He ran his fingers along the cement between the rocks and it crumbled away.

Dori shivered as she thought about going to bed tonight.

"And see here? Someone cut into this beam when they added plumbing to the downstairs bathroom."

She obligingly looked up to where he was pointing. "And that's not good?"

"Not when the beam is supposed to support your house. Anyway, we're going to replace all of this with new 2500 psi, steel reinforced concrete and put in steel T straps to these girder beams." He reminded her of an artist who saw something beautiful on a blank canvas. "When we're done, this place won't go anywhere and none of the doors or windows will stick because the house will be level again."

"And the pipe?"

"My guy is going to look at it, and then after we get it retro-fitted, he'll come back and reroute the pipe. The downstairs bathroom won't have running water for two or three days."

"Really?"

"Sorry but-"

"No, I mean only for three days? You guys work fast."

"Well, it's how we-"

They both jumped when the door slammed shut at the top of the stairs. The force of it sent a rush of cold air against her back that zigzagged up her neck and sparkled across her scalp.

Damn him, she thought.

But Vicente wasn't done yet. The lights flared and then the dark dropped down on them. Dori held her breath. The dark was so thick that it felt as if it pushed her eyeballs back into her head.

"Hold on," Gavin said, moving beside her. "Stay where you are. I'll help you up the stairs."

"I don't need you to-"

She started when he stood close enough that she felt his warmth. His hand cupped her elbow. "It's just me," he said gently. "We'll take it slow."

His other hand slid across her lower back and then he led her through the dark.

"Here. Grab the banister," he said. Her sweaty hand found itself stuck to the splintery wood. His hand rested on top of hers.

"You can let go." She stepped away from the hand on her back and felt her balance wobble. "I can walk up the stairs."

He squeezed her hand, and she clenched her jaw. "You sure?" he asked.

She concentrated on lifting her foot onto the first step. Even though she knew the steps were there, the oppressive black made her feel like she was about to plunge off a cliff. When her foot touched the riser, relief rushed through her. She took each step slowly, holding her hand out before her.

"Did this happen when you guys were working today?" she asked.

"They would've told me if it did."

"Where were you?"

"Running my business." She could almost hear the smile on his lips. "I have other jobs, too."

"I just thought-"

"I've swung enough hammers to earn the right to manage things. I bought this business from my old boss."

Dori's heart jolted when her outstretched hand bumped into the door. "Got it."

"You can let go of my hand then," he said and she realized she'd climbed the whole way latched onto him.

"Sorry," she mumbled, snatching her hand back. She felt the door for the knob. Her eyes squinted from dim light of the hallway that cracked and widened as she opened the door.

When she stepped into the hallway, she walked into the now familiar invisible wall of ice.

"Man," he said, as he walked up behind her. "Weather stripping and insulation should be next on your list."

Dori pretended nothing was wrong as she scanned the dark corners for Vicente. She wondered if sprinkling holy water on him would have the same satisfaction as kicking him between the legs.

"I'll check the breaker," Gavin said.

"You don't have to-"

"Let me. Really. Somehow this could get back to your grammy and then she'd really let me have it."

Dori clenched her hand that was still warm from holding his. "In that case, knock yourself out."

He saluted her. "Will do."

She waited till he was out the back door before blowing out a long breath and pressing her hand against her chest. She wasn't sure what discombobulated her more; Vicente's trick, or the way her hand felt in Gavin's. If she wasn't so screwed up right now, she'd do anything to get him to hold her hand again. But with their track record, the last thing she needed was a vengeful ex working on the foundation of her house.

The back door opened, and Dori heard Gavin's heavy footsteps approach. "Everything looks all right. Did the lights come back on?"

Dori pushed the basement door open and peered down the steps. Vicente saluted her, glowing cheerfully at the bottom of the stairs.

She pulled so hard that the door slam reverberated up her arm. "No. Not yet."

"Here let me-"

She stepped right in his path. Gavin stopped just short of bumping into her. "Let it wait till tomorrow," she said, her hands itching to slide up his chest.

"Why?"

"Have your guys work on it tomorrow. It's not like I have to go down there for anything."

"Really?" He cleared his throat and shifted his weight. "I don't feel right about that."

She squeezed the doorknob so tight that her skin burned. "It's fine."

Dori waited for Gavin to remember the rules of personal space. Instead, he just stood there as the house went silent all around them.

"What are your plans tonight?" he asked quietly, shoving his hands into his pockets.

"My what?"

He rocked his weight from foot to foot. "Your plans."

Dori's pulse thrummed in her throat and her hand shot up, scratching a non-existent itch on the back of her neck. "Uh, nothing. Just doing some research online."

He looked up with a frown between his eyebrows. "Research?"

"Family stuff."

He yanked his hands out of his pockets. Neither looked each other in the eye. "If I, uh, take another look downstairs, I'll be out of here in two minutes."

Remembering Vicente waiting down there, Dori held her hand up to block him. "Gavin wait, it's-"

She forgot what she was about to say when he pulled a flashlight out of his back pocket.

"You had a flashlight?" she asked.

"Yeah, I always do."

He'd played her. Dori let go of the door knob and stepped out of his way.

"Be careful down there," she said, hoping Vicente scared the hell out of him.

Gavin opened the door and the lights turned themselves back on. "Looks like the problem fixed itself." He snapped off his flashlight. "I'll turn everything off and have the guys check out the wires."

Dori tucked both hands into her the back pockets of her jeans to keep from shoving him down the stairs. "Thanks."

"Not a problem. But don't forget next week," he said. Without looking back, Gavin strode across the hall and then out the kitchen door.

# CHAPTER SIXTEEN

"I'm ready," Grammy called out breathlessly like she was late for a date. She entered the kitchen wearing head-to-toe purple, finished by a shawl with an embroidered peacock on the back. Dori wondered how she was going to fit in the car without breaking off the real feathers glued to the peacock's behind.

"Take my picture so I can post it on my Facebook," Grammy said, handing over a blinged-out iPhone.

"Where did you get all this tech?"

"Your cousin got it for me with her employee discount."

In their family, an "employee discount" meant it was carried out the back door when no one was looking. Dori took her photo and then handed it back.

"So, what do you think of my outfit?"

"Very colorful," Dori said. She'd been waiting to be confronted about Bernice the phony psychic, but Grammy hadn't gone there. They were careful with each other, which was a good sign. If Grammy had really been mad at Dori, she never would've opened the front door and let her inside.

"Go cut me some of the roses by the kitchen door."

"How many?"

"All of them."

"Are you sure?"

"When am I ever not sure, mija? Now go. I have to check my comments."

"Since when did you get on Facebook?"

"Last week. I tried to 'friend' you, but you're not on it."

"What do you post?"

"Oh, this and that."

Dori would rather not know. She walked into the small laundry room and automatically reached for the cutters hanging from a nail hammered into the wall. The sun had broken through the gray clouds that hung low in the sky. But more were coming. The yard smelled of pepper trees and wet earth.

At this very moment, there were men digging trenches around the base of her house. She hoped Vicente didn't scare anyone to death. She'd left right after Gavin and his crew arrived. From the window, she'd watch him direct his crew easily, without being a jerk. But when he briefly spoke to her, he did it like he hadn't held her hand last night.

It was his fault he had hidden the flashlight, making her grab onto him in the dark. For a moment, when they'd climbed out of the dark basement, it felt like they could be friendly.

When Dori had a handful of roses, she paused in clipping off the thorns. She went back inside and wrapped them in a wet paper towel. "Are you sure you want to go out?" she called out from the kitchen. "It looks like rain."

Grammy hadn't heard her. Dori carried the roses into the living room where Grammy opened and closed the screen door. "Did you mess with my door?"

"I tried."

"But I keep telling you to leave it. Chuy said he was going to do it."

"But it never gets done."

The screen slapped against the doorframe. It made an ominous crack and then slumped down crookedly, hanging from the last screw.

"Look at what you did!" Grammy scolded. "I told you not to mess with it."

"Well, don't hold your breath waiting for Chuy."

"You know what your problem is?" Grammy jabbed the air with her house key. "You're too negative. You always think the worst, which is why Bernice didn't work."

"But-" Dori clenched the roses and a thorn she had missed bit into her hand. She dropped them on the floor.

"Ay, what is up with you, girl? Pick them up!"

Dori bent down and carefully gathered the roses. Broken petals scattered over the rug and she wondered how long it had been since the place had been vacuumed. She pocketed the petals so Grammy wouldn't see them.

"You ready to go?" Dori asked, her voice straining after getting yelled at. Her chest hurt because she hadn't done anything wrong.

"I'll call Chuy on the way. He'll fix it if I make him dinner."

With her nose lifted so high in the air that she might topple backwards, Grammy marched to the car. Her peacock feathers fluttered indignantly in the wind.

In ticked-off silence they drove to the cemetery. Patches of blue sky shone through the holes in the gathering clouds. A lone crow walked across steep road, waiting until they were almost upon him to fly away.

Chuy hadn't answered Grammy's phone calls, and his girlfriend claimed not to know where he was. Dori tried not to smile over that small victory while Grammy texted or Facebooked or whatever she did on that stupid phone.

As Dori parked in their customary spot, she seethed over how she was the only grand kid who didn't take advantage of her grandmother, but somehow, she got most of her crap. Maybe she ought to call Chuy or her brother, Robert to drive Grammy to the cemetery once a week. She bet they'd fall all over themselves to do it. But once again, Dori rounded the back of the car to help her out.

When they got to Grampy's crypt, a mishmash of wilted turquoise carnations, roses and dried eucalyptus branches bulged from his bronze vase.

"Look what that loca did!" Grammy shouted, her voice echoing off the marble walls of eternal slumber. The wind blew the peacock feathers against her back.

It could only be the work of Great Aunt Norma, Grampy's youngest sister who lived her life as if Catholicism was a full-contact sport.

"You know what? I'm gonna report her for going around and stealing from the other graves. She's nuthin' but a grave robber!"

"Why don't you take a picture for your Facebook page?"

Dori braced herself for a scolding. But Grammy stared at her, clearly stricken. "What the hell is wrong with you?"

Guilt seeped through the cracks of her anger. "Sorry, I was just trying to be-"

"Throw all that out!"

Dori pulled the arrangement apart, separating the freshest flowers.

"What are you doing?"

"Recycling." Dori stuffed the nicer flowers into the vase of a husband and wife who had died in the 1960s. Even if they came from Great Aunt Norma, Grampy's cemetery neighbors might appreciate the gesture. No one left them flowers anymore. If Kaylee had aimed higher, Dori wondered if anyone other than Grammy would remember to put flowers on her grave.

"Be right back," she told Grammy, who ignored her.

Crows cawed in the distance. Dori looked out over the cemetery and thought of Vicente. She slowed to a stop as it occurred to her that he might be buried here. She decided that Grammy could use more alone time with Grampy and walked past the sink, towards the office.

The hot, coffee-scented air made her face tingle. A bell jangled against door when she stepped inside. She could hear Dr. Phil on TV in the back room.

"Hello?" she called out.

"Be right there!"

A young guy with a goatee, pink guayabera and a fedora perched on his head stepped out. "Good morning!" he greeted jovially. "How's it going?"

Dori had been expecting someone a bit more somber. He was way too cheerful to work in a place like this. She eyed the name plate on the counter.

"Hi Richard, I was wondering how I could find out where someone is buried here."

He shrugged and rested his hand on the counter. A silver skull with little red eyes blinked up from his ring finger. "I just need a name and preferably date of death."

Of course, he did. All she had was a name and a mental image of really handsome man in a ripped-up suit. "His name was Vicente Sorolla and he died in 1932."

"That might complicate things." He now rubbed his goatee thoughtfully. "There was a fire here in the 1940's, and they like, lost all of those old records."

Dori nodded her head, backing towards the door. "Thanks."

"Hey, anytime," he said. "Is he like, a relative of yours?"

"Yeah, something like-" She hated it when people said 'like' all the time. "Yes, he was."

"Wait a second! Have you tried the history room at the library?" He plucked a business card out of a holder. He jogged over and handed it to her. "The gal running it is really cool. She can, like, find anything, know what I mean?"

Dori smiled at the thought of Meg. "Thanks. I met her the other day."

"She's come by and helped some of our families out. When you have the names and dates, I'll look it up in the system just in case."

Dori thanked him and then walked back out into the gray day to wash out Grampy's vase of all traces of Great Aunt Norma's floral poaching. So much for ten years of law enforcement experience, she thought. She knew how to find someone. There had to be news accounts of a man murdered in her house. She felt a little stupid for not thinking of it before.

As she tucked the office guy's card into her pocket, she thought of Meg again and her internal mumbling faded away. Maybe when she finished up with Grammy, she'd give Meg a call and see if she'd be interested in coffee or something.

"Come on! I brought you all the way up here for your visit."

Startled, Dori turned from the sink to see a dented and scratched Nissan Altima idling at the top of the steps. She'd been so deep in thought she hadn't heard the car approach. A woman bent over the front passenger seat. At first, Dori thought she was hollering at her kids.

"Vieja, I drove you all the way here," the woman said a little too loudly for a cemetery. "It's your man's anniversary."

Dori craned her neck, only seeing a pair of legs in thick support stockings. A pair of claw-like hands jerked up in surprise when the woman grabbed her by the shoulders.

"Fine. I'll slap you outta this car," the daughter said.

Dori watched them struggle. She caught glimpses of the older woman's hand, trying to push the younger woman away. She should mind her own business, but she left the vase in the sink and walked towards the stairs.

"Excuse me," Dori called out. "Can I help you?"

The younger woman's thick gold necklace clanked over her black sweat shirt when she turned. "Who the hell are you?"

Dori took in the thick eyeliner, tattooed angry-thin eyebrows and silvery pink lipstick. She wore tight black jeans and white Converse shoes. Dori glanced in the car. The older woman cried silently.

"Hello, ma'am," Dori said, making eye contact with her. "Are you okay?"

"I told you, mind your damn business," the chola said, stepping over to block the old lady from Dori's view.

"I'm speaking to your mother."

"She ain't my mother and she don't talk no more."

"It doesn't look like she wants to get out of the car," Dori said. "Maybe you should take her home and bring her back another time."

"Who the hell are you to tell me what to do, bitch?"

Dori automatically reached for her badge. But it wasn't there. Her Smith and Wesson hid in her holster under her leather jacket.

She dusted off her pants instead. "If she doesn't want to get out of the car, don't force her."

The old woman in the car leaned forward and met Dori's gaze. She looked like she'd scream for help if she could. A knitted bib covered the hole from a laryngectomy.

The chola jutted out her hip and waggled her finger in the air. "If you're gonna mess with my business, you gotta get through me puta cabrona."

"You think you can talk to my granddaughter like that and get away with it?"

Dori turned to her Grammy standing there, fists on her hips and peacock feathers flapping in the wind.

"Hell, yes I can, and I'll tell you, you old bi-"

Dori called out. "Hey, both of you stop!"

But neither paid her any attention, inching closer and closer while tossing insults at each other.

"I don't care how fat you are, I'll put you in a wheelchair," Grammy shouted.

The chola started down the stairs. "Okay, now you pissed me off good, old lady. I'll show you to shut your damn mouth!"

"What's going on out here?" Richard the office manager demanded, standing in the open doorway. "This is like, a cemetery. You can't be fighting out here."

Both Grammy and her nemesis barked at him to shut up.

"I got this," Dori told him and then was shoved backwards. Her arms flapped in the air, feet tripping over the other. She caught herself and then without thinking, Dori swept her left arm up, deflecting the woman's fist. Her right fist drove up into the chola's chin, and she heard the woman's teeth snap. The chola staggered back and then landed on the ground with the thunk of her head hitting the sidewalk.

Dori stepped over her and grabbed her shirt, yanking her up from the ground. Her fist cocked up. She vaguely heard voices calling out to her as she drove that fist into the woman's nose. The impact reverberated up her arm as she saw the first trickle of blood that turned into a gush that covered the woman's mouth and neck.

Dori came down on her knees, her hand reaching for her weapon. Someone yelled gun and for a moment, she was looking down into Kaylee's face.

But then she was hauled off, arms wrapped around her chest. There was more yelling.

"Stop, mija! Enough!"

Dori looked around the cemetery, confused as to where she was and why someone was holding her. Grammy stepped into her line of vision, her face taut with fear.

"Mija, it's okay. She's down."

Dori sagged in his arms, the fight rushing out of her.

No one moved. It was so quiet that the dead may have been peeking out from behind their graves to see what would happen next.

"Let her go," Grammy pleaded with Richard. Dori couldn't bear the look on her grammy's face.

"I'm taking her into the office," he said. "Then I'm calling the cops."

Dori could've easily thrown him off, twisted his arm over her shoulder and tossed him into the fountain. But she nodded. "Okay. I'll go with you."

They shuffled towards the office. Dori forced herself to look down at the woman lying unconscious and bleeding on the ground.

"Wait," she called out to Grammy. "Stay with her mother."

"What the hell you talking about?"

"Stay with her till the ambulance comes," Dori explained, her lips going cold and stiff as the consequences loomed before her. She began shaking. Thank God, she hadn't reached her weapon in time.

Richard's hold relaxed. Grammy looked from the old lady in the car to Dori.

"Go. I'll stay with him," Dori said. "I'm okay."

He let her go. She opened the office door and walked inside.

They got in the car and Dori drove out of the parking lot. She had managed not to get arrested for assault. Richard and Grammy told the cops the chola had come for her first. They took the chola and old lady away in separate ambulances.

But now she had a new problem. At least she'd called her union rep and then her investigating officer from the scene and explained what happened. He never gave any indication if he believed her story that it had been self-defense. He'd said he would get the report and they would go from here.

In the rearview mirror, she saw Richard watching them from the top of the stairs. She turned the corner.

"I left Grampy's vase in the sink," Dori said.

"Don't worry about it. I borrowed his neighbor's vase and put my roses in it."

They swept down the hill. Her left arm would be bruised from blocking that woman's punch and her right hand throbbed. She shouldn't have done it. She should've kept to her own business.

"Promise me something," Grammy said.

"What?"

"You won't never do that to me."

"I was trying to defend you! What makes you think I'd ever lay a hand on you?"

"Not that! I mean, yelling at the poor vieja like that vergüenza was doing. I'd rather die than be treated like that."

"When have I ever- What would make you think that?"

"Because that's what happens when people become old and useless."

Dori pulled over and yanked the brake. She turned to Grammy. "I would never do that to you. Look what I just did to that woman you started a fight with!"

"That's cuz you got your grampy's blood. He always upheld my honor. Not that I needed him to," she added hastily. "Thing is, you and me: we gotta take care of each other, and I know I got mad at you about the door and Bernice, but you proved your loyalty, and I respect that."

"You're welcome."

"How's this gonna look with your job and everything?"

Dori shrugged, releasing the brake and pulling out into the street.

Now all of her senses were on high alert. She could smell the musty air coming in through the vents and feel the tiny ridges in the steering wheel. Her stomach clenched with regret at her impulsive reaction. For a moment, she'd completely lost touch with reality. Dori shivered as she wondered if the shooting had irreparably broken something loose inside her.

"You better take me home so we can put some ice on that hand," Grammy said. "How's your side?"

"She didn't get me there." The light turned green and Dori turned right and headed up the hill towards Grammy's house. "But I'll be okay."

"No, it's not okay. You need ice and some hot soup."

"I'll do it when I get home."

"Didn't you say you can't go home till they're done?"

"Maybe I'll go see a movie or something."

Grammy sighed long and hard. They pulled up to her house, and Dori prepared to help her out of the car. "How come you don't let no one help you?" Grammy asked.

Dori looked up at the broken screen door, slapping the side of the wall in the wind. She almost turned that comment back on Grammy, but the adrenaline had swooshed out, leaving her tired and slightly nauseous.

"Because I don't need help."

"You will when you get old. Who's gonna be there for you when I'm dead?"

"You think I'll be a lonely old lady?"

Grammy looked her up and down. "You're gettin' there."

"Well knowing you, you'll haunt me so I won't have anything to worry about."

"If you don't think I got better things to do when I'm dead and reunited with your grampy, than you got another thing coming."

Dori stared out the windshield. "When will things just go back to normal." She hated the whine in her voice. "I thought I was getting better, you know. I saw her pointing that gun again and-"

Grammy laid a hand on Dori's which clenched tight around the steering wheel. "It's going to take time, mija. You got to walk away from that whole situation. Think about that."

"And now I'm a mess."

"But you're alive, aren't you? You got a second chance."

She didn't bother to argue with Grammy, who didn't understand. Dori made herself grin even though right now, she wanted to put her head on the steering wheel and cry. "It doesn't help that I always end up beating people up when I'm with you."

"Better than changing my diaper, don't you think?"

# CHAPTER SEVENTEEN

The camouflaged school bus was parked out front when Dori pulled into her driveway. She smiled at Oscar, Gavin's foreman, as she got out of the car.

"We didn't want to leave the house open," he called out from the doorway of the bus.

"Thank you. I'm sorry you had to wait so long."

He shrugged. "It's no problem."

"Everything go okay today?"

"Oh yeah. You okay going in there by yourself?"

Dori resisted the urge to turn and look up into the windows. "Of course."

"I'll go in with you. Just to make sure."

Oscar stepped down off the bus and walked alongside her. "If you were my daughter, I'd have second thoughts about you being in this big place all alone."

She couldn't help but feel touched by his concern. "How long have you worked for Gavin?" she asked, slipping her swollen hand into her pocket.

"Ever since he got outta school. Hell, he used to work for me. I'm his uncle."

Dori hoped Gavin hadn't told him of what she'd done way back then. Even though this was the first real conversation they'd ever had, she would hate to lose Oscar's friendliness.

"You already know this, but I'm Dori," she said, slowing down to offer her left hand.

"Oscar." He took her fingers and gently squeezed.

They chatted as she walked into the kitchen. They'd left the lights on for her.

"See you tomorrow morning," he said when he made her promise to lock the door after him.

"Good night and thanks for waiting."

Dori stocked the freezer with more meals Grammy had made for her. She heard the bus engine come to life and loneliness crept up on her as Oscar drove off into the night.

She stood in the center of the kitchen, wondering if she should walk lightly in case her house toppled into the basement. It felt sturdy. She should've called Gavin for an update, but she'd been watching QVC with a bag of frozen peas on her hand.

She heated up a bowl of macaroni and cheese and then made herself a salad of mixed greens drizzled with balsamic vinaigrette and a touch of honey. Dori flicked on the flameless candles she'd bought from QVC the other night at Grammy's house for fear that real ones would burn her house to the ground.

She was blowing on her first forkful of dinner when Vicente asked, "Don't you ever cook on the stove?"

Her mac and cheese landed in her salad. "Couldn't you say hello or make a sound to warn me you're here?"

"Hello," he purred, standing on the other side of the table.

"Not like that."

"Like what?"

She fished the noodles out of her salad, rather than play games with him. "Where've you been these past few days?"

He lifted his eyebrows.

"Right," she said. "Never mind."

"Where were you today?" he asked as if he knew she'd been up to no good.

"At the cemetery." He narrowed his eyes, and she quickly added, "I didn't find her there. I was visiting my grandfather."

"Oh. I'm sorry. How long has he been gone?"

"In a few weeks, it will be twenty-six years."

"Do you see him?"

Dori shook her head. "You're my first."

He grinned, now leaning back with his hands behind his head in the chair opposite her. "Every man likes to hear that."

She smiled and it seemed to please him that she found his machismo amusing. "I've been meaning to ask you something. Why did you appear to Gavin the other day?"

"Gavin?"

She wasn't buying that innocent face. "Gavin, the man I hired to remodel my house."

"I didn't do nothing to him."

"He saw you looking down at him from my bedroom window."

"Gavin's his name, huh?"

106

"Yes, the same one who was in the basement with me when you turned off the lights."

Smiling, he rested his hand on the table. His sleeve rode up, and she could read the numbers on his Elgin watch. "I was testing him to see what kind of man he was."

"Leave him and his men alone," Dori said.

He nodded but said nothing more. She finished off both the mac and cheese and salad and then carried her plate to the sink.

"How come you're not afraid of me?" he asked.

She lifted a shoulder. "Should I be?"

"Nope. What happened to your hand?"

"I hit a lady."

He laughed.

"She was going after my grammy so I uh, kind of lost it."

"You were protecting your own. Sometimes our instincts know better than our heads," he said proudly.

Dori didn't want to think how her instincts had changed. She'd full on snapped at the cemetery. It was like she'd dropped into an alternate reality.

She looked at him, thinking it must be like what happened to Vicente when he appeared and disappeared. "So, are you going to tell me what happened the night you met those guys on the beach?"

"You like my story? I thought maybe my dirty past would offend your morals."

"I'm a white lamb in a family of black sheep," she said as she got up to start the tea kettle on the stove. "But that doesn't mean I'm judgmental."

"Most cops I knew probably would've made better criminals than me."

Thinking of how close she'd come to choking that woman out, she said nothing.

"What? Did I offend you?"

"I was on my way to delinquency when I was in high school." She opened the rooibos she'd bought from Halcyon and told him the short version of her journey to becoming a cop. "And then I made something of myself outside my family."

The surprise on his face was almost funny.

"I can't arrest you now, so don't worry about telling me your dirty past," she said.

He glanced down at the table, as if he didn't know what to say.

"So, you met those men making a delivery," Dori prompted, carrying her teapot and cup to the table. "Did you help them?"

He made a dismissive sound. "Sure, did and I learned my first two lessons in villainy. Never work for free and never work for someone who doesn't have the law on their payroll."

## San Diego, 1925

The officer laughed as he kicked Vicente in the stomach. He'd hauled him out of the truck, and the palms of his hands stung from the grit embedded in his skin.

Vicente struggled to breathe as the officer grabbed a fistful of his hair and yanked him up to his knees. "You think you can come into my country and break my laws?" His breath stank of tobacco and beer. He gave Vicente a good shake. "Huh?"

"We got our haul, sir," one of the officers said. "We should take him in."

"What's your hurry, Rick?"

Rick was the youngest of the three officers who pulled them over. He was also the only one who hadn't taken a swig from the kegs of Tecate beer before emptying them into the black soil that was torn and tumbled from the harvest. The lights from the police cars shone into his blue eyes that looked directly into Vicente's. He shook his head ever so slightly, as if sending a silent warning to keep a cool head. But Vicente boiled with the rage and humiliation. His wrists were cuffed behind his back, and the metal bit through the skin.

"This spic didn't answer my question. You think I'm gonna let you break the laws I almost died for?"

"No," Vicente managed, feeling the hairs pop free of his scalp.

"No what?"

"No, sir."

The officer threw him down, disappointed that Vicente hadn't given him a reason to continue the beating. Or maybe he was getting tired and wanted to go home at the end of his shift. Vicente looked up through the hair hanging in his eyes. Moments ago, he'd been riding high, feeling like the hero of whole operation and his new friends praised his quick thinking for saving their skins. Then they were caught on the dirt road skirting the lettuce fields in Paradise Valley, just outside the city limits. The rising sun silhouetted the mountains, and the air was thin and dry. It would be another hot, Santa Ana day.

"Let's go," said the officer who beat him. "Rick, you drive that one."

"What about the prisoner, sir?"

"Stick him in the back of the truck." He ordered the other officer to take the two bootleggers away. They'd been put into the car, not even handcuffed, where they watched the whole thing.

Vicente spat dirt, blood and snot. His eyes burned with tears of rage and pain.

Officer Rick came around and lifted Vicente to his feet. "They didn't kill you," he whispered in Spanish. "But it was close."

The ground gave way under Vicente's feet, and they nearly fell.

A horn sounded. "Tie 'em to the bumper if he can't walk!" They laughed.

"You have to walk. Come on." Officer Rick yanked him up. They shuffled the short distance to the truck.

"How come you speak Spanish?" Vicente asked.

"I'm half."

"But they think you're white?"

"Yup. We're almost there."

"Rick, I'm leaving with these two," the other officer yelled. "Have a few go's at 'im."

The engine started. Dirt and tiny rocks shot against Vicente's pants as the car drove away. When they were gone, Rick said, "Here, lean against the truck."

Vicente jerked his arm free, angry that he had to be helped. He nearly lost his footing, but caught himself.

"Next time, I'll leave you in the dirt," Rick said. "This is your first arrest, isn't it?"

"So?"

"The cops are done beating you, but I don't know about the prisoners. When they ask how old you are, tell them you're under 18. They'll stick you in with the juveniles."

Vicente shrugged like it didn't make any difference to him. But his grandmother's words rang true. His father spent many a night drunk in jail. Now Vicente was following in his old man's footsteps, just like she'd always said. In just a few short hours, everything had changed. Here he was on the side of a dirt road in a ripped-up suit and his ears ringing from the beating.

"Rick Campbell."

"Vic-" He then threw up in the dirt.

Officer Rick handed him a handkerchief when he was done spitting out his last meal. "Get in the truck. You might get some sleep."

Dori sat there, stewing in guilt at the force she'd used on that chola today. She was no better than that officer who had beaten a young kid. At least Vicente had technically broken a federal law. She had the training and experience to have used some defensive holds and locks to control the woman. She'd been ready to annihilate her.

She didn't want to think about it anymore. "You went with Officer Rick and?"

His eyes snapped up. "I got sentenced to a work camp."

"For how long?"

"It was supposed to be a year, but I was hired in six months."

If Dori could find the arrest record, it would be one more piece of concrete evidence. But he just sat there with a faint smile on his face.

"And then you came home?" she asked.

"Nope. I went to work."

"Doing what?"

"Stop asking questions and I'll tell you."

She sipped her tea.

"When I was at the work camp picking oranges for free, these men showed up and bribed the guards to take some of us to pick up shipments off the coast. They sent me and this Japanese guy, Andy Munemitsu. I never picked another orange again in my life."

She stored Andy's name with Rick's in her memory to look them up later. Vicente laughed at a private memory.

"They liked using guys like me and Andy because we were expendable. If a Japanese and a Mexican ended up floating off Coronado, no one cared."

She stayed quiet with her tea, not wanting to interrupt him.

"We hauled champagne, brandy, cognac, whiskey and scotch off the boats from Mexico and then shipped it into San Diego and Los Angeles. Our clients were rich people who didn't want to go to Agua Caliente or a speak. Hell, we supplied the American Legion when they had their convention in San Diego in 1929. We supplied mayors, bankers, lawyers, you name it.

"Andy and me never got busted. He knew all the back roads and I negotiated with the Mexicans so they wouldn't call border patrol on us and share the take."

"Sounds like the Old West."

"Sure, as hell was," he said wistfully, reminding her of her grampy.

"Then, I got called up by the boss and I took Andy with me. I shook John Gilbert's hand and Greta Garbo sipped my champagne." He ran his thumb and finger along the lines that had bracketed his mouth. "In four years, I managed deliveries between San Diego and Santa Barbara."

"And you never came back home in all those years?"

"Why?"

She pushed her tea cup away. "You never thought about Anna or wondered how your grandmother and sister made ends meet?"

His face went flat but his eyes were bright as he stared straight into hers. "I didn't want to come back until I was somebody."

"So, you came back."

He nodded. "My boss sent me personally in April 1932 to solidify our operations and get rid of the competition. Repeal was coming and we were ready to go legit. So, I lived like a king in the penthouse of the US Grant Hotel and began consolidating."

He sat back and then put his hands on the table, such a human gesture that she almost forgot he was dead.

He then pulled his hands back on his lap and pulled down the cuff of his sleeves.

Dori waited him out, reading his nervous gestures. If she kept her mouth shut, he'd crack open.

## National City, 1932

Vicente drank the whole ride to the barrio. He'd been in San Diego for six months, buying out rival operations, or when that didn't work, permanently putting them out of business. He sent no check, no word to the old lady or Eugenia that he was back.

Now dressed in his tuxedo with a white gardenia pinned to his lapel, he made the thirty-minute drive down the Harbor Drive section of the 101, past the Navy yards towards home.

"How much longer we got, sugar?" Clara asked, her hand sliding down into his lap. "Maybe we got time to loosen you up."

He caught her hand and flung it away.

She hissed in the dark. "What's with you tonight?"

Vicente drank so much that his throat went numb from the whiskey's burn. It spread through his whole body, making him feel like he was floating through the night.

Clara shoved away from him, settling in the corner of the limousine. He lifted his finger and ran it down the taut leather that upholstered the walls. Tiny lights burned in the shadows like yellow eyes that saw through his slicked back hair and barbered face and knew exactly what he was. That he was still that pathetic boy with shoes so old they'd flap around his feet.

Vicente smiled to himself, wiggling his toes in the custom leather shoes hand stitched at the same shop where James Cagney and Clark Gable got theirs. He was going back to show all of them, especially her that he'd made something of himself. Vicente was an important man now; someone they'd address as Señor Vicente, holding their hats in their hands.

Clara tapped the end of her cigarette against her case, and then her face appeared briefly under the flare of the lighter. She looked up at him with the cigarette stuck between her red lips. The limousine filled with the smell of fresh tobacco.

"You gonna share any of that?" she asked, gesturing towards his flask.

Vicente held out the silver flask, and her pale hand snatched it away. He'd picked her from the pack of girls who regularly circulated in the hotel lobby. She looked like Jean Harlow with the short silver hair and fingernails sharpened to red pointed daggers. He'd personally sent for the gold lace gown with a long mermaid train and glistening silver beads. She'd squealed with delight when she opened the box and then gave him the best blow job he'd ever gotten from a whore.

It didn't take long for them to tire of each other. But tonight, he'd walk her into the church dance and let everyone see her clinging on his arm in all her finery. Afterwards, he'd set her loose in the pool of lady sharks in the lobby. If he was feeling generous, maybe he'd buy her a train ticket to Los Angeles with enough money to set herself up in Hollywood like she talked about.

Traffic thickened as they neared National City. Tonight, sailors and couples were heading towards Tijuana like ducks flying south for the winter. By this time next year, they wouldn't need to cross the border to drink their liquor in peace. Repeal would take the excitement out of the business, but then Vicente could cut down on expenses paid to the law.

The limousine lurched and bounced as they turned off onto 6th Street, which led straight into the barrio. Vicente didn't have to look out the window to see the rutted roads and cramped little houses that reminded him of broken teeth.

"Jesus, where the hell are you taking me?" Clara demanded, bracing herself against the red velvet seat. The flower vases rattled with each bump.

"I told you, a party," he answered.

"It better be worth it."

He imagined the look on Anna's face when she saw the blonde on his arm. As if he already stood there, the dancers stopped and looked over their shoulders at him, envying him, maybe even hating him. Didn't matter as long as they knew what he'd become.

Years ago, he'd been nothing. Even if his grandmother had the money, she would've let him rot in jail. She never even came to his hearing. Now, he could buy his grandmother's shack, her nephew's shack and the whole god-damned block up to the Vazquez house that stood proud at the top of Billy Goat Hill. Maybe he'd gobble up their pool hall and watch them dry up like a mud under the hot sun. He'd walk in tonight and then turn his back on the past, never to think about it again.

The flask landed in his lap.

"You hardly left me anything," Clara whined beside him. "You're a real killjoy, know that?"

"I don't want you falling down drunk," he said.

"What the hell has gotten into you? I'm not takin' the strap from you."

"Yeah? How the hell else are you getting back tonight? Bet the sailors wouldn't mind a go at you."

She held her arm out, her white glove glowing in the dim light and tipped her cigarette ash onto the carpet. Vicente toyed with the idea of stopping the car and shoving her out into the muddy street. Clara stared back, arms crossed over her chest. The tip of her cigarette glowed, and he had no doubt that she'd smile as she ground it in his face.

The giant car pulled up to the front steps of St. Anthony. Paper lanterns lit a path to the church hall where he could hear the throbbing guitarrón and mariachi singing in full passionate chorus.

When the driver held the door open, Vicente stepped out into the cool misty night. The smell of damp earth, eucalyptus and fog rolling off the tidelands stirred up memories that flitted through his mind so fast that he couldn't catch one and hold onto it. Laughter with the smell of tortillas and rich menudo floated out, pulling a chord of longing deep in his chest.

"What the hell is this place?" Clara squawked angrily. "Did you bring me to a goddamned church?"

Vicente looked down at her as she reached for the driver's hand to step out of the car. Her blue eyes burned fire.

"Shut up and walk with me," he ordered.

"Forget it. I won't walk in there with a bunch of Mexicans." Her mouth twisted nastily.

"What did you think I was?"

"Italian."

"Surprise. Now come on." He yanked her wrist and settled her hand on his arm.

He happened to look down the street, remembering he'd stood in this very same spot the last night he'd been in the barrio. But then he saw the black Model-T pull to a stop a short distance away, across the street. Vicente almost waved to Agents Campbell and Holner.

The whiskey's effect on his composure vanished as he walked towards the hall. His heart pounded as they came closer. Couples danced by the open doors. Inside the hall, the mariachi sang about soldiers returning home, broken hearted over their country and frightened they'd never see their wives and children again.

He kept his gaze forward as they crossed from the chilly night to the heat of the church hall. He set his face in the stony lines befitting a señor who knew his importance. As they stepped through the door, Vicente didn't recognize the first couple who stopped mid-polka to gape at him. The man nodded his head in grave respect, careful to keep his eyes off Clara for fear he'd be shot by Vicente, or slapped by his wife.

Sure enough, the wife scowled and pulled her husband deeper into the crowd. Like dominoes, people looked over, momentarily forgetting the music. His name swept through the room and Vicente nodded in greeting to the boys who used to buy his tobacco and score Señor Riley's homemade whiskey. They were now men with faces lined and hardened by the days working in the sun and not much to show for it.

The glamour of the 1920's skipped the barrio, but the Depression sunk its teeth in. His chest swelled with superiority that he'd been out in the world and taken what it had to offer. There was no glitter in the room; no gilt framed mirrors or soaring ceiling painted like those in European palaces. Here it was just a dusty floor and walls yellowing with age and tobacco. The band played tired old Mexican songs instead of slick jazz.

Standing in the same spot as he had the night Anna danced with Albert, Vicente searched the morose faces of the young and older women. They wore handmade cotton dresses, low-heeled plain shoes and their long hair braided and pinned up. But Anna wasn't here among them, and his heart thumped with disappointment.

"Vicente, buenos noches."

It took Vicente a moment to recognize the man who had the courage to greet him. "Alex. Buenos noches."

They shook hands, and then smiling, Alex yanked him forward into a hug. He pulled away from Vicente, gripping his upper arms. Vicente smelled cheap wine and figured Alex was one more drink away from starting a brawl.

"My wife doesn't know you're here yet."

"Who the hell would be dumb enough to marry you?" Vicente said.

"Your sister."

The last time he saw Eugenia was the day he'd given her the doll she so wanted. Vicente couldn't picture her grown up and married, much less to his old friend. But he smiled and asked, "What's a nice girl like her doing with you?"

Alex laughed, mopping sweat off his forehead. "Come have a drink with us in the back. Like the old days."

Vicente's first instinct was to say no, not yet. Not before he saw Anna. He scanned the dance floor, checking the faces of the people sitting on the opposite side. He expected the crowd would part revealing Anna in her girlish white dress with Albert's arms still around her. But they weren't there.

Alex stared at Clara as if he hadn't noticed her standing there. In his condition, that was quite likely. Clara stared off, pretending not to be ogled. Vicente wished he'd left her in the car.

He pulled his arm free. Clara snatched at it as if she were a drowning woman. "Where are you going?"

"Getting a drink."

"You can't leave me here."

He tipped his hat to her. "Go wait in the car then," he said and then strode out the door, following Alex around the corner. A bare light hung over the front steps of the church hall where a group of boys tried to look like men. Their chatter cut off when they saw Vicente. He felt their eyes eating up his tuxedo and the gold ring on his pinky finger.

"Is Señor Riley still alive?" Vicente asked as they came around the corner.

"He died after you left. Where'd you go anyway?"

That last night, when he'd waited out front in a new suit only to end up in the jail the next morning, flashed through Vicente's mind. He gave Alex the abbreviated version. "I went to Los Angeles."

Alex tripped over his own feet, catching himself on the rickety fence. Vicente reached out to help him, trying to process that his old crony was now his brother-in-law. He hadn't been here to chaperone while they were courting or walk his sister down aisle. Did he have nieces or nephews? Was Alex a good husband?

"Let's head back, compadre," Vicente said.

"Nope. The night is young." Alex turned into the yard of a dark house.

With a quick glance over his shoulder for Agents Campbell and Holner, Vicente couldn't remember who lived here. The Riley's were three more houses down, and if you didn't know where they lived, you could tell by line of men pretending they weren't waiting for their turn at the still.

Alex knocked on the gate. It cracked open, revealing a suspicious eye.

"You owe us five dollars," a voice said, and then the gate was shut in their faces.

"What? Wait a second," Alex yelled, slamming it with the flat of his hand.

"Hold on," Vicente said, his hand shooting to his breast pocket. "He's good for it."

These small-time operations could get violent. The gate men were usually paid with the product, and the last thing he needed was a gun pulled on him. He slipped a twenty through the crack between the gate and the post. It disappeared, and then the gate opened.

"Who'd you steal this from?" the gate man asked Alex and then he started in surprise, not expecting Vicente to be standing there. He froze, thinking they were about to get jacked.

"I'm here as a guest," Vicente said, holding up his hands.

Alex nodded and jerked his thumb over his shoulder. "He's familia, cabron!"

The gate man grabbed his cap off his head, holding it respectfully in front of his chest. "Señor Sorolla. It's been many years."

Vicente peered into the man's face, trying to remember his name.

"It's Fernando. We worked on the street cars."

"Of course," Vicente said, nodding as he followed Alex.

"This way," Alex said and then they walked the length of the house. Ghostly clouds swept by a pale sliver of moon. He passed a tall narrow window. The shade was pulled down, and he checked for movement inside. A brief glimpse through the crack in the shade revealed an empty room and a closed door.

Here the air was thick with the smell of rotting plants. Vicente had the sudden urge to run out to the tidelands and breathe in the salty marsh.

115

Maybe he'd find those son-of-bitch bootleggers and-

Alex stopped and stomped his foot on the basement door. Light peeked through the cracks. Vicente wished Andy was at his side. But he was back in Los Angeles.

Vicente curled his hands into fists, ready for what waited underneath the house. The door swung up in a wide arc, pushed open by the skinniest boy he'd ever seen. The undersides of his sleeves were dark with sweat.

Alex bent down, placing his hand on the top beam for support as he took the steps down under the house. Vicente nodded to the kid holding the doors open. The kid stared at the ground, patiently waiting for them to go down.

When Vicente touched down on the floor, he had to bend slightly so as not to scrape the top of his head against the beams. Alex turned and held out his arms as if proud of the neighborhood bootlegging operation. Half of his face was lit by the tasseled reading lamp standing by a desk.

The dirt floor was clean and unlike most rotgut operations, it didn't smell of alcohol. Not even a whiff. No one was laid out on the floor. No bottles or barrels in sight. This was a neat and clean operation. The kind Vicente would've run if he'd been small time.

The skinny kid gently lowered the door and then came around to stand behind the desk. He ran his hands down his vest as if preparing to make a speech. Vicente noticed the silver watch chain. "May I help you, señores?"

"We want a bottle," Alex demanded and then looked to Vicente to pay up.

"Of course. That will be twenty-five cents."

"Twenty-five cents? You used to charge fifteen!"

Vicente held out his arm, keeping Alex on their side of the desk. The kid never blinked.

"With shortages, every business has to keep up," Vicente said. The president was easing the country off Prohibition and made allowances for near-beer and homemade wines, which drove up prices. In a year, little operations like this would dry up trying to keep up with more diversified businesses like Mr. McClemmy's. "We'll take one bottle."

Vicente reached into his pocket. The kid watched his hand as he placed a dollar bill on what had once been a fine desk. The leather blotter was torn and stained. Vicente held the kid's gaze in case he reached for the shotgun under the desk. The kid snatched up the money, his thumb rasping over the crisp paper. He placed it in his pocket and then politely excused himself, walking off into the shadows. Vicente counted the steps, and then a door opened and shut.

Footsteps sounded above, and dust sprinkled down on their heads. These guys were careful. While Vicente didn't like standing here, he admired their set up.

The door opened again, throwing light across the stairs. Vicente saw the plain brown shoes and then brown slacks. The light slid up her legs, and then she stood there, carrying the bottle by its neck. "Hi Vicente," Anna said. "I thought I recognized your voice."

The years had sculpted away her pale, plump face. She'd lost that dreamy, remote air about her, and she stared back at him as if she'd fully expected him to walk dressed to the nines into her basement tonight. Her blue eyes, so different from those of the overdressed, overdone woman he'd left in the church hall, never left his. Vicente swayed on his feet and then remembered to puff out his chest, like a male bird presenting himself for the female to see what she'd missed out on.

She handed the bottle over. "You paid for it. Aren't you going to take it?"

"Gracias Anna," Alex said, reaching for the bottle.

She jerked it out of reach, holding it over her shoulder. "How much did Vicente pay?"

"A dollar," Alex said. "And you didn't give us no change."

She looked ready to bring the bottle down on his brother-in-law's head. "You still owe me four dollars and seventy-five cents, and your son needs shoes."

Alex's mouth gaped with indignation.

Anna shifted her gaze back to Vicente, and his skin prickled. She walked by Alex, forcing him to step aside. She handed Vicente the bottle.

"Thank you for your business," she said, her lips twitching as if she were trying not to laugh.

He hardened his stare, but she tucked her hands into her pockets. She wore her hair braided and twisted at the nape of her neck. The sleeves of her shirt were rolled up and the buttons went straight up to her throat.

"You have any other business here?" she asked.

Vicente tucked the bottle under his arm. "Let's go," he ordered Alex.

"But she owes you change!"

She raised one eyebrow, daring Vicente to press the issue.

"How long has he owed you a debt?" Vicente asked.

"A year."

"She hasn't let me in here until tonight," Alex chimed in.

Anna nodded, not deigning to look at Alex. "For your family's own, good."

"Who are you to tell me what to do? You're the one breaking the law."

She lifted a shoulder, as if it were no matter. "I only to sell to men who pay."

Remembering her standing with Albert, looking down their noses at him as he lay in the dirt, Vicente barked out a laugh. "Well then, you haven't changed since I left."

He didn't bother to wait for her reaction as he turned and walked towards the double doors. The young man pushed them open. Albert was probably upstairs counting the till while her parents lived in their respectable, lace-curtained house.

"Good night, Vicente," Anna said behind him. "You sure you don't want a bottle for your lady friend?"

Vicente took the steps two at a time and never looked back as she laughed.

# CHAPTER EIGHTEEN

"There's someone here to see you."

Dori startled at Gavin's voice. She had just been looking on World Market's website for curtains to hang in the east-facing windows set above the built-in cabinets in the pantry.

"Who is it?"

He shrugged. "I didn't ask. She's got dreads and-" He shook his head as if he didn't have the words to describe the rest of Meg.

Dori smiled as she stood up from her chair. "Thanks. I didn't know you'd be here today."

"I just came to check in on the crew this morning. Everything's okay with you?"

"Yeah."

Gavin surveyed the home office she'd set up in the small room off the kitchen. "You got a nice set up here."

Dori couldn't stop the smile from reaching her face. The chestnut cabinets gleamed from her polishing. She'd cleaned the drawers and shelves and then lined them with clear rubber matting. A rug she'd rescued from her storage unit lay on the floor.

"Thanks." She almost told him about her plans to display her milk glass collection in the glass-fronted cabinets, but Gavin stepped out of her tidy sanctuary.

Dori smiled when she found Meg studying the chimney's herringbone pattern of bricks.

"Hey, you," Dori called out.

Meg straightened from the chimney, wiping the tip of her nose. "So, I heard you were asking around town about me."

"You did?" The morning was bright and chilly. When Dori hugged Meg, she realized she hadn't had any human contact this whole weekend. She'd fallen asleep at the table the night Vicente told her his story and apparently, she'd offended him because he'd been quiet these past two days. She could hardly believe it but she actually missed him and his stories.

"Richard from the cemetery called."

Dori only blinked. "So, what did he say?"

"Oh, that you were looking for someone who died in the 1930s and you punched out a woman."

"You did?" Gavin asked, startling her a second time this morning. She thought he'd gone down into the basement.

Caught between them, Dori bit her lip and then said, "Yeah, she threatened my grammy and so I-"

Meg removed her giant sunglasses, her eyes wide with delight. "You really punched a woman at the cemetery?"

Dori cleared her throat. "It got a little uh-" She almost said rough and instead rubbed the tip of her cold, numb nose. "They had to call an ambulance."

"I wish I'd been there to see it," Gavin said.

"Me, too," Meg purred. Dori looked at her, noting the sudden deepening of her voice.

She stepped forward, offering her hand to Gavin. "I'm Meg."

"Gavin." Staring into each other's eyes, they shook hands.

"Gavin is working on the foundation," Dori said. They let go, and her breath caught in her throat.

"And the staircase and your roof," Gavin added.

"Very nice," Meg said, and from the way she said it, Dori wasn't so sure she was talking about the house.

"I'll leave you ladies to it."

Meg sighed as he walked into the house. "So, you have the day off?" Dori asked.

"I do, and I brought this." Meg held up a professional camera. "I hope you don't mind, but I'd love to snap a few photos."

Of Gavin or the house, Dori almost asked. "Don't mind at all," she said, and they walked into the kitchen.

"By the way, Richard said he hoped you'd come back. He's never had a more exciting day at work than that. But before you get any ideas, he's married. To a man."

"Right." Dori wiped her hands on the front of her jeans. "Thanks for the heads up."

"I was hoping you'd be free for a lunch so I can tell you I've found no trace of your Anna Vazquez."

In her mind's eye, Dori saw Vicente in Anna's basement, buying a twenty-five cent bottle of liquor. She cleared her throat. "I have a lead."

"You do? Oh right. She may have had a lover in your house."

"Uh, yeah. Anyway, I heard a story that she may have run around with a bootlegger who lived at The US Grant Hotel."

"I know the perfect person you can talk to. He's an expert on the history of that hotel. Hold this." Dori took the camera while Meg dug out her phone.

"Who don't you know?" Dori asked.

"Your contractor for one," she said slyly. "Is he only your contractor?"

"Yes," Dori said before he walked in and heard them.

"Taken? Gay?"

Thinking of the night Gavin had kissed her under the streetlight, Dori cleared her throat. "Neither. So, who's this guy you're hooking me up with?"

Dori parked at Horton Plaza and bought coffees so she could validate her parking ticket.

"Now let me do the talking," Meg said as they walked past the Jessop's clock towards Broadway. Dori couldn't help but glance back at the alcove where she'd once made out with a sailor. She dug her hands deeper in her jacket pockets.

"He comes off as a bit stuffy, but truly, he's a sweetheart. His grandfather was the maître d' at the El Cortez."

Meg had briefed the historian over the phone while Dori drove them downtown. She gave over Vicente's name and the month and year he'd been in San Diego. Meg never asked how she knew his name and Dori didn't elaborate.

"I let him know what we're looking for. If there's any trace of Anna's suitor, he'll find them. Or would she have been his moll?"

Dori was at a loss to explain. Neither suitor nor moll described Vicente and Anna. "They were friends as kids, but after that I'm not sure."

"Lovers, then."

"Yeah."

"Such an old-fashioned word. Have you ever had a man who qualifies as a lover?"

"Almost."

"Well? What happened?"

She thought of her last encounter with Pete at the Hotel Del. She'd kissed him knowing his fiancée was in the ballroom downstairs and then turned her back on him forever. "Everything became a competition, and he couldn't keep up."

"Like up?" Meg pointed her finger in the air with a knowing wink. "Or, he feared you were better than him?"

"He thought that I thought I was better than him." Dori shook her head as they walked around the bronze doomed-fountain.

"I'm sorry about that."

Dori wished she hadn't answered the question quite so honestly. Thinking of Pete always depressed her.

She lifted her chin, looking down Broadway where it ended at the bay. A red trolley crossed the thoroughfare and pulled into the station across from the Santa Fe Depot.

"I'm so glad you invited me," Meg said. "I love field work, but I usually do it alone for my clients. This is more like a mystery."

"What clients?"

"I do a bit of freelance genealogy. I have to do something with my history degree." They crossed Broadway to The US Grant. The four flags over the main entrance hung limp. As they approached, thoughts of mobster movies played in Dori's head.

When she stepped under the twinkling chandeliers and smelled the perfumed air, she imagined Vicente striding across the checkered marble floors in a suit and fedora. She gazed up at the Corinthian columns, imagining flappers like Clara in beaded gowns drinking illegal highballs on the upper mezzanine which was bordered by an Art Deco brass railing.

While Meg announced their arrival with the concierge, Dori wandered over to the historic photos of Downtown San Diego. She lingered in front of one with horses and carriages parked along the thoroughfare they had crossed a few moments ago. Excitement percolated as she thought how close she was to finding more tangible evidence of Vicente. It would be huge, almost unbelievable that the guy she was talking to in her house had been, well, a real person.

She went from photo to photo until she came to the last of a man and woman posed before a tall window and a potted palm tree. Dori almost walked back towards Meg until she looked into the man's face.

He was dressed in a three-piece suit, smiling at the camera like he was your friendly general store owner. His curly hair shone with pomade and a watch chain stretched across his stomach. A stout matron frowned at his side, clutching a substantial leather purse under one arm. He was the man in her dream who'd sent Vicente to his death.

A brass plate was nailed to the frame. It read: James and Muriel McClemmy. Vicente had mentioned his boss' name plenty of times; always as Mr. McClemmy. But as she stared into those pale blue eyes from her dream – but were white in the old photo - she'd know this man anywhere.

Dori examined the background. A potted palm tree and table were behind them. Just beyond Muriel she saw a man's hand resting on the edge of the table. She inched closer, her nose nearly bumping the glass. The hand was tanned against the crisp white cuff and he wore an Elgin watch.

Recognition surged through her and she placed her finger on the image. Deep down, she knew it was Vicente.

Her face flushed and her stomach tightened with anger at what James

McClemmy had done to Vicente. Had he lived to be an old man? Had he ever wondered about the man who died for him, who left behind his family and the woman he'd loved?

"There she is."

Dori's heart kicked and she turned at the loud voice behind her. Meg embraced an impeccably dressed man. They kissed each other's cheeks, and Dori hoped she wouldn't be expected to the do the same.

As Meg and the man chatted, they held each other's hands. Meg momentarily forgot about Dori as they discussed a historical walking tour that was happening this weekend. She edged forward until she joined their group.

"Oh Dori, this is David Mumper who hides all the juicy secrets of this hotel," Meg said.

He looked from Dori's face to her hand and back, his warm smile fading. Dori wondered if she'd arrested him. He didn't look familiar, so she made herself smile. "Thanks for seeing us today."

"Oh my God," he said, backing away. "I'm sorry Meg, I can't- I have to-"

"David? What's wrong?" Meg turned to Dori. "Give me a minute. I'll be right back."

She followed him and he held up his hands as if protecting himself. Dori started towards them to help.

"Why don't you sit down?" Dori offered, pointing to a velvet sofa.

"I shouldn't be talking to you," he said.

Meg shushed him, leading him to the sofa.

Dread sprouted in the pit of Dori's stomach. "I can go get you something to drink," she said.

"Yes, why don't you do that," Meg said, giving her an apologetic look.

She escaped in search of a gift shop. She found it on the other side of the hotel, bought some waters and then hurried back. Through the potted palm fronds, she saw David with his arm over Meg's shoulder. In some strange reversal, he seemed to be comforting her. Dori took a deep breath and then stepped onto the square of rug.

"Here, I found these," Dori said.

David took a deep breath. Meg looked up at her and then cleared her throat. "Dori, I don't know how to-"

Neither took a water bottle from her.

Dori sank into the chair next to the sofa. "Just take your time."

He passed a glance at Meg. "I can't help you. My cousin was Kaylee Matthews."

All the air left her body and the plastic bottle crunched in her grip.

"I'm sorry, Dori," Meg said. "I had no idea and I- Well I've put all of us in such a position that I-"

"It's okay. It's not your fault." Dori turned to David, who stared at the floor, his jaw clenched. She forced herself to speak. "I understand and I-I'm sorry for wasting your time."

She tried to stand up but her legs wouldn't work.

"I grew up with her," David said. "She wasn't like that when we-" He paused, struggling to finish.

Legally, Dori should get the hell out of here and fast. But she couldn't. She had to let this man say his piece.

"She'd changed by the time you -" He looked away, his lips trembling. "By the time you met her, she wasn't the cousin I knew."

Her throat tied itself into a knot and she nodded her head.

"Her kids are with my aunt and uncle." He cleared his throat. "I did some preliminary work on the research you and Meg are doing-"

"It doesn't matter," Dori said, finding her voice.

"Why not? Isn't this what's important while you're under investigation?" he spat.

Dori held her breath.

He abruptly got to his feet and walked away, quickly disappearing around the corner.

"I'm so sorry about David. I had no idea."

Dori's side pinched as she twisted around to look before backing out of the parking space. "I know. You can stop beating yourself up."

"Still-"

"Don't worry. My job left me with a thick skin," Dori said, threading the car through a tight corner.

She was amazed Meg agreed to get into the car. They hadn't said much when Dori was finally able to stand up and walk out of The US Grant. They finally pulled up to the long line of cars at the exit.

"So, can I ask you what happened?" Meg ventured.

"David didn't tell you?"

"Well yes, but I-" Meg shifted in her seat, toying with the seat belt strap over her chest.

Dori squeezed her hands around the steering wheel to keep them from shaking. "Kaylee shot me and I fired back."

Meg nodded. Dori quickly added, "But the bullet hit my vest and pushed it into my side here." She pointed.

"And there were children there?"

Dori looked over at Meg and wished she'd not. Meg's face was twisted with horror and pity. For some reason, it brought back a vivid picture of Kaylee Matthews. She had simply turned around, her face absolutely a cold, stiff mask as she fired a shot at Dori for arresting her and putting her children in the custody of Child Protective Services.

It happened so fast. Dori had been standing there and then her duty weapon was in her hand. She'd fired three rounds, two hitting Kaylee and one the wall behind her. It wasn't until her knees hit the ground that she felt the flare of pain at her side. When she pressed her hand against the warm, sticky wet, she realized she'd been shot.

Dori blinked and she was back in the car, her hands gripping the steering wheel. She then remembered Meg's question.

"I'm under investigation, so technically I can't go into the details," she managed, her throat burning. "But yes, they were there."

Meg took a deep breath as she stared straight ahead. Dori imagined this wasn't what most girlfriends talked about on a girl's day out. The best thing to do now was get them back to her house so they could part ways as quickly as possible.

"Look, I know we'd talked about going to lunch but I understand if you-" Dori's eyes filled with tears, damn it.

"Pull over, Dori," Meg said gently.

Dori did and they sat there as she struggled for control.

"It seems ridiculous to tell you something like I'm sorry about what happened," Meg said after a long silence. "If you'd like to, I'd still like to go to lunch. I'm sure you did what you had to do."

All Dori could do was nod her head.

"We're still on?" A tissue appeared in Dori's line of vision. She took it and wiped her eyes. She looked over at Meg and only saw compassion and someone struggling not to cry, too.

"I know I shouldn't cry but, damn the whole thing," Meg said, reaching into her bag for another tissue.

"I don't know what it is about you but I feel like I've known you much longer than a few days," Meg said.

"How can you say that when on our second meeting you find out I shot someone?"

"Well, I- I don't know!"

They laughed and Dori accepted a second tissue.

"I imagine for all sorts of legal reasons you can't discuss what happened so I'll just say that I'm glad you're here." Meg breathed in deep and then let out a long sigh. "With that, let's go eat."

Dori couldn't agree more. She squinted as they emerged up into the daylight. The sun broke through, and she flipped the visor down before turning right on G Street.

# CHAPTER NINETEEN

Dori carried their tea cups to the back stoop. Meg had taken photos while she got an update on the day's work from Oscar.

Before they had lunch, Dori reported the meeting with David to her investigator. He sighed at the end of her explanation.

Her job might hang in the balance but she had to admit that right now, she felt okay. After lunch and some shopping, she and Meg had hung ivory damask sheer curtains in her little office. In the morning, when the sun hit this side of the house, they would diffuse the light.

Gavin's crew was still cleaning up downstairs. When she stepped out into the crisp evening, Dori warmed her hands with the cup of steaming rooibos with rose petals and grape seeds. She found Meg peering down at a pile of broken bricks.

"Tea time," she called out.

"I'm gasping." Meg came over and took the cup. "I think that was the original furnace. It might be worth saving."

"First the foundation and then the roof. The main staircase is also off limits. It might swallow you alive."

Meg sat beside her and they sipped their tea. The yard filled with lavender light. As Dori looked around her, a strange calm made itself comfortable in her chest. It felt enough to sit here, listening to the hollow sound of traffic in the distance.

She sipped her tea, not sure where this feeling had come from or how long it would linger. Maybe she and Meg really had the potential to be good friends. This might be all she needed to be content.

Dori took a deep breath and pulled her arms closer to her sides to keep warm.

"When will you go back to the hotel?" Meg asked.

"Not any time soon."

"Well I can't say that I blame you. Perhaps I can talk with David and he can get the information to me which I can-"

"It's okay," Dori said, even though it wasn't. "I'll try the history museum and maybe they'll have records."

Meg sipped her tea.

Dori then heard her cousin shout, "What do you want us to do with this old stove, Grammy?"

She twisted around to look through her office into the kitchen.

"Hell, if I know, boy!" Grammy shouted. "Just get that old piece of crap outta there!"

"Hang on a second," Dori told Meg. Her joints crackled as she stood up. She rubbed her warm fingers together, mentally preparing herself to face her grandmother and cousin.

When she stepped into the kitchen, she found her cousin and some old vato wheeling her stove out the door.

"Hey cuz," Chuy called out.

"Hey Chuy," she greeted, heading straight for Grammy.

"This is your early Christmas present," Grammy said and then held up her hand as Dori opened her mouth to protest. "Chuy got me his employee discount."

"But this is-"

"I know what you're thinking, but I swear on your grampy's name, this time it's really legit."

Dori took the paperwork Grammy brandished at her. It looked authentic enough, and as far as Dori knew, Chuy hadn't dabbled in forgery; that had been their Aunt Betty's specialty.

"Man, cuz, this is one helluva house you got here," Chuy said as he and his friend came back with a new stove. "Now I got somewhere to go when Linda gets mad at me, you know?"

"You tell Linda that she and the kids can stay with me anytime," Dori said.

Chuy's grin flattened. His friend snickered.

Dori met his nasty look, determined not to blink or look away. Of all her cousins, they were closest in age, with Dori beating him out by six weeks. They'd grown up competing for Grampy's attention, and it was never enough that he loved them equally. In the process, they'd given each other black eyes, skinned shins and bites. The fights Dori won weren't because she was a girl; he'd fought her like she was a guy, and some of the tussles she'd had on the streets would've gone a lot differently if it weren't for him. In a way, she should be grateful, even if he was a rat.

"Cut it out, you two," Grammy scolded. "When will you be done, mijo?"

"In an hour or so."

"Good. Make yourself at home."

Chuy's friend opened her refrigerator and helped himself.

"So-" Chuy jerked his chin up as he spoke to Dori. "Grammy told me you need me to work on the house."

"Did she?"

"Yeah. I can like give you a special discount."

"Doing what?"

"Painting and stuff. I'll have to do it on the side with my new job and all. I was thinking we could start with that fireplace in the hallway. We could haul it out tonight."

Dori's spine stiffened. Over her dead body. That fireplace was Carrera marble.

Grammy must've read the look on Dori's face. She moved to stand between them. "Mijo, you boys get to work."

"Hello," Meg chimed in. "Are you the infamous Grammy Cena?"

Grammy sized up Meg. "Infamous?"

"Yes, I heard about the Hotel Del and the video at the wedding."

"Did you now?"

Meg sent an apologetic look at Dori who quickly introduced them. Grammy pulled her hand away after Meg's vigorous shake.

"You have anything to drink around here?"

"Excuse us a minute, Meg."

Dori pulled Grammy into her office.

"I'm sorry, but you have to take this stuff back," Dori said. "Grammy, this is too much."

"Where'd you meet that girl?"

"At the library."

"Why does she talk like she's from Australia or something?"

"Because she's from England," Dori said. "Grammy, I'm serious. I can't let you pay for all this."

"She dresses weird. I don't know about her yet."

Dori crossed her arms, and Grammy huffed. "Can't you see that you need decent appliances?"

"I know but-"

"Just take the goddamned appliances!" She tossed up her hands with exasperation. "It's all top of the line. You can pay me back by taking care of me in my old age."

Meg tapped on the door. "Dori, I'll just run off now."

"Stay mija," Grammy said. "You go make us some tea and open up those lemon cookies I put on the table."

Dori mouthed "run" to Meg, who winked and exclaimed, "Absolutely!"

While Meg helped Dori make the tea tray, Grammy pointed exactly where she wanted Chuy and his friend to install the appliances.

She turned to Dori. "Bring those cookies and tea into the living room." To Meg, she smiled, "Tell me again where you're from and why you're hanging around my ungrateful granddaughter."

Meg walked Grammy into the living room while Dori did as she was told. She set everything down and then tried not to wince when Grammy asked if they had Mexicans in England.

"I had a friend who was from Mexico City. She came from a cement family."

"Cement family? What kind of family is that?" Grammy pulled out her flask and poured tequila into her cup.

Meg watched Grammy with delight. "Oh, her family owned a big cement company."

"What?" Grammy demanded when she caught Dori shaking her head.

"Nothing," Dori said. "What did you do this weekend?"

"Aren't you on that Facebook yet?"

"No."

"You should be. I figured out how to post pictures. I got me 26 friends."

"Do you know these people?"

Grammy shrugged and turned to Meg. "She's mad at me. I never make her happy."

"I don't like you spending all that money," Dori cut in.

"Why? You get the benefit, not me. And I can help my pobrecito Chuy out there." She turned to Meg. "He's what you might call, 'in transition.'"

Dori pressed her lips not to say anything about her cousin's probation status.

"See? This is what's wrong with your generation. Y'all are so uptight and stressed. In my day, we said thank you."

"It's not that I don't appreciate it but what's wrong with calling and showing respect for someone's personal space especially with a convicted felon?"

Grammy's eyebrows twisted as if Dori had just spoken in tongues. "But we're family!"

"What if I was with a guy?"

Grammy rolled her eyes as if that would never happen. "That's what locks are for."

Meg snorted and then clamped her lips shut.

"So how do you fit into all this?" Grammy asked her.

"I'm helping Dori find Anna Vazquez."

"Anna who?"

Dori nearly spit her tea. "My great-great-great grandmother, remember?"

Grammy frowned at her as if she were crazy. "Must be on your mama's side."

Meg cleared her throat. "You know a lot of the old families from the Westside, don't you?"

"Sure do."

"You should come in and do an oral history."

"An oral what?"

"Tell me your story and your family history and I'll record it."

"Why? Are you saying I'm old?"

Meg blinked.

"I'm just messin' with you. Sure. Now who is-"

"Meg's helping me with research on the house," Dori said.

"Does the name Vicente Sorolla strike a bell?" Meg asked.

"Let me think. There was a lady named Sorolla."

Meg and Dori looked at each other.

"And?" Meg prompted.

"I vaguely remember her. I think she lived next door."

"Do you remember her first name?" Dori asked, wishing she'd thought to ask Grammy before.

Grammy shook her head. "She lived by herself."

It hadn't occurred to Dori to look for Eugenia. If she was the same woman Grammy was talking about and she had children, then Vicente had family.

"Why did she live alone?" Meg asked. "Was she a widow?"

"Oh yes. It was so sad. My mama found her."

"Dead?" Dori asked, looking into the hallway for signs of Vicente.

Grammy nodded. "She had to bury the poor lady. There was no one to pay. I just remember them calling her Señorita Sorolla."

"Do you remember the year this happened?" Dori asked, remembering Vicente's story about the dance and how he'd found out his sister had married his friend, Alex.

Grammy lifted a shoulder and then blew the steam off her tea. "I was just a little girl."

Vicente kept to the shadows in the hallway. He could see the old lady's back and half of Dori's face as she listened to the sad tale of Señorita Sorolla.

If he had a heart, it would be aching now. His beautiful, delicate sister should never have died alone. When he last saw her, she had been married and she'd had her son and another on the way. They should've taken care of her when he couldn't.

He pulled away from the light that shone across the floor. He wished he'd stayed wherever it was that he went, but he'd been called by the sound of Dori's voice. He realized the front parlor was just a few steps away. He could feel it watching him.

"Oh shit!" someone shouted behind him.

Vicente swung around and faced two hobos who'd wandered into the hallway. Then again, they were both too clean-shaven to be bums. They had tattoos on their necks and their arms. They wore short kid's pants that sagged over their hips and long white socks.

The hobos just stood there, eyes blinking and mouths comically moving but no sound coming out.

Vicente couldn't help himself. "Boo," he said.

The bum in the white undershirt jumped up in the air, spun and then ran. His friend was right on his heels making a strange keening sound like a small animal about to be eaten. The first one skidded, nearly missing the wall and then shouted, "Jesus save me!"

Not feeling any better, Vicente stuck his hands in his pockets as he turned back to the living room.

"What the hell was that?" the old lady asked.

"You stay here," Dori said. The floorboards creaked under her footsteps.

She stopped short when she saw Vicente. She pursed her lips with exasperation.

"I was minding my own business, listening to you talk about me," he said. "I can't control who sees me."

They both turned at the sound of a truck starting and driving away.

Dori walked into the kitchen. "Damn it. Couldn't you have scared them after they installed the appliances?"

Vicente appeared beside her. The refrigerator had been pulled out of the kitchen and partially blocked the door.

Dori pressed her hand to her forehead. "You've got to be kidding me."

"What happened to my sister?"

She turned back to him. "What?"

"My sister. You were talking about her."

"I can't deal with this right now. I have a refrigerator on my deck and no stove."

"Tell me."

"I don't know what happened to her. I was trying to find out."

"Mija, who are you talking to?"

Dori's eyes went wide, and Vicente almost laughed at her.

There stood the old lady and another woman wearing a puffy sleeved blouse that reminded him of his grandmother's clothes. He stepped out of their line of vision.

"Wait!" Dori cried out. "Uh, go wait in the living room. I'll take care of this."

"Why was your cousin screaming?" the younger woman asked.

"Where the hell did he go?" the old lady asked.

Dori's lips twitched. "He ran so fast I didn't have a chance to ask."

"Don't be so mean." The old lady pulled out a thin little box from the pocket of her sweater.

"It's been fun but maybe I should go," the younger woman said, walking to the door.

Vicente turned as she walked by, deliberately eyeing her backside to torment Dori.

"You don't have to go, but I don't blame you," Dori said as the old lady squawked into the little box.

"I've stayed long enough," she replied, hugging Dori and then heading out the door.

"Where'd you find her?" Vicente asked.

Dori glared at him but waited for her grandmother to finish yelling into her little box.

"What happened?" she asked as the old woman sighed and shoved the box into her purse.

"He said he saw a see-through man. Your fantasmo."

"Sounds like the mota talking," Dori said.

"Don't give me that. You doing anything about getting rid of him like you said?"

Vicente turned to Dori, but she pretended he wasn't there. "Yes."

The old lady stared at Dori like she could see straight through her. "That's the research you got going through la librarian, ain't it?"

"Yeah, but I messed up my lie. I forgot if I told her Anna Vazquez was my great great grandmother or my great grandmother."

"So, who is this Anna Vazquez?"

She glanced at Vicente, looking him in the eye for a moment as she gave a slight shake of her head. "First thing's first, is Chuy coming back to put all this together?"

"Nope."

Her lips curled into a sly grin. She couldn't help but ask, "Was he crying?"

"You didn't answer my question. Wait-" The old lady's eyes went wide as she looked around. "Is he here?"

Vicente cleared his throat.

Dori looked at him. "Yes. But he'll go away."

"When I damn well feel like it," he shot back.

"Anyway, Anna lived in the Westside. She was his girlfriend. Kind of."

"Kind of?" Vicente demanded.

"She had a still and she lived in a big house on Harding," Dori said, maintaining a straight face that even impressed him.

"How do you know all this, mija?" the old lady asked warily.

"Yeah, explain that," Vicente added spitefully.

Dori cleared her throat. He could tell that the old lady was getting scared. But she had pride like her granddaughter.

"What kind of pain killers did that doctor put you on?"

"I'm only taking Motrin."

He turned to Dori. "Take her home."

Dori took in a deep breath before she asked, "Do you need a ride home?"

"I drove my own damn self, thank you. Chuy was supposed to take me back,"

"It's dark out. I'll take you back."

"I'll do it myself."

"But you don't like driving at night."

"How you gettin' back?"

"I'll come back in your car and then return it in the morning."

Their voices grew fainter as he willed himself to go. "I have to come right back," Dori said and Vicente knew she was saying that for his benefit. "So, I can't stay for dinner."

"Who said I was cooking for you?"

# CHAPTER TWENTY

Dori slammed her car door and then crossed the street. A saw whined, interrupted by the pounding of a hammer.

It was almost lunch time and Dori wished she'd stopped for something to eat before coming here. She recognized Gavin's truck parked in front of a 1920's Spanish-style bungalow where Oscar had said he would be. Eucalyptus trees swayed in the breeze and hid the busy 8 freeway below the Mission Hills neighborhood.

A box of tiles propped the front door open. She called out hello but no one could've heard her over the racket.

Dori followed the trail of plastic sheeting that protected the wood floors. She took her time through the tiny house with a rounded fireplace, niches and a built-in hutch with leaded-glass doors. She peeked into the lone bathroom with a red tulip stained-glass window.

"Oh, it's you."

She jumped. Gavin wiped dust off his hands. "Oscar told me you'd be here," he said.

"Well I um- This is a nice place."

"It's small."

"I tried knocking."

"I didn't hear you. I just came to use-" He gestured to the bathroom.

"Right."

She stepped out of his way. Rather than linger by the door, she went into the kitchen. Plastic sheets lay over a vintage stove and refrigerator. Wires and bare pipes stuck out of the broken walls. Dori stood in the sunny breakfast nook. The built-in table and bench spoke of a simpler time, or those who believed that life was simpler in the past. From what Vicente was telling her, there was no such thing as the good old days. Suffering, self-inflicted or otherwise, was the same then as it is now.

Dori rubbed her burning eyes. She hadn't slept very well. Grammy hadn't said much during the ride to her house last night. She didn't come to the house to pick up her car, nor had she answered her phone when Dori called.

"I got it in auction."

Dori started at the sound of Gavin's voice.

"The stove and refrigerator were in the garage, but they'd trashed the cabinets and took all the light fixtures," Gavin said, joining her in the kitchen.

"They left you a bath tub."

"You'd need a crane and dynamite to move that thing. It's cast iron." He opened an ice chest. "Water? Coke?"

"No thanks. Are you planning to live here?"

"Fix and flip," he said. "So, what brings you here?"

She took in a deep breath. "I have a problem."

He waited for her to explain.

"My grandmother bought new kitchen appliances and my cousin can't finish installing them."

A crack sounded between them as he twisted the cap off a water bottle. He took a long drink and she looked out into the back yard through the watery glass.

"And so, you want me to..." He deliberately paused for her to fill in the blank.

"I need you or one of your guys to finish the job."

He leaned his hip against the stove. "Are we talking reconfiguring the kitchen? It's out of the 1970s and the cabinets weren't built for new appliances."

"They'll fit, for the time being."

"Might be a good time to- Never mind. This is killing you to ask me, isn't it?"

Dori fought the urge to grin. "I'll survive."

"Thought so. I can come tonight."

"Well, I thought maybe one of your guys might-"

"Nope. I also want to get you started on the hallway." He chucked the empty bottle into a box. "Remember? You need to put some muscle into the place."

"I remember."

"Now that I think about it, the kitchen might be a better place to start."

"I'd really like to work on the hallway." She thought of Vicente taking his last breath on the floor. "I'd like to paint it and maybe polish the marble a bit and refinish the floor."

"You should call in my wood guy."

Dori imagined thousands of more dollars going out of her bank account. She'd wanted to pace out the restoration projects over time.

"I need to take a break," Gavin said. "There's a store I want you to see."

After talking with him, she'd planned on going to the history room at the downtown library. Instead of politely refusing, she got into his truck.

"We could've taken the color sample to Home Depot," Gavin said when they carried out her paint supplies later that afternoon.

Dori propped the door open with her foot. "I helped a small business. Go ahead."

He hesitated. "It's against my programming to go before a lady."

"Oh, just go. The door is heavy."

He shook his head.

"Fine," she said on a sigh, stepping out into the parking lot.

Gavin tried to slip through but the door slammed against his arm and the bells jingled merrily. He struggled. She stood there watching, and the grin he gave her once he slipped free made her smile back.

"Impressive," she said.

"I know. I use it on all my dates."

She almost asked why he wasn't married. Not that it was any of her business. But he hadn't really changed from the brief time they'd dated. He'd taken her to the old-fashioned paint store that specialized in vintage homes and then patiently explained what she'd have to do to her hallway.

"You know that you're setting yourself up, don't you?" Gavin asked as they walked to his truck.

She prepared herself for criticism. "What?"

"You're going to end up spending the rest of your life working on your house."

"I always planned to live in one house so that'll be fine with me."

"Old houses need loyal owners."

She braced herself for the inevitable conversation about her lack of loyalty. Dori wasn't quite sure that she heard him right when he said, "You seem to fit the bill."

"Would you be disappointed if I sell?"

He shook his head. "Nope. I might even buy it from you. And if you're nice-" He paused to grin at her. "I might even let you stop by for a visit."

She lifted an eyebrow. "I could come over for tea."

"Tea? Yeah, I noticed you drink that stuff by the gallon. I'd never have pegged you as a tea person."

"Why? It's good for you."

"Okay you could come for tea." The look he gave her made her coil her fist against her thigh. "Only if you bring the cookies," he said, and the alarm chirped when he unlocked the truck.

She couldn't help herself. "What kind of cookies do you like?"

His cheeks turned red. He'd always blushed easily, even in high school.

"Oatmeal chocolate chip. What about you?"

"I'm a straight forward and simple girl," she said, her lips quirking. "I like shortbread."

"With the sugar crystals on top?"

His arm brushed against hers, and chills radiated over her skin. Dori cleared her throat. "Exactly."

She stood beside him, waiting for him to open the truck's back gate. As a boy, Gavin had nervously shuffled when he was about to kiss her. But the man stood with both feet planted on the ground, his eyes dark and watchful.

Something buzzed between them. He pulled out his phone. "It's mine," he said, frowning.

He held up his finger and took the call. Disappointed but hoping they'd decide to go out for a bite to eat, Dori finished loading the brushes and plastic trays.

"Oh, hi Meg," he said. "Yeah, I remember."

Dori's ears pricked up, and then she told herself it was petty to eavesdrop.

"Tomorrow night? Oh. Can I call you back?"

Dori left him the heavy paint cans and walked to the passenger side of the truck. Her hands were shaking and her armpits wet. Of course, Meg would ask him out. She'd asked if Dori was interested in him and if he was gay, so there was no reason for anyone to be weird about it.

"It's unlocked," Gavin called out to Dori.

Dori wished she'd driven her own car, but got in and shut the door. She shivered even though the cab was hot. The truck shook when he slammed the bed gate shut.

"That was your friend Meg," he said, settling into the driver's seat.

She couldn't look at him until she got her nerves under control. "Yeah?" she asked casually.

"She, uh, asked me out," he said as if he couldn't quite believe it.

"You should go," Dori said. "She's really cool, but if you mess up on her-"

"Hey, I'm not like that."

Dori looked up at the tone in his voice. "I know."

He rested his arm on the steering wheel, watching her. "So, you don't mind?"

They weren't moving. A car was waiting for their spot. Dori wet her lips and shook her head. "Of course not."

He hesitated and then turned around to look out the back window. "If you say so."

As she aimed straight at the chest of the zombie target, Dori breathed in and on an exhale squeezed the trigger. But she flinched just when the hammer clicked against the LaserLyte Training Cartridge in her Smith and Wesson. If it had been a live round, she would've pecked the zombie's shoulder.

Her shoulders ached and her knees trembled ever so slightly. Dori had been dry-firing from her bedroom door to the end of the hallway for almost an hour, trying to rid her mind of that look on Gavin's face when he'd told her to bring cookies. With a sigh, she pulled the slide open and poked a pen through the barrel to pop the cartridge loose.

As she reloaded her weapon, Dori wished she'd given him another signal. She wished Meg hadn't called him. She wished he had crossed the distance between them to lift her chin so they'd look eye to eye before he kissed her.

Dori shook her head to clear away pointless fantasies and regrets. She grabbed her zombie target and then turned off the lights, walking back to her room in the semi dark.

Securing the gun under the bed, she hoped the tight ball in her chest would unravel now that she was in her sanctuary. From now on, she would keep things friendly between her and Gavin. No flirting and no looks. But now under the covers, she craved oatmeal chocolate chip cookies.

He cleared his throat. "Is this a bad time?"

Vicente spied on her through the bathroom door she'd left cracked open.

She sat up, strangely relieved he was here. "No."

"What did you find today?"

"Your boss shouldn't have trusted his arresting officer."

Vicente cocked his head to the side, not following.

After Dori brought home her paint supplies, she ran out of time to go to the library. So, she logged online into the Nexis database of historical newspapers. She found the James McClemmy trial for violating the Volstead Act chronicled in the Los Angeles Times. She then got ambitious and used Ancestry.com to find his intake record at McNeil Island Prison, his marriage certificate and his San Diego address in the 1920 census.

"He thought by pleading to the charges that they'd let him off," she said. "We use that line all the time. How come they didn't arrest you?"

Vicente stared at her and then vanished.

"What?" She sat up straight. "It's a legitimate question."

"I know, but he wasn't a stupid man." He now lay on the bed beside her, his hands behind his head. She was about to protest, but in truth, it didn't bother her. "He really went in, huh?"

She cleared her throat. "Yeah. I'm going to look for his probation record tomorrow."

Vicente nodded, staring at the pattern on her quilt. "I worked for a dairy company." He looked at her and winked.

"You're not disappointed?"

He shrugged and she knew him enough to know that was his way of deflecting the truth. "It's not every day you find out that you died for nothing. The whole point for me to step inside this house was so they'd stick the charges on me and let him off. Fucking cops."

She resisted the flare of indignation. She'd been hearing it her whole career, mostly from her family who had been guests of the federal and state penitentiary system. "He broke the law and he paid the price."

"You ever been beaten with your hands cuffed behind your back by men who are supposed to uphold the law?"

"No."

"Then you don't know nothing."

The chola's blood-soaked face flashed in Dori's mind and her righteousness dried up. "Sometimes we have to make tough decisions," she said, her voice shaking. "I'm not saying what they did was right but-"

She couldn't remember what she was about to say.

"What?" he asked, his eyes narrowing as if he sensed the turmoil churning in her chest.

Dori looked away. "I killed a woman. Just a few weeks ago. She drew a gun and fired-" She lifted the covers and her shirt to show him her bandage.

He eyed the bandage but never said a word.

"It was me or her and I-"

"She's dead?"

Dori nodded. "If I could go back-"

"Yeah I know."

She jerked her chin up. "I'm not like those men who killed you. They were almost gleeful about the whole thing."

He stared down the length of the bed. "Do you think Eugenia's the old lady your grandma found?"

Dori blinked, not quite following the abrupt change of subject. It was her great grandma who'd found her, but she didn't correct him. "I don't know. I hope not."

She reached for her notebook and made a note to herself to look up the property record.

"I tried to stay away from the barrio after that night," he said with a long sigh. She looked up from the to-do list she'd started. "But I had to take care of my sister and my grandmother. They barely scraped by."

"Your grandmother accepted your money?"

He grinned, but his eyes were sad as if the rejection was still fresh. "Eugenia did. She had her baby boy to feed and another on the way."

"What was her son's name?"

"I can't remember. I never met the baby because I-" He lifted a shoulder instead of stating the obvious.

"Right." Dori eased back onto the pillows, turning towards him to prop her head on one hand. "So, you went back."

## National City, 1932

"At this rate, you might as well marry me for all it's costing you."

Vicente looked over at Clara, who clutched the leather strap above the door as they sped south towards home. "You'd kill me in my sleep," he said.

"Puh, what makes you think I'd wait that long?" She winked at him. "You know, we could be quite a team. You're not so bad when you laugh. You got a good sense of humor."

He rolled his eyes and kept a firm grip on the wheel. The red Cadillac's powerful engine pulled against him, wanting to break loose and run wild till it met the water.

Clara counted on her fingers. "We're not stupid, we've made good on our agreement and I could help you move up."

Vicente tore his mind away from the memories of seashells under his thin shoes and his lips sticky from mint candy. "Yeah, how?"

"I could be your Mata Hari and seduce secrets from your rivals."

He couldn't help but laugh at her. "No, you couldn't."

"Why not?"

"'Cause I can read what you're thinking by just looking at your face. Maybe you should be in the movies."

"Did you just insult me?"

She grabbed her hat when he jerked the wheel and turned off the main road. "Close your damn window," she said. "It's letting in the dust."

He obliged her. Rocks pinged off the insides of the wheel wells as the car bounced along the dirt road. Autumn turned hot and dry. He remembered the taste of the red dust in his mouth and the pain of it shredding his eyes.

The sunlight slid over the curves of the roadster and children stopped their play to watch him drive by. He pulled in front of his sister's house. According to Alex, the old lady lived in the front house, which still had the plate glass window from its time as a small store. Eugenia, Alex and their little boy, whose name Vicente already forgot, were in the back house.

Clara brushed her white suit jacket with a handkerchief. Yesterday, he'd ordered her back up to his penthouse to try on the all-white ensemble, including gloves, shoes and hat. She'd wanted to throw it in his face. But in the end, she couldn't resist.

He helped Clara out of the car. A faded curtain hung in the plate glass display window. Someone had attempted to scratch away the name of the store, which had been owned by a German family. Just one street over was

Anna's parents' house with its roses and starched white curtains.

"Hold this," he said.

Clara took the hat box. "What did she get?"

"I didn't get nothing for her."

She looked confused. "This is a woman's hat, ain't it?"

He stupidly thought Clara had been asking about Anna. He never told her where he'd gone the night he left her at the dance. He'd given the bottle to Alex and then found Clara smoking in the back of the limousine.

"Just give it to my sister like you picked it out," he said. Clara frowned, trying to figure him out. He wished her luck. "Come on. Let's go."

They headed into the small yard. He caught movement behind the neighbor's curtains. Vicente turned and tipped his fedora. The curtains abruptly dropped and the nosey woman stepped back from the window.

He grinned as word spread at this very moment of his fancy car and his fancy woman carrying expensive presents to his family. By the time he was back at the penthouse tonight, everyone would know he'd really come back a rich man.

"Eugenia," he called out.

Clara kicked at a curious chicken. "The old lady catches you doing that and she'll strip your hide," he said.

"I hate these damn things."

He knocked and called out Eugenia's name. When she didn't answer, he tried the handle and it opened.

Clara curled her lip with disgust as they walked into Eugenia's tiny sala that hadn't been tidied in days. Dust lay thick on the small table between two mismatched wingback chairs. His nephew's toys were left on the floor. The window let in just enough light that kept the place in perpetual shadow. His dead mother's portrait looked out in the cold, still room.

"Stay here," he ordered Clara, setting the boxes on one of the chairs.

"But-"

He left her there to search the tiny kitchen. Breakfast plates and cups remained on the table pushed up against the wall. Vicente whispered Eugenia's name as he peeked through the curtain that replaced the bedroom door. The beds were made and a patchwork rabbit doll with button eyes lay on the small trundle bed. He wondered what happened to the doll he'd given her seven years ago.

Vicente stepped back into the kitchen and noticed the exposed raw wood where it looked like the door hinges had been ripped out. He ran his fingers along the sharp splinters. His blood simmered. Had Alex done this? Eugenia should've known better than to marry a man like their father. If Vicente had been here, he would never have allowed it and made her wait to find a proper man who could provide more than this.

"They're not here," she said behind him.

He nearly jumped out of his skin. Turning, he found Anna standing in the back door, wearing an apron soaked through with a basket of clothes on her hip.

"What are you doing here?" he demanded, his breath locked tight in his chest.

"Helping Eugenia with her laundry. They went for a walk."

"In her condition?"

"Yes," Anna replied, setting the basket down and then straightened up. In the light of day, her face was tanned with a spray of freckles across the tops of her cheeks and nose. Her hair frizzed around her face and came loose from the chignon at the base of her neck. In her button-down shirt and trousers, she was no longer the pale, unblinking doll.

He didn't know what else to say, and she wasn't helping. He stuck a cigarette between his teeth and pulled out his silver lighter.

"Is laundry your side business?" He flicked the lighter open. She watched the hissing flame as it touched the tip of the cigarette.

"No, this was a favor." She reached behind her and he paused, watching her back arch and a piece of hair dangle over her cheek. She pulled the ties loose and then peeled away the wet apron. The white shirt stuck to her skin. He could make out the lace pattern of her chemise underneath, and his legs felt heavy.

She leaned her shoulder on the doorjamb, her blue eyes traveling up and down his suit as if he were there for her inspection. "You're going to run out of lighter fluid," she said.

Vicente flicked the lighter shut and stuck it in his pocket. His neck tie strangled, and sweat built up under his shirt. He'd be damned to let her know it. "So, did Albert retire and make you work for him?" he asked.

"I help Eugenia when I can." Anna glanced down at the flowers he held at his side. "Those will make her happy."

He then remembered Clara waiting in the sala. He stepped outside, and Anna reared back, losing her balance on the steps. She caught herself. Her smug grin popped when he didn't stop. They were now outside under a giant pepper tree. The red peppercorns popped underfoot. He could all but taste the sweat collected in the v of her shirt. He shoved the basket aside with his foot.

Anna watched him, her lips parted, waiting to see what he'd do next.

"You need to shut down your operation," he said and tossed his cigarette into the dirt.

She frowned as if he wasn't being clear enough.

"I said-" His hands itched to press her against him.

"I heard you." She pocketed her hands, regaining her easy stance. "But why? I'm hardly a threat to people like you."

He didn't like the inflection she'd placed on you so he inched towards her. She didn't back down, but she had to lift her chin to look him in the eye. She still smelled like mint candy and he wanted to dip his finger in her pocket to see if she still carried them.

"Prohibition is ending and if you're smart, shut down. You could always do laundry."

She eyed him, assessing how serious he was. "I could."

Vicente wasn't used to being taunted. After driving down here with Clara, he had no more patience. "I can burn you down like that," he said, snapping his fingers close to her face. "I'd hate to see that kid you have working the desk get hurt."

She didn't blink, but he heard her sharp intake of breath. "Me, too."

Curiosity bled through the wall of hostility he kept between them. But Anna must have had a layer of ice under her skin. She wasn't giving much away, and that little smart grin on her face told him she enjoyed playing with him. Who was that kid to her? He was too old to be her son, and Vicente already knew her brothers and sisters were dead.

She shifted her weight, coming close enough that chills rolled down his back. "I should know why I need to give up my livelihood. Consider it a professional courtesy."

He hated that twinkle in her eye. She laughed at him like he was some blustering boy in a cheap suit. He pulled out a fifty and tossed it into her basket. "Thanks for doing the laundry. That should tide you over."

The recoil on her face soured his stomach. But Vicente turned on his heel and went back into the house, nearly running into his sister.

"Vicente?" Eugenia cried.

He caught her by the shoulders, her large stomach between them. Vicente needed more time to catch his breath and slow down the hammering in his chest. Anna had played him but good and for it, he'd make her pay. As soon as he got back, he'd send the cops straight to her, and she'd know he wasn't the foolish boy who panted for her attention.

"I can't believe it's you," Eugenia stammered, her eyes filling with tears. "It's been so long, and I thought Alex was just drunk when he-"

Vicente tightened his hold on her and forced a smile on his face. "Miss me?"

She openly cried, blubbering about him standing in her kitchen.

"Enough of that," he said, handing her a clean handkerchief. "You'll upset the baby."

"I can't use this. It's so nice and-" she stammered as he dabbed her cheeks dry. "Did you see Anna?"

The hairs stood up on the back of his neck. He glanced over his shoulder expecting her to walk in on them. He urged Eugenia back towards the sala. "She's finishing up your wash. Come sit down."

She refused to budge. "But I should see if she needs-"

"She's fine." The last thing he wanted was to make small talk with the two of them together. "You need to get off your feet."

"Can I get you something to eat?"

"No." He turned her around and nudged her into the dark, cool sala. The hat he'd bought for the old lady had been tossed back into the box. "Where's Clara?"

Eugenia rushed to put the hat away. "Grandma asked her to leave."

Vicente could just imagine how. "She was here?"

"Well, when she saw you were here and-" Eugenia straightened her spine. "You shouldn't have brought all of this."

He looked down at the wingback chair. It was a cheap imitation piece of crap. But he sat down and horsehair stuck him in the ass through his trousers. "You deserve nice things. I can afford them. Open them."

Eugenia reluctantly took the box he handed her. He half listened as she protested every toy and piece of clothing she unwrapped. He kept one ear trained on the back door for Anna. But she never came into the house and he tried not to wonder where she'd gone or what she was doing. His blood started to move again and he instantly remembered her damp skin and her lips. He shifted to adjust himself.

"Alex isn't going to like this," Eugenia said. "He's very proud."

Alex wouldn't like it if Eugenia knew how much they owed Anna. And yet she'd been out back, scrubbing their clothes like a servant.

Vicente lit another cigarette. "If Alex has a problem with it, he'll discuss it with me."

She opened her mouth to protest but said, "Thank you. Aren't you going to check on your lady friend?"

"She can take care of herself."

A sly grin eased the worry lines on Eugenia's face. "I heard all about her at the dance."

He grinned and exhaled. She rolled her eyes.

"When's the baby due?" he asked.

"Another month," she said, her shoulders slumping.

"Alex treats you, all right?" he asked, glancing at the ripped door jam.

"He's more like a child who needs to be managed."

"Why'd you marry him?"

She handed him an ashtray. "He's a hard worker and you were gone."

They were quiet. She neatly folded a piece of tissue paper and placed it into the box.

"I didn't realize-" he struggled to remember his nephew's name. "The boy was so big. I'll get him some bigger clothes next time."

"Neto," she said. "His name is Ernesto."

"Who're his padrinos?"

"The Ramirez family down the street."

Vicente looked down at Neto's wooden train. If he'd been here, he would've been the boy's padrino. Maybe they would've named the boy after him.

"The baby can use these when it's big enough," she said, patting the clothes he'd brought for Neto.

Vicente leaned forward, "Look, instead of having someone like Anna do your laundry, hire a woman to come in," he said. "I'll pay her myself."

Eugenia shook her head.

"You can't do all this on your own."

"I want to discuss this with Alex."

"There's nothing to discuss. I'll send a woman over myself."

He sat back, the matter settled. But then she turned on him. "Vicente, this is not your home. I appreciate all of this, but it's my family."

He didn't know what to say. He'd never seen her like this. "Look at where you live, Eugenia," he said and then lowered his voice. "This place is a mess and you don't even have a decent door to your bedroom."

It took her a moment, but she rose to her feet, her face hard with anger. "I'm proud of what we have because we earn it honestly."

"Don't be so high and mighty when you got a bootlegger and a rich man's whore out there doing your dirty laundry."

She sucked in her breath, but she didn't crumple. "You don't know Anna enough to say those things about her. But I'll tell you one thing; she doesn't come into my home and insult me and my husband."

Apparently, Anna wasn't the only one who grew a backbone while he'd been gone. If they were both willing to live with the smell of chicken shit in the front parlor, to be slaves to worthless men, who the hell was he to stop them?

He got to his feet and jammed his hat on his head. "She goes in and out the back door, huh? So, people won't talk?"

"Vicente, don't."

"I won't send a woman over. But if you need anything I'm at the US Grant Hotel."

Eugenia's eyes widened and he should've felt a thrill of satisfaction. Instead he just wanted to get the stink of this place off him. "Just send word, and I'll be here."

# CHAPTER TWENTY-ONE

Dori stared up at the ceiling, thinking of half remembered names and vivid faces. She'd fallen asleep to the sound of Vicente's voice. She stretched her arm to his side of the bed. It was cold. There was no indentation on the pillow to show that he'd laid there. She rolled onto her side, sad that he wasn't here.

She wished he'd told her where he went. Then again, having come close to death herself, she wasn't so sure she wanted to know. If she hadn't reacted or the shooter had aimed higher, Dori wasn't so sure she would've left this world freely. She had too many regrets hooked into her.

A knock sounded downstairs. Dori threw off the duvet and gritted her teeth as she pulled a hoodie over her pajamas and jammed her feet into Ugg boots. She couldn't wait for the day when she had rugs for all the floors. When she answered the door, Gavin looked up from his phone.

Her cheeks tingled, just imagining what she looked like with her hair tangled and sticking out of her head every which way. "Uh, hi," she said.

He tucked his phone in his back pocket, giving her the charming grin that all Latin men perfected by puberty. "If you'd give me a key, I wouldn't have to wake you up this early in the morning."

Clearing her throat, Dori thrust her hands in her pockets. "What are you doing here so early?"

His eyebrows winged up at her question. He jerked his thumb at the refrigerator standing just a few feet behind him on the porch. "I thought I'd help you get started before I fixed up the kitchen."

"You are?"

"Well, yeah. We talked about it yesterday."

She shivered from the stark cold. The sky was so clear and blue it hurt her eyes. She stepped back to let him in. "Do you need coffee?" she asked.

"I never say no to coffee."

Rather than get into another conversation about cookies, Dori busied herself with making coffee.

"So, how's it coming along in the basement?" she asked.

"You haven't peeked?" Gavin leaned against the counter.

"No. Why? Is it bad?"

"We have a few problems, but nothing we didn't expect."

"You're saying that to make me feel better."

"The place in Mission Hills had dead animals under the house. I don't know how the neighbors lived with the smell."

"How do you clean something like that up?" She got milk out of the refrigerator, and he stepped out of her way.

"I hired someone and didn't stick around to watch."

Not sure what to say next, Dori heated milk in the microwave. She was about to ask how many vintage homes he'd restored when Gavin cleared his throat.

"I'll go down and check what they've been up to and then be back to get you started."

"The coffee is almost done."

He was half way across the kitchen. "I'll come back and pour myself a cup." He paused. "How did the curtains turn out? Meg told me you two did some decorating."

Dori didn't spill the coffee she was pouring into her mug. "We did. They look great."

"Cool. Mind if I look? She'll ask if I did."

She cleared her throat. "Sure, go ahead."

He stepped into her home office and then continued out the back towards the basement stairs. Dori stared out the window, not seeing the trees brushed with the gold light of the morning. It was cool, she told herself and picked up her coffee to go upstairs and get dressed. He'd be good for Meg, and she bet Meg would be good for him. But her chest squeezed tight as she thought of them together.

An hour later, Dori bent down and dusted off the tops of the paint cans for something to do. In preparation to strip a hundred and twenty years' worth of paint, she put on her Wonder Woman red MAC lip glass for moral support.

The crew had rolled in. Their radio and power tools started up and the house rang with purpose and productivity. With the floor vibrating under her feet, the house literally came to life. She smiled, thinking of the promise she'd made to her house. She patted the floor as if to say, we're doing all right.

"So, first, you have to wear these," Gavin said. He walked over, holding out a pair of goggles and plastic gloves. "I have a feeling you're going to come across milk paint underneath the first hundred layers, so I brought a heat gun."

He held them away from her. "But you're not to touch the wood work with this thing. Leave that to the professionals."

She promised, taking the goggles and face mask. "I'm not going to end up with cancer, am I?"

"We'll open the doors and windows."

He bent down and rummaged through all the stuff they'd bought yesterday. She caught herself staring at the muscles in his back moving under his shirt. She went to the door and propped it open with a paint can.

"How long will this take?" she asked, rubbing her frozen fingers together.

"If it's a straight sanding and paint job, maybe two weeks. But we have to make sure to cover this wood work good and tight." He seemed to disapprove of her plan. "You know, paint isn't going to solve all of the issues in this hallway."

"I know but it's a start."

"And while you're at it, get rid of the bookcases," a familiar voice chimed in.

Dori closed her eyes and thought, why now? As Gavin went on, she casually glanced over and saw Vicente standing in front of the fireplace, arms crossed over his chest and feet planted wide.

"If you don't, I'll start slamming doors," Vicente said to her, eyeing Gavin like he was encroaching on his territory.

Dori frowned at him to go away.

"Don't give me that look," he said as Gavin went on about how to use the scraper.

Turning to Gavin, Dori cleared her throat. "We have to get rid of those bookcases," she said.

Gavin eyed the bookcases that flanked the fireplace and then back at her. "You sure you want to do that?"

"You do, trust me," Vicente answered behind her.

"Yeah, why not?" she asked as if she weren't having two conversations at once.

"I'll bet money that whoever put in those bookcases cut into the chair railing and then you'll have these two blank cut outs next to the fire place," Gavin said.

"I want to take them out," she said remembering to add a smile at the end of her sentence.

Gavin narrowed his eyes. "You're gonna have to cover your hair and close off the rooms so you don't get dust everywhere."

"Thanks, Gavin."

He did a double take, suspicious of the sweetness in her voice. "You're sure?"

She nodded.

"I'll be right back."

When he was gone, Dori turned to Vicente about to tell him to beat it.

"You like him don't you," he teased.

Taking her chances that Gavin would walk in and find her talking to the wind that blew in through the open door, Dori's curiosity got the better of her. "Is there something behind those book cases?"

Vicente lifted one shoulder. "Like what?"

She looked down at the place where she'd found him that night. "Evidence of your demise."

"Doubt it. I just don't like them."

Before she could reply, Gavin returned with one of his guys.

"Last chance," he said.

She did a double take at the young, cute guy beside Gavin. Maybe Grammy had been onto something about making men out of boys. "I'm committed," she said.

"We'll take this out in a couple of minutes," Gavin said, watching her watching his worker who now rolled out a drop cloth.

"What do I do," she asked, hoping to look innocent.

"We don't want to damage the walls or the paneling behind the bookcases," Gavin said, sliding a shiv between the wall and the bookcase and then tapping it down with a hammer.

"Just let him do it," Vicente said right in her ear, and she jumped.

"You okay?" Gavin asked.

"Fly in my ear." She swatted the air around her head.

Gavin's eyes searched the room for the make-believe fly, and then he jerked his chin at his helper to start working.

Dori clasped her hands behind her back, seething with the same frustration she'd felt as a girl when the boys decided they could do it better and faster. She considered pouring herself another coffee as they hammered and tugged and then stood back staring at the bookcase that refused to budge.

"You know, they should just take a sledgehammer to the thing," Vicente said, standing by the younger one.

Dori eyed the sledgehammer they'd laid on the floor. The men were shaking their heads at the bookcase as if standing there would finish the job.

She sighed as she picked up the sledgehammer and carried it to the other bookcase.

They were too busy talking as she pulled the goggles over her eyes and the mask over her nose and mouth. She lifted the sledgehammer over her shoulder, careful not to pull her side. Her muscles stretched without pain. Dori focused on the bookcase and brought the sledgehammer down. A spectacular crash of broken wood exploded in the room.

A smile broke out on her face as she took in the bashed in bookcase. She looked over at Gavin who stood there with the same expression on his face as his helper and Vicente.

With a powerful yank, she freed the sledgehammer and tore out of a piece of the bookshelf. Kicking it aside, she planted her feet and readied herself for the next blow.

Five minutes later, the bookcase was a pile of rubble. Only the back remained attached to the wall.

Gavin's helper blew out a whistle. "Guess you don't need us." He held up his hand for her to give him a high-five.

Dori did.

"Okay thanks, man" Gavin said, grabbing his shoulder and patting his back. "Why don't you head back downstairs?"

The kid gave Dori a wink and then walked down the hallway to the basement door. She waited for Gavin to acknowledge her work. Instead, he kicked away some of the mess so he could run his hand over the wall.

"Well they didn't cut away the woodwork, but they scarred it up pretty good," he said as if assessing a patient. "We'll need a really good wood guy to replicate the panels."

She glared at Vicente, imagining how much this was going to cost her.

"It already looks much better," Vicente said and was gone.

"Check this out," Gavin said, holding up a fire truck toy in the palm of his hand.

Awe fluttered between Dori's ribs as she traced the number painted on the tiny door. Some little boy in the past had lost it. He'd probably searched everywhere for it; his mom scolding him for not putting it away.

"Take it," Gavin said. "It's yours."

"Are you sure? Finders keepers."

He looked her straight in the eye. "My daughter's too old to play with toys and besides, you did the work."

The word daughter went through her like she stuck her finger in socket. Did Meg know? How old was his daughter? Would she like Meg? Was he divorced or had he not married the mom?

Dori played it cool as she held out her hand. He tilted his so the truck fell into hers. Their hands touched for a moment.

"What? No questions?" he teased.

In spite of her best efforts, she couldn't hold back her grin. "Only a few."

He stood up, looking her in the eye. "Well, you have my attention."

"How old is she and what's her name?"

"Isabella is six."

Dori had packs of young cousins that age. But she'd never been a kid-friendly tía. "Oh. So, she's in kindergarten."

Gavin nodded. "She is. So, let's clean this up and then get working on the next one." He patted her shoulder. "If I'd known you were this good, I would've hired you a long time ago."

His touch lingered as he carried the sledgehammer to the other bookcase. She stood there wanting to know more about Isabella even though it was none of her business. Maybe she should tell Meg, or would that be meddlesome? She couldn't decide as she-

"Stop it," a rough voice shot out at them.

Dori spun around. Not Vicente. Gavin was saying something about the redwood chair rail, not having heard the voice. Her hands went jittery as she forced herself to look into the front parlor. Staring back at her was a black figure, more like a shadow without a face or eyes.

Keeping her eyes on it, Dori said to Gavin, "We should do this another time."

"What? Why?"

"I uh, don't feel well and-"

"That's okay. I can take care of this."

It never moved or faded away. It simply watched them. "No really. You have better things to do."

Gavin rested the head of the sledgehammer in his hand. "What's going on here, Dori?"

"Nothing. I just don't feel right."

"Are you that freaked out about my kid?"

She glanced into the front parlor. The room was empty.

"Hey boss." They turned at the sound of Oscar's voice. He pointed to the basement door, his face tense. "Freddie needs to go the hospital."

"I'll take him." Gavin hurried over, deliberately stepping around so not to brush against her.

"What happened?" Dori asked.

Gavin disappeared down the stairs. Oscar turned to answer her. "It's a serious cut, but he'll be fine. Just part of the job."

He then turned and followed Gavin into the basement. They left her alone with the breeze rippling across the drop cloth.

She turned and stared into the gaping doorway. It had resembled Vicente in stature and shape. What the hell was that thing? Vicente had been here, appearing as he always did. She unclenched her sweaty hands, thinking of crazy Bernice and her promise that he would go bad.

"Miss Orihuela?"

An involuntary sound shot out of her mouth.

"I'm sorry. I didn't mean to scare you," Oscar said.

Finally, Dori shook her head, her pulse kicking in her neck. "I'm good."

She moved down the hall to shut the front door, keeping her eyes averted from the room.

He gestured to the mess at her feet. "You need my help?"

She shook her head, seeing his wariness through her watery eyes. "I'll clean this up."

"It's no bother."

She threw her hands out, keeping him from walking over. "No, no. It's my mess. I got it."

"He's gonna be all right," Oscar said.

It took her a moment to remember Gavin had taken his worker to the hospital. "I know. I'll call in a little while."

"Okay." He started backing away. "I'll be downstairs if you need me."

# CHAPTER TWENTY-TWO

Dori stayed away from the house for the rest of the afternoon. She'd left a message with Gavin asking about his guy. He texted her that everything was fine and he went work on his house.

She spent the afternoon practicing at the gun range. Her hands shook and she flinched when the casings flew at her face as the bullets ripped out of the barrel. When her rounds were spent, she'd reload and do it again until her right arm and shoulder felt like noodles. Dori rolled up her targets that smelled of gun powder. It felt a hell of a lot better than therapy.

But the tension in her stomach returned as she walked across the parking lot, thinking about what was in the front parlor. Was it one of those guys who'd killed him? What if Vicente didn't know there was something in there, or what if it tortured him by replaying his death as she'd seen in her dream.

Apparently, thank God, it couldn't cross the threshold.

Dori put her gun case in the Rav-4's back compartment and then locked herself in the car. Bernice's face floated in her mind, but she shook her head to clear it. Grammy had questioned Vicente talking to her and made that comment about pain killers. The only person she might trust with this problem was Meg.

She stuck the headphone in her ear. When Meg answered, Dori forgot the script she'd thought up so not to appear nuts.

"Dori?" Meg asked again.

"Yeah, it's me."

"Where are you?"

"I uh, went shopping and I must've, uh, butt dialed you." Dori squeezed her eyes shut for lying.

After a long pause, Meg said, "Oh. Well it's a good thing you have a nice tush."

"Okay then, I'll talk to you later."

"Wait! I have something for you. It's a painting of an orchard that was done from your home."

"No way. Really?"

"I'll pop in after work. Would you mind if Gavin met me there?"

Dori's eyes fluttered shut. "Sure," she heard herself reply. "That'll be great."

Oscar's bus was gone but Grammy's car and a smart little green Fiat waited in the driveway. Dori smelled like gun powder and incense but at least she felt calmer from her visit to Botanica Mama Roots. The woman who helped her didn't bat an eye when she told her about bad energy in her old house. She'd bought a smudge stick of sage, white candles and some crystals.

Dori took a deep breath as she reached for her bag of supplies and then got out of the car to bring in her gun case. She warily glanced up at the windows, not sure what she dreaded more: evil shadow people, or making small talk with Meg and Gavin before they left for a date.

She smelled dinner as she walked up the steps to the kitchen door.

"Hello?" she called out. Grammy wasn't in the kitchen. Gavin's guys had installed all of her new appliances.

She heard a man's voice in the front parlor. Dori eyed her bag of New Age, not sure it had the same effect as proton packs and nuclear containment units. She walked into the hallway, squinting from the sunlight that angled straight through the front windows. They were in the front parlor. Her heart thudded in her chest and her throat squeezed tight.

"Hey, there she is," Gavin said.

Dori blinked as he and Meg walked out into the hallway. She set down her New Age bag on the floor behind her gun case. "Hi guys," she said, her face stretched tight into a smile.

"I've been dying to show you this all day," Meg said, coming at her with arms wide open. They hugged. Over her shoulder, she met Gavin's watchful eye and then he glanced away.

Meg looked great with her dreads let loose in their full glory. A long white scarf draped over her tight pink tank, giving coy glimpses of the purple bra underneath. Her dark jeans hugged her lean legs and she wore heeled black mini shearling boots.

"Here. Open it."

Dori opened the manila file in which Meg paper-clipped a copy of an 18th century water-color painting of an orchard that once stretched from her house to the edge of National City Boulevard.

It pre-dated Vicente's death.

"Where did you find this?"

"It's on display at the History Museum in Balboa Park. I was, well, a bit sneaky and took a few snaps with my camera."

"Thank you."

Dori and Meg smiled at each other and then looked over at Gavin.

"Your grammy let us in," Gavin said.

"Where is she?"

"In your office," he said. "I think she might be addicted to Facebook."

"Gavin showed me the basement and where you ripped out the bookcase," Meg said.

Dori grimaced at the second bookcase she'd left behind. "I still have a lot of work to do."

"What color will you paint these walls?"

Out of the corner of her eye, Dori saw Gavin back away from them, his hands in his pockets. "I'll check my messages and let you girls chat," he said.

As he walked by, he looked great and smelled even better. She wondered if he'd brought Meg flowers on their first date as he had done for her. Dori heard herself say, "I don't want to keep you guys."

Gavin looked at Meg. "You ready?"

"Of course."

"Ready for what?" Grammy asked, marching into the hallway from Dori's office. "Dinner's ready and there's more than enough for everyone."

"That's so sweet of you," Meg said, hugging Grammy. "But we're running out of time."

"What? You don't think my cooking is any good?"

Dori didn't dare look at Gavin. "Meg and Gavin have to leave for their, uh, dinner."

Grammy looked from Meg to Dori, her eyebrow arching up. "Oh really?"

"Yes really," Dori said.

"They could stay for a glass of wine," Grammy offered.

"Another. Night," Dori insisted.

Grammy pressed her lips together. Meg took Gavin's arm. Dori knew exactly what Grammy was thinking. Gavin was supposed to be for Dori, not Meg.

"Ohh what is that smell?" Meg broke away from Gavin when they entered the kitchen. She peeled back the foil and peeked. "Are these tomatotello?"

"What did you say?" Grammy asked.

"A tomatotello," Meg persisted.

"Mija, is that one of them English things?"

"You mean a tomatillo?" Dori offered.

Understanding dawned on Grammy's face and then she turned back to Meg. "Girl, you're in America. You gotta speak Spanglish right or you'll get hurt."

Meg shook her head. "Is that how you pronounce it? Say it again."

Grammy replied, "To-mah-tee-yo."

"That would crack my British tongue in two."

Dori stepped between Grammy and Meg. "You should-"

"We should-"

Dori and Gavin looked at each other and then quickly dropped their gazes to the floor. She could feel Grammy's stare boring into the side of her head.

"Open the wine," she ordered Dori and then went to Meg. "Now mija, let me show you how to make the sauce."

Grammy elucidated Meg on the finer points of enchiladas suizas; both of them ignoring Dori and Gavin.

"I'll get the glasses, if you tell me where they are," he said.

She cleared her throat. "They're in the cabinet above the microwave."

Dori poured four glasses of Malbec and considered downing hers to loosen up her knotted throat.

"Here we go," Dori said, passing out the glasses. Her hand brushed against Gavin's hand and they both stood as far as apart from one another as they could.

"To new friends," Meg said.

Grammy eyed Dori and Gavin and then shook her head. "Salud."

Gavin warily raised his glass and took a sip. Grammy sent Dori a disapproving look.

Resting her hip against the counter, Dori told herself that she was a mature woman. She was drinking a great Malbec. Meg brought her a beautiful, thoughtful gift and her Grammy had made enchiladas suizas and the kitchen windows were slightly misted with rice-flavored steam.

If she and Gavin didn't have this awkwardness between them, they all might have been comfortable with each other, like they did this sort of thing all the time. But once Gavin finished the project, Dori found Anna Vazquez and Meg finished her internship, everyone would drift their own separate ways and life would return to normal. She would be back by herself; eating on the run or at her desk. She finished off her wine, feeling more wilted.

"Tell us about your work, Dori," Meg said out of the blue. Apparently, she was in no hurry to go on her date. "What was the first case you ever solved?"

Dori sensed Gavin turning and watching her as she answered. "My first call was an assault."

"She was first in her police academy," Grammy added.

"And so, what happened?"

"There was this woman who had been suing her husband, and he was suing her. They went back and forth, back and forth. So, on the day I came into the picture, he had her served at her work. She was a barista at Starbucks and threw coffee at the process server."

"Was it hot?" Gavin asked with a wince.

"Scalding. So, I had to taser the wife when she threatened me with the coffee pot."

"But surely a coffee pot is harmless," Meg said, setting her glass on the counter.

"Not in the hands of an angry soon-to-be ex-wife."

"Couldn't you have talked her down?" Gavin asked.

Dori paused, feeling the sting of Gavin's question. Would he have had a problem with her being an officer? She then reminded herself that he was going on a date with Meg, not her, so it didn't matter.

"The second rule in law enforcement is to make sure you and your partner go home at the end of the shift," she said. "If I didn't get her under control she could've hurt me or my partner or someone else."

"So how come you're around so often," Gavin asked. "Are you on some kind of sabbatical?"

Grammy bristled and Meg stared down at her glass.

"If people behaved themselves, then my mija wouldn't have a job, see?" Grammy said. "Now, where are you two going for dinner?"

Dori caught the confused expression on Gavin's face.

Meg made some noise about how they should get going to make their reservation. Tuning them out, Dori just wanted them to go. She eyed the bottle. Gavin edged closer to the door and Meg practiced her pronunciation of tomatillo. Dori set down her glass when footsteps thumped in the front parlor. A door opened and then slammed shut, cutting off the chatter.

"Who's still here?" Gavin asked quietly. "I thought my guys all left."

"It's an old house. They make-" Dori started to say when a man shouted. His words were unintelligible but he'd cried out in pain and fury. Vicente.

She was three-quarters down the hallway when she stopped so suddenly that she nearly fell forward. The sage bundle that had been in her bag had exploded across the floor.

"Who's in there?" Gavin asked, now behind her.

She held up her hand behind her, motioning for him to stay put. "Stay with my Grammy."

"What about you?"

"Like hell I'm standing around by myself!" Grammy called, poking her head out of the dining room with Meg at her side.

A heavy thump vibrated the floor under her feet. Meg clapped both hands over her mouth. Dori went cold all over, remembering her dream.

"Just go," she ordered, approaching the front parlor even though she wasn't sure what she could possibly do. "All of you, go!"

She peeked through the doorway. She pressed her arm against her mouth and nose. The cold air was soaked in foulness.

Gavin came around Dori.

"No wait," she called after him. He looked from the bay windows to the fireplace in the empty room. "What the hell made that noise?"

"You need to get out of there," Dori ordered as the cold damp reached out towards her.

"This is going to sound crazy, but that guy-" He moved his foot over the floor where they all had heard what sounded like a body falling. Dori tensed knowing exactly what he was trying to say. "The one I saw upstairs the other morning-"

She walked in and grabbed his arm. They didn't have time for explanations.

"Who is he? Did he do this?" Gavin asked.

Dori heard the crackling over their heads. She shoved Gavin out of the way. He grabbed her arms and their feet tangled. They hit the floor as plaster crashed down from the ceiling.

Dust tickled her nose and she felt ceiling crumbs against her back. Gavin sneezed and his fingers dug into her skin. He'd pulled her against him, taking the brunt of the fall. Her hands rested against his chest, thighs against his, and he was warm and smooth and rough in all the right places. As she stared down into his face, she could've kicked herself for breaking his heart sixteen years ago.

Gavin reached up and gently pulled something loose from her hair. His dark eyes locked with hers. Heat flashed through her. His lips parted and his hand pressed ever so slightly against the back of her head, lowering her to meet him and-

"Oh!" Meg said from the door.

Dori jerked her head up. Looking over her shoulder, her friend stood in the doorway while Grammy rose up on her tippy toes to get a good look. Through the haze of dust, she couldn't read the look on Meg's face. Perhaps the dust was thick enough that she couldn't quite see Dori draped over her date.

She scrambled off Gavin. That was it, Dori decided. Tomorrow she would call an exorcist and go hardcore, old school medieval Catholic on whatever was in here. By the time she was done with him, the devil would have trouble putting its pieces back together.

"I told you not to go in here," Dori said to Gavin through the thickness in her throat. She left him there on the floor.

He got to his feet and followed her into the hallway. Meg and Grammy had vanished. "Why did you lie to me?"

Dori whirled around. "I was a stupid kid. I-"

"I wasn't talking about that," he said quietly. "I meant the guy I saw in

the window a few weeks ago."

Dori hugged herself. "Oh. Right." She took in a deep breath and all the dust and grit burned her throat.

"Why do you have to lie about everything?"

She made herself look him in the eye, searching for condemnation in him. He simply waited for her answer. "I didn't think you'd believe me."

"But I told you I saw him."

"I know, it's just that-" She started to look away but stopped herself. "After what I did in high school, I didn't want you to have an even worse opinion of me."

He clenched his jaw. "Well, let's just deal with one thing at a time," he said. "How many times have you seen that guy?"

Dori jerked her chin up. "A few times."

"He doesn't scare you?" he asked.

"No. I don't think that was him-" She pointed to the front parlor. "He wouldn't have done something like that."

"What was it?"

She shook her head as if she didn't know. He reached for her and Dori took a step back. "You should go. Meg is…"

"Has he hurt you?"

She shook her head. "No."

"Do you know why he's here?"

She looked away, trying to figure out how to answer that question in such a way that it wouldn't break their fragile truce.

"You're figuring out how to shine me off aren't you?" he asked.

"No, it's just-"

He backed away. "Why would I think otherwise when you've lied since the day we met?"

"I'm so sorry about all that, okay? I'm not like that anymore."

"Okay," he said, shoving his hands in his pockets. With the white dust in his hair, she could imagine what he'd look like as an old man. It made her chest ache. "I better go try and-"

Gavin shook his head as if there was no point in finishing what he was about to say.

"Go ahead," Dori said, moving further out of his way. Gavin refused to look at her as he walked away.

# CHAPTER TWENTY-THREE

When Dori finally entered the kitchen, Grammy sat at the table with a glass of Herradura and her iPad.

"She left and then he went after her," Grammy said, giving Dori the once over. "You should clean up before you eat."

Dori picked up her wine glass. "Pour me a shot."

Grammy did what she asked. "It's about damn time you jumped him. But I think your timing was off."

"I was pushing him out of the way." She pointed to her fine coating of plaster. "I'd never- I mean, I don't do stuff like that anymore."

"If someone had been fool enough to get between me and your Grampy, I'd stop at nuthin' to get him."

"I told you it was- Never mind."

"Too bad. I liked her." Grammy pointed to the enchiladas waiting on the stove. "You gonna eat or what?"

With the tequila warming her from the inside out, Dori made a plate for Grammy. Grit was wedged into the underwire of her bra, and her arms and head itched. Anger boiled in the pit of her stomach, rising up and burning her throat. When was all of it going to stop? The investigation, Vicente, her family and now her friend and Gavin?

"Were they sleeping together?" Grammy asked.

Dori eyed the tequila and then thought that another with the Malbec would only make things worse. "Tonight was their second date. I think. I didn't ask."

"Well you could still-"

"I don't think so."

"Hell, call that girl up and explain it was an accident." Grammy thanked her for the plate. "I like her. A woman can't get through life without a comadre," Grammy said emphasizing her point with a fork. "You need one. Especially now that you got- How many ghosts running around here?"

Dori shrugged, too tired to count. If that thing hadn't acted up and she hadn't tackled Gavin to the floor, everyone might have parted ways with no hard feelings, at least on their part. She would've stewed in her own regret.

"Ay mija," Grammy said with a sigh. "You look too old for your age."

"Gee, thanks."

"You know what I mean." She patted her shoulder, and Dori's throat burned. "Take your shower and I'll make you some of your tea. Or do you think el fantasmo-"

"I doubt it."

"I could always bring Bernice back."

"I don't think so."

"She was right about him getting dangerous." Grammy paused in cutting her food. "You heading upstairs now?"

"Yeah."

She picked up her plate. "All right then. I'm coming with you."

"Get him!"

The voice startled Dori out of sleep. She lay on her stomach, her ears pounding with the blood rushing through her head. They were moving around downstairs again; their shoes scuffing against the floor and knocking into the wall. It was just as she'd heard them that night she found Vicente in the hallway.

When they moved towards the back door, she checked the time on the clock. It was 4:07 a.m. and they went silent. She should've stayed the night at Grammy's house. But no, she had to be brave.

She was about to pull the blanket up and hide when a pair of leather shoes appeared in her line of vision.

"The ceiling wasn't my fault," Vicente said.

"What the-" She struggled free of the blankets. "It just fell by itself?"

He actually backed away, holding up both hands as she sat up ready for battle. "That's just you messing in places you don't belong."

"It's my house. What the hell is in there?"

"Nothing. No one."

"Then what brought the ceiling down on me?"

Dori yanked the chain of her mica lamp. He wasn't answering. "Vicente!"

"It wasn't me. That's not me," he said roughly.

"What if there's a part of you in there?"

"So now they all know about me."

"Don't change the subject. And yes. Well sort of. I didn't tell anyone I talk to you."

"Cause that would be crazy."

"Exactly. But that's the least of our problems."

"Our problem?"

"Yes."

He lifted a shoulder and then slightly hitched his pants before sitting elegantly in the chair. "That day when I-"

She forced herself to relax, to not say anything that would give him a way out.

"I went from walking out of The US Grant to ending up in this house. I thought I was alive again and at the time I had no idea that I was..."

"Dead," she finished for him. "Maybe you need to go in there and-"

"No."

"I'm just saying from personal experience-"

"What? You went to that lady you killed and said you were sorry."

Her throat went stiff. "No."

"Well you could. I'm stuck here. I can't do shit."

Dori thought of the day she'd last walked into Kaylee's apartment. What if she'd left Kaylee in there? It was much easier to tell him how to fix his problems than face hers.

"You can go into that room and face what's in there," she said. "Maybe you don't need to know what happened to Anna. Maybe what's in that room is what's keeping you here."

Vicente flickered and then he was on his feet. He moved so fast she didn't have time to flinch or show any sign that he scared her. Half his face was lit but his eyes glittered. "You find her."

"You really didn't bust up my ceiling?" she asked.

"I just told you I didn't. What the hell more do you want?"

"I'm sorry. In my line of work, I'm used to being lied to"

The surprise on his face was almost comic. But then he went from standing over to her, to sitting back in her chair. "Who isn't?"

Dori pulled the blanket over her shoulders.

"How's your side?" he asked.

She touched it. A week ago, a mere brush would set off stinging arrows of pain. She had to press deeper to feel a twinge. "Better. Is that why you woke me up at four in the morning?"

"Time doesn't work the same for me. I need energy and-" He paused and looked her straight in the eye.

"I know."

They both then stared at the floor, awkwardly recovering from their first real argument. When they spoke it was at the same time.

"So you left your sis-"

"I wanted to tell you-"

Dori gestured to him to finish.

## San Diego, 1932

Ever since that afternoon when Vicente had left Anna in his sister's yard, the Santa Ana winds swept down from the mountains like dragon breath. Without pomade, his hair stood on end. His throat scratched with a perpetual thirst and sweat collected in the folds of his clothes.

There was no woman lying next to him to help him forget the girl he'd never even kissed. After seeing her, he wouldn't let someone like Clara put her hands on him. He never carried booze on his person, or kept it in the Penthouse.

This morning, his first waking thought was if Anna's skin tasted like candy. He rolled over the cold sheets, staring at his dim reflection in the mirror over the dresser. There was nothing more pathetic than a proud, lonely man. He'd walked into that barrio, ready to show her what she could've had. She all but laughed in his face.

He jumped out of bed, determined to fill his day with business. He ripped the seams of two shirts and nearly drove his foot through his socks in his hurry to escape his loneliness

Now riding in the back of the limousine, solitude and the early morning crowded in, giving him nowhere to hide from himself. Itching for some distraction, he glanced in the mirror he'd affixed to the wall separating him from the driver. He saw the feds tailing them two cars away as they'd been doing for months.

"Stop here," he ordered the driver.

Eli looked in his rearview mirror.

"I said here!"

"Right away, sir."

Vicente braced himself against the seat as they swerved to the right. Cars honked and delivery trucks heading down Market Street veered around them. He burst out of the door before they came to a stop.

The Model T screeched to a halt, its tail sticking out into traffic. Agent Campbell bounded out of the car, his face set with determination. Vicente rolled his shoulders back, the fight simmering in his gut.

"You need to get her," Campbell barked.

"Get who?"

Campbell was usually smart and recognized a man looking for a fight. But he stood right up to Vicente. "Miss Vazquez. She was arrested last night working for you."

Vicente almost blurted she didn't work for him. But then he remembered the dairy business was his cover. "Doing what?"

"I'm not fooling around. Do you know what those guys want to do to her?"

Vicente went cold, his face stiff with memories he didn't want in his head. "Where is she?"

"Hey there, I got what you want right here," a woman called out, her face squeezed freakishly between the bars of her cell.

Vicente walked under the lights of the city jail, his shoes tapping smartly on the concrete floor. There were two large cells reserved for the women prisoners. Unlike the men, they were usually a quiet lot. Most of them sat prone, staring at nothing.

"She must be something special," Watch Commander Sprague commented as if they were passing through a party. "Her English is even better than yours."

Vicente stared straight ahead, angry enough to take Sprague by the neck and slam his nose into the wall. Never mind that Sprague and Mr. McClemmy were close friends. He flexed his fingers as they reached the end of the corridor. He had to get Anna out first.

"Here she is," Sprague said, gesturing for the officer accompanying them to open the doors.

A former resident of jails up and down the state, Vicente felt the clanging and grating of steel doors in the pit of his stomach. He stepped inside the cell, his breath squeezing through the fear in his throat at what he might find.

If it weren't for her man's shirt and beige pants, he might not have recognized Anna. She huddled in the corner, facing the wall and knees hugging her chest. Her hair had been shorn so that he could see the back of her pale neck. Her hands were caked with dirt and blood.

He wanted to rush over and wrap his arms around her. But the cops he kept on retainer were watching. If they saw any tenderness in him, he'd be vulnerable. They needed to fear him.

He sucked in a deep breath and ordered, "Let's go."

She flinched as if he'd woken her from a deep sleep.

He stepped forward to take her arm and see if they'd done what Campbell had said. But Anna moved so fast he didn't realize she'd slapped him until he was looking over his shoulder.

"I hate you!" Her voice echoed off the cold walls.

The cops snickered and his driver moved toward the cell, ready to break Anna's arm if Vicente so much as snapped his fingers. He stopped them with a gesture to stay put.

He caught her by the forearm when she swung her hand back to land another hit. He caught her arm, locking his eyes with hers. He swallowed down the surge of rage at the sight of her swollen left eye.

"Do that again and you can stay another night," he said.

Anna tried to throw him off. He yanked her to him, the feel of her

164

whole body pressed against him made him dizzy. "Say nothing or we both spend the night here," he hissed in her ear.

"Let go of me!" His fingers sprang loose and she staggered backwards. Her good eye stared into his, hating him with all she had as she rubbed her arm where he'd held her.

"Act like a lady and you can come with me," he said for the benefit of their audience. "Or stay here. It's your choice."

He turned with deadly precision to Sprague. Sprague backed up, and his junior officer hesitantly put himself between them.

"She put up a fight," Sprague said, almost pleading.

"Remember where you are," the junior officer stammered, his fingers sneaking towards his night stick.

"Shut up, you idiot!" Sprague stepped around the officer. "Just take her and get out."

When junior's hand dropped from his nightstick, Vicente turned back to Anna. He took her arm and pulled her out into the corridor.

"Wait," the junior officer said. "He's gotta sign her out!"

Vicente held out a crisp fifty dollar bill, nearly half of what junior made in on month. The young officer snatched it before it fell to the ground.

When he climbed into the car waiting behind the jail, Anna stared straight at the divider between them and the driver. Vicente inventoried the blood on her clothes, the short hair and the shaking hands that she clenched into a tight ball in her lap.

Rubbing his stinging cheek, he rapped his knuckles on the roof and they pulled away from the curb. Even though he'd spent days twisting his guts into knots over her, he didn't know what to do with her now that she sat beside him.

"What happened?" he asked.

She didn't so much as blink.

Impatient for an answer he almost asked again when Anna quietly said, "They drove us into a ditch."

He couldn't talk as the Cadillac slid under the palm trees lining Broadway. "That's how you got the shiner?"

Still not looking at him, she shook her head. "After. They said they'd take Michael to the hospital. But they left him in the truck and I don't know if he's alive."

He looked out the window. "What did they do to you?"

"Nothing when one of the feds said I was your employee."

Campbell. Thinking of how easily he could've lost her, he automatically answered, "I'll look for Michael. I'll make sure he's taken care of."

She finally looked up at him. "Did you tip them off? You saw my place. I'm not a threat to you."

"The tip didn't come from me," he admitted. "Not directly." He remembered Campbell and Hollner had had followed him to the barrio that night. Campbell was good. He must've shadowed Vicente right up to Anna's door.

Then why did he arrest her only to have Vicente haul her out of jail?

He turned to her and recognized the doll-like mask on her face. The fight had left her. "Drop me off here," she said.

"Where do you think you're going?"

She didn't have a purse, and there had been no personal property to collect. Without a corset, or whatever women wore under their clothes, her breasts were loose in her shirt. The car bounced over the road and he looked out the window as his fingers dug into the seat. "You don't have to go back to him."

"Back to who?"

"Albert."

Anna looked at him like he was crazy, and then she laughed softly. "Albert is gone. He's been gone for years."

The joke was on him. He should've known. He had the contacts to have gotten a full dossier on her, but he'd been blinded by his emotions. "I thought he was behind-"

"I know exactly what you thought. Just drop me off. I'll take of myself."

"With what?"

"I have something set aside."

He couldn't help but ask, "What happened to Albert?"

Anna stared out her window. "He was already married. My mother died before that little secret came out. But my father had to die with the knowledge they'd made me a married man's whore."

Vicente couldn't resist and moved a hank of her clumsily shorn hair away from her face. "Their mistake doesn't make you a whore."

She blinked, stunned for a moment before she jerked away from his touch. "Those were my father's last words, not mine."

Vicente brought his hand back and rested it on the seat. "You can go back, but they've probably confiscated your operation by now. You're right. I'm responsible for this. I led them to you."

She made no move to punch or kick him. He would've welcomed it more than her blank stare, which took him back to those first days on the beach before she gave him her trust He'd taken that golden gift and flung it far. He was just as guilty as her father and mother. All those years ago, he should've waited under her window and taken her far from them.

She slapped her hand on the window separating them from the driver. "Stop here," she shouted. "I'll check into this hotel."

She'd picked one of those buck-a-night flophouses teeming with streetwalkers and drunks. Vicente decided she wasn't getting out of this car without him. "No."

"Get off me!"

He almost grinned at the tone in her voice. "Why? I won't do anything to you," he said. "Besides, I need to find your boy, right?"

He could see her thinking through her options. Anna nodded her head. "After that, I'm no longer your merchandise."

"I had to say that in front of them," he explained, about to touch her shoulder and offer her some comfort. She shrugged in dismissal.

He shook his head, staring at the tips of his shoes. For a moment, he was the kid on the beach fumbling to make her notice him. He felt the need to please her again, to earn a piece of a candy and the possibility it could just be the two of them and nothing else. Just like that, he remembered what it was like to be a boy in love.

"At least enjoy my penthouse until you can show your face back home."

She swung around, fire glittering in her good eye. He was showing off again and she wasn't buying it. They turned off 5th Avenue onto Broadway and pulled up to the hotel.

Sighing, he stepped out of the car. Vicente was aware of the doormen waiting and his driver looking up in surprise to see him holding the door open. Finally, her slim ankle appeared, and then she firmly planted her mud-caked shoe on the ground. He offered his hand, but she deliberately stood up without his help.

"I want my own room," she said. With her torn clothes and banged-up face, Anna walked like the queen through the doors into the lobby.

"He was married all that time?" Dori asked. "What a disgusting piece of filth!"

Anna and the hotel vanished. Vicente was back in Dori's bedroom, but he could still feel her hair on his fingers.

He wanted to stay in that memory and live every second of it again. Every time he came back to the present, he had this feeling that somehow, he could take over his old self and do everything different. If he could go back to that first night in her basement, he would've gotten on his knees, wrapped both arms around her legs and never let her go. He should've held her, kissed her, told her how much he loved her.

He sat there helpless as the chances he'd once had slipped away so long ago.

He heard Dori ask, "What happened to that boy who worked for her?"

"He was dead," he said, looking up at her.

Morning was coming with its gray light. "Who was he? The boy named Michael."

"Some kid whose mother took Anna in when her father died and Albert couldn't marry her."

"And so, Anna started bootlegging to support herself," Dori said as if she wanted to go back in time and shake her hand.

Pride in his Anna, with her pluck and pugnacious nature, swelled in his chest. "She took over Old Man Riley's still."

"Was her stuff any good?"

"The booze? No. It was some of the worst I ever tasted," he said, laughing. "I don't know how she made any money off it."

"Did you ever tell her that?"

"There was no time. But if I had, she would've hit me."

"Wait!" Dori jumped up and messed around with the stuff on the table by her bed. "When was she arrested? Do you know the date?"

"Why do you need to know that stuff?"

"I can look it up in the old records, and if there's an address I can find her through property records."

"If she was smart, she wouldn't have used her real address. She also wouldn't have had a record because I paid enough to make sure she wouldn't."

From the look on Dori's face, he'd offended her principles. He could feel himself fading. "But it's worth a try," he said in an attempt to reassure her.

"What if it doesn't work?" she asked. "What if I find that something terrible happened to her?"

"You'll tell me the truth."

"I know that. But what will you do?"

Her voice traveled across a long distance. He hoped she saw him smile as he was swallowed into the light.

# CHAPTER TWENTY-FOUR

Dori hesitated at the top of the stairs leading to the Local History Room. As she got dressed this morning, she realized she had no idea where Meg lived. All this time, it had been about her and her secrets.

She sighed, ashamed of her selfishness.

Maybe she should've texted or emailed Meg to get a sense of what she might come up against. Dori put on her cop face and took a few steps and then shook her head. Meg didn't deserve the cop face.

She took in a deep breath and tried to relax, but the longer she stood there, the more ridiculous she felt.

When Dori walked in, Meg remained focused on her work. "I was wondering how long it would take you to cross the threshold."

"Do you have a minute?"

Meg looked across the empty history room. She wore white gloves, carefully handling a collection of tiny bottles in a cracked leather case.

Dori managed a weak smile as she walked over to the desk and then set the bag of tea she'd picked up Halcyon. "What's this?" Meg asked.

"I'm sorry about what happened last night-" She cleared her throat. "With Gavin on the floor and everything."

"Oh. Well. Hmmm."

Dori didn't know whether to sit down and have it out, or run like hell.

"You don't owe me an apology," Meg finally said.

"But I was-" Dori stopped herself from saying, on top of him. She frantically searched for the right way to say it. "It wasn't like that. I pushed him out of the way. The ceiling came down and- I'm sorry. I'm not the kind of woman who goes after another woman's man."

"But you knew we were going out that night."

She took in a deep breath. "I did."

"And I made sure you weren't dating him."

Dori nodded her head. A high-pitched whine erupted in her ears.

"I appreciate the tea by the way," Meg said, pulling off her gloves. "But I don't think I can accept it. You haven't been completely honest with me from the very beginning."

"It's hard to tell a complete stranger that you have a ghost in your house."

Meg flinched at the word, stranger. "I don't mean that. I mean this whole charade about Anna Vazquez as your great grandmother. Your Grammy didn't know her name. You've backpedaled and you never told me about your past with Gavin."

Dori's mouth went dry.

"He told me last night," Meg said.

"Oh."

"I don't think he-" Meg paused and crossed her arms over her chest. "I've had enough dishonesty in my life. I can't have friendships with people who only tell me half the story."

Thinking of the married man Meg had upended her life to be with, Dori withered under her piercing stare.

"Thank you for the tea and um, well I-" Meg paused to search for the polite way to tell her to get the hell out.

"I understand and I-," Dori managed, grabbing the bag of tea and hurrying the long length of the room to the door before she made a bigger fool of herself.

She raced down the stairs, humiliated to think she could patch things up with a stupid bag of tea. She'd been selfish; caught up in all her issues that she walked into one wall after another. The bag exploded when she dumped it into the trash can by the door. Instead of stopping to pick up the leaves, she kept on walking.

The crew was ending their lunch break. Dori ended the call with the San Diego Police Museum. Even though Vicente hadn't told her the date of Anna's arrest, she could search between April and December 1932. For the past few days, she'd thrown herself into research, hunting down Eugenia Sorolla. She'd come up with women who weren't in National City during in the 1930's. Vicente hadn't told her Alex's last name.

The breeze swept in through the back door that she'd propped open. Gavin was due to come by to get her started on stripping paint in the hallway. She walked through the house to stretch her legs and ease the nerves in her stomach.

"Are you around?" she called out, her ears straining for some sign of Vicente. A car drove by. Two crows squawked at one another. The floor board under her weight cracked.

Even though now wasn't the best time for him to show up, she was dying to know what happened once he and Anna walked into the hotel. She wished she had the courage to return to The US Grant and see the lobby, or talk her way into the Penthouse suite.

Instead, Dori heated up water for a cup of tea that she really didn't want as Gavin's truck pulled up the drive. Her stomach shriveled into a tight ball of dread. He shut the door to his truck, talking to someone on his cell phone.

She wiped her palms down the front of her jeans, about to open the front door so he could walk in. But then he might think she was waiting for him, which she was, but not in the way one might suppose. Dori couldn't get the idea of Gavin telling Meg about their past. Had they talked over the phone or in a cozy, candlelit corner? Did they make up or was it over before it started?

Before she got caught up in that train of thought, she opened the door. Gavin stood on the porch, negotiating plumbing supplies. She held up her hand in greeting, he jerked his chin up and then asked the person on the phone about fittings.

With all of his guys working in the basement, she'd technically be alone with him. If she were 17 again, that would've been plenty of time to get what she'd wanted and then send him out the door with a grin on his face.

The microwave beeped at her. She took her cup out and then set it on the counter.

"You ready to get started?" Gavin asked, startling her.

Her face burned. "What?"

"The front room." He pointed up. "Your ceiling."

"Oh but they already cleaned it up." The crew had swept away the rubble that day she'd seen Meg. She shuddered at the raw memory.

"I thought I was stripping paint today."

"I thought you'd want to repair the big gaping hole in your ceiling."

"I can live with it for now."

His glance told her that he highly doubted it. "It's your house."

She waited for him to bring up Meg or Vicente, or that she'd dumped him in high school. But he had other things on his mind. "It would only take maybe three or four days to tear it all down and then re-plaster," he said.

"It's never just three or four days."

He lifted a shoulder. "It's not like you don't have other rooms to work on."

"Exactly."

He eyed the cup on the counter, playing with his ball cap. "You going to make your tea?"

"No, it's okay. I can reheat it later."

They walked to the hallway in relatively comfortable silence. At least they were both pretending to be comfortable.

"Wow, you look like you're prepped for surgery," he said, bending down to pick up a paint scraper. He walked over to the front corner of the hallway across from the front parlor.

"Can I start there instead?" she said, pointing to the far end of the hallway.

He looked around and realized they stood across from the front parlor. He then nodded in understanding and picked up a paint can. "Anything else happen since last night?" He started carrying it down the hall.

"No." She bent down to pick up some of the tools. As she straightened up, she caught a glimpse of movement in the front parlor. The memory of Vicente bleeding out on the rug flashed before her eyes. Dori blinked and it went away. But the chills lingered on her bare arms.

Gavin cleared his throat. "Well, that's good. I was kinda worried to be honest."

She wished he hadn't said that. "I'm good at taking care of myself."

"Let's start here in the corner and see what we've got," he said. He lightly scraped off paint only to reveal a layer of pink then blue and then a miasmic white.

"You don't secretly think I'm crazy, do you?" she asked.

He scrapped some more at the white and then gave up with a sigh. "I was hoping it wouldn't come to this."

Dori jerked back. Gavin looked over his shoulder. "You have milk paint."

She stared at him with no idea how milk paint was relevant to her question.

"You ever use a heat gun to remove paint?" he asked.

"Not yet." Dori looked at walls she had to scrape, zap and sand. Suddenly arson seemed like a perfectly viable option.

"And no, I don't think you're crazy. I saw that guy in your window myself, and then I was here with all that going on. The thing I want to know is how do you sleep here alone? It's not like you can shoot things like that."

She was going to get a headache at the pace with which Gavin switched subjects. "He doesn't scare me anymore. Plus, he might be afraid I'll sic Grammy's fake psychic on him."

He laughed and shoved the scraper in his back pocket.

"So, you believe in-" She couldn't quite use the word ghost and instead said, "-this stuff?"

"Sure. It's better than thinking that once it's over it's over."

Dori's phone buzzed in her back pocket.

"You need to take that?"

Dori sent her mom to voicemail. "It's fine."

"So how long do we have you till you go back on duty?"

Had Meg told him about the shooting, too? "Things haven't been decided."

"Were you really hurt?"

Damn it, she wished he hadn't asked. "It was serious but I'm okay."

Her phone rang again. Her mother wasn't giving up. "I need to take this in the other room," she said.

"Bad news?"

"It's my mother."

"You sound like my sister."

Dori walked down the hall towards her office. "Hi, Mom."

"Where are you?" Brenda shouted.

She held the phone away from her ear. "I'm at home."

"What are you doing there?"

"Tell me what's going on. Are you hurt?"

"Don't you care anymore?" Brenda demanded. "You sound like I'm bothering you."

She sank into her chair while her mother raged. When Brenda finally wore herself out, Dori cleared her throat. "I still don't understand what the problem is. Tell me."

Brenda sighed. "It's your grandfather's anniversary. Your brother got a frantic call from your grammy to take her the cemetery today because you didn't show up."

Her chest went cold and tight. Grampy's anniversary was next Thursday, not this Thursday. Grammy would've reminded her.

"So, did Robert take Grammy to the cemetery?" Dori asked, her voice trembling.

"Of course not. He's busy with patients while you're just at home," Brenda said.

Anger surged up hot and thick until it became hard for Dori to breathe. "Let me get this straight, Grammy called Robert who then called you to call me?"

"Yes."

"Would it have killed either of you to take her to the cemetery?"

"B-but that's your job," Brenda screeched. "I mean it's not like you're back on duty. Why are you making this our fault?"

Dori shot up to her feet, determined not to get sucked into her mother's tangled logic. "Where is Grammy?"

"At home, waiting for you."

Dori highly doubted Grammy was pining away at home.

"So, what are you going to do?" Brenda demanded.

Dori hit the end button and shoved the phone back in her pocket. She vaguely heard the men working under the house through the screaming in her head. She swept her purse strap off the back of her chair on her way through the kitchen and out the door.

Without fail, for almost a year, Dori had taken Grammy to the cemetery every week. And of all days for her to forget-

As she drove to La Vista, Dori could hardly breathe through the guilt and panic. Did she have time to go to the liquor store for Grampy's bottle of Wild Turkey? No, best to get there as fast as possible.

She made it to the gates of La Vista in exactly eight minutes.

Grammy's car was parked across two spots. A funeral was taking place just a few feet away from Grampy's crypt. When Dori spotted Grammy sitting on the bench with Richard, the weird happy guy in the cemetery office, she imagined the worst: Grammy had fallen or fainted or all of the above.

Her car started to roll back. Dori yanked the parking brake into place and then hurried out of the car, forgetting to lock the door.

"Are you okay?" she called out as she came down the stairs.

Grammy glared at her. She turned to Richard. "Thank you for sitting with me. It's time for me to go."

He eyed Dori and then his expression brightened with recognition. "Oh hey, I remember you. I found your grandma coming down those steps by herself and-"

Dori could barely register what he was saying. "I'm so sorry I'm late. Wait. Where are you going?"

Grammy stood up and walked by without a word.

"I'm sorry. I got busy with-" Damn. She realized she'd run out on Gavin. "I mean, I got caught up in stuff and-"

"I already spoke with your grandfather. I'm ready to go home."

"But-"

"If you want to talk to him, he's where he's been for the last twenty years."

"I know you're angry. At least let me apologize."

Grammy started up the stairs.

Anger flared up, burning her guilt and shame to ash. "I've been driving you here every week ever since I moved back!" The words burned her throat. "Does this one time make me the bad guy?"

"It's the time that counts," Grammy snapped over her shoulder.

"I know and I'm sorry. But I'm here, aren't I? I didn't just call my mother like Robert did."

Grammy spun around and if Dori wasn't spitting mad, she would've worried about her falling.

Never mind that there was a funeral taking place behind them, Grammy's voice shot hell and brimstone across the cemetery. "Don't pretend that you liked driving me here every week! You did it out of duty, not love!"

The priest faltered in his graveside service, and out of the corner of her eye, Dori saw the mourners turn and stare.

"Um, excuse me," Richard said, holding up finger to his lips. "There's, like, a service going on right-"

Dori hurried up the steps and moved to take Grammy's arm. "Let's take this somewhere more private."

"To hell with private!" Grammy threw her arm off. "That young man had to sit with me because you weren't here to help me with the goddamned flower vase! It fell, and I made a fool of myself over it and broke the damn flowers and got water all over my pants and now all those damn people think I'm an old lady who pees my pants!"

Dori looked down. Grammy's pants stuck to her legs. The priest raised his voice to keep the crowd's attention on the burial.

"Why didn't you call me?" Dori asked, lowering her voice. "I would've come right away."

"Because I shouldn't have to. I'm a burden as far as you're concerned."

"I never said that!"

"You didn't have to," Grammy said, her voice trembling. "You throw my gifts and my attempts to help you back in my face."

Dori's throat burned. The muscles around her mouth twitched as she fought back tears.

"You're not saying anything," Grammy said quietly. "I was the only one in the family who has supported you, defended you even though you think you're better than us."

"That's not true," Dori said, despair ripping her up inside.

"I can't even look at you right now," Grammy said before walking away.

To her shame, tears spilled over. But Dori wiped them away before anyone could see them.

If Grampy was here, he would've taken her side. He wouldn't have let Robert or Chuy get away with their shit. He would've called them out on it. Dori wouldn't be cut off by everyone, looking at their backs and wondering what terrible thing she had done to deserve it.

As the wind pushed against Dori, she swallowed the hard truth that Grampy wasn't looking over her. Vicente's love for Anna Vazquez had chained him to this world; pitting him against the impossibility of ever seeing her again.

But her grampy had moved on when he died. He must've felt he'd done everything he could to prepare Dori for life without him. Even though she wished against all sense and logic that he was here, she wasn't going to let him down. She'd let herself cry when she went to a place where no one could see. The fact was that she was on her own. People came and went, even family. No one was going to step out of thin air to take care of her.

Dori hugged herself tightly and walked to her car.

# CHAPTER TWENTY-FIVE

In the 80 years or so he'd been dead, Vicente liked to think he'd had enough time to become a wiser man. He could see where he'd gone wrong with Anna. He could even admit to himself that if he'd placed love higher than pride and ambition, he might have died a poor, old man instead of a rich, young one.

The dark hallway appeared before him. He was alone, but he didn't feel lonely. Hope fit him like a baggy suit, and he wasn't quite sure what to do with it. Dori was all he had and piece-by-piece she found crumbs of his life. Eventually, dead or alive, she would find Anna and perhaps he would know peace.

Shafts of blue light pooled on the floor. If he looked hard enough, he could almost see James McClemmy standing before the front parlor, sending him to his death. He started down the hallway, testing his mettle. He'd already lost everything. Well, mostly everything. He'd stonewalled Dori last night when all along he knew there was a part of him in that room. If he could face it, then maybe he would be free.

When he turned to the gaping doorway, he only saw an empty, pathetic room. He waited for it to appear. He then stepped into the room. Nothing happened. The walls didn't melt away; nor did the furniture reappear from the past.

"You-" He cleared his throat. "We did our best. We could've made it but-"

The rage simmered inside him. He held up his hands that were turning black like burnt wood. "I did my best," he repeated in voice that was his but raspy.

He struggled against the voice that told him he'd been betrayed; his life taken and tossed away.

A door opened in the house. Vicente leapt back, staggering in the hallway. The thing remained in the room, a dark silhouette of where he'd just stood.

He held up his hand. It was normal. He'd had no strength against what waited in there.

With relief, he recognized Dori's footsteps through the house.

Vicente appeared in the doorway to the kitchen. Dori leaned against the refrigerator, a note crumpled in her hand. Someone – not him – had left the light on. Vicente glanced at the clock over the stove. It was almost midnight.

Something was off about her, as if there was no spark. Vicente tried to think of the best way to make his presence known without startling her. Frankly, there was no way to go about it when you were dead, so he cleared his throat and stepped into the light.

"You look like hell," he said, hoping outrage would shake loose the blankness of her face. "What happened now?"

Dori didn't take the bait. Thinking it was the silent treatment, he dug down deep for something nice to say. Kindness and soft words had never been his way.

"Uh, if you want I can-"

She came towards him and he flinched as if avoiding a blow. But she walked right through him and continued up the back staircase.

Vicente found Dori in her bathroom. Bottles fell into the sink as she pawed through the cabinet over the sink. She twisted off the top and he said, "What are you doing? What the hell is wrong with you?"

Dori froze and then slowly looked up into the mirror.

"I can't do it anymore," she told him.

"Dori," was all he could say when he saw the emptiness in her reddened eyes.

She pulled in a shuddering breath. "I have to pull myself together."

He didn't dare break eye contact. Even though he didn't know what she was talking about, he said, "You're fine."

She shook her head. Her voice trembled as she struggled through her tears. "I'm losing everything that matters to me and-" Her eyelids fluttered shut. "I can't help you."

"You promised me you'd find her."

Dori tossed her head back and covered her mouth with her hand. She swallowed the pill dry. She gripped the edges of the sink, her shoulder blades pointing up sharply against her shirt.

He watched helpless as she flickered and then faded away. Vicente staggered back, scanning the now empty bathroom for her. Dori would come back. She gave him her word that she would find Anna. He knew her word was her bond, but if something happened to her-

He watched as the walls vanished. Hell was not a dark, fiery pit of suffering. It was blindingly white and limitless with a suffocating silence that pressed against his ears. He called out Dori's name but no sound came from his mouth. He called for her over and over again and then a figure appeared before him.

He yelled at it that he was here, that he was lost. It approached, and he froze when he saw a faceless woman walk by him. The light absorbed her, and then he saw he was surrounded by beings like her, moving silently around him.

Dori no longer anchored him and he was nothing more than a kite cut free from its string.

In time, he would forget everything, even Anna's face and his own name. He begged God, Jesus and the Devil to let him free. He'd give anything, do anything, for one last chance to find Anna and see the light in her eyes when she heard him say he loved her.

But none of them answered. They'd forsaken him in this netherworld where he'd eventually end up like the unblinking souls around him.

Vicente started to run. He had no idea where he was going. If there was a way in, there had to be a way out.

Faintly he heard a man over a loud speaker. He quickened his pace towards the sound as it sharpened into the voice of a conductor announcing the train from Los Angeles.

Glossy brown octagonal tiles appeared under his feet. In the distance, a door waited for him. Vicente ran faster before it disappeared and left him here forever. When he was within a few feet, he stretched out his hand. He grasped the cold brass handle. His shoulders strained as if he were pulling it open under water.

### San Diego, October 1932

He stood against the full blast of color and sound of the Santa Fe depot. Pigeons fluttered over the wood benches. Newsboys hollered the morning edition's headlines and the ground rumbled underfoot as the train appeared alongside the windows.

He hurried his pace and his men did the same. They should've been on the platform so Mr. McClemmy could see them from his private car when he arrived.

Vicente pushed through the doors and weaved through the crowd of passengers and porters and luggage carts. Mr. McClemmy's private car was glossy silver and black, and the tasseled window shades were pulled exactly half shut.

"Wait here," he ordered his men who stood sentry at the private entrance, discouraging onlookers from getting too close.

Vicente climbed up the steps, and the door was opened by a red-haired man he'd never seen before.

"This is a private car-"

"Who are you," Vicente said, stepping through the door, forcing the man back.

"What the-" the little man stumbled back but then grabbed Vicente's collar.

With his forearm, Vicente pinned him to the wall by his throat. "I asked who are you?"

"Mr. Sorrelle," Mr. McClemmy said behind him. "You haven't met Mr. Dearbourne."

Still holding the little bastard by the throat, Vicente turned to see his boss pouring himself a cup of coffee from a silver samovar while his lawyers and clerks sat frozen, staring in shock.

Vicente released the little shit. Mr. McClemmy dropped four lumps of sugar in his cup. "Apparently Mr. Dearbourne neglected to introduce himself over the telegram."

Vicente eyed his boss, taking in the bags that hung under his blue eyes. Lines had cut deep around his mouth, and his blue-black curls were silvered.

He waved his cigar at his lawyers. "I've seen enough of you today. Good day, gentlemen."

The lead lawyer looked to Dearbourne and Vicente didn't like it. They should've looked to him to confirm Mr. McClemmy's orders.

Vicente stepped forward, reclaiming his rightful place. "You heard him," he said to the lead attorney. "You can either walk or take the taxis parked outside."

The others refused to budge, waiting for their leader's next move. Vicente locked eyes with him, deliberately slowing his breath and loosening his muscles. Not that this pencil neck would get physical, but he'd learned never to be taken by surprise.

The lawyer eyed him up and down, a sneer of disgust twisting his lips to save face. He stood up and took his time buttoning his jacket. Mr. McClemmy shook his hand, wished him a good day and then said, "Dearbourne, please see them out."

They shuffled past Vicente, taking care not to look him in the eye. "You too, Dearbourne," Mr. McClemmy added. When the door was shut, Vicente walked to the samovar to pour himself a cup of coffee.

"You shouldn't be here," he said to his boss, who now sat in his leather chair near the window.

Mr. McClemmy glanced around the private car as if searching for something. "I'm going to damn prison so who the hell cares." He jiggled his knee.

"But you haven't been sentenced yet."

"Next week."

Vicente tilted his head to the chairs vacated by his legal team. "What do you have them for?"

"Exactly. Why the hell do I have any of you?"

Vicente waited for Andy to step out but then decided to sit with his boss.

"Your reports are unsatisfactory," Mr. McClemmy said, perched on the edge of his seat. "You were supposed to be looking out for things for me."

"I have. I shut down our biggest competitors."

"But not all of them."

"Look, if you shut down every operator, it's gonna be-"

Mr. McClemmy slapped him. His coffee cup flew out of his hands and landed on the rug with a thump. In an instant Vicente was on his feet, fist drawn and ready to smash the old man's face. "What the hell?" he said, spitting in his face.

Mr. McClemmy pointed his cigar in Vicente's face, his eyes cold. "Remember who I am."

"I do," Vicente said, struggling to put his fist down. "But what the hell was that for?"

"I don't trust you. I don't trust no body. So I'm here to make sure all the mice get exterminated."

"The bigger mice are gone. The smaller ones can't compete. Not with the shortages and rumors that Roosevelt's gonna give over on wine and beer."

"But I worry about my house and the damage they'll do." Mr. McClemmy fidgeted, which was unlike him. "I want Muriel to live comfortably till I come back. I want all of them gone."

A solid mass of anxiety formed in the pit of Vicente's stomach. Anna was still at the hotel. Her operation was shut down. She was no threat.

"Vince?" Mr. McClemmy called him back, watching with a dangerous gleam in his eye. "I have no need for men I can't count on."

He sat down opposite his boss. "I know. But you've been able to count on me. I've followed your orders to the letter."

"You're not afraid of me, are you?"

Vicente chose his answer carefully. "I've had nothing but respect for you, sir."

Mr. McClemmy's stare eased and a grin stretched across his face. "You remind me of a new father. Do you have something you need to tell me?"

He knew better than to be fooled by Mr. McClemmy's paternal joking. His boss had outmaneuvered the feds and the mob during Prohibition. He could order Vicente's permanent replacement as easily as he ordered bacon instead of sausage for breakfast.

"You should get one for yourself," Mr. McClemmy continued as if Vicente's pant legs weren't stained with coffee. " A wife, I mean. Just so I don't envy you."

Even though he was having trouble breathing through his nose, Vicente forced himself to smile as if enjoying his boss' father-son council. "Duly noted, sir."

Always a patient hunter, his boss let the silence stretch out. He then tapped cigar ash on the carpet. "Yes, you're the man for the job I have in mind."

Vicente set his handkerchief on the marble topped table, listening for Andy to walk in. "I thought I already had a job."

"This is something particularly sensitive."

"What do you want me to do?"

"Join me at a meeting with law enforcement."

Vicente nodded, mimicking Mr. McClemmy's now relaxed posture. "I'll make arrangements."

"It's arranged. Just you and me will finalize the last part of our agreement. Then when repeal is official, our business will be perfectly legitimate."

"I know who should accompany us."

He stared across the room, calmly smoking. "No security. No guns," he said. "Just you and me, my boy."

Vicente deliberately relaxed his shoulders. "Yes, sir. But I don't-"

Mr. McClemmy groaned as he pushed himself up to stand. "I know. You don't like the sound of it." He winked as if they hadn't nearly come to blows.

Vicente got to his feet and then followed him to the door, opening it for him as he'd been trained. "I'll be ready."

His boss' hand landed on his shoulder, the amethyst sparkling on his pinky. "Good. Because we're leaving straight away. I have to return to Los Angeles."

He looked into Vicente's eyes almost sadly. He then squeezed his shoulder before stepping out of the car.

Two men Vicente had never met before escorted him and Mr. McClemmy from the train to the hotel. They were Dearbourne's. The elevator slowed and then stopped after a slight bounce. The operator opened the door and held it as Vicente stepped out on the penthouse floor.

"Mr. Dearbourne wants you out of here and down the hall," one of them ordered.

"What's your name?" Vicente asked.

He looked puzzled. "Donny."

"Donny, you tell Dearbourne he can make the request himself."

Vicente entered the secondary bedroom. He'd always left the master bedroom for Mr. McClemmy.

He walked through the short foyer and then slipped behind the wall, reaching into his coat for his revolver. Donny and his friend lingered outside the door, their voices buzzing as to who would go deliver Vicente's message to their boss. He crossed to the armoire, reached in and pulled out the Western Field 12-gauge shotgun.

When they didn't break down the door, he walked straight to the door leading to Anna's room. Without knocking, he opened it and stepped inside.

She'd left behind the imprint of her body on top of the blankets. The brown dress with its matching feathered hat, shoes and gloves remained hanging by the dresser. Apparently, she'd taken the new shirt and pants he'd ordered for her.

He checked the bath and touched the damp towel she'd used.

Perhaps it was best she'd run out on him. By tomorrow at this time, Vicente would either be dead or turned over to the feds. He didn't want her anywhere near of this.

But the timing of her arrest and Mr. McClemmy's arrival didn't sit right with him.

Vicente listened for sounds of Dearbourne and his men. He pulled on a coat over the 12-gauge and slipped out through the service entrance to the suite, taking the stairs down into the kitchens and laundry. He paid the manager cash for the Ford truck. He was on Harbor Drive when he saw the smoke curling up through the tops of the Eucalyptus trees into the cloudless sky. He jerked the car into the wrong lane, passing the meandering truck. An oncoming car zigzagged, unsure what to do, as Vicente swung left onto 6th Street.

They were flinging buckets of water at the fire, held back by the withering heat and thick smoke. Vicente could hear the snapping wood and explosions of glass. He abandoned the truck with the motor still idling as he pushed through the crowd towards Anna's house. The fire brigade hadn't yet arrived.

He grabbed the person next to him. "Where is she?"

The man reared back as if he'd struck him. "Where the fuck is she?" Vicente shouted.

"Who? Who?"

"Anna!"

Frightened, he shook his head. Vicente shoved him out of his way and went to the next.

Ignoring a chorus of voices telling him to stop, Vicente ran down the side of the house towards the back. Heat seared through his clothes. He ripped off his jacket and held it over his face, racing through the narrow space between the house and fence.

He found the boy lying down on the back steps. Smoke curled off his pants, his feet trapped under the burning door. His back was peppered with shot gun blast. They'd used his body to make it look like the still had blown. Vicente knew because he'd used that tactic before.

He stood there, trying to calculate if she'd left the hotel in time to have made it inside the house. Or, if they grabbed her while he was on the train with Mr. McClemmy. He started for the door when he was grabbed from behind. Men held him down on the hard-packed dirt. A face came into his line of view. Andy. He yelled in his face, but Vicente couldn't hear through his own screaming. Finally, Andy stood up, pulled his flask out of the waistband of his pants and threw the contents in Vicente's face.

Vicente coughed and spluttered.

"Get up. We gotta run."

The flames now consumed the body on the steps and the smell of roasted hair and human meat reached down into Vicente's throat. Anna was in there, burned beyond recognition.

Andy yanked Vicente up to sitting. Another man stood next to him, helping him to his feet.

"Get up, compadre," Alex ordered. "If we stay here, it's all over."

Smoke licked the trees, smearing across the sun. The wind blew pieces of ash in their faces. Vicente caught his footing and stood up; Alex and Andy led him away. With each step, he went numb inside.

"Get rid of him."

Vicente's head snapped up at the sound of the old lady's voice. He was now seated at Eugenia's table in her dark kitchen, wondering how he'd ended up here. Andy stood by the door smoking. Alex was nowhere to be seen. The old lady still wore black, her hair now completely white and her face sunken from the loss of her teeth.

Eugenia placed a cup of steaming coffee in front of him. "Drink this."

"He's got no business bringing trouble to our door," the old lady screeched. "He turned his back on us-"

"Abuela, enough," Eugenia said without conviction.

"He left us. Why should we take him in and that-" She flapped her hand in Andy's direction. "That Japanese he brought with him."

Vicente thought how much she sounded like Anna's mother did on the morning they woke up on the benches. He didn't care what happened to him now. He couldn't talk or cry or feel anger at what had been done. He was just a body now that waited to die.

"Drink it," Andy said, pointing to the coffee. "This Japanese could've died saving your ass."

"You had this coming," the old lady said. "Good riddance to bad rubbish! Go to hell for all I care but don't take this family with you."

The table blurred, and he was so tired that he rested his head on the cool wood. It occurred to him to ask Andy how he'd found him. But then he thought no more.

"Vicente, wake up." He tried to open his eyes. But they wouldn't budge.

"Come on, I know you can hear me." Her cool fingers slid under his hand. "Please wake up."

He grabbed the hand hovering over his face, holding on tight so he wouldn't drift back into unconsciousness.

"You're awake. Finally." Anna pressed a wet cloth against his cheek. He opened his eyes and saw her face lit by the bedside lamp.

"You're not dead," he croaked.

"Obviously."

He doubled over coughing. She rubbed his back. When he caught his breath, her hand slipped away. He reached for her. "Don't go," he said.

"I'm not. I just have some water for you. Here."

She helped him sit up. She held the glass to his dry mouth. He felt the cool water slide down his burnt throat and through his aching chest.

"I made Andy drive us here," she said calmly. "We're safe. For now, anyway."

Vicente just stared at her, his throat squeezing tight. She actually sat next to him, her thigh pressed against him and her hand safely nestled in his. He wanted to cry with relief and admiration for her quick and matter-of-fact appraisal of the situation. A woman like Clara would've pushed him in the fire and dusted off her hands as she walked away. But Anna was here; his Anna, wiping his filthy face with a cloth. He wanted to laugh but breathing hurt like hell.

He looked around the room lit with an old oil lamp. His suit coat and shoes were missing. He sat in a narrow bed. The curtains were shut against the night. It wasn't his sister's house. He'd been moved. Right now, he could give a shit where they were. Anna was alive and this wasn't a dream.

"Thank you," he said and she took the glass away.

"I tried to clean you up while you slept-"

He grabbed her hand as she pulled away to dip the towel into the basin by the bed.

Her eyes met his and without hesitation he pulled her close to press his forehead against hers. Waiting for some sign that she didn't want him, he then angled his head to brush his lips against hers. She jolted but didn't pull away. He stayed there, silently asking for more, weaving his fingers through her hair. When her hand slid up his shoulder, he kissed her, coaxing her lips apart to taste her. He went dizzy, holding back the desperation of so many years of wanting her. She slipped her tongue between his teeth, and his hand fisted her hair.

She shoved him away. Just when he thought he'd pushed her too far, she began unbuttoning her shirt.

"Touch me," she whispered as she pulled her shirt open. "Hurry-"

He slipped his hands under her cotton undershirt and his hands filled with the heat of her skin. Her breasts were heavy and her nipples already tight beads. With a sound, he'd never heard her make, she arched into his hands. He squeezed and tasted and when he couldn't hold back, he dug his hands into the waistband of her pants, tugging them down. Anyone could walk in on them. That only made him more frantic to get to her, to finally make her his.

She unzipped them and then wiggled free. The feel of her bare skin against his sent a shock through him. The dark room filled with the sounds of their kisses and ragged breath. They both cried out and went still when she slipped him into her.

Afterward they lay facing each other, foreheads touching and her leg hitched over his hip. She kept her eyes closed, and for a moment, he thought she slept.

She grinned when he slid his hand up her spine. "That's the first time it-" Anna went quiet and her hand curled into a fist against his chest.

"It what?" he asked.

She didn't move or make a sound.

A hole started to open in his chest. "I hurt you, didn't I?"

Anna shook her head, her breath hitching. "It was the first time it felt good."

He should've felt rage at what Albert had done to her. But he kissed her and tasted her tears as if he could take her pain inside and carry it away with him. "I'm that good, huh?"

They laughed.

"Are you going to tell me what happened?" he asked.

"Michael is dead," she said. "I saw the house go up and-"

"You what?"

"I was going to run but then I thought, what if you followed me and you thought I was dead." She pressed her hand against his cheek.

Vicente held her tighter, his throat burning as he remembered the heat of the fire and the smell of smoke and flesh. He thought of the boy he'd found over the back steps. Mr. McClemmy set this up. Vicente wondered if Campbell or Hollner were in on the deal.

He released her enough so he could look her in the eye. "You and I, we need to disappear."

"I know." Her fingers flexed, tightening her hold on his shoulder. "But we're going together."

He had nothing but his burned-up clothes. He'd left the shotgun and the truck in the barrio. But none of that mattered with her in his arms. They'd grab their chance and run like hell. He kissed her. Her hands glided down his back, exploring and heating his skin. Her hip pulsed against him, and he gently rolled her onto her back, pressing her into the mattress, tasting and feeling her for what would be a lifetime of nights like this. They'd ride this out, cast off their names and all this ugliness to start new.

As they lay together, holding each other tight, she whispered, "Promise me, no matter what, we stay together."

He kissed her temple and said, "I promise. I'll never leave you behind again."

# CHAPTER TWENTY-SIX

Dori yanked open the door at the third knock.

"Are you Dori Orihuela?"

"I am."

"I'm serving you with-" The process server stepped back, her mouth dropping open with surprise as Dori came out the door. "Hey hang on there."

"I'm not going to do anything to you," Dori said, taking the papers from her. "I have to get to work and you're in my way."

On a January night, she should've worn something warmer than her leather jacket. But it and the scarf Sela gave her for Christmas were the closest things at hand when she got the call for an armed robbery outside a bank on Adams Avenue.

She tossed the papers onto the passenger seat, flicked on the headlights and pulled away from the house. She had just made a pot of tea with Melody Gardot on the iPod to celebrate that she'd finished her last Lexapro and was no longer on desk duty. Dori frowned at the waste of that beautiful dragon pearls green tea.

When she arrived at the scene, Dori breathed in the misty night air and the sense of calm of having been back on the job for almost two months. She had been free of ghosts and panic attacks and Gavin. He never asked for an explanation as to why she'd disappeared on him the day she'd fought with Grammy, and for that she was grateful. But he put Oscar on the job who said they'd be done with everything at the end of the week.

She locked the door of her car and shoved her key into her pocket. As her boots crunched over glass and grit, her life was becoming a neat, manageable package. At least that's what she told herself when she thought about the papers she left behind in the car. But mostly Vicente weighed heavily on her conscience. And Meg. Grammy, too.

Dori pushed those thoughts into a corner.

The mist hovered in the beams of the cruiser lights and she found her partner, Elliot Markle, talking with one of the paramedics.

A uniformed officer questioned a well-dressed couple. The wife held a French bulldog in her arms. As Dori walked towards her partner, she grabbed her flashlight out of her pocket and aimed it on the ground. A rhinestone earring glittered on the pavement and she marked it with a tissue. No ripped clothing, tire marks or loose bills on the ground. She peered up at the bank, noting the camera aimed at this side of the lot.

"We catch you on a date or something?' Elliot asked when Dori walked up to him.

She spotted the Starbucks cup in his hand and ignored his greeting. They had a few conversations about the shooting but things weren't the way they'd been. Although, he appeared to come out of it better than she had.

She nodded at the paramedic, with the name Jimmy Cardenas on his uniform. "Hey detective," Jimmy said.

"How's it going?" she returned in greeting and then to Elliot. "What do we have?"

Elliot sipped his latte, taking his time to answer her question. Dori kept her stare steady but uncertainty squirmed in her stomach. Even though she'd been cleared and reinstated, there were a few on the force who were testing her. But Elliot really seemed determined to keep her at arm's length.

Suddenly, she remembered what she'd once told Vicente - she'd faced bigger and badder guys than him. The macho grin on Vicente's face was so clear in her mind that she blinked and then came back to the parking lot.

Elliot cleared his throat. "Two store employees were dropping off the day's deposit bag when two guys came out of nowhere, of course, and held them at gun point." He pointed to the ground where Dori had marked the earring with tissue. She waited for him to notice it but he continued.

"The couple with the dog over there found them lying here. Didn't see the robbers, but they think they heard tires squealing and saw the girls lying in the parking lot."

Jimmy caught her attention. "Let me know when we can take her to the hospital," he said.

Dori turned to the 20-something girl sitting on the bumper of the ambulance and met defiant, black-rimmed eyes. She was trying to be tough, but she hugged herself tightly. The other victim was in the back of the ambulance with a female paramedic.

"I want to chat with them first. I'll be right there."

Jimmy nodded and then walked back to the ambulance.

The cold worked its way through her boots. But this was right where she was meant to be.

She scanned the parking lot. It was well-lit, facing a busy street in a neighborhood where people were out walking with their kids or dogs. The movie theatre across the street had enough people coming and going to deter most armed robbers.

Elliot touched her sleeve. "Ready for more?"

"Bring me up to speed."

"So, the first guy grabs-" He paused, handing his cup to Dori to hold. When she didn't take it, he put it on the ground to fish out his notepad. She refused to feel petty for playing games with him.

"He grabs Mia, the assistant manager with the cash bag," he said, after scanning his notes. "Her co-worker Yvonne gets pushed to the ground; gunman presses her face down and threatens to shoot if Mia doesn't hand over the bag."

Dori wondered when he'd pick up his latte. "How much was in the bag?"

"Eight hundred cash."

She stared across the parking lot at the tissue, picturing what had happened in her head.

"Mia drops the cash," Elliot continued. "Guy throws her down, and he and his friend run for it. Two witnesses find the girls and then call us."

"I used to make cash deposits like this when I was in high school," Dori said, eyeing the coffee by her foot. "Amazing this doesn't happen more often."

"Where did you work again?"

"Remember Suncoast Motion Picture Company? I worked at the one in Plaza Bonita."

"Yeah, I remember those stores," he said. "It'd be smarter to hire an armored truck to make the deposits with cash like that."

When she couldn't stand it any longer, Dori bent down, picked up the latte and handed it to him. "Hey, thanks," he said, genuinely surprised as if he'd completely forgotten it.

Maybe she'd been the one imagining he was playing a game. As he sipped it, she thought that a latte didn't sound too bad about right now. "They don't make enough every night to warrant an armored truck, nor do they want cash in the back safe," she explained. "Did you get a hold of the store manager?"

"He's not answering his phone. Why? What's that look about?"

Dori turned away from the girls. "The one sitting there, is that Mia?"

"Yup. The other one won't talk."

With another look at his latte, she said, "See you in a second."

"You want one?" he asked, holding up his cup. "There's a place across the street."

She grinned and nodded.

"With two sugars, right?"

"Yes, please."

He winked like it was old times. "Got it."

As she walked towards Mia, Dori nodded to the patrol cops. One raised his hand in greeting; the other one only gave a curt nod. For a fraction of a second, she wished she was at home with her slippers on her feet and a cup of dragon pearls tea in her hand and maybe Gavin's arm around her shoulders.

The image of him came out of nowhere. She nearly halted mid-stride but she recovered and pretended that the empty feeling in her chest was from the cold.

"Hi, I'm Detective Orihuela. How are you holding up?" Dori said, holding her hand out to Mia.

"Are they taking Yvonne to the hospital or what?" Mia asked, eyeing her from head to toe and back before deciding to take her hand. "She drove, and my car's back at the mall."

"Did you call your parents?"

"They're in Vegas."

"Is there anyone you can call for a ride?"

Mia hesitated and then glanced away as if she were looking for someone. "My boyfriend."

Dori sat on the bumper next to her. "Have you called him yet?"

"No."

"You can if you don't mind waiting a little longer."

"For what?" She edged away.

"For you to tell me who jacked you guys."

"I saw you talking to your partner. Didn't he tell you?"

Dori stayed quiet and noted that Mia was wearing two dangly earrings.

"We were depositing the cash and checks," Mia finally said. "We closed up and drove over here. These two dudes came out of nowhere, grabbed me and then threw her-"

Her voice cracked, and she blinked rapidly to keep the tears at bay.

Dori held out a tissue from the small package she kept in her pocket. "Take your time, okay?"

Irritated by the gesture, Mia snatched it out of Dori's hand. She was careful not to smudge her make-up.

"Keep going. You're doing fine."

"I had the deposit bag, and they said if I didn't give it over, they'd shoot her," Mia continued. "Aren't you going to write any of this down?"

"I will. I just want to listen to what you've got to say."

"Whatever. I have class tomorrow and she needs to see a doctor."

"Yvonne was on the ground, and you had the deposit bag," Dori prompted, checking the girl's tights for rips and tears from having been on the ground.

"He held a gun to her head. I thought he was going to shoot her and I froze. The other guy, he grabbed my hair, and that's when I thought they were going to do it. The bag just fell and he took it and then he pointed the gun at me and told me to get on the ground. Then I heard them run and drive away."

"Where did they drive off?"

"I didn't look."

"Can you show me where you were standing?"

Mia slid off the bumper and took Dori to the spot where she'd found the earring and pointed.

"Is that yours?" Dori asked, gesturing to the earring.

Mia shook her head.

"Is it Yvonne's?"

"I don't know," she said, her voice was high and tight. She hugged herself, and Dori could see her knuckles turning white.

Elliot was still at the coffeehouse across the street, so Dori waved Jimmy over. "Check and see if this earring belongs to Yvonne."

"Sure thing." He looked down at it and then took off.

Dori looked over at Mia. "You want a coffee or something?"

"What? No."

"Has this thing happened before?"

"To me?"

"To anyone at the store or the mall."

"No."

"Were one of the guys wearing this earring?"

Mia's mouth opened and then she shut it and shook her head.

Dori repressed a grin as the whole thing started to take shape in her mind. She let Mia stew in the silence, wondering how long it would take for the girl to come out with it.

Jimmy came back. "The other girl isn't missing an earring."

Dori looked at Mia. "Guess we'll have to test it and find our guys that way."

Mia's face stiffened with fear.

"Call your boyfriend," Dori said.

"Why?"

"Unless you have some reason you want me to drive you home."

"Here you go," Elliot said, returning with the coffee. "How you holding up, Mia?"

Mia stared down at the earring, her jaw clenched tight. Elliot raised his eyebrow at Dori, but she gave nothing away.

192

"So, the manager called me," Elliot said. "He's on the way over but the store has been having problems balancing their drawers with the cash."

Dori then asked, "You know anything about that Mia?"

She came home the next morning at 7:30, confident that as long as there were stupid people in the world she would always have a job. She should've been crawling on her hands and knees from exhaustion, but she still rode the high of having made two arrests. Elliot was a bit warmer. They had a little ways to go but her life was right back where she'd left off.

"That's a rather satisfied look on your face."

Dori stopped and then realized it was Meg standing up from the top step and dusting off the back of her skirt. Two cups stood next to her purse.

"How long have you been waiting here?"

"Maybe five minutes." Meg opened her arms for a hug, and Dori realized how much she'd missed her.

"Sorry, I've been working since ten thirty last night."

"I was hoping it was something more illicit than that," Meg teased as if months hadn't passed since the last time they'd talked.

"Is that for me?" Dori asked.

"It's tea. I figured if you were working or doing more stimulating things, you needed something soothing."

"Thanks, Meg." She didn't know if she should hug her or just sit down. "I'm sorry for-"

Meg held out her hand. "Actually, I should apologize. I was embarrassed more than hurt."

"You were right about me being dishonest. I was pretty messed up but it doesn't make it right."

"Come sit. I've been home for the holiday and well, I've been meaning to give you something."

Feeling nervous, Dori sat down on the step next to Meg, breathing in the morning air perfumed by her neighbor's juniper trees. She allowed the moment to be simple: the heat of her cup in her hands and her friend sitting next to her.

"You don't need to give me anything."

"So, did justice triumph or can you not talk about work?"

"It triumphed all right, but frankly, it was so easy it's almost embarrassing."

"How so?"

"This girl was stealing from her store with her boyfriend. They staged a robbery and threatened her coworker, but the boyfriend's earring fell off at the scene. So, when he showed up at the station to pick up the girlfriend, they broke like that."

Dori thought again how much Mia kind of reminded her of her teenaged self, except she had never been that ruthless. For eight hundred cash, Mia had cruelly set up an innocent girl so her whole scheme would look authentic.

"You like your work again?"

"I never stopped liking it, I just-" Dori shrugged, not wanting to think about the unraveling mess she'd been when they first met. That period in her life made her more compassionate, but it also made her grateful to be back to normal. "Let's just say I took a detour."

Meg nodded.

"So, what's up?" Dori asked.

"You mean why am I sitting on your porch after months of not talking to you?"

Dori nodded.

Meg took in a deep breath, as if debating what to say. Dori braced herself for it. "I found Anna Vazquez."

A little earthquake shook her at the sound of that name. She'd given up the search after that night she started her medication. Guilt and all sorts of feelings she couldn't name kept her from seeking out Vicente. The house had gone completely quiet. No more replays of the scene downstairs, or his sudden appearances that she'd once looked forward to.

And yet, she'd wondered what happened after he got Anna out of jail. But then she'd snuff out her curiosity. What did it matter? She knew the end to his story and there was no going back to change things.

"And?"

"She's dead."

"When?"

"Would you believe she died four days ago?"

Feeling slightly nauseous, Dori set the cup down between her feet. "Are you sure it's the right one?"

"I did my cross referencing, using the dates and names you gave me. It was the same woman, except her married name was Campbell." Meg handed her a manila file folder. Neon colored tabs fluttered in the slight breeze.

Dori's hands were numb as she flipped it open and saw that Meg had found Anna's New Mexico birth certificate from 1911, her parent's death certificates, her marriage certificate and finally, her obituary. Anna lived to be 101 years old and would be buried next week from today at La Vista Cemetery. Chills radiated from the top of her scalp down through her body.

"I can't believe you found all of this."

"There's more." Meg handed her another folder. "This is from David."

Dori took the folder and opened it. It was a ledger page and next to the date, April 15, 1932 was the bold signature Vincent Sorelle. He'd signed into the Penthouse. She covered her mouth, the page shaking in her hand.

Vicente's signature went blurry. She remembered the desperation in his voice that last night. He'd come so close to begging but she'd still turned her back on him.

Meg held out another tissue in Dori's face. "Thank you," she said, carefully setting the folder down between them.

"It all matched up, and once I started looking, I found her," Meg said. "Read the interview with her."

"What interview?"

Meg reached down and opened the file. She handed Dori a photocopied news story from 1985. Three Old Town National City women had been crowned barrio queens and profiled about the old days. Anna stared straight into the camera, her lips touched with a serene, regal grace that Vicente had described so well. She had been in her seventies, but she looked ten years younger.

"Well then, I'll leave you to it," Meg said, getting up.

Dori grabbed her arm. "You don't know what this means to me."

Meg looked down at the ground as if embarrassed.

"How about dinner? My treat," Dori offered.

"There's no need to pay me."

"Who said I was paying you?"

"Let's do lunch after Anna's funeral. You, me and Grammy will toast to her long life."

Dori's eyes stung.

Meg smiled. "But dinner tonight would be a good start."

They set a time to meet at Café La Maze, hugged extra tight and then Meg walked to her car. Dori stayed on the step, reading the article. She'd married Rick Campbell, a former federal agent, on August 16, 1933. She flipped back to the obituary. He'd died in 1982, and they had three sons and a daughter. They had lost one son to the Korean War.

She almost went to the ledger page, wanting to trace his name with her finger. But the guilt hovered and Dori walked into the house on stiff, cold feet. She paused in the doorway, staring at the dark butler's pantry where Vicente had materialized out of thin air. She owed him the truth.

"Vicente?" Her voice sounded too loud in the kitchen. "Vicente? I found her."

Something snapped in the wall upstairs. Dori hurried up the servant's staircase, clutching her file that contained proof of his and Anna's life.

The upstairs hallway was just as she'd left it: lights off and doors closed. "Vicente, she lived."

He didn't even make a cold spot.

"Where are you?"

Dori waited until she was certain he wasn't going to step out of the walls or tap her on the shoulder. She leaned on the banister, feeling as if she'd lost her best friend. It wasn't right - much less normal - to think of him that way, but there it was. If she'd moved faster, maybe hadn't fought with Meg, she might have shared the contents of the file in her hand before he'd disappeared.

She jumped when a banging noise rang through the house. "Is that you?"

The knocking sounded again followed by Oscar, Gavin's foreman, calling her name. Dori closed her eyes and straightened her spine. She told herself to accept it for what it was. As she walked down the stairs, towards the smell of drying paint in the hallway, she left behind the promise she'd made. Maybe he was at rest and now it was time to move on. This would be a memory - a fantastic, weird one - but it would belong to a chapter that had made her stronger.

The foreman knocked again, and she hurried to open the door.

Standing next to Oscar, her mother's face popped out from behind a potted tree.

"Wow you look great but can I just say that I was hoping you'd quit?"

# CHAPTER TWENTY-SEVEN

Brenda's greeting was like a smack in the face.

Oscar took a step back. "Just wanted to say hi," he said. "We'll get started."

"Thanks Oscar," Dori said. "There are sodas and snacks up here if you guys need anything."

He waved, already at the other side of the deck.

"Hey mom, what are you doing here?"

"May I come in?"

Dori hesitated but stepped aside to let her in. "Perfect timing," she said. "I just got back from my shift."

"Do you have to work again tonight?"

She shook her head, wary of her mother's cheery attitude. "I go back on Tuesday."

Brenda tried to set the plant on the table but it scraped the ceiling. She placed it on the floor and then stood, not sure if she should sit down. "It looks like the house is coming along."

"They're almost done with some painting and plastering. I'm getting the wood refinished in a couple of months."

"Oh, that's good."

They stood there, not knowing what else to say.

"So, do you want-"

"I just came by to-"

They both paused and then told each other, "You go first."

Dori gestured for Brenda to speak.

"I wanted to apologize for the last time we spoke," she said, gripping her hands together. "Cleve has been talking to me about it all this time and well I..." Brenda's voice shuddered and then drifted away.

Not knowing what was safe to say, Dori asked, "Do you want to see the house?"

"You're not mad at me?"

"Not anymore," she said, somewhat surprised that she actually meant it. "I was hurt and uh, disappointed but I-" She then placed her fists on her hips. "What do you mean you wish I quit?"

Brenda dropped down on the chair. Dori braced herself for an outburst, but instead her mother cleared her throat and said, "I thought you'd quit everything. The police and the house. I guess I-" She looked down at her hands.

"You guess what?"

"I thought that you looked so defeated that I- Well maybe for the first time, you would need me."

Dori's insides got all shaky as she went about the business of making tea. Her mother had been almost gleeful that day they met for lunch. Is that what she'd wanted all this time, for Dori to get some kind of comeuppance? But for what?

She set down two cups and then took a seat.

"Ever since you could walk, I never felt like you needed me," Brenda said, breaking their silence. "And so, when you were in the hospital with the whole-" She pointed at Dori's side. "I thought you might need me and well, you didn't. You were so together and once again, I didn't know what to do."

Dori tried to sort it out in her head. The only response she came up with was, "I wasn't together if that's any consolation."

Brenda's chin shot up. "That's not what I meant."

"I've been seeing a therapist since I was in the hospital." She then detailed her panic attacks, the fear she'd lost her mind and finally, the meeting with David, Kaylee's cousin.

She paused, wanting her mom to feel the weight of her burdens. "I just finished my prescription for antidepressants and I'm not sure I'm ready to stop seeing my therapist."

Brenda blinked four times and then on a long sigh said, "Fuck."

"Mom!"

"Cleve had a feeling and I- What kind of mother am I that I was so blind?" Brenda shrank in her seat. Dori waited with her fists clenched for her mother to turn it all around on her and make it her fault.

"You three kids were the best things that came out of my marriage to your father. I went about a lot of things the wrong way and I-" Brenda shook her head. "I realize that I was so caught in my own stuff that I wasn't there for you guys. It's my fault that we're all so broken."

Dori wished she had something stronger than tea as she entered strange new territory with her mother. "Do you regret marrying dad?" And having us, she thought to herself.

Brenda titled her head and said with a note of surprise. "No. I had a-What do you call it? An ephemera?"

"Epiphany."

"You were always so good with words," she muttered. "Yes, one of those. If I hadn't married your father, I wouldn't have had you kids. And then, if it hadn't been for Robbie's wedding, I wouldn't have had that terrible fight with your father and I wouldn't have left and then found Cleve."

Brenda sat back, daring Dori to debate her logic.

"Nothing is wasted," Brenda continued. "Not even the bad stuff. Actually, I think we really need the bad stuff. It's like plant fertilizer."

Dori stared at the person who looked like her mother, but sure as hell didn't sound like the woman she'd known her whole life.

"Anyway, I got you something," Brenda said, pointing to the plant in case Dori missed it.

"Thank you." Dori peered down at the clay pot. It was in a swirling pattern of red, blue and purple. There was writing etched into the side.

Brenda squirmed with cautious pleasure. "You like it? You don't think it's too much?"

"What does it say," Dori said, moving closer to read the inscription. May your home always be too small to hold all of your friends.

"I took a pottery class and I made it as your Christmas gift."

Dori laid her fingers on the writing. They had only talked on the phone during Christmas. She'd spent it in New York with Sela.

"Well? What do you think?" Brenda asked. "It's okay if you don't like it. I could always take it home."

"I won't let you do that. I really like it. Thank you."

"So, we're good?" Brenda asked.

"Of course."

"Oh that's-" Brenda blinked and then pointed to the kettle. "The water's boiling."

Dori hurried over and made them a pot of peach vanilla tea. "Thank you for the gift. I'm going to put it in the front hallway." She slid the sugar bowl towards her mom.

Brenda used the silver tongs to pull out two cubes of sugar. Her hands shook ever so slightly. She sucked in her breath. "I'm glad you stuck with your career and this house. I hope we can be friends."

Dori sat back and sipped her tea, seeing her mother differently after all these years. "Me, too."

Dori pulled as close to the backyard as she could. Today was the first day without Gavin's crew. The house was lonely without them and Grammy. But the landscape team she found was now working behind the house.

Clouds created a lavender and pink sky. Dori stared up at them, smelling her neighbor's laundry. She sighed, thinking of the old dramas now resolved and the new drama she faced. She finally remembered the papers she'd been served with the other night and read them. The chola she'd taken down at the cemetery was suing for physical damages. Unlike a few weeks ago, a dart of anxiety didn't pierce her chest. She paused, staring up at the clouds moving across the sky, dissolving and then reforming.

Dori would hire an attorney and then it would be just a matter of time and money which she would've spent on the house. As she opened the back door of her car to unload her haul, she decided to focus on how she'd carry all this stuff to the back yard.

She'd planned to leave Home Depot with some houseplants and a welcome mat for the door. Rather than make a martyr of herself, she carried two rose bushes to the back yard and ask one of the men to help her with the rest.

The air was thick with the tang of fresh cut grass and lawnmower gas. The dead vines that had once clung to the brick wall were tossed into a pile. One of the gardeners dug out ancient hedges that were nothing more than skeletal sticks.

The trio of workers looked up at her. One whistled to his boss who fought a lawnmower through the thick, overgrown grass. He cut the motor and walked over to her.

"We have a lot of work."

"We do." She held out her hand and he shook his head, showing his dirty hands. Dori insisted and with a smile, he obliged her.

He pointed to the rose bushes she'd set on either side of her. "You want these in?"

"Yes, and there's more in my car."

He called over one of his guys. "We clean up first and then plants."

"Sounds like a plan. Mind if I help?"

"Sure. But give us an hour to clear up."

"Thanks."

She walked with the guy to the car, and his eyebrows shot up when he saw the potted orange and pink roses, trellised jasmines, gardenias, purple princess flower and twin, topiaried rosemary shaped into neat balls. At least she'd shown some restraint by not bringing home the bird bath and statue of St. Francis of Assisi. He would've looked great next to the brick wall in the shade of the jasmine. Then again, she had till the spring when the morning air would be saturated with its sweet smell.

They carried everything out back and Dori thought how she could prop open her back door and look out at the garden from her home office. She stood there, seeing the jasmine draped over the brick like a shawl and the roses blooming in colors like sunsets over the ocean. Some fruit trees would look good at the back where there was full sun, with a vegetable garden box filled with healthy green tomato plants, beans and zucchini.

"There you are," Gavin said behind her.

She blinked and the garden was once again a small jungle of weeds with a giant pine tree that needed a trim two decades ago.

"Doing some gardening?" Gavin asked, now standing beside her.

She fought the urge to squirm. "Trying. The cleanup is taking longer than I thought."

He cleared his throat and then stuck his hands in his pockets. "Well, it looks like we're done."

"You did a great job."

"We try."

She had to finish things with Gavin on the right foot. "I kinda blew our deal, didn't I?"

"You fed us."

"Yeah but-"

"Don't worry about it." He pulled an envelope out of his back pocket. "Here, I brought this for you."

"Thanks." The envelope was still warm.

"What are you doing with those old bricks?" he asked, pointing to the pile in the back corner. "You could get some good money for them."

"Do you want them?"

He looked at her and their eyes met. "Serious?"

"Sure."

"Thanks. Can I take a look?" Gavin was already walking across the yard.

"Of course." She followed him.

He bent down and inspected what looked like a broken-up heap of bricks. "I bet this was the incinerator. People burned their trash outside in the old days."

"What do you think you'll use it for?"

"I might pave the patio behind the Mission Hills house," he said, pushing against a small column. It easily gave way and landed with a thump.

"Sorry about that," he said, tearing up weeds to get to the smaller pieces lodged in the dirt.

She edged away from the pincher bugs racing over the exposed dirt. "No problem."

"Hold on. Here's something interesting." He pried a bottle loose from the dirt. "Cool."

She smiled at the wide-eyed wonder in his eyes as he held it to the light. "It's like playing archeologist," she said.

"Ask the guys if they have some small shovels."

She did a double take at his commandeering tone, but then did what he asked.

By the time she returned with a garden shovel, Gavin had a small pile of buttons, two glass bottles and rusted sewing scissors. She bent down. "Here you go."

"Thanks." His eyes met hers but then he quickly looked away. Something fluttered in her chest. When he bent down to dig, she watched him with interest while a part of her secretly hoped he'd ask her to dinner again. Meg had said they weren't dating.

The shovel scraped against something hard. She peered over his shoulder and when she saw the glimmer of bone through the dirt, she grabbed his arm, stopping him. "Wait a second," she said, her fingers stiffening with cold. "Let me try."

He handed her the shovel and she nudged him aside. With her trembling fingers, she carefully brushed away the dirt. When the surface was clean, she rested her hand on it, knowing deep in her gut what it was and who it had belonged to.

"It's probably just a dog or cat," Gavin said.

Before she could call the cops, she had to make sure. She carefully dug around the bone, careful not to nick or scratch it. Gavin started to push away the pile of loose dirt.

"No, don't touch it," she said.

He paused, and she felt him waiting for her to look at him. When she did, he wasn't mocking or doubtful. "What are you thinking? That it's him?" Gavin tilted his head towards the upstairs window.

"I want to be certain, and if there's evidence, we have to be careful with it."

"Okay. What do you want me to do?"

"Can you take photos or a video on your phone?"

"Sure."

He stood up and aimed his phone over her shoulder. It took her a moment to realize he was taking this seriously; he never once questioned her or teased her.

Dori returned to digging. She tried to detach herself; she told herself this was evidence, not a human being, especially one whom she'd abandoned. But she had to pause momentarily to breathe through the tightness in her throat. Finally, she revealed the top of his skull.

She sat back on her haunches, her body heavy with loss. She looked up at the house. She silently told Vicente how sorry she was that this had happened to him. But the windows stared blankly down at her.

Gavin eased down to his haunches and put his arm around her shoulders. Dori clenched her jaw to keep it together.

"I got it all on video," he said quietly.

When she could speak, Dori replied, "Now, we call the cops."

# CHAPTER TWENTY-EIGHT

### Bonita, October 1932

For the first day of the rest of his life, Vicente looked like hell. But he never felt more alive watching Anna brush her hair with her fingers.

"I should've taken the dress," she said, meeting his smile in the reflection of the mirror.

"They'll think you beat me up."

"Good," she said and walked out of the mirror's reflection and closed the bedroom door behind her.

After they calmed down last night, Anna explained how she used the lonely, red-tiled bungalow as a hiding spot. The garage was packed with bottles of whiskey.

"We could take a few and sell them," she'd said, sliding her arm under her pillow as they lay in bed. "We'd have more than enough to get settled."

He shook his head. "I want to be free of all this."

"You say that now."

"I mean it. If we're getting a second chance, let's do it right."

She'd smiled at him like he was a foolish child, but said nothing more.

Vicente smelled like an ashtray, but he put on the jacket that Andy tried to clean when he'd been unconscious. He smiled at the rumpled, narrow bed as he tugged the cuffs of his shirt down so the links would show as his tailor had once instructed. He'd like to stay here and make love with her in every room of the house. But he had her and Andy to protect. Mr. McClemmy had to return to Los Angeles for his sentencing. If they could get across the border into Yuma, they would be far enough away. For a while.

His face brightened when he found her in the living room. "I'm hungry but not for-" His good cheer popped when he saw Mr. McClemmy sitting in the chair by the door. Through the sheer curtains in the huge window, he could see the Cadillac and two Fords blocking the drive.

"Morning, Vince," Mr. McClemmy said, uncrossing his legs. "Your girl is charming."

Vicente turned away from Mr. McClemmy to Anna. Unlike the girl she'd been, she stared daggers at his boss, clutching a pillow in her lap like it was his throat.

"But we have to go, my dear," Mr. McClemmy said to Anna, standing up.

Vicente smoothed his hands down the front of his jacket, tugging it slightly to straighten the lines. He had to get her out of here. "I'll see you later, sweetheart," he said, keeping his voice casual. He bussed her cheek and slipped the money into her hand.

She jolted back, shocked to find the twenties crammed in her hand. "Where are you going?"

"On an errand," Mr. McClemmy said, his voice strained. "We leave now, Vince."

Anna asked in Spanish, "What the hell is going on?"

"I'll meet you in the car, sir," Vicente said, grabbing her arm roughly and pulling her towards kitchen where there was a back door. Anna locked her knees, but when he pinched her, she leapt forward.

"Don't wait for me here," he said in Spanish.

"Where are you going?"

He heard Mr. McClemmy open the front door, calling to his men outside.

Vicente lowered his voice. "You're getting out of here and not going home. Understand me?"

"What about you?"

His heart raced painfully. Instinct told him to run with her now. If he hadn't left the 12-gauge in the Ford truck, they might get away. Then again, if he started shooting, they would too and he couldn't risk her in that way.

But he'd put two hundred cash in her hand. She'd have enough. "I'll find you and then put a ring on your finger and never look back."

"But how will you-"

"I found you once. I'll do it again."

Someone moved by the kitchen window. Vicente jerked her behind him. It was Andy who appeared in the door. They locked eyes. Andy wasn't in his butler's get up. He looked like any Japanese farmer who got up and dressed for work.

With no guarantees, Vicente shoved her forward as Andy opened the door, reaching for her. "I'll take her," Andy said. "Go."

Anna spun around, betrayal burning in her eyes. She looked ready to fight and Vicente would keep this image of her with him until he saw her again.

He hoped she'd understand as men tramped through the door. If he ran off with them, Mr. McClemmy would kill them all. With Andy, she had a chance.

Vicente turned his back on her and Andy, stepping into the living room to give them time. "Let's go."

"Where is she?" Mr. McClemmy eyed him, teetering on the verge of sending his men after her.

"Going back to her husband," Vicente said with a shrug.

Mr. McClemmy smiled and shook his head. "You won't have to worry about him," he said, putting his arm around Vicente's shoulders as they walked out into the cool morning. It smelled sweet and wet.

"You're doing me one helluva favor," Mr. McClemmy said.

Vicente stepped into the back of the Cadillac, his hands shaking. He hid them in the folds of his coat. His boss slipped in, smiling and eager as if they were going to a party.

"What kind of favor?" Vicente asked.

The driver shut the door.

"I need you to turn yourself into the authorities. I know it's lousy, but you'll do a bit of time and then have a job when you come out."

"That's it?"

Mr. McClemmy rapped his fist on the window separating them from the driver. The car lurched forward. "That's it, Vince. Piece of cake."

They turned onto Sweetwater Road, heading west to National City. As his boss talked about how he'd spring for the appeal, betrayal and relief warred within Vicente. Why was he going in? Why not someone else further down the food chain?

He'd been replaced by Dearbourne. That was clear enough. Vicente didn't know what to think. Had he done right to give Anna over to Andy? How did Mr. McClemmy know to find them here? Had Andy betrayed them?

There was nowhere for him to go, but wherever this car took him. Vicente closed his eyes and brought her face to his mind. He saw Anna smiling at him, her hair spread over the pillow. The vision changed and then she glared at him, Andy behind her waiting. If she was angry, she would survive. The twisting in his chest loosened, and he knew he made the right decision. Vicente opened his eyes and saw the farms rolling by as they sped out of the country.

He could face anything as long as she was safe.

The road faded and Vicente and his dark silhouette stood side by side, staring at their reflections in the window. Dori found him. He fought hard not to think about the last thing he'd seen that last morning of his life; the blue sky filtered through the pine tree. As he bled into the dirt, he pictured Anna and told her in his mind how much he loved her; how hard he'd fought to stay alive as they beat him. He lived just long enough to remember they stripped the clothes off his body. He'd passed out before they burned him.

The Shadow from the front parlor stood next to him, whispering dark, angry things at him.

The yard had now grown dark and the cops were switching on giant floodlights as they dug out what was left of him. He saw someone offer Dori a cup, and she shook her head, refusing it.

Despair draped over him, threatening to suffocate him with the pain that he'd failed Anna, possibly shoved her into the arms of the enemy. Pride was what killed him. He'd wanted to be the big man and save her and come out on top. But for all he knew, after they'd killed him, hacked his body and burned it in the incinerator, they could have easily slit her throat.

He turned to the shadow and it inched towards him. He felt it merging with him and then he willed them to fade away from the window and float in the light. This time he decided they'd never come back. If the wakefulness started, he'd just let it go and stay in the light where the memories couldn't find him. He placed his hand on the window, his finger over Dori as if giving her a benediction. Of course, she'd left him. She had a life and a future. He couldn't blame her, and no matter where she went and who she ended up with, he wished her well as the silence closed in on him.

# CHAPTER TWENTY-NINE

They buried Anna Vazquez Campbell next to her husband at the topmost point of La Vista Memorial Park. Dori could see her grampy's mausoleum and the thin strip of ocean in the distance.

Three generations of Anna's family crowded around the pink-and-gold coffin loaded with white roses and gardenias. Photos of her husband, Rick, and her comadres, all who had gone before her, were framed and displayed in places of honor on easels.

From the eulogies given by her grandchildren and the surviving children of her life-long friends, Anna had lived a good life. They shared her story of having been the last surviving child of her parents, of coming to National City from Anthony, New Mexico, and laughingly, of how her husband had arrested her for bootlegging. From what Vicente had told Dori, it all matched up. Except for his part in her life; Anna had kept him secret.

Dori's throat burned thinking of Vicente, who had imprisoned himself in her house, terrified that he'd failed Anna. He shouldn't have feared. Anna had been loved.

She searched the crowd for Anna herself. Instead she held her breath when she spotted a Japanese family in attendance. Goose bumps spread over her arms. She knew deep in her gut that they were Andy Munemitsu's.

When the last speaker stepped back into the crowd, the young priest asked if anyone had memories to share. Just as enough silence indicated they were ready to leave, there was a buzzing at the front row where Anna's children sat.

Dori craned her neck to get a better look. Two younger men helped an old gentleman stand. When she saw the way, his white hair swept up off his forehead, her whole body tingled with recognition.

The priest watched respectfully as the old gentleman, dressed in a gray zoot suit with a white carnation pinned to his lapel, bent over his mother's coffin. He whispered something only she could hear and then kissed the place where her cheek would be. He then turned to the crowd, thanking them for coming.

Dori should've been shocked. But a strange calm settled over her. When she saw his face and heard his voice, of course he looked and sounded like an older version of his father.

He held up a flask to toast his mother and Dori laughed out loud. Several people turned in her direction. She pressed her fist against her mouth, trying to stop the tears. Meg put her arm around her shoulders and that only made it harder not to cry.

The funeral slowly broke apart. Without thinking, Dori started for the knot of people surrounding the family. She vaguely heard Meg ask what she was doing, but kept moving in case she came to her senses and chickened out.

"Excuse me," she repeated like a mantra as she wound her way deeper into the crowd.

She found Vicente's son shaking hands and thanking people for coming. One of his grandsons held his silver flask.

Dori walked right up to him, ignoring the line of mourners waiting to greet him. He looked at her with surprise, taking in her gaping mouth and hair blowing crazily in the wind.

"Hello," he said.

She opened her mouth and then shut it before she blurted out everything she knew. "Hi," she finally said just as her silent staring got awkward.

"How do you know my mother?"

Dori's mind went blank and then she heard herself saying, "I- I'm here for my grandmother. She's sick."

"Oh, and who is your grandmother?"

"Azucena Orihuela."

He smiled politely. "Oh, I'm so sorry. Please send her my wishes for better health."

"I'm sorry for your loss," Dori said, unable to tear herself away. "Your mother seemed like a very special woman."

He took the hands of the woman standing next to her and nodded at Dori's comment.

"I'm Dori," she said, thrusting her hand at him.

The crowd was starting to notice that something strange was happening. He glared at her, and the old lady gave her that look that Dori was muscling in on her man.

"Ceferino Campbell," he said, more puzzled than anything. He looked to his grandson to get rid of her.

"Did you know Vicente Sorolla?" Dori asked.

His face went blank. He lifted his chin and looked down his nose as his father had often done to her. "Who are you, and what do you want?"

"No one. I mean I-"

The grandson moved towards her and she held up her hands in defense. "Sorry, I shouldn't have- Excuse me."

Dori quickly turned on her heel and nearly slammed into a woman using a walker. She wormed her way out of the crowd, walking as fast as she could without running. As she stepped on headstones and nearly twisted her ankle on a plastic floral arrangement, the stares of the mourners clung to her back.

Meg caught up with Dori at her green Fiat parked at the base of the hill. "What on earth did you say to him?"

"Let's go. I'll tell you in the car."

The Fiat beeped when Meg unlocked the doors. They ducked in and before Dori clicked her seat belt, the tiny car buzzed out of the cemetery.

"I got his name," Dori said, still breathless from her flight. She rubbed her arms, pebbled with chills. "He's Vicente's son. He looks just like him."

"How do you know?"

"Oh. I uh-" For a moment, Dori considered trying to skirt around the truth about Vicente.

"Never mind. It doesn't matter," Meg said, disappointed.

"Let's drive to the tidelands. I think I'll have the guts to tell you by the time we get there."

As they drove, Dori thought how she could, for lack of a better word, resurrect Vicente. Maybe she could find a real psychic. But then Grammy's friend hadn't seen him when he'd literally stood in her face.

All kinds of crazy ideas went through her head. Perhaps she could find out where Ceferino lived and write him a letter. Or, maybe she could invite him to the house and see if Vicente would reappear.

Meg took them through the old Westside barrio into the marina. They pulled into a small park where the Sweetwater River emptied into the bay. The wind pushed against the door as Dori stepped out of the Fiat. She stood at the edge of the rocks that tumbled down into the gray green water. Dori closed her eyes, picturing Vicente and Anna on the sand, way back before this land had been paved and fenced in.

This is where it all ends, Vicente had said to her.

Dori opened her eyes when she heard Meg walk to stand next to her. She watched a sailboat bob in the choppy water. Maybe Vicente had disappeared because Anna had come for him. He might already know.

She uncurled her fists and let her arms fall at her sides. "I'm telling you this because you seem pretty open minded."

Meg wisely stayed silent as Dori told her about the night Vicente greeted her at the kitchen door, including her phone call to the police, all the way up finding him in her backyard last week. When she was done, she forced herself to turn and look at Meg's reaction. "So, do you think I'm nuts?"

"Yes. Because you could've told me months ago and I would've believed you." Meg smiled at her. "I come from a country that crawls with ghosts."

"But do you talk to them on a regular basis?"

"I never told you about my gram. She knew my grand dad was dead when he appeared to her at the foot of her bed. She said he stood there just like as he had when- Well you know." She took a deep breath. "He told her, 'bye.' And then he was gone."

Dori nodded. A year ago, she would've had some cynical thought that gram was off her rocker, or it had been the wishful imagination of a grieving woman. But now she was different and feeling foolish for having hid Vicente from her friend.

"Now that you know Anna and Vicente have a son, you can't just blurt it out to this old man and his family," Meg said. "What if he doesn't know he had a different father from his brothers and sisters?"

"But he knew Vicente's name. Maybe she told him before she died."

"When did you mention Vicente's name?"

Dori explained how her encounter went down, and Meg kicked at the dirt.

"I can't let Vicente be forgotten and unknown. He has a son and grandkids and maybe great-grandkids."

Meg shook her head. "You have to let things be. Think on it: if you told him and his family that the dead man haunting your house, whose body was in your backyard, is his father, how would you make him believe you?"

"We could do DNA tests."

"And how will you get Vicente's son to give you his DNA sample? Will you snatch his toothbrush in the dead of night?"

Dori's embarrassment was burned up by her irritation. Meg didn't understand.

"Come off it, Dori. You did not fail Vicente. You found Anna and you found his son. That has to be enough."

"But it can't be enough that I'm the only one who knows," Dori said.

Meg stiffened with indignance. "You forget me, your partner in crime. I bear witness, too."

Just when Dori was starting to get good and angry, she had to say that.

"When they release Vicente's remains to me, I want to bury him as close to Anna as I can."

Rather than say she had finally come to her senses, Meg slid her arm through Dori's as they were buffeted by the wind. "I'll come to the funeral and bring flowers for both of them."

# CHAPTER THIRTY

For insurance purposes, Dori carried a lemon haystack cake from George's World of Cakes up to Grammy's door. The dogs peeked through the window and then let out a chorus of excited barks when they saw her. Grammy shouted at them to shut the hell up, and then she yanked open the door. When she saw it was Dori, she put her fist on her hip.

"I know you're mad at me," Dori said. "But I figured if I got shot again, it would be too late for me to say sorry."

Grammy tried to keep her mad face on, but her lips twitched. "You want tea or tequila with your slice of cake?"

Dori followed Grammy inside. The *Maltese Falcon* played on TV. Grammy's iPad was propped by her easy chair.

"So, what's this I hear you spreading lies that I'm sick and dying?" Grammy shouted from the kitchen.

Dori set the box on the table. The day hadn't ended and already word spread faster than a preschool flu epidemic. "I went to Anna Vazquez Campbell's funeral."

A drawer slammed. "What were you doing there?"

"Vicente."

Grammy appeared in the doorway with plates and forks. "Oh. And?"

Dori took a deep breath and then sat down.

"That bad, huh?" Grammy set the plates on the table. "Have you had dinner yet?"

"It's in the pink box."

Grammy opened the box as Dori proceeded to tell her everything. They washed down the cherry pie with tequila-spiked tea.

When Dori finished, Grammy leaned back in her chair. "Well, that's one helluva circumstance. You think they'll find his family?"

"If they can identify him, but I doubt they have any of his DNA records from 1932."

"So, you'll take care of him."

Nodding, Dori scraped up the crumbs.

"You're like your grampy, you know. He kept his word till the end."

Thinking of that night she'd turned her back on Vicente, Dori wasn't like Grampy at all. She pushed her plate away. "Do you know Ceferino Campbell?"

"Not really."

"Do you think he knew?"

"Who his real daddy was?" Grammy tilted her head, staring out the window. "Hard to tell. They lived in Chula Vista, but his sister married a guy from my neighborhood."

"Who was Rick Campbell?"

"Far as I knew he worked for the railroad. I was just a kid so I didn't pay no attention."

Dori wondered what it had been like for Anna to live so close to all those memories and sleep alongside the man who had known Vicente. Had she ever walked up to Dori's house, looking for him? Had she known his spirit walked those halls, chained to her for all time?

Before the questions pulled her down, she scooted her chair back and then carried her and Grammy's plates to the sink.

Grammy sighed. "You're selling your house. I've been getting calls from everyone about it."

"I can't stay there after we found him like that."

Grammy nodded.

Dori made an attempt at levity. "You should see the inside. My realtor went a little crazy."

"Yeah?"

Dori didn't want to, but she told Grammy she'd take her on a tour of the rooms that no longer echoed with dust and shadows. Within an afternoon her realtor named, Gwen, had filled up the bottom floor rooms with antique furniture. The dining room table was set with dishes and real silverware. Potted palm trees filled in the corners and a clock ticked away on the mantle.

The hallway and the living room had been given the same treatment. Curtains had been hung, period style lamps sat on tables next to comfortable sofas and wing back chairs. They'd even placed andirons and screens in front of the fireplaces.

The furniture and accessories gave the impression that someone could just write a check and then plop down with a good book.

"Where'd you put your stuff?" Grammy asked as Dori rinsed the plates.

"They put it in storage for now. I only have my bed upstairs and my little office in the back."

"Well, at least you got to be there a little while."

Dori nodded even though her chest tightened at the thought that one day she'd close the door behind her for good. She dried the plates and placed them back in the cupboard. She filled up the teapot and put it back on the stove.

Returning to the dining room, she almost sat back down but instead she stopped and looked down at her grammy.

"I'm sorry about forgetting Grampy's anniversary. I won't let that happen again."

Grammy blinked and then sat back, startled by Dori's blatant apology. In their family, there was the unspoken agreement that it was best just to act normal and not acknowledge whatever started a fight.

But then Grammy nodded. "Thank you, mija. But I know you love him."

"And you." Dori put her hand on Grammy's shoulder. Grammy grabbed her hand and squeezed. They agreed without saying that life was too short for hard feelings.


On her way to work the next morning, Dori headed east on 18th Street. The sky was a tender purple and the defroster roared its breath against the mist that clung to her windshield.

She drove through the old Westside barrio. The houses that still remained sagged behind chain link fences, squeezed between auto repair shops and tile warehouses. Most of the old families had left; their names and lives erased by time.

Instead of turning north on Harbor Drive towards Downtown, Dori jerked the wheel and the tires squealed in protest as she turned left on Hoover. She slowed as she drove by her mom's tiny childhood home crouched next to St. Anthony's Church.

This was the last thing she'd do for him, Dori told herself as she searched for the house that matched Vicente's description. There it was, the last on the paved street before it became a dirt road that dipped down into the gully. The roofline barely peeked over the tops of overgrown trees.

Dori swung around in a U-turn and then parked. She stepped out into the hollow silence of dawn and surveyed the street. This was Olden Boys territory, and even though some of her cousins and their kids were affiliated, she kept a keen eye on the street.

As she walked alongside the crooked and rusted iron fence, she caught glimpses of Anna's house through the tangle of shrubs and vines.

Wind swept up the hill, rustling the tree overhead. Dori stepped up to the gate. When she touched the iron rosette, she turned and looked across the street. She could almost see a teenaged Vicente standing in his shabby but clean clothes, hoping for a glimpse of the girl he loved.

She tried the gate latch and rust particles rained down. The hinges squawked and groaned as she shoved it open just enough for her to slip through.

Remembering Vicente's description of roses in the garden and crisp lace curtains, the house now bore little resemblance to the grandest home in the barrio. Dori walked up the path, ducking under the grasping arms of the dying trees. Dead rose bushes stuck up from the ground like broken bones. Flower boxes clung beneath the tall windows, some of which were boarded up.

Dori should've felt sorry for the house. But it was fitting for what this place had been to a girl whose innocence had been sold by her own parents.

She walked around the perimeter, then stopped and looked up at the second-floor window that faced the mountains. Deep in the pit of her stomach, Dori knew that had been Anna's view of the world. She turned to the sun, which burnished the edges of the rain clouds in pink and gold. Anna had found her freedom and from what people had said at the funeral, happiness, too.

Dori walked away from the falling-down house, smiling for Anna. She had done enough and now she, too could be free.

"Hey! What the fuck you doing here, hyna?"

She swung around and there was the chola from the cemetery. "I'm looking at this house," Dori said, counting four hard-core boys, each with tattooed tear drops on their faces, backing up the chola.

They stared at each other, no emotions crossing their faces. One move and they'd be on her. Dori would never make it out through the front gate. She might make a run for it down the hill. But they'd probably nail her with a rock or a bullet and when they ripped her to pieces, no one would come to the rescue. Not if they wanted to sleep safe in their beds at night.

Dori held her hands out to her sides. "Well?"

"I heard you fucked my lady up," one of the guys said, breaking from the group to approach her. The pack tensed, waiting for his signal.

She held her ground. He had no weapon that she could see, which didn't mean he didn't have one. "She came after my grandma."

"Who was calling her a bitch." He moved into her personal space. If she backed off, the others would smell fear and circle around her.

Dori kept her eyes locked with his as his chest bumped against hers. He hadn't brushed his teeth this morning. "I ain't gonna let no lawyer do what a man's gotta do."

She said nothing.

"Just cut her up," the chola yelled.

Neither Dori nor el vato loco here so much as blinked. Whoever struck first was gonna strike fast and with maximum power.

"Did she tell you what she was doing to her mother?" Dori said with one last hope to get out alive.

His eyes flicked to the side and then back on hers. "Bitch, what you talking about?"

"The old lady in the car. The one with the scarf around her neck. Your girl here was this close to back handing her."

"What?" He turned away from Dori. "You didn't tell me that!" he yelled at the chola.

The chola's smug expression turned to fear. "She's lying, mijo. You gonna believe her over me?"

He swung back to Dori. "What's your name?"

"Dori Orihuela."

His eyebrows lifted up. "Chuy Orihuela related to you?"

Dori resisted the urge to roll her eyes. "He's my cousin."

"And you say she was disrespecting my moms?"

"She was. I told her to stop and take her home."

He stared at her and then yelled, "Shit, woman!" He walked back to his group. Now the boys were looking down at the chola. "You was messing with my moms again?"

"You told me to take her and she was giving me attitude!"

"Yeah but-"

"Hey, it's cool," Dori called out before he struck his woman.

"Mind your own damn business and get the hell out."

A normal person wouldn't wait to be told again. But Dori wasn't going to walk off and let four guys beat on one woman. "You're not beating on her. Not in front of me."

He turned back to her. "You want a turn, foo?"

"Look, listen," she said, adopting her cousin's parlance. "You want cops here taking you down?"

"I'm lettin' you go cuz I owe mi carnal a favor."

"Fine but if you fuck her up, what do you think she'll do to your moms when you're in jail?"

Now she had him weighing his options. But she couldn't put him in a weak position in front of his homies so she added, "Let her walk outta here and when I'm gone-" She held up both hands. "I won't see nothing. You see what I mean?"

His lip curled into a grin. "Yeah, I hears you." He turned to his lady. "Get the hell out, hyna. You better run."

The chola nearly slipped on the loose dirt in her hurry to escape. Dori expected she'd be getting a different answer when she called the lawyer listed on her subpoena papers.

"We're cool, right?" Dori said, giving him the last word.

"Yup, we cool." When he jerked his chin that she was dismissed, Dori nodded with respect. When Chuy found out, she would never hear the end of it.

# CHAPTER THIRTY-ONE

Gwen and her assistant argued downstairs as Dori gathered up the crime scene tape in the backyard. The gardener finished planting the last rose bush. They had sprung for fresh mulch to create a little path so potential buyers and lookey-loo's could wander about with tea or a glass of wine during today's first open house.

"We're done," the gardener said, pulling off his gloves.

"Thanks for coming on such a late notice," Dori said.

He shook his head as if it were no consequence. "You be okay, right?"

"I will."

He glanced at the envelope she pulled out of her pocket. He took it. "That body you found, my wife and I asked our priest to pray for him."

"Thanks."

"You know who it was?"

"Not yet."

She told him she appreciated his prayers, and then he walked to his truck.

Dori checked the time on her phone. Gwen had kindly but firmly "asked" her not to be here during the open house. If she left now, she'd have to think of something to do, or she'd have to wait almost two hours before she met Elliot for lunch.

The gardener's truck drove away. Dori walked across the yard, doing her best to ignore the voice of the wind through the pines and the forest smell of the mulch that called at her to stay.

When she stepped into her office, Gwen or her assistant were stomping around the house. Dori reached for her bag and debated whether to say good bye or get the hell out.

She found Gwen in the front parlor, primping in the mirror they'd hung over the fireplace. The pocket doors had been squirreled away in the basement and velvet curtains graced the new window.

Even with the open windows and the faint smell of fresh ceiling plaster, Dori detected that strange wet creepiness in the air. She stayed near the doorway. "I'm out of here," she said.

Gwen turned from the mirror, and her face instantly broke into a smile. "Okay great! Are you doing anything fun?"

"Lunch with my partner," she said. "Good luck."

"It's going to be fabulous! I have so many people coming who are in the restoration business, and Tracy will be tweeting pictures of the open house in real time." Gwen crossed the rug that had been rolled over the scarred floor.

Dori's stomach turned at the memory of Vicente bleeding out on the rug that had once lain here. "Sounds great. I'll be back tonight, so just lock up."

She escaped and headed out to her car. Maybe she should get some tea at Halcyon in Golden Hill or window shop for a place to rent before lunch. Then again, Golden Hill and South Park were treacherous places with old houses all in various stages of restoration. It might depress her.

Dori mentally cast around for ideas of how to use up her time, which was why she didn't see the car blocking the driveway until she drove into it.

An awful crunching sound ripped through her and then all went silent as she processed that she'd literally crashed into a parked car.

Then again, crashed might have been too strong a word. At the speed she'd been going, Dori had nudged and bounced off the passenger side of the car. She forced herself to release the steering wheel and then realized Ceferino Campbell stared at her from inside his sparkling gold 1978 El Camino. When they made eye contact, he held up his hand and waved.

Her face burning with embarrassment, she turned off the engine and then got out of the car.

"You live here?" he asked.

"I do. Are you okay?"

"Oh sure," he said as if car crashes were routine.

She pointed a shaking finger at her glove compartment. "I'll give you my insurance information-"

"That's not important, mija." He made a face as he reached into his pocket and took out a candy stick. "Want one?"

She forgot to look at the damage. "Yes, thank you."

Ceferino peeled the plastic wrapper. "Don't worry. It's my grandson's car and he owes me money."

"That sounds like something my grammy would say."

He smiled and she shivered. The brim of his fedora shaded his eyes, but his voice and his stance were too familiar. "Now, why did you come to my mother's funeral?" he asked and then stuck the candy in his mouth.

She held onto the door for the support, trying to wrap her mind around the fact that she was talking with the living version of his dad. "How did you know I live here?"

"Everyone at the funeral knows your grandma, so I called her up."

And she didn't think to warn her? That'd be the last time Dori would buy Grammy a whole pie. "You did?" she said. "What did she say?"

"She told me that I needed to talk to you."

"They're having an open house today so I'm not-" Dori pointed to the open house flags flapping in the breeze as if they weren't obvious.

He was amused by her attempt to hold him off. She might as well as let him in after having hit his car.

"Come in. Just park your car in the drive."

He flapped his hand as if her invitation were a fly. "I'll walk."

He started up the driveway. Dori looked from him to their cars and then caught up with him in case he fell.

Grinning, he held out his arm for her to take. "You can call me Cef. How old are you, doll?"

"Old enough to handle you." She threaded her arm through his. He laughed and patted her hand.

"I'll cut to the chase, Dori," he said, staring straight forward. "My mother and father kept no secrets from me. When I was 17 and told them I signed up with the Navy, they told me everything about my father."

Dori shivered and tried not to show it.

"It's okay, mija." Cef stopped just before they crossed into the shadow cast by the house. He turned and faced it, clutching her hand tightly. He wasn't as nonchalant as he appeared.

"Of course, I was angry when they first told me and I said things I never should've said to my mother. But you know, time moves so fast, especially in war. When I came back, she never spoke of it, but my father did. He told me about this house and what he'd pieced together."

"Did they ever come here?"

He shook his head, his eyes clouded with old memories and regret. "Not that I know." He then cleared his throat and turned to her. "But I've come here from time to time. Never stood this close before."

"You're welcome to come inside."

He nodded. "Yes. I need to. When I see my mother and my father - well, fathers-" His mouth trembled, but he straightened his shoulders. "When I see them again, I can tell them that I knew and I understood. But first thing, how did you find me?"

Dori mentally scrambled for ways to edge around the truth. She swallowed before she lied, "I was researching the history of the house."

Cef accepted her answer and she walked him inside. Debussy was playing softly from speakers hidden in the potted palms. Gwen swept out of the front parlor with her realtor's smile on her face. Her pleasure dimmed when she saw it was Dori. "Back so soon?"

Dori had no patience for her. In her best command voice, she said, "Gwen this is Ceferino Campbell. He's here to see the house."

"Oh, of course!" Gwen stepped back in retreat. "I'll just be in here waiting for guests."

"We need this room," Dori said.

Gwen looked at her laptop set on the table with fliers and business cards.

"I'll let you know when we're done," Dori added, softening her tone.

"May I bring you some wine or lemonade?"

"Wine in fifteen minutes, por favor señorita," Cef said, his voice smoldering.

Gwen actually swayed and then giggled as she backed out of the room.

Dori should've asked for two glasses, but instead she led him into the front parlor. She took a deep breath and tried to ignore the clammy air crawling over her skin. He wrapped his candy in the plastic and stuck it in his pocket.

"Tell me what you know," Cef said, standing in the doorway. "Through your research."

Dori looked around the room that still dripped with sadness in spite of the beautiful furniture.

"From what I know, Vicente was supposed to be arrested but they-" She tried to hedge around the truth but then she lost her place and didn't know what to say next. What if he called her crazy or worse, asked how much money she charged to talk to the dead?

She sucked in her breath and braced for the worst. "This is where they killed him."

Cef's eyes closed and for a horrifying moment she thought he would have a heart attack or something. But he nodded and then opened his eyes. "How do you know it happened here?"

"I saw- I mean, I don't know for sure." She couldn't look at him as she told half-truths.

"My father," Ceferino started and then paused. "The one who raised me, told me even though my father was a bootlegger and money launderer and worked for murderers and thieves, he thought he was the bravest man he knew. He admired him."

"Did Rick love Anna?"

Cef's eyes widened, as if surprised by the question. "Very much so. When I was a young man, I accused him of setting up my real father to die so he could have my mother." He shook his head as if he still couldn't believe he'd done such a thing. "She loved him, too."

Dori took a deep breath before she told him the rest. "There's more. We found his remains in my backyard. I told the coroner if they didn't find family that I would bury him."

"You did? How do you know it's him?"

"I just know."

Cef grinned like he was onto her. "You know both my fathers' names. You knew my mother."

"Well, I just pieced things together and-"

He held up his hand. "I came here with my secrets. Now you can tell it to me straight."

"I don't want anything from you. I did it for- To make things right and-"

Thinking of Bernice, the phony psychic, Dori had the sick realization she was doing the exact same thing. "Okay fine. Vicente was uh- I saw him and I-"

"You said you'd come out with it," Cef teased.

She looked up in surprise that he hadn't called her out as a swindler.

"Vicente and I were friends," she said. "Yes, he was a ghost or a spirit or whatever you want to call him. But he was my friend."

When she was done, she felt the last of her burden fall away. Her chest no longer burned, and she felt her shoulders melt from where they'd lodged up under her ears.

"That's an interesting way to put it," Cef finally said.

"Look, I'm not psychic or anything like that. It was just- He came to me for help. He needed to find your mother and make sure she was okay, so I helped him."

When he still hadn't called her names, Dori said, "I didn't believe in this stuff so I was trying to- Never mind. There's no excuse for lying."

"Lies and fibs are the tools of cowards," he said with approval. "But you're no coward. If my father chose you to find us, you made good."

She didn't know how to respond to that, considering she missed her chance to tell Vicente about Anna and their son.

Cef held out his arm for her take. "Show me where you found him."

As they walked out of the room, it lost its coldness. The sunlight glowed through the curtains and the antique tea cups and silver demitasse spoons sparkled on the table Gwen had set by the fireplace. All of the windows were open letting in air sweetened by fresh cut grass. Dori led Cef into the back garden and down the steps.

"You made this a very beautiful place," he said as they made their way to the spot where she'd planted white roses and gardenias over the old incinerator and the crime it had concealed.

"I'd be honored if you and I both laid him to rest," Cef said. "There's a plot next to my mother and father's."

Dori couldn't say thank you through the swelling in her throat. Instead, she hugged him.

"How are you going to explain things to your family?" she asked.

"Heh, they already think I'm old and crazy. I can handle them." He winked and then turned his face to the sun.

# CHAPTER THIRTY-TWO

Dori walked around the table pouring wine into seven glasses. She paused at the eighth place setting at the head of the table.

Grammy cleared her throat. "Give him the tequila, mija."

Dori switched bottles and poured Vicente two fingers.

Sighing, she started for the kitchen to help Meg carry out the food. They buried Vicente this morning and Gwen left her voice mail that they had an offer for the house. Dori decided it could wait till tomorrow. In the meantime, she needed to keep busy as this part of her life approached its end.

"Perfect timing," Meg said, handing her a tray of empanadas at the doorway. "How are you holding up?"

Dori shrugged. "Holding up."

Meg nodded with approval and then rushed back into the kitchen.

The hot December day turned the house into an oven, and they decided to have dinner out in the backyard. Cleve had put up a cover with mosquito netting to which Brenda and Meg added lanterns. Grammy set the table with her vintage linens and Dori used her "nice" plates before she had to pack them up. Cef's grandson, Victor brought the wine.

"What is that girl doing to my mole?" Grammy asked. Last week she'd emailed her secret recipe for mole negro to Meg. She'd been giving her cooking lessons and Dori was happy to taste their efforts.

"Smells great," Victor said, making eye contact with Dori. "Here let me help."

He stood up and held open the mosquito netting for her to duck into the tent. She sensed Grammy and Cef watching the two of them. His brother had been the one who witnessed her awkward encounter with Cef at the funeral. But it was his El Camino she drove into. She liked Victor enough that if he asked her out, she'd say yes.

"Try one," Victor said, startling Dori back to the present. He held out an empanada for her to bite.

"Yes, mija," Grammy said. "You should try one before they're all gone."

Dori caught the emphasis in Grammy's voice. She took it from him with her fingers, and his friendly grin widened. She didn't dare look at Brenda or Grammy as she ate it.

Meg came out with the main course and everyone oohed and ahhed over her work. She wiped a piece of hair stuck to her forehead. Dori handed her a glass of wine.

"You ground the spices by hand like I told you?" Grammy asked.

"I did," Meg said.

"You used corn oil not olive."

"Yes. Just like you told me."

Dori handed Grammy her plate. "You be the first taster."

She continued serving the plates and passing them out. Grammy took a delicate bite and then closed her eyes. Meg kept her cool, calmly sipping her wine.

Grammy nodded and then opened her eyes. "Damn girl, you did good."

Everyone broke out into applause, and Meg's eyes were suspiciously bright. Dori squeezed her shoulder and then took her plate to fill it. When she sat down between Victor and Meg, Dori eyed Vicente's place.

Cef stood up. "Thank you for your friendship and kindness to my family," he said. He looked at Dori with a smile that silently expressed that by family, he meant his father for whom they'd made a place of honor.

She returned his secret smile. Victor, her mother and Cleve were the only people at the table who didn't know the whole story. They'd agreed his family would never believe them and so as far as Victor knew it was Dori's "uncle" they were mourning.

"It just goes to show you're never too old to meet good friends." He lifted his glass, and the tent was filled with the sounds of clinking glasses.

Cef sat down and resumed flirting with Grammy. As Dori cut into her chicken, she thought of that day he came to the house and they sat out here during the open house. Cef finished where Vicente had left off, explaining that Andy Munemitsu brought Anna to Rick Campbell. Andy's family stayed close to his parents, Cef and his sisters having grown up with their kids. When they'd been relocated under Roosevelt's Executive Order 9066 of 1942, Rick and Anna leased their home and kept it until they returned after the war. Eugenia had been widowed when Alex broke his neck while digging a well. She raised her two boys and was Cef's godmother. Unlike the woman Grammy had remembered, Eugenia lived up till 1996 and died of old age.

Dori never found out what happened to James McClemmy after he'd been incarcerated at McNeil Island Prison on February 15, 1933. He'd been sentenced on December 5, 1932, a year before the 21st Amendment passed, ending Prohibition.

Dori slipped the mole-soaked chicken into her mouth and let it linger on her tongue. The present moment had no room for regrets or anger she told herself. Anna had lived her life. She hoped that Vicente's absence meant that he knew and he was free.

"Excuse me," came a voice.

They looked over, and Gavin stood outside the mosquito netting. Dori nearly dropped her fork. He held the same porkpie hat he'd worn the first day she almost shot him in the living room. His dark hair glistened as if he'd cleaned up before coming over.

"Mijo! Come and eat with us!" As Grammy rose from her chair, he ducked into the tent.

"Thanks, but I was just stopping by," he said and then looked at Dori. Her heart bloomed in her chest. "Have you talked to your realtor yet?"

It took Dori a moment to process his question. "No. Not yet."

"Oh. Well, I brought this." He pulled out an envelope. "Maybe I'll just leave it by the door."

Her heart beat double time. "You could sit down and have dinner with us."

He glanced at Meg and smiled bashfully. "I'm intruding."

"Sit down next to me," Grammy insisted, pointing to an extra chair in the corner of the tent.

"I don't believe we've been introduced," Brenda said, offering her hand. Gavin shook her hand and then Cleve's before sitting.

Dori tried not to think about Gavin now across the table from her. When she looked his way, he paid attention to Grammy.

She forced herself to eat, not really tasting the food as she went all shaky inside.

"Are you going to miss your house when you sell it?" Victor asked.

Dori swallowed and then nodded. "I will. I made a lot of good memories here in a short time."

"My grandpa said you planted the garden."

She glanced across the table, admiring the strong elegance of Gavin's hands. She then remembered that Victor had commented on the garden. "I did, but with a lot of help."

"You don't seem like the kind of person who asks for help too easily."

She hesitated before answering, not sure if that was an observation or criticism.

"I don't." Dori glanced at Gavin to see if he was listening. But he was talking to Cef, his fingers now tapping the tablecloth. "But I'm getting better at it."

"So, are you going to stay in National City?"

"I'm looking for a place closer to work."

"You might have to wait awhile. It's probably going to be hard to sell a place like this."

Maybe she wouldn't say yes if he asked her out. "I just have to find the right owner."

"You've had offers?"

"I have and none of them were the right fit."

"Seriously, I don't get it. Why buy it, patch it up and sell it? Cops make pretty good money. You could work on it bit by bit."

She looked for a resemblance to Vicente in Victor, but couldn't find it. "I'll always love this house but I don't think I'm the right person for it."

"I should go," Gavin said, abruptly standing out of his seat.

She watched him shake Cef's hand, kiss Grammy's cheek and then he paused to nod his head at Dori. His eyes glowed, and he seemed to want to say something to her. She held her breath, forgetting her mother watching and Victor's flirting.

"Good night," Gavin said and then was gone.

"Looks like we ran out of wine," Victor said, starting to rise from his seat.

"I'll get it," Dori said. She caught Meg's smile and her head tilt in the direction Gavin had gone.

"I'll help you," Meg announced, throwing her napkin on the table and then nudging Dori along into the house. Dori grabbed one of the bottles off the counter and nearly turned into Meg.

"What are you doing here?" Meg suddenly asked.

"I'm getting the wine."

"Like hell you are! Go after him."

"But-"

Meg grabbed the wine, and they had a brief tug of war before she said, "Go or I'll fetch him for you!"

"Are you sure?"

"Yes."

"We might need some water," Dori said and retreated into the kitchen to fill a glass pitcher.

Even with Meg's blessing, she held the pitcher under the running water, wondering what she would say to him without making a bigger fool of herself. She'd had her chance, and she blew it. The gulf between them was too vast. It would take nothing short of her showing up naked on his doorstep, which she would've done when she was seventeen and ten pounds lighter.

He'd probably driven away by now. It was time to go back and see through the rest of the dinner party. She patted down her hair and then froze when footsteps approached behind her. Her heart leapt, and she spun to see Gavin standing in the kitchen door.

He handed her a folded-up piece of paper. She almost didn't take it, but he flapped it at her impatiently. When she took it, he gave her a lopsided grin and then left.

Meg never saw that he'd been there. "Ready?" she asked from Dori's office.

"In a minute," Dori called out, impatient to read the note in her now shaking hand.

"Come out when you're ready."

Dori waited for Meg to step outside, and then she walked into the dining room and sank into one of the chairs. She unfolded the paper and for a moment took in his bold handwriting. She could see where he'd pressed the pen deep into the paper.

Dori-

I'm the one who made the offer to buy your house. I came with another letter much different than this one but I can't give it to you. All I can say about buying your house is that you know I'll take care of it with my own two hands. Yes, I've loved this house the same way you do and you were pretty suspicious of me in the beginning. But I'm also buying this house because I couldn't drive by it knowing someone who wasn't you lived in it.

Call me crazy but I'm still that pathetic kid in school who wants you to be his girlfriend. At first, when your grammy came to me asking for help, I was hoping to make some money and possibly make you jealous. I even thought you might make the first move and then I'd get the chance to turn you down. But there's no way I'd be able to do that to you. The plain truth is that I wanted to be around you. I wanted to see if you were just something I'd made up in my head.

I'm probably embarrassing us both by writing this. I understand that if you saw me at the store, you'd pretend you didn't see me to avoid a really awkward moment.

Then again, there were times when I thought I saw something in you. When you said you were planning to leave for good, I couldn't risk losing this chance, slim as it probably is. If this was the wrong thing to do, I'm sorry. But if I'm right in feeling what I feel, give us a chance.

Yours, *Gavin*

With the note still clutched in her fist, Dori found him sitting in his truck across the street. He rested one hand on the steering wheel while staring out the window.

She stopped at the curb, perched on the very edge. The fading sunlight turned purple and blue. On stiff legs, she crossed the street.

Gavin turned when she came to his open window, resting her hand on the edge. He stared at her, not sure what to expect. When she smiled, he opened the door. She slipped her arms around his waist and held on. Wrapped in his warmth, she shivered and then settled in to listen to his heart beating.


## The train, April 1932

"More coffee, Mr. Sorolla?"

Vicente looked over his shoulder at Andy Munemitsu, who like him, had been recruited from the orange groves to transport product from the midnight deliveries along the coast. Now Vicente was James McClemmy's personal secretary and Andy the butler.

For some reason, he was overjoyed to see him as if it had been decades not minutes since they'd last spoken. Tears burned his eyes, or maybe it had been the bright sun that blinded him. All he could make out was Andy's white coat and his silhouette against the open windows facing the hazy ocean.

"Go to hell."

"Very good sir," Andy replied and then snorted.

Vicente fought to keep from smiling.

"Good thing he's not here to see this," Andy said, whipping out a towel and then mopping up the spilt coffee.

Rubbing his aching forehead, Vicente asked, "When are you heading back?"

"Right after I make sure you're fed and diapered."

Andy finished with the coffee and returned to the private car's kitchenette.

Vicente stared across the new airport tarmac at the San Diego Bay. It was a hazy blur of blue, but he could almost smell the brine and hear the crunching sand under his shoes. If he closed his eyes, he might feel the wind and see her-

He staggered when the train pulled to a stop.

"Here," Andy said, holding the camel hair coat open for Vicente to slide his arms into the sleeves.

"Give it over."

"Let me do my job while I still have it."

Vicente gave him a dirty look and then yanked his coat free. He nearly caught his watch on the satin lining. Andy sighed. "At least let me open the door."

He had this feeling he'd done this before. Vicente shook it off and started for the door that Andy held open.

"See ya later," he said, about to step out into the sunlight.

"Not this time, Vince."

Vicente stopped, grabbing the railing. He turned to Andy, who was gone.

When he touched down on the wood floor, he looked up and froze. He was in the front parlor again. Confused, he looked for the two men who beat him to death and the thing that whispered rage in his ears. A fancy rug was underfoot and conversation drifted in from the back. Nothing moved.

Unlike the last time, he remembered everything: James McClemmy's betrayal, Anna and Dori.

Vicente spun when the front door opened. Its hinges groaned, and he moved to a spot where he could see who walked in without being seen.

Footsteps sounded and then stopped. She appeared in the doorway, smiling right at him as if she'd known he would be waiting there.

Vicente didn't dare blink as she crossed the room to him. Just like the night in her basement, she wore the white button-down shirt, pants and brown lace-up shoes.

"You're not real," he said, his voice choked off by the emotions that made him shake like a leaf caught in the wind.

Anna reached up and cupped his cheek in her hand. He grabbed her hand and pressed his lips against the warm skin and thin bones.

"But this means you're dead," he managed, not hiding his tears from her.

Anna blinked. "Do I look dead to you?"

He laughed and cried at the same time. Her eyes shone with joy. He grabbed her around the waist and kissed her.

She pulled away and then kicked him. "You said you'd come back!"

He welcomed the pain where she got him in the shin. "I know. But Anna, I-" He choked and then said, "I've been waiting here for you the whole time."

## The house, present day

Dori had just made the decision to go home with Gavin and make up for all the years they'd missed when she heard them shouting her name.

"Ignore them," he said when she broke the kiss and looked over her shoulder.

"What if the house is on fire?"

He pushed her backwards, trying to get out of the truck.

They had just made it across the street, when Dori slowed to a stop. The front door was open.

"Come on," Gavin called after her.

She shook her head and veered off towards the porch. Dori's heart pounded and hands went slick with expectation. She walked into the shadowed hallway and froze in place when she saw the flare of gold light in the front parlor.

"Vicente?" she called.

She vaguely heard the panicked group outside. Dori walked into the front parlor. The smell of candy and cologne lingered in the air.

Dori pressed her hand to her heart banging against her chest. She looked frantically for them in the dark corners when the smudges in the mirror caught her eye. The group chattered that all the candles flared up and nearly burnt the tent down.

Ignoring them, Dori stepped up to the marble hearth and saw that the smudges were words. She read in the waning light: *She came for me.*

# THE DORI ORIHUELA PARANORMAL
# MYSTERY SERIES CONTINUES

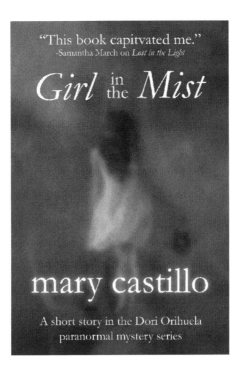

"This book capitvated me."
-Samantha March on *Lost in the Light*

*Girl* in the *Mist*

# mary castillo

A short story in the Dori Orihuela
paranormal mystery series

Thanks so much for reading, *Lost in the Light*! If you enjoyed Dori's first step into the world of the paranormal, please let other readers know by leaving a review, or sharing your thoughts on GoodReads, Facebook or your favorite place to show off your favorite books!

Also join my newsletter for free reads, pre-orders of new books and more!

Check out the sexy excerpt from the e-book novella, *Girl in the Mist*.

After driving under the redwood shadows, the crescent-shaped beach seemed to burst before them in shocking white and heavenly blue. In that moment, Dori forgot to be suspicious of Gavin poking into her personal stuff to plan their first romantic trip. She was mesmerized by the ocean that sparkled as if diamonds had fallen from the sky.

"Is this my surprise?" she asked.

"Part of it," Gavin said, leaning over the steering wheel to get a better look at Carmel River Beach. "Wow. It's usually fogged in."

She rubbed her goose pimply arms to warm them up, welcoming the heat of the late afternoon sun. A month ago, Gavin told her he had set up a surprise just for the two of them.

Dori's first instinct was to demand how he knew her work schedule when she hadn't told him. But he had been so full of glee and mischief that she stretched her lips into a grin and asked if she should pack for warm or cold. He replied both and then during these past weeks left her clues throughout the house – a pine cone, beach sand in an antique glass bottle and this morning a vintage tea cup hand painted with a fairytale cottage.

"It's been killing you, hasn't it?" he asked, cutting into her thoughts. "What?" she asked, stalling.

Laughter made his lips tremble. "Don't what me." In such a short time, he knew her too well. "You've been dying to know how I knew you'd have this week off."

"It crossed my mind."

"Okay, I'll tell you. You left your work calendar on the kitchen table." "When?"

"A couple of months ago. You didn't think I'd poke around your stuff, did you?"

Yes, she had but opted to keep it to herself. In her experience, men didn't react well when challenged. One wrong word and they'd be yelling and then all the juggling he'd done to make sure his daughter was taken care of and his work calendar rearranged would be ruined.

"Come on admit it," he said, sneaking his hand over to grab hers which she held balled tight in her lap.

Dori took a deep breath and then admitted, "Okay I did. But I didn't make a big deal of it because it's not like I have anything to hide."

He squeezed her hands. "I know my limitations. I just wanted this to be special."

He then let go of her hands to hold onto the wheel. Dori uncurled her fingers. She rolled down her window, breathing in the cold air tinged with ocean, pine and cypress. The road took them by the 18th Century Carmel Mission and whimsical cottages with thatched roofs, stone chimneys, and diamond-paned windows tucked into the forest. Eventually, they turned and headed down Ocean Avenue that cut through the center of the small downtown. Couples and families, almost all accompanied by dogs in jackets, strolled in and out of the boutiques and cafes. After seven hours in the car, she wanted to walk up and down these streets, with Gavin's hand in hers.

Gavin pointed out his favorite restaurants and the bookstore he wanted to show her. Her eyebrows lifted when he pulled into the porte-cochere at the Del Mar, a Mediterranean resort built in the 1910s. It was a few streets away from the shops and restaurants. The ocean's roar could be heard through the trees.

A bellhop took them out of the lobby and across the street to a cottage hidden by overgrown hedges. A crooked river rock chimney reached up to the sky and green moss decorated the shingled roof. Adirondack chairs with colorful pillows were grouped around a brick fire pit. A path meandered alongside the cottage to a second, smaller one in the back.

The bellhop opened the Dutch door. "Go on, check it out," Gavin said.

Dori walked inside while he tipped the bell hop and sent him away. Burning logs snapped in the fireplace and a bottle of champagne waited in an ice bucket. A bouquet of her favorite flowers, sweet peas that were so dark they were almost black, rested on the giant bed.

Her chest went hot and tingly as she stood there taking it all in. He did this for her. The long drive. The lucky break finding her schedule and juggling his work crew and his daughter. He'd worked late last night. But he brought her here. No man had ever done something like this for her before, because, well frankly she never let one get past her defenses. When she hadn't been paying attention, Gavin saw the romantic heart she kept hidden and had known just what would make her eyes fill up with tears.

The door shut. She turned and saw that knowing grin of his stretched proud and unrepentant.

"Oh, shut up," she said, looking away when her voice cracked under the strain of not crying in front of him.

He got to work on the champagne while she stopped being such a girl. It only took 36 years for it to happen, but with one letter from him, Dori tripped and fell deeply, truly, completely in love. He had offered to buy her house and when she told him she was keeping it, he just smiled like he'd known she would do that. They spent every other weekend together unless Dori was on duty, or he had his six-year-old daughter, Bella, whom she still hadn't met. Gavin respected her job and his laid back, his creative mind the antidote to long days on the job. He even survived a cop barbeque without getting intimidated by her male colleagues who initially froze him out. He started talking with her sergeant's wife and, before Dori knew it, Gavin was like an old friend of the family. Now when her colleagues invited her to barbecues, they always asked if Gavin was coming too.

As happy as she'd been these three months, she also lived in terror. There were nights she'd jolt awake that it had all been a dream like Bobby Ewing's death in Dallas. She always screwed up. But as Meg told her, maybe she wouldn't this time. She cleared her throat and joined him by the fire.

When Gavin handed her the flute, glittering with golden bubbles, she trusted herself to talk. "Thank you," she said, sinking into the impossibly comfortable sofa.

"I did good, didn't I?" He clinked his glass against hers then nudged her over so he could sit with his arm around her shoulders.

After a few sips of champagne, she let her head rest on his shoulder. "This is all-" she choked up again.

"We have an hour and a half before sunset," he said easily as if her tears were safe with him.

The fire warmed her face. She could fall asleep to the sound of his heartbeat. "You know, I'm worried about something," he said, putting his flute on the table. "What?"

He took her drink and set it next to his. He then looked down at her lap. "Your jeans look too tight."

The warm fuzzy bubble in which she had been floating popped. "What?"

"Mmm hmm." Just when she was about to get good and offended his fingers traced the inseam up her thigh. His hand cupped over her, fingertips pressing ever so slightly to make her squirm for more.

"I don't want you to be uncomfortable," he said quietly, just before he sucked her ear lobe into his hot mouth.

With a hiss of surprise, she arched up from the sofa, loving the feeling of being teased by those strong, dark fingers. He then firmly took her chin and turned her face to him. His eyes met hers and then he kissed her. Holding her in place, his tongue invaded her mouth, mimicking what he'd do once he got undressed. She grabbed onto him and he made a dark sound that sent a vibration from her mouth straight to where his hand played her.

With Gavin rhythmically stroking her, she lifted her hips in a silent plea for more. He smiled against her mouth before catching her bottom lip between her teeth. Her zipper hissed down.

"Lift your hips," he said.

She did and for a fleeting moment, realized the curtains were wide open. Gavin yanked her jeans and panties down in one pull and she forgot all about the windows.


Get *Girl in the Mist* at www.Mary Castillo.com.

Want to see a sneak peek of *Lost in Whispers*, the next book in the Dori O. Paranormal Mystery Series? Sign up for my newsletter at MaryCastillo.com!

Thanks so much for reading!

# ACKNOWLEDGMENTS

Every book begins as a solo trip into the unknown. As I go along, feeling my way through the dark, I meet people who influence and inspire changes in the story. Or, they confirm that my instincts were dead on.

This story was seeded by the tales told by my Grandma Nana (Great Grandmother Eduvijen Holguin Melendez) and my Grandma Margaret Melendez Castillo. My Grandma Nana arrived in National City in the 1920's with her ornery grandmother and little brother. I have photos of her on the tidelands, but as far as I know, she didn't operate a bootleg operation. But she did marry Alex Melendez, who inspired the name of my business, Reina Books. When I was a baby, he walked around Westside National City with my picture and told all the old ladies that I was his reina. By the way, he didn't break his neck in a well. That happened to my Great Grandmother Inez Vasquez's second husband. However, my Grandma Maria Mendez may have dabbled with a bootlegger or two in her time. Her rebellious spirit inspired Anna Vazquez.

Mary Allely, formerly of the National City Public Library's Local History Room, helped me locate my great grandparent's addresses in the 1926 city directory, and pointed me to the oral histories given by a few Mexican Americans who lived in the Westside barrio, including my Great Uncle John Mendez. Hearing his voice from across the decades, reminiscing about his mother who worked for one dollar a day, seven days a week in a laundry was truly a magical moment in which I saw how far my family had come.

I'm also indebted to Sergeant (ret) Dean Carr of the National City Police Department for his open and honest discussion of post-traumatic stress disorder and procedures following an officer-involved shooting. Thank you to Blair Stephens of the San Diego Police Department who answered mundane questions with patience and good humor. After having been in Dori's head for two years, I appreciate the work of police officers everywhere.

I am grateful to the independent author community where everyone generously shares their expertise. Literary Agent Leslie McLean started me on the indie author path when I took her online seminar. After her presentation, I wanted to cry with excitement. Instead, I ate chocolate and then got to work on my business plan! I'm also grateful to Debra Holland for her workshop on self-publishing through the Orange County Chapter of Romance Writers of America.

Thank you to my editors, Ryan Gilmore and Jennifer Mahal, who taught me the finer points of guns and commas, respectively. I had hoped they would let me get away with a few things but they gave me the push to make this story even better than I had imagined.

Most of all I am grateful to you, dear reader, for holding this book in your hands. You will never know how much I appreciate that you choose to read this story.

Love,
Mary

# ABOUT THE AUTHOR

Mary Castillo's novels have turned romance and paranormal mystery readers into dedicated fans. Her latest paranormal mysteries, *Lost in the Light* and *Girl in the Mist* have been widely praised by critics, book clubs and readers. She is the author of *Switchcraft*, *In Between Men* and *Hot Tamara* and novellas featured in the anthologies, *Orange County Noir*, *Names I Call My Sister* and *Friday Night Chicas*. Mary and her family live in Orange County California and are owned by a black pug named Rocky. Visit her at www.MaryCastillo.com, on Facebook, Twitter, Pinterest and Instagram.

Made in the USA
Columbia, SC
28 March 2018